KU-180-538

01. MAR 10   0 7 FEB 2014

10. AUG. 10   − 3 NOV 2014

21. DEC 10.

02 APR 11

14. JUL 11

X000 000 036 8540

ABERDEEN CITY LIBRARIES

KEEPING SECRETS

A bittersweet saga set in the 1930s

Gillian Finch and Dorothy Prosser are firm friends as well as cousins. For four years they have kept their friendship secret in the face of a bitter family feud. But this is not the only family secret. When Gillian and Dorothy fall head over heels for the same man, the repercussions lead to other secrets being exposed. Everyone, it seems, has something to hide...

*Gwen Madoc titles available from
Severn House Large Print*

Mothers and Daughters
Take My Child

KEEPING SECRETS

Gwen Madoc

Severn House Large Print
London & New York

This first large print edition published 2009
in Great Britain and the USA by
SEVERN HOUSE PUBLISHERS LTD of
9-15 High Street, Sutton, Surrey, SM1 1DF.
First world regular print edition published 2008 by
Severn House Publishers Ltd., London and New York.

Copyright © 2008 by Gwen Madoc.

All rights reserved.
The moral right of the author has been asserted.

British Library Cataloguing in Publication Data

Madoc, Gwen.
  Keeping secrets.
  1. Cousins--Wales--Fiction. 2. Wales--Social
  conditions--Fiction. 3. Large type books.
  I. Title
  823.9'2-dc22

  ISBN-13: 978-0-7278-7804-5

Except where actual historical events and characters are being described
for the storyline of this novel, all situations in this publication are
fictitious and any resemblance to living persons is purely coincidental.

Printed and bound in Great Britain by
MPG Books Ltd, Bodmin, Cornwall.

To the memory of my dear husband, Harry. Always in my heart and in my thoughts.

One

The Kardomah in High Street was crowded as it usually was, being one of the most popular restaurants in town.

Gillian Finch sipped her tea and then bit into her cream cake with satisfaction. She glanced across the table at her cousin Dorothy Prosser, similarly occupied.

'We got here just in time for a table,' Gillian remarked and then gasped in annoyance as a large woman carrying many shopping bags bumped into her shoulder, knocking her tam sideways and making her almost spill her tea.

Gillian adjusted her tam on her head, feeling foolish.

'Some people have no manners,' Dorothy declared loudly, glaring at the woman, but she, doggedly searching for an empty seat, had her back turned.

'I love coming to the Kardomah,' Gillian said edgily, still fiddling with the angle of her tam. 'But I'm worried that we'll be spotted together. One careless word to my mother and I'll never hear the end of it.'

'Aunty Vera wouldn't mind all that much,

7

would she?' Dorothy asked and then nodded. 'But then my father says his sister can be fearsome.'

Gillian stopped munching and frowned. She wasn't sure she liked that remark about her mother, even if it was true.

Uncle Henry was hardly a paragon of virtue himself. There was no doubt, in her mother's mind at least, that he had been underhanded when it came to Grandma Prosser's will. He had inherited the family business and her estate while Vera had been left only a measly five hundred pounds. Vera and Henry were at war over it.

Gillian put her half-eaten cake back on her plate. She did not want to quarrel with Dorothy, who was not only her cousin but also her very best friend. They had shared a secret friendship for the last four years, ever since Gillian was thirteen. They got on so well together despite their feuding families, and shared each other's innermost dreams and secrets.

Dorothy was looking at her quizzically. 'Did I say something wrong?'

Gillian forced a smile. 'Not really, but I think we should keep off the subject of our families,' she said. 'I don't want to be mixed up in their quarrels.'

'Nor I,' Dorothy agreed with feeling. 'I'm so bored with it all.'

'Let's talk about us,' Gillian said cheerfully. 'Tomorrow I'll get the results of my shorthand and typing exams. If I pass Dad says he'll speak to Uncle Henry about getting me a position as

8

typist in the yard office.'

She had set her heart on getting an office job at Prosser & Knox, Building Contractors. Earning a wage, no matter how small, would mean a measure of independence from her mother.

'At my father's office?' Dorothy's expression stiffened. 'Really? Do you think that's proper for a young girl? I mean, being surrounded by men all day?'

'Men?' Gillian raised her eyebrows in surprise. 'There's only Uncle Henry and Mr Meeker who does the accounts – and he's ancient. And Dad says your brother Andy is rarely at his desk.'

'The tradesmen and apprentices are back and forth in the yard all the time,' her cousin persisted with a pout.

Gillian shrugged. 'I'll be in the office all day. I won't see much of them.'

Dorothy's nostrils flared. Puzzled, Gillian could see that for some reason her cousin was piqued.

'There's also Ronnie...' Dorothy hesitated, her cheeks turning pink. 'I mean Mr Knox, my father's partner.'

Gillian picked up her cake again. 'Mr Knox is hardly ever in the office according to my dad,' she said. 'He's always out checking on the work at the various building projects and getting the men's backs up as well.'

Gillian chewed for a moment while her cousin glared. She dabbed at her lips with a napkin.

'The older tradesmen don't like being spied on and criticized,' she continued. 'Dad says, as young as he is, Mr Knox is a real sharper just

9

like his grandfather, Charlie Knox.'

Dorothy tossed her head. 'Uncle Arthur is just an employee of my father's company,' she said tetchily. 'He should watch what he says about his bosses.'

Gillian glanced up in surprise. 'Dot, what's wrong?'

'Nothing.'

Gillian wondered if her cousin was jealous of her prospects.

'Why didn't your mother enrol you in commercial college?' she asked. 'I know you went to high school, but you're eighteen and you still haven't got a job.'

Dorothy stretched her neck, obviously put out by Gillian's probing. 'My mother says it's common for a young lady to work.'

'Common?' Now Gillian was really annoyed. 'Most of us have to,' she said smartly. '*My* father doesn't own the biggest building contractors in town. Aunty Gloria doesn't know what she's talking about.'

'I don't know about you having to work, Gill,' Dorothy countered. 'My father says Aunty Vera is not all that badly off for money. Uncle Arthur earns the top wage as a plumber and your parents own their house outright.' She sniffed disparagingly. 'Not to mention earnings from the lodgers she takes in.'

Gillian ignored the remark about her mother's boarders.

'I want my independence,' she said firmly. 'I've no intention of sponging off my parents for the rest of my life or being dependent on them

10

either.' She lifted her chin. 'I intend to be my own woman when I'm older.' She looked keenly at her cousin. 'I thought you felt the same, Dot.'

Dorothy bit her lip, hesitated a moment and then grinned sheepishly. 'I'd love to have a job,' she admitted. 'But my mother won't let me. She expects me to marry well.'

The girls stared at each other for a moment and then burst into giggles.

'Mothers! Who'd have them?'

They giggled again and the tension between them was broken.

'Come on,' Dorothy urged with energy. 'Finish up your tea. Let's stroll around Ben Evans' store. I've heard they've got some lovely hats on display.'

'Gill passed her exams with flying colours,' Arthur Finch said heartily to his wife the next day. 'Surely you're proud of our girl, Vera?'

'Of course I am,' his wife said touchily. 'But I baulk at asking Henry to give her a job.' Vera gritted her teeth. 'I won't be beholden to that scoundrel brother of mine.'

'Scoundrel is a bit harsh, Vera love,' Arthur said gently.

'He cheated me out of a decent share of my mother's estate, so what else would I call him, except a snake in the grass?'

It was a Saturday afternoon, Arthur's half-day off. He was sitting in the kitchen, his feet on the fender before the fire and a pipe of tobacco between his teeth, watching Vera iron his shirt ready for chapel the following morning.

11

'I can't imagine your mother Rose being persuaded to do anything with her money that she didn't want to do,' he ventured to say. 'In fact, if you ask me it was your mother that did you down, not Henry.'

'Well, I didn't ask you!' Vera snapped. 'Anyone would think that you're on Henry's side.'

Arthur shifted uncomfortably in his seat. He had to go careful in what he said to his wife. If she ever found out that his brother-in-law Henry was not only his employer but his best friend and that he was Henry's confidant, his life wouldn't be worth living. He knew more about Henry's private life than Vera could ever imagine.

Arthur took his pipe out of his mouth, and pressed down on the tobacco in the bowl with the blunt end of his pocketknife.

'I'm only saying that there are two sides to every story,' he said carefully. 'You don't know what your brother has to put up with at home.'

Vera rounded on him, staring. 'What?'

Arthur flicked his tongue nervously. 'Well, it's no secret that he and Gloria don't get on,' he said. That was putting it mildly, Arthur reflected. 'They're not happy like we are, love.'

'How do you know?' Vera's eyes narrowed. 'Have you been talking to Henry behind my back? Have you been telling him our business?'

'Of course not!' Arthur sat up straight in his seat. 'Ronnie Knox told me,' he lied and then felt guilty at deceiving her.

Vera put the iron on the stand and looked at him, hands on hips.

'Well, it doesn't surprise me,' she said, nodding. 'Gloria got very snooty after she married Henry.' She sniffed disparagingly. 'You would not know to look at her now that her father was no more than a rag-and-bone man.'

'Yes, I remember Old Man Skinner,' Arthur said, nodding. 'Now there was a scoundrel for you.'

Vera shook her head in wonder. 'Why my brother married her I'll never understand. She wasn't even pretty as a girl.'

Arthur was silent and thoughtful as he knocked out the contents of his pipe into the hearth and then scraped inside the bowl with his pocketknife.

Henry had had no choice in marrying Gloria after he had got her in the family way at seventeen. His brother-in-law had confessed to him that he bitterly regretted the marriage from the start.

'What about our Gill, though?' Arthur asked, changing the subject. 'I think it's better that she find employment with Prosser and Knox than with strangers.' He played what he felt was his trump card. 'It's her birthright. After all, let's not forget that her great-grandfather Samuel founded the company.'

Vera looked thoughtful. 'Well, that's true enough.'

'And when she's working in the yard office I can keep an eye on her.'

'You're out on building sites all day,' Vera pointed out.

'Yes, but she'd be with family, not strangers,' Arthur persisted.

13

Vera stretched her neck, not yet convinced.

'You didn't mind Sam and Tom taking apprenticeships with Prosser and Knox,' Arthur said with alacrity. 'Why treat our daughter different to our sons?'

'It's different,' Vera insisted. 'It's family tradition that sons go into the business, but daughters...' She shook her head doubtfully.

'Gill wants to find a job,' Arthur said. 'It might as well be in the family business.'

Vera grimaced. 'I'd be mortified if Henry refused to have her work there,' she said. 'He'd do it out of spite and malice.'

Arthur could not tell her that he and Henry had already agreed on it – very amicably, too. 'I've spoken to Ronnie Knox,' he lied again, wishing he did not have to. 'He's agreed to it. Henry won't go against him.'

'No, I suppose not,' Vera said. 'Well, if Gill really wants the position I suppose it's all right.'

'Of course it is,' Arthur agreed enthusiastically. 'Our daughter working in the family business is as right as rain.'

In the last week of May one of her three boarders, Mr Brundle, announced to Vera that he was leaving immediately. His mother in Stockport had taken sick and he had to go home.

'I'm sorry to go, Mrs Finch,' he told Vera regretfully. 'It's home from home here and I do appreciate your cooking.'

Vera, though disappointed at losing his rent, was mollified. 'Sorry to see you go, Mr Brundle,' she said. 'And you had such a good

14

job at the gas works, too.'

He shrugged. 'Family. Can't let one's family down.'

Some people can, Vera thought bitterly. When your own brother does you out of what's rightfully yours the world has come to a sorry pass.

Mr Brundle, bags already packed, took his leave after breakfast. Vera decided to get around to the newsagent after lunch to put a postcard in their window advertising the vacancy. The room probably would not be unoccupied for long, but on the other hand she was very fussy about who she took in.

Early afternoon she was in the hall, about to put on her hat and coat to go to the newsagent, when she heard someone at the front door. Opening it she found a tall elderly man on the doorstep, a big leather suitcase at his feet. He had a bronzed weather-beaten complexion and wore a long dustcoat of coarse cream linen and a strange hat of the same colour with a very wide brim.

Vera blinked at him, feeling confused and disorientated for a brief moment. She had a strange feeling that she had met him before. But he looked like a foreigner, so that wasn't likely. Disturbed she moved to close the door.

'Mrs Finch?' the man enquired.

Vera hesitated. 'Yes, I'm Mrs Finch.'

'I understand you have a room to let.' His accent was very strange, too.

Flummoxed, Vera blinked at him again. 'How did you know?' she asked suspiciously. 'I only

15

knew myself this morning.'

He pointed down the street. 'The lady in the corner house said you might have a room vacant.'

'You mean Mrs Turner?' said Vera.

The elderly man shrugged. He was sparely built and looked wiry for his age. 'Didn't have time to ask her name. She had a vacancy card in her window, but she said she was full up when I enquired.'

Vera pulled in her chin. Elsie Turner had a thing about foreigners. They were all axe murderers according to her.

'I expect she was full,' Vera said. 'I'm not sure that I—'

'You did say you had a vacancy,' the man said quickly. He smiled at her. 'I'm quite harmless, you know, and I'm willing to pay extra.'

'Oh!'

'I was born around these parts,' he continued eagerly. 'I've been sheep-farming in Australia for the last thirty-odd years.'

Vera's sharp ears did detect a slight Welshness in his voice beneath the accent. He had a nice manner about him, a gentleness that impressed her. Relenting she opened the door wider.

'Come inside,' she said. 'See if the room suits you.'

He picked up his suitcase and followed her in. They stood in the hall.

'You are Mr...?' Vera queried.

'Oglander,' he said. 'Bill Oglander.'

Vera frowned. 'That's not a local name.' She wondered with misgiving whether she had been too hasty in inviting him in.

'My parents were born in Swansea, not far from here.'

Vera was dubious. 'I've never heard that name before, not around here.'

'It was long before your time, I think,' he said easily. 'Probably before you were born. You can't be much over thirty years old.'

Vera touched her hair self-consciously, smiling, delighted at the compliment. 'Not much older,' she said.

It pleased her to think that at thirty-eight she looked thirty to a complete stranger.

She turned towards the staircase. 'You'd better see the room, Mr Oglander,' she said. 'It may not suit, although it is one of my best.'

The vacant room was first floor forward, overlooking the street. Vera was proud of the big bay window. It gave the room airiness.

'This will do very nicely,' Bill Oglander said. Vera was pleased at the satisfaction in his voice. 'How much is the rent, Mrs Finch?'

Vera told him. 'That includes laundry, cleaning of your room and all meals, which will be taken along with the family.' She paused. 'No cooking in the rooms, Mr Oglander. I'm very fussy about that.'

'That's very satisfactory, Mrs Finch,' he said and put his case on the bed. 'I take it I can move in now?'

'Yes, of course.'

He reached into the inside pocket of his jacket under the dustcoat and took out a wallet. When he opened it Vera saw that it fairly bulged with crisp banknotes.

'There you are, Mrs Finch,' Bill Oglander said, selecting some notes and holding them out to her. 'Here's a month's rent in advance.'

Vera took them eagerly. 'I'm afraid you've missed lunch, Mr Oglander,' she said. 'But I'll be making a hot meal at supper-time.'

Vera started chatting about her family and the other residents. And her worries about her daughter's new job.

'Thank you,' he interrupted. 'I'm going to take a nap now. I've been on the go all day and I'm not as young as I was.'

Vera took the hint. 'Well, I'll leave you to it, Mr Oglander.' She paused again. 'The facilities are along the landing.' She smiled. 'See you at supper-time. Six o'clock on the dot.'

The big basement kitchen smelled deliciously of roast beef. Gillian laid out the table as she was expected to do: eight place settings – the family and three boarders.

'When you've finished that,' Vera said, 'go up and sound the gong.'

The dinner gong was kept in the hall at the bottom of the staircase. Gillian thought it pretentious and totally unnecessary to sound it since Vera always served supper at six o'clock on the dot and family and boarders were usually gathered in the drawing room in readiness, but knowing better than to disregard her mother's instructions she picked up the stick and hit the gong resoundingly three times.

Mr Gilmore and Miss Philpot were the first out

of the drawing room. They had both been lodging with Vera some years and seemed part of their family now. Her brothers Sam and Tom strolled out next, arguing as usual. Gillian hung back, waiting for her father. She was excited at the prospect of starting work at the yard office and wanted to ask him more about the place.

Arthur Finch came out at last, pausing to knock the contents of the bowl of his pipe into the flowerpot that stood on the hall table.

'Dad, what do you think I should wear on my first day?'

Her father looked perplexed. 'Something sensible, I hope,' he said as they strolled towards the stairs that led down to the kitchen. 'You're going to a place of work not to a dance.'

'Yes, but I want to look smart,' Gillian said. 'I want to be taken seriously. Sam told me that I'll be the first female they've had working in the yard.'

'That's true,' Arthur said thoughtfully. 'I'll have to have a word with Henry about the ... er ... facilities for you.'

'You mean the lavatory?' Gillian asked. 'Surely they have lavatories at the yard?'

'For the men, yes,' Arthur said. 'For women, no.' They were about to go into the kitchen and her father touched her arm in caution. 'Don't talk of lavatories in front of your mother. It might put her off. I'll work something out.'

They were all seated and her father, at the head of the table, was about to start carving the meat. One chair was empty.

'Where's Mr Oglander?' Vera asked sharply. 'I

told him six o'clock.'

'I'll miss Mr Brundle,' Miss Philpot said sadly. 'He had such good conversation.'

Mr Gilmore gave a sharp cough. Miss Philpot's cheeks turned pink.

'Not that Mr Gilmore doesn't have good conversation, too,' she said, smiling at him coyly. 'He keeps me entertained.'

Gillian hid a smile. Poor Miss Philpot. Anyone could see she had a soft spot for Mr Gilmore. But they were both too set in their ways for it to develop. What a pity.

Her father was busy carving the piece of beef. The sight of the juices running and the smell of the vegetables made her tummy rumble.

Vera paused in arranging the food on the plates and frowned.

'Tom! Go and fetch Mr Oglander,' she said sharply to her younger son. 'He must be still asleep.'

Tom gave an irritable growl. 'I want my supper,' he said morosely, hunching down in his chair and scowling.

'I'll go, Mam,' Gillian offered, giving her twin brother a baleful look. 'Tom's too lazy to get out of his own way.'

Gillian ran up the stairs and on the half-landing stopped abruptly, finding a tall old man standing there.

'Supper's ready, Mr Oglander.'

Mr Oglander seemed old to her compared to her mother's regular boarders, who were usually people of working age with steady jobs.

'You must be Gillian,' Mr Oglander said,

smiling genially.

She was surprised he knew her name. 'Yes.'

'I see the family resemblance.'

They went down to the kitchen together. Everyone had started eating. Vera's glance at Mr Oglander was stern as he took his place.

'You're late, Mr Oglander. Now there's no time for introductions.'

'Plenty of time for that later, Vera,' Arthur said soothingly. 'Welcome, Mr Oglander.'

Vera looked affronted. 'Meals are always on the dot, Mr Oglander,' she said tightly. 'Seven thirty, one and six. Please don't be late again.'

'No, Mrs Finch, I won't,' he said in his interesting accent.

Sitting next to him Gillian ventured a sideways glance. His head was bent over his food, but she saw the ghost of a smile playing around his lips. Immediately she knew she liked him. And there was something else about him that drew her, something familiar, but she was flummoxed to know what it was.

Two

Her first day of work! Gillian was bubbling with excitement as she rode the tramcar with her father into town where Prosser & Knox had their builders' yard at the back of St Mary's Church.

Vera had prepared a packed lunch for her. Gillian decided she would eat it quickly and then spend the remainder of her lunch break window-shopping with Dorothy, with whom she had arranged a secret meeting.

The first thing Gillian noticed as she went into the yard office was how untidy it was. In the outer office, where the accounts manager Mr Meeker worked, ledgers, brown files and sheets of paper were scattered everywhere. She would soon get that sorted out, Gillian decided.

Mr Meeker was a skinny little man with a lined and worried face.

'Norman, this is my daughter Gillian,' her father said. 'She's a good girl and I know she will work hard.'

Mr Meeker shook hands with her quite cordially but she could see there was a nervousness about him. Obviously, he wasn't used to sharing an office with a girl. Well, he would have to get used to it!

'This is your desk, Miss Finch,' Mr Meeker

said formally. He had a squeaky voice and a wheezy chest. 'And this is your typewriter.'

It was an Imperial and Gillian viewed it with some disappointment. Imperials were very good machines but this one looked ancient. Never mind. She would make the most of it.

'Is Henry here yet?' Arthur Finch asked. 'I want a word with him.'

'Mr Prosser's gone up to Treboeth,' Mr Meeker said. 'There's a good chance of us getting a contract to build six houses. Speaking of which, Arthur,' he continued in a sharper tone, 'shouldn't you be getting on with that job in Manselton?'

'I had to see my girl was settled in first,' Arthur said plaintively. He nodded his head towards Gillian. 'I wanted a word.'

She knew exactly what he was going to say next and felt her cheeks flush with embarrassment.

'It's about the facilities for her.'

'It's all taken care of,' Mr Meeker said, averting his gaze from Gillian. He held up a key. 'She can use the management facilities. Only Mr Prosser and Mr Knox use it – and myself, of course. But she must always bring the key back to me.'

Gillian felt her flush deepen. It would be very embarrassing to have to ask Mr Meeker for the key every time she wanted to use the lavatory.

'Can't we leave the key on a hook somewhere?' she asked in a small voice.

'Oh, very well,' Mr Meeker said. 'But I won't take the blame if it gets lost.'

'You go now, Dad,' Gillian said to her father. 'I'll be all right.' She longed to get on with the job and prove that she was capable.

'All right, my girl,' Arthur said. 'See you at supper-time. Here is some money for the tram fare home.'

When her father had finally left, Gillian turned to Mr Meeker. 'What do you want me to do first, Mr Meeker?'

'Eh?'

'Do you have any letters to write or invoices to type up?'

'No. I do that myself.'

'But I'm here now, Mr Meeker,' Gillian said firmly. 'I've got my certificates for shorthand and typing, you know.'

Mr Meeker gazed around helplessly. 'Well, just tidy up, Miss Finch. I have to go out for a while.'

'Shall I answer the telephone when it rings?' she asked eagerly.

'Eh? Oh, yes. Take particulars,' he agreed. 'But be careful. It could be someone important. We don't want to upset customers.'

He put on his trilby and left. Gillian tightened her lips as she watched him go. She could tell by his expression and tone that he really did not approve of her being there. She glanced around at the untidiness. Well, she would soon make herself indispensable.

An hour passed and Mr Meeker had still not returned. Neither had her uncle put in an appearance. Gillian had been busy in their absence: rearranging the contents of the cabinet and filing all the loose files and papers. Not one brown folder or piece of paper was left lying around, while the ledgers were now neatly stacked on the shelf behind Mr Meeker's desk. She could not wait for him to come back to see her handiwork.

She had just come back from the lavatory, which was situated in a small courtyard reachable only from Henry Prosser's inner sanctum, when she was aware that someone had come into the outer room.

She rushed in expecting to see Mr Meeker, but instead a tall broad-shouldered young man stood there, staring around with a bemused expression on his face, his trilby hat in his hand.

Gillian pulled up short when she saw him. The first thing she noticed was how handsome he was and secondly how well his broad shoulders were set off by the excellent cut of his expensive-looking three-piece suit.

'Am I in the right office?' he asked with a smile, and Gillian thought her heart would stop, quite bowled over by his looks: dark hair and violet-coloured eyes ringed by long black eyelashes.

'I ... umm...' She felt tongue-tied.

'You must be Gillian, Arthur Finch's daughter,' he said. She loved the sound of his voice. 'Pleased to meet you, Miss Finch. Or can I call you Gill?'

Gillian opened her mouth but no words would come out. She felt mortified. He must think her an idiot. She swallowed hard and tried again.

'Yes, I'm Gillian Finch. Are you a customer?'

He let out a roar of laughter and Gillian

flushed with dismay.

'I'm sorry, Gill,' he said. 'I should've introduced myself properly. I'm Ronnie Knox, your uncle's business partner.' He held out a hand. 'How do you do, Gillian Finch?'

Gillian tentatively put her hand in his. His grip was strong yet gentle. 'How do you do, Mr Knox?'

'Call me Ronnie. Everyone does.' He held on to her hand and her confusion mounted. 'My word, you are a pretty little thing, Gill. Just what we need in this dusty office. I don't usually spend much time here but from now on nothing will keep me away.'

She stared into those fantastic eyes and felt her head swim. At that moment the office door opened and Mr Meeker walked in. Ronnie Knox dropped her hand as if it were a hot cake.

'Ah, Norman,' he said in a businesslike voice. 'The very man. Littlejohn is complaining about some oversight in the estimate we sent him. Will you look into it?'

'Yes, Mr Knox,' Mr Meeker said and walked to his desk. Then he stopped and stared around. 'What the hell...?'

'Tidy, isn't it?' Ronnie Knox said with a grin.

Mr Meeker could not answer because his mouth was hanging open.

'Our Miss Finch here has done sterling work, don't you agree, Norman?' Ronnie Knox continued.

'Where are the estimates I left on my desk?' Mr Meeker wheezed. 'The ones I've been working on all week.'

'They're quite safe,' Gillian said shortly, stung by his tone of dismay – and in front of Ronnie Knox, too. 'Everything is in the cabinet and in the proper order.'

'They were already in order.'

'It was a mess!'

'I knew where everything was,' bleated Mr Meeker. 'I could lay my hand on anything I wanted at a moment's notice.'

'Well, I'm sorry!' Gillian blurted angrily. 'You told me to tidy up.'

'I meant for you to dust around.'

'Dust!' Gillian was livid. 'I'm a qualified shorthand typist. I don't dust!'

Ronnie Knox gave a little cough. 'I'll be off,' he said. 'See you again, Gill. We'll have a longer chat. Get to know each other.' He saluted her, put on his hat and left.

Gillian was mortified that Ronnie Knox had witnessed the scene between her and Mr Meeker, who was fussing about the room shaking his head and sighing. She would not speak or even look at him afterwards and was glad when her uncle Henry came in. His appearance broke the awful tension.

'Oh, Gillian!' Henry exclaimed on seeing her. 'I'd forgotten about you. Are you settling in?'

Gillian darted a glance at Mr Meeker. 'Yes, thank you, Uncle Henry.'

'Good.'

'She's made a right ramshackle of the office,' Mr Meeker commented peevishly.

Henry looked around. 'Ramshackle? I've never seen it so tidy.'

'Huh!'

'Where's Andy, Norman?' Henry asked in a harder tone.

'Your son hasn't been in the office today so far, Mr Prosser,' Mr Meeker said.

Henry Prosser's lips tightened and Gillian could see he was angry. 'When he does deign to turn up, tell him I want to see him immediately.'

'Yes, Mr Prosser.' Mr Meeker hesitated. 'Did we get the contract, Mr Prosser?'

Henry Prosser nodded, his humour returning. 'Yes, and very profitable it'll be, too. I want to talk to you about it later.' He glanced at her. 'You can take your lunch now, Gillian,' he said and went into his inner office.

Gillian was relieved as she had had all she could stand of Mr Meeker for the moment. She had always liked her uncle Henry despite the situation between her mother and him. He was tall, lean and really quite good-looking, she always thought. Since the terrible bust-up over her grandmother's will she had not seen much of him, but he was always pleasant to her.

Not bothering with eating her packed lunch, Gillian lost no time in going off to meet Dorothy outside Ben Evans' store. She had so much to tell her cousin, especially about Ronnie Knox. Gillian gave a huge sigh. He was so handsome.

Dorothy was standing on the pavement outside the store. They had planned to go up to the Kardomah but her cousin did not make a move or smile a greeting as she usually did. Her gaze was dour as she searched Gillian's face.

'How did your first morning go?'

Gillian was still smarting at the belittling attitude of Mr Meeker and gave Dorothy a blow-by-blow account of their disagreement.

'Me! Dust!' Gillian laughed. 'My mother didn't pay high fees at Clarke's College just so I could dust some office.'

'Who else was there?'

'Well, your brother Andy wasn't for a start,' Gillian said flatly. 'Uncle Henry was really cross about it.'

Dorothy waved a hand impatiently. 'Who else?'

'Ronnie Knox came in.' Gillian smiled broadly. She had been longing to tell her cousin about their meeting. 'Oh, Dot, Ronnie is so handsome. He reminds me of Rudolf Valentino.'

Dorothy's expression became sour. 'He's Mr Knox to you, Gill. You're just the typist,' she said sharply. 'Ronnie is my father's business *partner*, after all.'

Gillian tossed her head. 'He *told* me to call him Ronnie,' she said firmly. 'He said I was pretty and he wants to get to know me better.'

'You're making that up!' Dorothy burst out. 'Ronnie is too elegant and sophisticated to bother with some office girl like you.'

'Well!' Gillian was cross. 'That's all you know!' She tossed her head. 'He held my hand as a matter of fact,' she said triumphantly. 'He was very impressed with me, I could tell.'

'Oh!' Dorothy stamped her foot in fury. 'You stay away from Ronnie,' she exploded. 'I saw him first.'

'What?' Gillian stared at her cousin in

astonishment. She could hardly believe they were quarrelling over him, but at the same time she disputed her cousin's claim. 'You don't even know him.'

'Yes, I do. I know him very well,' Dorothy asserted. 'Ronnie has been over to dinner at our house several times. My mother says he's the perfect match for me. It would keep the business in the family and all that.'

Gillian stared at her open-mouthed.

Dorothy lifted her chin in triumph. 'My mother says she's going to see to it that Ronnie marries me. He's already in love with me. Last time he was at our house he kissed me.'

'I don't believe it!'

Dorothy looked smug. 'My family are well off and Ronnie is, too. We're the same class.' She gave Gillian a disdainful look. 'I can't see him taking any interest in the daughter of a mere plumber and a boarding-house keeper.'

'You stuck-up cat!' Gillian exclaimed, enraged at the slur on her family. 'How dare you say that about my parents? At least *my* father is honest. He didn't cheat his family out of their inheritance.'

Dorothy spluttered in fury. 'You spiteful thing, Gill,' she gasped. 'You're just like Aunt Vera. Out for everything she can get. That's what my mother says, and it's true.'

Gillian was outraged. During their four-year friendship they had had their disagreements but had never quarrelled so bitterly before. It looked like their friendship was about to fall apart.

'Well, Dot,' said Gillian, 'you're showing your

true colours at last. And to think I was prepared to be your best friend. Snake in the grass, that's what my mother calls your father, and you're a chip off the old block.'

'You hussy!' Dorothy squealed in wrath. 'You're throwing yourself at Ronnie. But there! My mother says you're common, and she's right. Thank goodness she doesn't know how I've lowered myself even speaking to you, let alone being your friend.'

'Friend!' Gillian spluttered. 'You don't know the meaning of the word.' She glared at her cousin. 'This is the last time I'll speak one word to you, Dorothy Prosser. You and I are finished.'

'That suits me!' Dorothy flared.

Gillian swung away on her heels and then turned back. 'And don't think you're getting Ronnie Knox either,' she said passionately. 'I'll be seeing him every day from now on. You don't stand a chance.'

With that she stuck her nose in the air and turned away to stalk off along the pavement. She longed to look over her shoulder to see what Dorothy was doing, but she would not give her cousin the satisfaction.

She hurried down to the tram stop outside the middle market gate, still seething at what had been said. After all these years Dorothy had shown what she really thought. She could hardly believe she had been taken in by her cousin for so long.

She was on the tram halfway home when she suddenly realized she should have returned to the office at Prosser & Knox. Would Uncle

31

Henry sack her? She hoped not. She really wanted the job but she could not face going back now. She was overwrought and had had enough of Mr Meeker for one day.

By the time she was walking along Marlborough Road towards her mother's house it was all she could do to stop herself bursting into tears. She had lost her best friend. Worse than that, she had discovered that her so-called friend secretly despised her.

Tears and rage fought for supremacy. What was so aggravating was that there was no one she could confide in or discuss the quarrel with. Suddenly she felt so alone.

Feeling very dejected Gillian hung her coat and tam on the hallstand and then crept quietly towards the staircase, hoping to find sanctuary in her bedroom. But at that moment Vera came out of the drawing room. She stopped abruptly when she saw Gillian on the stairs.

'Gill! What are you doing home at this hour and on your first day at work?'

Gillian swallowed hard, trying not to cry, unable to reply.

Vera hurried to her, her face showing concern. 'What's wrong, my girl?'

Gillian shook her head. 'Nothing.'

'You're as white as a sheet,' her mother said. 'Something's happened.' She grabbed Gillian's arm and pulled her towards the drawing room. 'You'll tell me what's happened this minute.'

Gillian could not hold back the tears any longer and let herself be dragged into the room.

'Now then,' Vera said firmly. 'This has something to do with my brother, hasn't it? Has Henry been uncivil to you? Has he sacked you?' She nodded sagely. 'That would be just like him.' Her lips thinned in anger. 'Well, you're not going back there. I knew it was a mistake from the start.'

Gillian gulped. 'No, no! It's not Uncle Henry's fault,' she said in a small voice, suddenly fearful for her job and the opportunity of meeting Ronnie Knox again. 'He was very nice to me, as a matter of fact.'

'Well, someone's upset you.'

Gillian dare not admit her friendship with Dorothy. Vera would be incensed at what she would see as a betrayal.

'It's Mr Meeker,' Gillian said quickly, wiping her nose on her hanky. 'He wanted me to dust the office. He's the one that upset me.' It was partly true, anyway.

Vera raised her brows. 'Is that all?'

'I'm a qualified shorthand typist,' Gillian said hotly. 'Not a common cleaner.'

'Well, it doesn't matter now because you're not going back.'

'Yes, I am, Mam,' Gillian said firmly, surprising herself. She very rarely found the courage to contradict her mother. 'I want to go back. I'm not letting Mr Meeker beat me.'

Vera stared at her and Gillian held her mother's shrewd look with difficulty. She was determined to see Ronnie Knox again. He was interested in her, she could tell. And she was a little bit ashamed to realize that deep in her heart she wanted to spite Dorothy.

'Your father will have a word with Mr Meeker tomorrow,' Vera said.

Gillian was appalled. 'No, Mam. That would make things worse.' She straightened her shoulders. 'I'm out in the world now, and I have to fight my own battles.'

She caught a fleeting flash of admiration and satisfaction in her mother's eyes. 'I knew I'd brought you up properly,' Vera said. 'You've got the Prosser spirit all right.'

'I'll just wash my face,' Gillian said, relieved. 'And then I'll come down and help you in the kitchen.'

After supper that evening Gillian was in the kitchen doing the washing-up when her brothers strolled in too nonchalantly by half. She gave them a wary glance, wondering what they were up to. They hardly ever came down to the kitchen unless it was for meals.

'Everything all right, our Gill?' Sam asked lightly.

Older than her by two years, he was a carbon copy of their father, medium height, stocky build and with the same genial expression. He had shed his dirty overalls, which he wore as an apprentice electrician with Prosser & Knox, and had cleaned himself up before supper.

'Why wouldn't it be?' she retorted tartly, eyeing them suspiciously.

'We heard tales,' her twin Tom said, teasing her.

He sat on the edge of the kitchen table, still

34

wearing the dingy dungarees he wore as an apprentice bricklayer and plasterer at the yard. He had sat down to supper like that and Gillian was surprised her mother put up with it. But then – tall and lean like most of the Prosser men – Tom could do no wrong in Vera's eyes, and Gillian was keenly aware that her twin brother was their mother's favourite.

'Tales?'

Tom grinned disarmingly. 'What do you think of God's gift to women, then?'

'Do you mean Mr Meeker?'

Sam laughed.

'No,' Tom said. 'I mean Ronnie Knox.'

Gillian turned her face away to hide the flush rising to her cheeks. 'I think he's very charming and handsome,' she said carefully.

'Oh, no!' Tom chortled. 'And another one bites the dust!'

Gillian rounded on him. 'What do you mean?'

'You've fallen for him,' Tom said. 'They all do.'

'I have not!'

'Well, you want to be careful, sister, dear,' Tom said jeeringly. 'Ronnie will have you in the family way before you can say knit one, purl one.'

'Ooh!' Gillian was thoroughly shocked.

Sam stepped forward swiftly and gave his brother a clip across the back of the head. 'Watch your tongue, squirt!'

'Ouch! That hurt!'

'Push off,' Sam ordered. 'And clean yourself up.'

Scowling, Tom left the kitchen.

Sam hung back a moment. 'Sometimes I can't believe you're really his twin, our Gill,' he said. 'The stork dropped him at the wrong house.'

Gillian managed a smile. 'At least we're not identical. That's something to be thankful for.'

Sam smiled at her but still hesitated to follow his brother.

'About Ronnie Knox—' he began.

'Oh, not you, too, Sam!'

'I'm serious,' her brother said. 'Ronnie does have a way with the girls. I've heard rumours about him, and not very pretty ones either.' Gillian was reminded sharply of Dorothy's admission that Ronnie had kissed her. Was it true, after all? 'Whereas you *are* pretty, and knowing Ronnie he'll be after you.' His grin faded. 'Just be on your guard, our Gill.'

Sam and Tom had gone out. The rest of the family and boarders were in the drawing room listening to the wireless broadcasting dance music: Carroll Gibbons and his Savoy Hotel Orpheans.

Feeling wretched, Gillian could not bear to join them but instead sat in the fading light on the staircase above the half-landing, out of sight of anyone coming into the hallway. From there she could hear the music and yet be alone.

In a house full of people she felt so lonely; there was no one she could confide in. There was Sam, of course. He would not betray her confidences to their mother, but at the same time he would not understand either. He had lots of pals

36

and she had only Dorothy for a friend.

If only she had not been so exclusive. She should have made other friends, and yet with Dorothy there seemed to be no need for anyone else. Her heart felt heavy with it all and she knew it would not be relieved until she could discuss everything openly with someone.

Gillian was startled by a sound of a soft footfall on the stairs behind her. Turning to see who it was, she recognized their new boarder, Mr Oglander. Snuffling into her handkerchief, Gillian stood up out of his way as he descended.

'Hello, Gillian,' he said. 'What are you doing all alone here on the stairs?'

Gillian felt embarrassed. 'I could ask you the same thing, Mr Oglander.'

They stood on the same stair and he looked down on her from his height. 'Are you crying?'

'No,' she denied. 'I've got something in my eye.'

'I'm sorry,' he said and lowered himself to sit on the stair next to her.

Surprised, Gillian sat, too.

'It helps to be alone to sort things out, doesn't it?' Mr Oglander said. 'I do it all the time, especially when I'm feeling sad.'

'I'm not sad.'

'Aren't you?' His voice was gentle with sympathy. 'Why don't you tell me about it?'

Suddenly Gillian wanted to pour it all out. Mr Oglander was a stranger; he wouldn't judge or blame her. She gave a little sob.

'It's about my cousin and very best friend, Dorothy,' she said. 'We had an awful quarrel and

I can't tell my mother because – well, I'm not supposed to know her.'

'Dorothy? That would be Henry's daughter,' said Mr Oglander.

'Do you know Uncle Henry?' Gillian was curious.

'No, but I've heard your mother talking about her brother. And your father likes to chat about the Prosser family.'

'The thing is,' Gillian went on, 'my friendship with Dorothy is finished and I'm so upset about it. Now I've got no one to confide in.'

'Well, I'm sure the quarrel won't last,' Mr Oglander said cheerfully. 'It'll be forgotten by tomorrow.'

'No, it won't,' Gillian said. She hesitated, wondering whether to mention the real cause of the rift, then decided it did not matter. Mr Oglander was a stranger. 'We quarrelled over a man.'

'A man?' There was a change in Mr Oglander's tone. 'What man?'

'Uncle Henry's business partner, Ronnie Knox.'

'Knox?'

'Ronnie is so handsome,' Gillian confided. 'And he was very nice to me when I met him today. But Dorothy was jealous. She reckons she's going to marry him.' Gillian sniffed plaintively. 'I'm sure he prefers me, anyway.'

Mr Oglander was silent.

'You won't tell anyone about my friendship with Dorothy, will you, Mr Oglander?' Gillian asked. 'Especially my mother. She'd be ever so cross. She'd say I was disloyal. But Dorothy and I got on so well.' She gave a little sob. 'It was a very happy friendship.'

'Until Mr Ronnie Knox came between you,' said Mr Oglander.

'He hasn't come between us.'

'Hasn't he? Are you sure?' Mr Oglander stood up. 'Come down to the drawing room, Gillian. Let's join the others.'

Gillian felt better for having got things off her chest and followed him down the stairs. Maybe Mr Oglander was right. Things had been fine between her and Dorothy until she met Ronnie.

Oh, but he was so handsome.

Everyone had gone to bed. Arthur still sat in the drawing room, smoking his pipe. Mr Oglander sat with him, also puffing away at a pipe.

Vera put her head around the door. 'Don't stay down too long, Arthur,' she warned. 'And don't wake me when you come up.'

'I won't, love.'

Arthur stretched out his legs before him, pipe between his teeth. 'This is the time of day I love best,' he said to his companion. 'Peace and quiet.'

'Am I in the way?' Mr Oglander said, attempting to rise from the armchair.

'No, no,' Arthur said, waving him down. 'It's good to have someone intelligent to talk to for a change.' He took his pipe out of his mouth and looked across at Mr Oglander. 'Not that Vera isn't intelligent,' he added quickly. 'In fact she's too sharp for my own good sometimes.'

'I know what you mean,' Mr Oglander said. 'Your daughter Gillian is an intelligent girl, too.'

Arthur nodded. 'Oh, yes. She gets it from the Prosser side of the family, you know.'

'Really?'

'Know-how.' Arthur nodded sagely. 'That's what the Prossers have in bucketfuls: know-how. They know how to make a shilling, or even twenty. They're a family to be reckoned with, Mr Oglander.' He spoke with such pride that his listener might have believed Arthur was a Prosser himself. 'Gillian's great-grandfather Samuel started the business,' he went on. 'He was a shrewd one, and a hard taskmaster.'

'You knew him, then?' asked Mr Oglander.

'Hardly!' Arthur chuckled. 'Samuel Prosser was long dead when I started my apprenticeship in 1906, but I listened when the older tradesmen, like Bert Tomkin, talked about him – they respected him.'

'The salt of the earth?' Mr Oglander suggested.

Arthur nodded. 'Don't see his like nowadays.'

'You're right, Mr Finch. So what became of the business when Samuel had gone? Was there a change in ownership?'

'No, not really.' Arthur frowned. 'Old Samuel did a strange thing. When he died he left only sixty per cent of the business to his only son William and the other forty per cent to a young employee named Charlie Knox, barely twenty-three years old.' He shook his head. 'A bit of a mystery about that to tell you the truth, Mr Oglander. No one knows why he did it.'

'Must have had his reasons.'

Arthur shrugged. 'Whatever they were, Charlie Knox fell in lucky. At the time of Samuel's death William Prosser was still doing his apprenticeship so Charlie was in full charge.'

'Strange indeed,' Mr Oglander agreed.

'Charlie was still running things in 1906 when I started there,' Arthur said. 'And he was doing a good job of it, too.' Arthur puffed at his pipe for a moment while Mr Oglander remained silent, waiting. 'Charlie was a real sharper, Mr Oglander, even in his older years,' Arthur continued at last. He tapped the side of his nose. 'Canny and clever, with his eye on the main chance and made damn sure he got it, too.' He gave Mr Oglander a knowing look. 'Both in business and in private.'

Mr Oglander raised his eyebrows in query.

'Women,' Arthur explained. 'Charlie couldn't keep his hands off the women.'

Mr Oglander digested that while Arthur puffed on his pipe.

'What about Samuel's son?' Mr Oglander asked at last.

'William finished his apprenticeship, got married, and had a couple of kids, Henry and Vera. He and Charlie remained partners until—'

Arthur stopped speaking abruptly, realizing he was talking too much on matters about which he knew very little.

'Until?' prompted Mr Oglander.

Arthur leaned forward to knock out his pipe in the hearth.

'It's getting late,' he said quickly. 'Vera will be after my blood if I stay down here much longer.'

41

'What happened to William Prosser?' Mr Oglander asked. 'You've aroused my curiosity, Mr Finch. Don't leave me on the edge of my seat.'

Arthur's glance slid away. 'He died,' he said matter-of-factly. 'And then his widow Rose, Vera's mother, married Charlie Knox.'

He stood up and stretched. Mr Oglander stood up, too.

'The Prosser family seem to have a fascinating history, Mr Finch. I'd like to learn more.'

'We'll chat again,' Arthur said offhandedly. He was anxious to leave his companion. 'Goodnight to you, Mr Oglander.'

Three

Hafod, Swansea, January 1889

William Prosser let himself into his father's house on Aberdyberthy Street and crossed the high, wide hall, floored with black and white tiles. The dark January day made the place seem gloomier than usual – or did the pall of death still linger?

William took off his hat and coat and squared his shoulders, ready to face any mourners still remaining in the house.

Samuel, his father, was gone. This was his

house now, his inheritance. He must take his father's place and run the business to the best of his ability. It was a big responsibility at his age, but he felt up to the task, as young as he was.

Someone came out of the drawing room and William turned to see Mr Simmons, his father's solicitor.

'William, where have you been? You should have been here to thank mourners for attending the funeral. Everyone has gone now.'

William took objection to the solicitor's chiding tone. Simmons would never have dared speak to his father that way.

'I took my fiancée home. Rose wasn't feeling very well,' he said shortly. 'She was overcome by it all.'

'But surely her father could've done that. Didn't he attend?'

'Rose's father is deceased,' William said curtly. 'It's just her and her mother.'

'Oh, I see. Well, nevertheless, your place was here. It was rather embarrassing that you left the house so quickly. Your sister had to stand in for you.'

'Cissie is very capable,' William said. 'And she is the eldest child.'

'She's not the head of the house now, William. You are. Well, let's waste no more time. The will has to be read.'

Mr Simmons led the way back into the drawing room: a long, narrow room darkly furnished in the early Victorian style.

William paused at the door, looking towards the far end of the room where two people sat on a black leather chesterfield. He had expected to see his older unmarried sister Cissie, but he had not expected to see one of his father's young employees, Charlie Knox.

William caught Simmons' arm. 'Why is Charlie Knox still here?'

Mr Simmons hesitated before replying. 'He's a beneficiary, William.'

'What?' William frowned. 'A beneficiary?'

'If you'll let me get on with the reading, all will become clear.'

Cissie gave him a sad little smile as he sat down opposite her. Poor Cissie. Ten years older than he was, but he always thought of her that way. Tall and thin, she looked gaunt in the black mourning dress she wore.

Cissie had devoted herself to their father since she was sixteen after their mother had died and had never had a life of her own. Now she was free, in a way.

William glanced at Charlie Knox and nodded acknowledgement. Charlie's returned glance was full of confidence as usual. He was a tall, well-built handsome man and, although married two years, still had an eye for the ladies, so it was said. William found that trait distasteful.

Mr Simmons sat down and fumbled with some sheets of paper.

'William, you may not know that your father made a new will recently,' he began.

'What?'

'He knew he was dying,' Mr Simmons said gravely. 'He was very concerned about the future of the business, Prosser and Son, and

44

therefore he made a change.' Mr Simmons glanced at Charlie Knox. 'Samuel decided you would need help running the business, William, and so he secured help for you.'

William was bewildered. 'I don't understand.'

'Samuel felt you needed a business partner. Someone in whom he had the utmost confidence.' Mr Simmons wetted his lips. 'In his new will Samuel left sixty per cent of ownership in the business to you when you reach the age of twenty-one and have finished your apprenticeship. The other forty per cent is left to Mr Charles Knox. Mr Knox is now your partner.'

'What?' William stared from one man to another. 'Are you saying that my father had no confidence in my ability to run the business alone?'

'It's not for me to say what his motives were,' Mr Simmons said. 'I'm here to see that his wishes in his will are carried out.'

William was stunned and very hurt. His father had not believed he was capable. He felt humiliated, especially in front of Charlie Knox, who had been merely an employee yesterday.

'He didn't even give me a chance to prove myself,' William said.

'You're only twenty years old, William,' Mr Simmons pointed out. 'And you have a year still before you finish your apprenticeship. Your father acted in your best interests and the interests of Prosser and Son.'

'That name will have to be changed now.' Charlie Knox spoke up for the first time, his tone already authoritative. 'We'll change it to Prosser and Knox.' His confident gaze met William's glare. 'I think that's only right, Will, since I'm now a partner.'

William was astonished at the other man's self-assurance and composure. Knox, just three years older than him, had just inherited almost half of a flourishing building contractors and had taken the news in his stride.

'You don't seem surprised at what's in the will, Charlie,' William said tetchily. 'Did you know?'

Charlie Knox nodded. 'Yes, as a matter of fact, I did. Mr Prosser told me about it a month ago. He warned me to speak of it to no one.'

Anger stirred in William's heart against his father. Samuel had confided in an employee but had not bothered to take his own son into his confidence. His pride was hurt and it rankled.

He caught Cissie's glance and suddenly felt ashamed. So wrapped up in himself he had forgotten about provision for her. What about poor Cissie?

'Did my father leave anything for Cissie?'

'Miss Prosser is left a reasonable annuity, which will increase on a yearly basis for the rest of her life unless she marries.'

'That's all?' William frowned.

'The annuity is adequate,' Mr Simmons said. 'I believe your father expected that Miss Prosser would continue to live here with you.'

'Yes, of course.' William nodded. 'Cissie and I were born in this house. This is her home and always will be as long as she wishes.'

Cissie, sitting quietly, smiled at him in gratitude.

'Apart from the business side, the rest of the estate including this property now belongs to you, William,' Mr Simmons told him. 'Your inheritance is sizeable. You are a wealthy young man.'

William was hardly listening. He had known his father was dying and had prepared himself for the heavy responsibility that would eventually rest on his shoulders. Now he felt cheated and outraged that his father had had so little confidence in him. Samuel had saddled him with a partner he did not want, and in truth did not trust.

There was nothing he could do about the situation, but something warned him that he should never turn his back on Charlie Knox.

Mr Simmons, having finished his business with the will, took his leave.

There was an awkward silence between the remaining three in the sitting room. William, still angry and humiliated, was at a loss to know how to treat his new partner. It was Cissie who broke the ice.

'Your wife must be very pleased at your good fortune, Mr Knox,' she said. There was no rancour in her tone.

'Yes, indeed,' Charlie Knox said. 'Now that I'll be earning extra, Freda wants us to buy a house. She thinks it will be good for our boy George rather than living in rooms as we are now.'

'How is your son?'

'He's a year old and thriving,' Charlie Knox told her, his voice thick with pride. He glanced at William. 'I suppose you'll be bringing your wedding forward now?'

'No,' William answered abruptly. 'I see no reason to change our plans. Rose and I will marry next year when I come of age.'

'That's probably wise,' Charlie said, nodding. 'Rose is young. She probably won't be able to cope with the responsibility of this house. It is a bit of a mausoleum, Will. You should sell and buy something more modern.'

'My father built this house by the sweat of his brow.' William was angry. 'It's a monument to his hard work.'

'Damned difficult to keep up to scratch, though,' Charlie Knox remarked evenly, seemingly unmoved by William's anger. 'I still think it'll be too much for Rose.'

'Cissie has managed this house perfectly well since she was sixteen,' William said curtly. 'Rose will have my sister to rely on when the time comes.'

Charlie Knox stood up, ready to go. 'I'll go around to the sign makers tomorrow, first thing,' he said. 'To get the new sign painted.'

William stood up, too. 'I haven't agreed to a name change yet,' he said brusquely. 'I'm still the major shareholder.'

Charlie's jaw tightened imperceptibly. 'Nevertheless, Will, I am now your partner whether you like it or not. You need me. Your father believed in my ability to help the business prosper.'

He paused, and William thought he detected a smirk on the other man's face.

'You still have a year to reach your maturity, Will,' Charlie continued, 'and to finish your

48

apprenticeship before you are a full partner.'

William gritted his teeth. 'Don't rub my nose in it, Charlie.'

'I'll take the helm in the meantime,' Charlie said with confidence. 'It was what was discussed with your father. He made it quite clear. I am to run things until you are twenty-one.'

William turned his head away and did not speak. It was galling that Charlie was to become his boss for at least another year. The arrangement made him look like a complete fool.

'I'd better go,' Charlie said. 'I'll see myself out, Miss Prosser.'

William turned his back and heard Charlie leave the room. He felt mortified.

'Will?' Cissie's voice was soft. 'Why don't you have a glass of sherry to soothe your nerves? It's been a difficult day for you.'

William turned eagerly to her sympathy. 'Why did Father do it, Cissie? Did he think so little of me?'

'Quite the reverse,' his sister said. 'He was thinking only of you. Admit it, Will. It would have been a great strain, running the business, coping with the men, most of them years older than you.'

'I would have managed.'

'Now you have Mr Knox to rely on.'

'He's trying to take over already.'

'Then don't let him. Assert yourself.'

'Oh, Cissie!' He went to her and grasped her hands in his. 'Thank God I have you.'

'I'll always be here, Will.'

'There's nothing stopping you from marrying

now, finding a new life.'

Cissie smiled wanly, her head on one side as she gazed at him.

'Look at me, Will. I'm thirty already. An old maid. I know I look like a long drink of water. No man would want me.'

'Don't deride yourself, Cissie,' William said earnestly. 'I've never met a woman more capable than you. You're loving and giving. You'd make a wonderful wife for any man.'

Cissie withdrew her hands. 'I'll get you that sherry. At least let me look after you as I did Father.'

'I won't make a skivvy of you, Cissie,' William said. 'It's not right.'

'I like my life, Will,' his sister said. 'I always have really.'

He sat down and she brought him a glass.

'Mr Knox is right, though,' she said as she handed it to him. 'You could bring your wedding forward. I'm sure Rose wants that.'

'Yes, she does,' he admitted. 'But I don't.' He glanced up at her. 'Don't misunderstand. I love Rose dearly and I want to marry her. But first, I have to make my mark in the business – with or without Charlie Knox.'

'You'll do the right thing, Will,' Cissie said. 'You're that kind of man. Father knew that.'

William said nothing. He had always thought his father believed in him. Now Samuel had proved him wrong. Charlie Knox's partnership spoke volumes about what Samuel had really felt.

William was disconsolate. He would never

now be able to prove that he had it in him to succeed, as his father had done, with Charlie Knox continually overshadowing him.

'Can I get you another sherry?' Cissie asked, breaking into his morbid thoughts.

William shook his head.

'I think I'll have one,' Cissie said. She went to the chiffonier, half-filled a glass and then came back and sat down opposite him, taking a sip. 'If Father could see me now,' she remarked. 'He'd be frowning. He never liked to see me at rest.'

'That's over,' William said firmly. 'You're still in charge of the house, Cissie, but I'm going to hire extra help. No more hard work for you.'

She clicked her tongue. 'Nonsense. I thrive on hard work.'

William was silent; his thoughts were on what was ahead of him with Charlie Knox in charge. It would be galling. The men would despise him. How could he live with it?

'Charlie Knox is not the man you are, Will,' Cissie said, as though reading his mind. 'He's go-ahead, I grant you, but there's something lacking in moral fibre.'

William glanced at her in surprise. 'You don't know him well enough to say that.'

'I know he's carrying on with a young widow living on Odo Street,' she said flatly. 'And his mother-in-law told me that his wife Freda has just had a miscarriage. Perhaps the poor girl found out he's deceiving her. They've only been married two years.'

Again William was astonished. 'How do you know all this, Cissie?'

51

She smiled. 'I may be a spinster, old before my years, but I'm not totally unworldly. You'd be amazed what I learn about people, Will.'

He gave her a long speculative look. 'You know about Rose's background, then?'

'I know her mother was never married.' Cissie shrugged. 'It doesn't matter one iota, does it, Will?'

'Not to me. I love Rose. Her illegitimacy is irrelevant.'

'Everything will work out, Will,' his sister said. 'Within a year you'll have finished your apprenticeship and reached maturity. You'll be able to take charge of the business then.'

'I suppose so.'

'Just keep your wits about you,' she warned. 'Take nothing for granted where Charlie Knox is concerned. He has already proved himself a cheat.'

Four

Brynmill, Swansea, 1931

Henry gingerly negotiated the turning into the driveway of his house in Brynmill, bringing the big Humber motor to a stop outside the door. He sat for a moment, thinking and trying to control his anger.

Andy had not shown his face at the office all day, and it wasn't the first time. If his son made an appearance more than three times in a week it was a miracle. Well, enough was enough. No matter what Gloria would say, Henry was determined to have it out with Andy this evening. There would be no more excuses.

He climbed out of the car and let himself into the house. His maiden aunt Cissie was in the hall.

'Good evening, Henry,' she began, her eyes bright and inquisitive. 'Everything all right?'

Henry sighed. The old girl had a nose for impending trouble. She had lost height over the years and at seventy-two was slightly stooped, but he knew her mind was as sharp as his own, perhaps sharper.

'Good evening, Aunt Cissie. Where's Andy?'

53

'In the drawing room with his *dear* mother Gloria.'

Henry resisted a smile at the mockery in her voice. He knew that with her wry humour and forthright way of speaking his aunt was a thorn in Gloria's side. His wife's hoity-toity airs and graces cut no ice with Aunt Cissie. It amused him as a rule, but this evening he was too angry to find anything even vaguely funny.

'Where's Dorothy?'

'In her room.' Cissie paused, frowning. 'She seems upset about something. She's been crying.'

Henry grunted and turned towards the drawing room. His aunt followed him in. He strode purposefully to the fireplace and stood with his back to it, scowling, while Cissie took a seat near the window.

Gloria was in an armchair, her well-corseted figure resplendent in a floral silk afternoon dress. Her hair was set in a marcel wave with not a hair out of place.

'Oh, Henry,' she began in a high, affected voice. 'I'm so glad you're early this evening. We have the Bartletts and Heslop-Joneses dining here tonight. They'll be our neighbours when we move next month to the new house in Sketty. I do want to make a good impression.'

Henry ignored her. He looked at Andy, sprawled carelessly on the chesterfield nearby. His son was tall and lanky and a carbon copy of him except in the ways that really mattered. Andy was lazy and without ambition.

'Where the hell were you today, Andy?' Henry

bellowed. 'I'm sick to death of you swinging the lead. I won't put up with it any longer.'

'Henry!' exclaimed Gloria. 'Don't speak to Andy like that. You know what a sensitive boy he is.'

Henry ground his teeth. 'Stay out of it, Gloria. This is between me and my son.' He glanced at Andy. 'Well, what've you to say for yourself, eh?'

'I had other things to do,' Andy said in a surly voice, keeping his gaze downcast and making no attempt to stir himself.

'What things?' Henry barked. 'Wasting time and money. *My* money. Sometimes I can hardly believe you're my son.'

'Huh!' Gloria flared. 'You don't treat him like a son! You'd have him slaving in that office every hour of the day if you had your way.' She sniffed into a handkerchief. 'You don't even try to understand him.'

'Oh, I understand him all right,' Henry growled. 'He's a lazy little swine. I've a good mind to kick him out.'

'Don't be stupid, will you?' Gloria spluttered, her posh accent slipping. 'Andy is your only son. He'll inherit your share of the business one day.'

'And run it into the ground,' Henry said. 'He doesn't have it in him, Gloria, and I'm ashamed to say it. He's no Prosser.'

'What are you suggesting?' Gloria's shrill voice rose. 'Of course he's a Prosser.'

'Andy takes after your father, Gloria,' Henry blared. 'A layabout, a waster living by his wits.'

Gloria sprang to her feet, her face crimson.

'Cissie! Leave the room, please.'

'Stay where you are, Aunt Cissie,' Henry commanded in a loud voice.

'Why do you always humiliate me in my own home?' Gloria bleated, dabbing at her nose with the handkerchief again. 'My father was *not* a layabout. He had his own business.'

'Business, my arse!' Henry exploded. 'Old Man Skinner was a scavenger, collecting rags, bones, skins and any other old tat he could find.'

'Oh!' Gloria flopped back into the armchair, the handkerchief covering her face. 'How could you?'

Henry was feeling vengeful for the way she had tricked him into marriage and for all the years he had suffered her cold scheming ways. 'And if you ask me, your father was a thief as well.'

'Henry! You go too far.' She clutched dramatically at her chest. 'My heart won't stand this.'

'You have a heart of stone, Gloria. Nothing can touch it.'

Gloria sat forward in the chair, her face livid. 'You beast!' she shrieked. 'Sometimes I hate you.'

'Well, you never loved me, that's for sure,' he said mockingly. 'I was your ticket out of the slums.'

'Ooh!'

Henry turned to his son. 'You'd better be at that office first thing tomorrow, earning your wage, Andy. Or you'll be sorry. Let's see how you get on without money.'

'You can't do that to me!' Andy jerked to his

feet. 'You'll make me a laughing stock.'

'You heard what I said.' He turned to Gloria. 'I'm going out. Don't wait up.'

'But what about our dinner guests?' Gloria exclaimed, horrified. 'You can't leave me in the lurch, Henry. How can I explain your absence?'

Henry shook his head. 'You'll scheme your way out of it, Gloria. You always do.'

Henry drove the Humber into town, parked it in Lower Oxford Street and walked the rest of the way to Fleet Street. Using his key, he let himself into the humble two-up two-down, terraced house.

A wireless was playing dance-band music. Florrie loved her dance-band music. The aroma of freshly baked bread teased his nostrils. Immediately he felt his sour mood lift. He was home.

'Florrie! Florrie love, it's me.' He hurried eagerly down the passage to the back room. 'Florrie!'

In the back room an older man was sitting reading a newspaper beside the range fire. He looked up when Henry came in.

'Hello, Bert,' Henry said hesitantly. 'Where's Florrie?'

'My daughter has just slipped next door to give old Mrs Phillips something to eat.' Bert Tomkin's tone was not friendly, but then it never was. 'She'll be back in a minute. Are you stopping?'

'Probably,' said Henry.

Bert's disapproval of him was tangible, but he

never voiced it. Henry was his employer, after all.

Henry sat on a chair near the table. 'Where's Jimmy?'

'Your son is in our bedroom reading,' Bert said. 'His nose is never out of a book. The times I've had to try to sleep with the light on.'

His tone was curt and Henry knew the older man would never forgive him for Jimmy's illegitimacy. Bert didn't seem to take into account that Henry loved Florrie with all his heart and Jimmy, too. Florrie was the woman he should have married.

'Bert, listen, I've been thinking,' Henry said, leaning forward. 'Jimmy will be seventeen next week. I want him to take an apprenticeship with Prosser and Knox. I thought he could train as a plumber under Arthur Finch.'

Bert lowered the newspaper. 'Arthur is a good man,' he agreed and then frowned. 'But would it not be better if Jimmy apprenticed elsewhere? Think how shamed he'd be if the truth got out.'

'My son has never reproached me for his background,' Henry said stiffly.

He and Florrie had decided to tell Jimmy the truth as soon as he was old enough to understand. For all Bert's disapproval they were a real family. He bitterly regretted his marriage to Gloria. The only good thing to come out of it was his daughter, Dorothy.

'No, it must be with Prosser and Knox,' Henry said firmly. 'I've decided that Jimmy will take over the business after my days.'

Bert stared at him in astonishment. 'What

58

about your other son, Andy?'

Henry swallowed hard. It pained him to admit the truth about Andy.

'He hasn't got it in him, Bert,' he said quietly and with regret. 'No backbone, no ambition.' He shook his head. 'He's a bitter disappointment to me. I blame his mother. She has spoilt him.'

Bert's face clouded with doubt. 'You'd better think again, Henry. Your wife will make trouble if Jimmy gets the business over her boy.'

'Gloria knows nothing of him or Florrie,' Henry said. 'Faced with my will she'll have no choice but to accept it when the time comes.'

'Well, it's your business, of course, you can do as you like. I'm only concerned for my daughter and grandson.'

'You know I'll take care of them,' Henry said. 'I always have, haven't I? I made sure Florrie owns this house free and clear and she's never short of anything.'

Bert grunted and turned to his newspaper again.

Henry watched him for a moment. 'Jimmy can start his apprenticeship this coming Wednesday.' He paused before adding, 'I want him to get on in life, Bert. He's got a good brain and I want him to get what's due to him.'

At that moment someone came in through the back door and the next moment Florrie was in the room. A smile lit up her face when she saw him.

'Oh, Henry love, I didn't know you were here.'

He rose quickly to embrace her and kiss her cheek. 'Hello, love,' he said, looking down at her face. 'I've missed you.'

'Get away with you!' she said, teasing. 'You were only here yesterday.'

'It seems longer,' he said sincerely.

At thirty-nine, Florrie was a year older than his wife, but the difference between the two women was remarkable. To Henry, Florrie was always the lovely young woman he had met by chance when one day she had called on her father at the yard nineteen years ago.

Already married to Gloria for two years, he was wretchedly unhappy and fell head over heels in love with Florrie. The miracle was she fell for him even knowing he was married. He often thought that if he didn't have Florrie to come home to, his life wouldn't be worth living.

She touched cool fingers to his cheek. 'Have you eaten yet, love?'

He shook his head, his arms still around her waist.

'I'll make a meal now,' she said.

He put his lips close to her ear and whispered, 'Can I stay the night?'

She gave a sigh. 'Yes, of course.'

Bert gave a noisy cough and rattled the newspaper. 'Any chance of some grub, our Florrie?'

'Coming up on the lift, Dad,' she quipped cheerfully. She detached herself from Henry's arms and went into the scullery. 'How about some nice liver and onions with mash?'

Later Florrie was delighted with Henry's suggestion that Jimmy should start an apprenticeship, and there were tears in her eyes when Henry told her of his intention to leave the business to their son.

'You're so good to us, love,' she said. 'Jimmy couldn't have a better father.'

Henry was silent for a moment. 'Florrie, do you resent the fact that I don't publicly acknowledge him as my son?'

'Of course not,' she said and smiled at him. 'You know you're the love of my life, Henry, and you gave me a wonderful son. I'm happy the way things are, and if people talk, well, let them. I've got you and Jimmy. That's all I want.'

'And you two are all I want,' Henry said, and meant it.

'Come to bed,' she said.

Henry went back to his house in Brynmill for a change of clothes after an early breakfast in Fleet Street. Gloria was still asleep and he was thankful that recriminations for being absent all night would come later. He could not have faced her now.

He was about to make his getaway down the stairs when Dorothy, still in her nightdress, came out of her bedroom along the landing.

'Dad, I want to talk to you.'

'I'm in a bit of a hurry, Dot,' he said. 'Can't it wait until this evening?'

Tears began to glisten in her eyes. 'You never listen to me.'

He remembered then that Aunt Cissie had told him that Dorothy had been upset the day before and felt sorry that he had ignored his aunt's warning.

'What is it, chick?' he asked kindly. 'What's

wrong?'

'Everything,' Dorothy said, her lips quivering. 'You've got to put it right, Dad.'

He was concerned. 'Fetch a wrap and come down to the drawing room,' he said. 'We can talk there.'

He sat waiting for her and when she came in to the room, spoke kindly again. 'Sit down next to me, Dot. Now what's the matter?'

'It's Gillian Finch,' Dorothy blurted out. 'I want you to sack her, Dad.'

'What?' That was the last thing he had expected.

'She's ruining everything for me. I thought she was my friend, but now I find out she's my worst enemy.'

Henry was stumped for a moment. 'You and Gillian are friends? Does my sister know?'

Dorothy shook her head. 'No one knows. Gillian pretended to be my friend for about four years, but now she's showing what she's really like.'

Henry scratched his head. It seems he wasn't the only one keeping secrets.

'Are you put-out because I gave Gillian the job at the office instead of you?' he asked. 'She is qualified, Dot.' He patted her hand. 'But I'm sure I can find a place for you there, too, if you've set your heart on it. Except your mother would create merry h—'

'I don't want to work at that stupid office!' Dorothy flared. 'I just want you to sack Gillian.'

'But why? What do you think she's done to you?'

62

Dorothy's lips quivered again. 'She's a hussy,' she said petulantly. 'She's throwing herself at Ronnie. It's cheap and disgusting.'

He was puzzled. 'What?'

'Gillian says Ronnie is making up to her, but I know it's the other way around. It's me Ronnie wants.'

He was alarmed. *'What?'*

'Everything was going splendidly until Gillian put her oar in,' Dorothy said huffily. 'Well, you know he's been to dinner here quite often and Mother says it won't be long before I bag him if I'm clever, and she'll help me. Mother says we must keep the business in the family.'

This time Henry was utterly speechless.

'I don't ask much, Dad,' Dorothy continued. 'I mean, I'm not like Andy scrounging money from Mother all the time. It's my future I'm thinking of and that of the business.'

Henry's stupefaction turned to outrage. 'Has Ronnie Knox laid a hand on you?' he bellowed. 'You know what I mean, Dorothy.'

'Dad! Don't shout and don't look at me like that!' She lifted a shoulder. 'Of course he hasn't. He has kissed me a few times. I am eighteen, after all. Although Mother says I shouldn't be too strait-laced, I won't allow anything but kisses, not until we're married.'

'Good God!' Henry stood up and towered over her. 'Now look here, my girl,' he growled, straining not to shout, 'you're to ignore what your mother says in future, and you're to stay away from Ronnie Knox. Do you understand me?'

'No, I don't!'

'Ronnie has a bad reputation where women are concerned,' Henry said. 'He's not to be trusted.'

Dorothy waved a dismissive hand. 'Yes, but that's all in the past. Mother says now he's met me, he'll change.'

'Your mother is a scheming, unscrupulous cow!' stormed Henry.

'Dad!' Dorothy looked appalled. 'What a terrible thing to say about Mother.'

Henry was unrepentant. 'She ruined my life. I'm not going to let her ruin yours because of her greed.' He took in a deep breath to steady himself. 'Ronnie Knox is no longer welcome in this house. And I'll tell him so today.'

Dorothy sprang to her feet. 'But you can't do that, Dad!' she wailed. 'Mother says I'll marry him.'

'Over my dead body!' Henry howled in fury. 'And that's the end of it!'

Arthur Finch clocked in at the yard at eight thirty on the dot Tuesday morning, before going off to the plumbing job at Beach Street. He was about to be on his way, on foot as usual, when Henry's big Humber swung in through the yard's gateway.

His brother-in-law waved his arm through the car window, indicating that he wanted a word with Arthur.

'You're early, Henry,' Arthur remarked cheerfully.

'Come into my office,' Henry said curtly, as he climbed out of the car. 'I need to talk to you.'

Arthur followed him in, wondering at his foul mood. He hoped that whatever the matter was it didn't involve the dispute with Vera. All he wanted was a quiet life.

The outer office was empty. Mr Meeker and Gillian hadn't yet arrived. They went into the inner office; Henry closed the door firmly behind them. The planes of Henry's face were tight and sharp and Arthur could see he was in a right old state.

'What's up?'

'It's that bloody wife of mine—' Henry began and then checked himself.

Arthur rubbed his chin with his thumb. 'I'm no good at giving advice on domestic matters, Henry,' he said. 'I can hardly cope with Vera.'

Henry shook his head impatiently. 'It's not that. It's about our girls.'

'What? Our Gillian and your Dorothy?'

'Did you know they've been friends for years, despite Vera's quarrel with me?'

Arthur sniffed. 'Yes, I've known for some time,' he admitted. 'Can't see any harm in it as long as Vera doesn't find out.'

'Well, the friendship is over,' Henry said. 'The girls have quarrelled over Ronnie Knox.'

Arthur was flummoxed. 'I don't understand.'

Reluctantly Henry related in full his earlier conversation with his daughter, and Arthur was disturbed. Gillian and Ronnie Knox? He could hardly believe it. He would have judged his daughter to have more sense.

'Gloria is encouraging Dorothy to entrap him,' Henry continued. 'Same way she entrapped me.

Not that Ronnie needs much bloody encouragement.'

'Here! I don't like the sound of this,' Arthur said. He had not given a thought to it before. It never occurred to him that Gillian might be at some risk working so close to his brother-in-law's young partner. 'Our Gillian working in the same office with Romeo Ronnie. I don't like it at all.'

'How do you think I feel?' Henry said angrily. 'With Gloria inviting him to the house with the sole purpose of getting him hitched to my daughter.' Henry's glance slid away. 'Any bloody way she can.'

'The thing is,' Arthur said thoughtfully, 'Gillian is so taken with working here. I would hate to disappoint her.'

'Well, I'm going to have a word or two with Ronnie as soon as I see him,' Henry said decidedly. 'Let him know where he stands as far as Dorothy goes.'

Arthur said nothing but cogitated. He intended to speak with Gillian and leave her in no doubt about his opinion of Ronnie Knox. She would listen to him, he knew she would.

'Well, I'll be off then,' Arthur said. 'I'm running late for that job on Beach Street.'

'Wait a minute,' Henry said. 'There's something else I want to talk to you about.' He paused. 'It concerns my other son, Jimmy.'

Arthur felt embarrassed. Henry had confided in him a long time ago about his relationship with Bert Tomkin's daughter Florrie, and about their illegitimate son Jimmy, but Henry had never referred to the boy as his son so openly before.

'I want Jimmy Tomkin to do his apprenticeship with us, Arthur, and I'd like you to train him.'

'What does Bert say?'

'It's none of Bert's business.'

'But Bert is his grandfather.'

'And I'm his father,' Henry blurted out. 'I've got plans for that boy.' He lowered his voice. 'I'm changing my will. I'm leaving my share of the business to Jimmy.'

Arthur was startled. It was Charlie Knox all over again.

'That's a drastic decision, Henry,' he said. 'Gloria will go mad if she finds out.'

'I'm sick to death of my conniving wife and her spoilt brat of a son.'

'Andy is your son, too, Henry.'

Henry looked away. 'Don't remind me. He was the reason why I had to marry Gloria.'

'You shouldn't hold that against him,' Arthur cautioned. 'It wasn't the boy's fault.'

Henry sat down heavily in his seat. 'You're right, Arthur,' he said dejectedly. 'It was my fault for being such a blind young fool. She took me in good and proper.'

'Well, the same trick won't work with Ronnie Knox,' Arthur opined. 'He's far too fly.'

'Yes, but Dorothy could get badly hurt by Gloria's scheming,' Henry said. 'Dorothy is under her influence and sometimes I feel that Gloria has no sense of morals.'

Arthur felt embarrassed again at Henry's

frankness.

'I'll take Jimmy on as my apprentice, Henry,' he said quickly. 'If that's what you want.'

Henry stood up and held out a hand to shake his. 'Thanks, Arthur. You're a good man and I trust you. Jimmy will start tomorrow.'

Arthur left the yard, his mind churning. At the first opportunity he was determined to have a quiet word with his daughter and get to the bottom of this matter. He trusted her, but it was better to be safe than sorry.

He was also disturbed by Henry's revelation about making Jimmy Tomkin his heir. History seemed to be repeating itself. Samuel Prosser had done something similar and it had led to a great deal of bitter family feuding.

It was about time he delved into the Prosser family's secret past, and the man to tell him all he wanted to know was Bert Tomkin. Bert had started his apprenticeship when Samuel Prosser was still in charge and before Ronnie's grandfather Charlie had been given a share of the business.

Arthur would bet a pound to a penny that Bert knew the truth about what really happened to William Prosser. Arthur suddenly felt it was very important he knew it all.

Five

Gillian was surprised to find Uncle Henry was already in the office when she arrived. He seemed rushed and in a bit of a temper, too. His greeting to her was curt and she wondered what she had done to displease him.

She heard him tell Mr Meeker that he would be at Glynn Neath for most of the day, negotiating yet another new contract, but would be back before the office closed up.

Andy Prosser swaggered nonchalantly into the office mid-morning. He was tall, like his father, but weedy, Gillian thought disparagingly, and he did not have Uncle Henry's pleasant expression.

Although they were cousins, she hardly knew him. As children they had met very occasionally. Vera did not like Andy's mother, and even before the quarrel over her grandmother's will there had been tension between the families.

But Gillian was willing to be civil now despite the friction between their parents and she nodded, giving him a smile. To her annoyance he ignored her completely.

Well, two could play at that game.

Mr Meeker indicated the wall clock. 'We start at nine o'clock, Andy, remember?'

'Shut your face, you old goat,' said Andy.

The older man sat down without another word. Gillian was not sure that she liked Mr Meeker, but she felt sorry for him then.

'Shall I make you a pot of tea, Mr Meeker?' she asked kindly. 'I think we've got some ginger snaps left.'

Mr Meeker looked at her. 'Thank you, Gillian. That's very kind of you.'

Out of the corner of her eye Gillian saw Andy's lip curl in contempt. He reached into a drawer of his desk and took out a comic book, then sat back, boots resting on the desk, reading it.

Gillian felt her own lip curl. A twenty-year-old reading a kid's comic. She wondered what Uncle Henry thought of his son and heir.

For the rest of the morning Gillian got on with the work Mr Meeker gave her. Andy continued to lounge and smoke. Lunchtime came and he had not done one stroke of work. Gillian was disgusted with him.

Vera had given her some money for a hot midday meal as a treat and so she went to the little Italian café nearby in Wind Street and had pie and mash. On her way back to the yard she caught sight of Andy Prosser in an alleyway. Who should be with him but her brother Tom.

The two young men seemed to be arguing and Gillian was alarmed when Andy grabbed roughly at the straps of Tom's overalls, almost yanking him off his feet. Andy was shouting, but Gillian could not make out the words. She was relieved when Tom pushed Andy away and walked off down the alley in the opposite direction.

Gillian moved off, too, so as not to be seen by her cousin. There was something very unpleasant about Andy Prosser and the thought of Tom associating with him made her uneasy. She decided she would have a word with her twin brother and warn him.

Andy did not return to the office until well after three o'clock. Mr Meeker ignored him this time, but Gillian watched her cousin avidly. He lounged in his seat, smoking one cigarette after another until the air in the room grew dense.

'I can hardly breathe in here for smoke,' Gillian said pointedly.

Andy ignored her and that made her furious. When Mr Meeker left the office briefly to talk to someone in the yard, Gillian decided to speak up.

'Andy, what were you and Tom arguing about this lunchtime?'

He glanced briefly across at her but did not answer. His high-handed attitude got her goat.

'I spoke to you, Andy,' she flared. 'Haven't you the manners to be civil?'

'Shut your mouth,' he growled. 'And mind your own bloody business.'

Outraged, Gillian sprang up. 'Don't you speak to me like that,' she cried, 'you long streak of dirty water!'

He jerked to his feet, his expression vicious. 'You're asking for a thumping, you slut.'

Her mouth dropped open in shock at his violent reaction. At that moment Mr Meeker came back into the room. He glanced at Andy and then at Gillian, his eyebrows raised.

'What's the matter, Gillian?'

Andy sat down glaring at her. Gillian flicked her tongue over her lips. 'Nothing, Mr Meeker. I'm just looking for the key to the washroom.'

'Oh, that reminds me,' he said. 'I've had a duplicate made especially for you. Don't leave it lying around, there's a good girl.'

Usually his patronizing tone irritated her, but she was grateful that he had been thoughtful on this occasion. Her own key to the lavatory. That was a step up.

'You can go now, Gillian,' Mr Meeker said at five o'clock. 'Finish that filing first thing in the morning.'

Andy had marched out without a word an hour since. Gillian was glad to see him go. Uncle Henry had not returned and she wanted an excuse to remain.

'I don't mind staying behind for a while,' Gillian said.

She had been waiting all day for Ronnie Knox to make an appearance, but he hadn't shown his face. It would be thrilling to be in the office alone with him when he did arrive.

'No, it's my duty to make sure the office is safely locked up,' Mr Meeker said. 'You go now.'

Reluctantly Gillian put on her cardigan and retrieved her handbag from under the desk.

'What about Uncle Henry or Ronnie – Mr Knox?' she asked hopefully. 'They might come in and need me to write a letter or something.'

Mr Meeker looked at his pocket watch. 'Your

uncle won't come back here now and as for Mr Knox, he always finishes work at four,' he said putting on his trilby. 'He is a boss, after all. He can come and go as he pleases.'

'Oh.'

At that moment her father appeared in the office doorway. Gillian was surprised to see him.

'Dad! You don't usually finish work until five thirty.'

'I'm making an exception today.' He looked at Mr Meeker. 'Evening, Norman,' Arthur greeted. 'How's the wife?'

Norman Meeker's lips twisted. 'In rude health, Arthur. Never ruder.'

Arthur chuckled. 'I know what you mean. Same here.' He glanced at his daughter. 'Well, come on, Gill. Let's get home to some grub.'

Gillian knew her father usually walked home. It kept him fit, he said. But she had no intention of walking all the way to Marlborough Road in new shoes. She wasn't all that used to high heels yet.

'I'm catching the tram, Dad,' she said firmly.

'I'll join you,' he said affably.

She had the feeling he had called in at the office for the express purpose of escorting her home.

'I'm not a little girl any more, Dad,' she said. 'I'm seventeen.'

'I'm well aware of it,' he said. 'The tram ride will give me a chance to talk to you without your mother overhearing.'

'What about?'

'Ronnie Knox.'

73

'Eh?' Gillian stopped walking and for some reason that she could not define felt guilty. 'What about him?'

'Come on,' her father urged. 'We'll miss the tram and your mother will go off the deep end if we're late for supper.'

They boarded a tram almost immediately and luckily found seats. Gillian was silent, waiting for her father to speak his piece.

'You and Dorothy have quarrelled, then,' Arthur said quietly. 'What a pity to end a friendship like that.'

Gillian was startled and turned her head to stare at him. 'You know about me and Dorothy? How long have you known?'

Arthur shrugged. 'Couple of years now.'

Gillian quailed. 'Does Mam know?'

Arthur chuckled. 'No. Let's hope she never finds out.'

Gillian lifted her chin. 'Well, she won't now. Dorothy and I are finished.'

'Like I said,' Arthur continued, 'it's such a pity. But it's what the quarrel was about that worries me.'

'What do you mean?'

'Ronnie Knox,' Arthur said. 'He's a thoroughly bad lot, Gill. Where women are concerned anyway.'

Gillian was annoyed. 'Oh, not you as well!'

'What?'

'Sam and Tom have been making horrible jokes about Ronnie – Mr Knox. It's not fair. They're only jealous of him.'

Arthur nodded sagely. 'I can understand Ron-

74

nie turning a young girl's head, Gill. He's well off, single and handsome, I suppose,' Arthur said. 'But do you know what the men call Ronnie behind his back? Romeo Ronnie. That's because he has a different woman on his arm every week.'

'That's not a crime,' Gillian said.

'No, but it says something important about his morals, doesn't it?'

'I don't see—'

'Gillian, you're seventeen now, a woman, so I won't beat about the bush. I'll be frank. Ronnie isn't chasing after women just for their pretty faces.'

Gillian squirmed, knowing what he meant and felt her cheeks grow hot at her father's bluntness. She was always going on at her parents about how grown up she was. Now her father was treating her as a responsible adult and she baulked at it.

'Some men are like that, Gill,' Arthur warned. 'Only after what they can get from a girl and then throw her aside like a worn-out shoe.'

'Dad!'

'Young as he is, Ronnie Knox is that type of man,' Arthur insisted. 'So, Gill, either you curb your enthusiasm for him or you leave your job at Prosser and Knox, because I'll not have him ruin you.'

'Dad, I'm not stupid.' She was annoyed that her father thought her so.

'My girl, you have no experience of the world or men,' Arthur said. 'Ronnie has made such an impression on you already that you broke up a long, happy friendship because of him.'

'Dorothy was beastly about it,' Gillian said defensively. 'She says she's going to marry him.'

'I fancy your uncle Henry will have something to say about that – and in strong language, too.'

Gillian was silent. She did find Ronnie thrilling and she would love to be seen about with him on his arm. He was so handsome and dashing.

But at the same time she was beginning to realize that perhaps she was seeing him through rose-tinted glasses and behaving like a silly schoolgirl with a crush. She wanted to prove she was grown up and responsible.

'I like working at the office very much, Dad,' she said at last. 'I promise I'll not be silly over Mr Knox.'

'Good girl!' Her father gave a huge sigh. 'I knew I could trust you to be sensible.'

Gillian had a thought. 'What about Dorothy?'

'That's your uncle Henry's problem,' he said flatly. 'You be thankful you've got a good and blameless mother, Gill. Dorothy is not so lucky.'

All through the day Henry found his mind was only half on the negotiations for the important contract he was hoping to get in Glynn Neath. He could not stop thinking about his daughter and what she had told him about Ronnie Knox. The more he thought about it the more appalled he was.

What kind of a mother was Gloria to instil such loose behaviour in her own daughter? And

76

loose behaviour was what it amounted to; encouraging the girl to entrap a man into marriage by any means she could. In other words, offering herself up on a plate. Henry felt his blood boil at the thought.

And Arthur Finch was right. Ronnie was too shrewd and worldly to fall for such a trick, but young Dorothy could get very hurt.

By midday the meeting with his prospective client was over. Henry decided he would not return to the office but instead go straight home to tackle Gloria.

His wife was in the hall when he arrived; viewing her reflection in the hall mirror, adjusting the angle of her fashionable cloche hat. She was wearing too much rouge and Henry thought that for all her fashionable clothes she looked common compared to the still fresh beauty of Florrie.

'Gloria, I have to talk to you.'

'It must wait, Henry.' She waved a white kid-gloved hand dismissively. 'I'm meeting Lillian Langley. We're having lunch together at the Baltic Lounge.'

'You're not going anywhere until we've had our talk,' Henry said firmly.

She turned her head to stare at him. 'Don't be absurd!' She turned back to the mirror again. 'You're forgetting who Lillian is married to. Mark Langley is a Member of Parliament and stinking rich as well. They have that lovely manor house in Bishopston.'

'I don't care if he's the bloody Prime Minister,' Henry shouted. 'You're not going anywhere until we've talked.'

'Oh! Why must you swear? It's so vulgar.'

'Vulgar!' Henry grimaced. 'That's rich coming from you when you're trying to turn our daughter into a prostitute.'

'Henry! What utter nonsense!' She tossed her head. 'I can't think what you mean.'

'Can't you? You're pressuring her into setting her cap at Ronnie Knox,' Henry said. 'Urging her to entice him so that he'll have to marry her.'

'He's a good catch,' Gloria said pertly. 'And his mother is all for it. Miriam was only saying last time she and Ronnie had dinner here that Dorothy and Ronnie make a lovely young couple.'

'I don't care what Miriam Knox thinks or wants,' Henry said. 'I will not have it.'

'But the marriage would bring the two halves of the business together.' Gloria lifted her chin defensively. 'We have an obligation to see that the money stays in the family.'

'Money! That's all you think about,' Henry said angrily. 'You trapped me with your loose wiles, but Ronnie is far too astute. He'd chew up our daughter and then spit her out.'

'You have the crudest way of talking, Henry,' Gloria complained. 'And what you say is pure nonsense. Ronnie is every inch a gentleman and well off, too. And he knows a good deal when he sees one.'

'He knows an easy target when he sees one!'

Gloria ignored him and went on talking. 'Dorothy is very pretty and attractive, and after all, Ronnie knows he'd get her share of the inheritance from you.'

'You're living in cloud cuckoo land,' Henry said disparagingly. 'You never had any brains, Gloria, only animal cunning.'

Gloria fumed. 'How dare you say that?'

'How dare you cheapen our daughter for the sake of your greed and avarice?'

There was a footfall on the staircase behind them. Henry whirled to see Dorothy standing on the stairs.

'Dorothy!'

'Why must you always quarrel?' Dorothy said, her eyes glistening with tears. 'Can't a day go by without upset?'

'I'm sorry, Dot, love,' Henry said, moving quickly towards his daughter. 'I didn't realize you were in the house.'

'It's your father's fault,' Gloria accused quickly. 'He's always criticizing me, and all I want is the best for my children.'

'Best for you, you mean!'

Gloria spread her hands. 'You see what he's like?' she cried. She pointed her finger at him. 'I'm trying to protect Andy's future and Dorothy's happiness. That's more than you're doing.'

Cissie came out of the drawing room. 'Well, she won't find happiness with the likes of Ronnie Knox,' she said emphatically.

Gloria rounded on her furiously. 'Keep your nose out of it, Cissie,' she flared. 'You're not a member of my family. I don't know why we tolerate you and your interfering ways.'

'Don't speak to Aunt Cissie like that!' Henry exclaimed.

'It's all right, Henry,' Cissie said calmly. 'I'm used to it.' She cast a scornful glance at Gloria. 'You're an empty-headed fool, Gloria.'

'Well! Really! I don't have to put up with this in my own home.'

'I've watched young Ronnie when he's been here to dinner,' Cissie said. 'He's just like his grandfather.'

She moved to the bottom of the stairs next to Henry and looked up at Dorothy. 'Charlie Knox was a handsome devil, too,' she said. 'Couldn't keep his hands off other women. Young, older, single, married; it was all the same to Charlie. And his poor wife Freda suffered in silence. Is that the kind of husband you want, Dorothy?'

'You're a poisonous old witch!' Gloria shrieked.

'Charlie Knox did terrible damage to our family,' Cissie persisted, a catch in her voice. 'That's why my brother, William—' She stopped abruptly and a guarded look appeared on her lined face. 'Our family was never the same again,' she finished.

'That's all ancient history,' Gloria snapped. 'And neither here nor there.'

With a studied nonchalance she glanced in the mirror and tweaked the narrow brim of her hat.

'I'm not going to turn away a good catch like Ronnie Knox because of an old woman's spite and gossip,' she continued forcefully. 'Ronnie will always be welcome in this house and in our new home in Sketty when we move in next month.'

'We're not moving,' said Henry.

80

'What?' Gloria turned to stare at him. 'But the contract is about to go through.'

'I've backed out of the purchase.'

'What? But why? It's not because we can't afford it, heaven knows.'

Henry compressed his lips. His reason for backing out had been pure spite and revenge on Gloria but now he hesitated to admit it before Dorothy and Cissie.

'I have my reasons.'

'But you can't do this to me,' cried Gloria, a hysterical tone in her raised voice. 'I've told all my friends about our beautiful new home. I've arranged a house-warming party.'

'Well, you'll have to cancel it.'

'But people will wonder why,' said Gloria. She sounded tearful. 'There'll be talk. I'll be made to look a fool to all my friends.'

Henry found some pleasure in his wife's distress and then felt ashamed. Cancelling the purchase of the new house had been done on impulse at the height of his anger that morning. It was a petty gesture, he saw that now.

In fact, he had been looking forward to the move himself, hoping that living in the new house would ease the never-ending friction in their lives. All at once he felt regret for his hasty actions but he would not show it in front of Gloria.

'You'll get over it, Gloria,' he said flatly. 'Far more quickly and easily than Dorothy would get over a bad marriage.'

Gloria glared at him and he saw she was not taken in. 'You did it to spite me!' she screeched.

81

'You beast, Henry! I'll never forgive you for this.'

She snatched off her hat and, pushing through Cissie and Henry, ran quickly up the staircase past a startled Dorothy.

His daughter came and put a hand on his arm.

'Dad, what have you done?'

His shame was so acute he could not look her in the eye.

'I'm sorry, Dorothy.'

'Shouldn't you be apologizing to Mother instead of me?'

Henry bit down hard on his lower lip. 'There are things between your mother and me that you don't understand, Dot,' he said.

'Is it because of me?'

'No, Dot love.' He shook his head. 'You're quite blameless.'

He glanced at his aunt and she turned and walked into the drawing room again, leaving them alone. He turned to look at his daughter.

'The truth is, Dorothy, your mother and I are not happy together, and haven't been for a very long time.' He lifted his hand in a gesture for silence when she appeared about to speak. 'Our differences are not because of you.' Henry paused, knowing he must be honest with himself. 'Or Andy.'

'What's going to happen?'

'Nothing, love.' He sighed. 'We go on as before. But I want you to promise me that you'll not let your mother persuade you to act foolishly. You know what I mean. Ronnie Knox is not for you.'

'But, Dad, I think I'm in love with him.'

Henry put his hand wearily to his forehead. 'Dot, you're too young to understand what real love is.'

'I'm eighteen.'

'And I was only eighteen when I met your mother and believed I was in love.' He shook his head, remembering his folly. 'It wasn't love or anything like it. Don't make the mistake I did, Dot.' He grasped her hand and held it tightly. 'If you don't find real happiness with the right husband it'll break my heart.'

'I'll be sensible, Dad. I promise.'

Gillian's bedroom was a space partitioned off from a much larger room where her brothers slept. It was cramped but at least she had it to herself and was grateful for the privacy.

She went to bed at the usual time but left her door open a crack so that she could hear when Tom came home.

Although her father had put a curfew on his youngest son, Tom sometimes broke that rule. Her parents slept on the floor above and were unaware, especially with Sam covering for Tom's absence.

Gillian often wondered what her twin got up to, staying out so late. He was only seventeen, after all. After seeing him with Andy Prosser she was even more concerned.

It was five minutes to midnight before she heard a stealthy footfall on the stairs and crept out of her room to intercept him. He was just a tall slim shadow on the landing.

'Tom?'

'Eh!' He was startled. 'Bloody hell, Gill,' he gasped. 'You didn't half give me a turn.'

'How did you get in?' she asked. 'Dad hasn't given you a key, has he?'

'Sam left the back scullery window open for me,' Tom answered.

Gillian clamped her lips together. She would have a sharp word with Sam about that. Brotherliness was all very well, but Sam was taking it too far.

'Where have you been?'

'Out,' he said shortly.

'With whom?'

'Never you mind, our Gill.'

'I saw you with Andy Prosser earlier today,' Gillian whispered. 'Are you pals with him?'

'What if I am?'

'Come into my room a minute,' she said. 'I want to talk to you about Andy.'

He edged away. 'It's late,' he said. 'I've got to be up early.'

'You should've thought of that earlier. If you don't talk to me now I'll tell Mam about you being friends with Andy Prosser. She'll be cross.'

He followed her into the small bedroom where she lit a candle. 'Now I want the truth,' Gillian said firmly. 'What do you and Andy get up to when you stay out late?'

'Nothing!'

She shook her head. 'I don't believe you, Tom. I'm your twin, remember. I can read you like a book.'

'What business is it of yours what I do?'

'Why have you got to be pals with Andy Prosser of all people?' she said. 'I don't like him, Tom. There's something about him that's not – normal.'

'Tsk! You're talking daft.'

'He doesn't do one stroke of work and he treats Mr Meeker like dirt,' she said. 'And – and he called me a slut today.' She felt outraged remembering. 'Normal people don't behave like that.'

Tom shrugged nonchalantly. 'That's the way Andy talks. He says all women are sluts, including his sister.'

'Oh! That's awful!' Gillian was disgusted. 'Dorothy is a sweet, lovely girl—'

'How do you know?'

'Never mind.' She had almost said too much. 'Tom, don't have anything more to do with Andy,' she pleaded. 'I don't trust him. If you ask me, he's no good.'

'Gill, you don't understand,' Tom said. 'Uncle Henry and Aunt Gloria are always rowing, Andy told me. They hate each other apparently. They're not a happy family like us.'

'That's no excuse for him to be so beastly,' Gillian said.

'I'm going to bed.'

'Tom, promise you won't be pals with Andy in future. He'll get you into trouble, I know it.'

'Goodnight, Gill.'

Six

Arthur got to the yard extra early the next morning, intent on cornering Bert Tomkin for a quiet chat before any of the other men were about. Bert, six months off retirement, was in charge of the stores; he was a conscientious man who always clocked-on well ahead of time.

'Arthur, I don't have time for chatting now,' said Bert with obvious irritation when Arthur approached him in the stores.

'I won't keep you long, Bert. It's information I'm after,' Arthur said, leaning his elbows on the stores counter. 'About the Prosser family, especially William Prosser.'

'William Prosser?' Bert's expression was guarded. 'What for?'

'It's for the wife. She wants to know about her father.'

'After all this time?'

'Who understands women, Bert?' Arthur hedged.

He wasn't sure himself why it seemed important to know.

'I'm busy, Arthur.'

'Look, Bert, I'll tell you what,' he said. 'I'm doing a job just around the corner in Wind Street today. Why don't I buy you a cup of tea and a pie

86

at dinner time in that Italian café opposite the bank?'

'Right you are, Arthur,' said Bert. He sounded more interested now.

'Right, Bert! I'll see you then,' Arthur said and left.

Henry was before his usual time, knowing Ronnie was always on hand early to check that the men clocked in personally and on time. He was a stickler for timekeeping. Henry wished his partner would be as careful with his personal life.

Henry was surprised to see Arthur Finch hanging about near the stores and was about to have a word with him about Jimmy when he saw Ronnie Knox about to go into the office.

Henry changed his mind about speaking to Arthur and followed Ronnie instead. This was as good a time as any to face him.

Ronnie glanced around and grinned when he saw Henry.

'Up with the larks this morning, Henry,' he joked. 'Gloria kicked you out of bed, did she?'

Henry's mouth tightened at Ronnie's tasteless joke. 'I want to talk to you, Ronnie,' he said. 'Come into my office.'

'Can't stop,' Ronnie said casually. 'There's been a complaint about a plastering job up at Cedar Crescent. The house-owner is livid.'

'Well, he can wait,' Henry said harshly. 'This is personal.'

Ronnie gave him a quizzical look. 'What's up?'

He followed Henry into the inner room and Henry closed the door. He did not want anything overheard.

'It's about Dorothy,' Henry began. 'I want you to stay away from my daughter.'

'What?'

'Don't look so innocent!' Henry exclaimed. 'I know what's been going on behind my back.'

Ronnie spread his hands. 'Don't know what you're talking about, old chap,' he said casually.

'I know my wife has been encouraging intimacy between you and Dorothy. And your mother has had a hand in it, too,' Henry said, shaking his head. 'Well, it has to stop. In no circumstances would I allow my daughter to marry a skirt-chaser like you.'

Ronnie looked angry now. 'Now steady on! There's no call to insult me, Henry. What I do in my private life is none of your business.'

'It is when it concerns Dorothy. She told me that you've taken liberties and that you plan to marry her.'

Ronnie stared for a moment and then burst out laughing. Henry felt his hackles rise. His fist itched to knock the other man down.

'Do you deny it?' he thundered.

Ronnie stopped laughing and suddenly looked arrogant. 'Of course, I deny it,' he said scathingly. 'I'm well aware that Gloria sees me as a prospective husband, but I can tell you now that Dorothy is not the wife I have in mind. Besides, it'll be a while before I'm ready to settle down.'

Henry was not convinced. 'Do you deny the proposed marriage is an attempt by you to combine our separate halves of the business?'

Ronnie's glance was contemptuous. 'Presumably Andy will inherit your share of the business, not Dorothy,' he pointed out, his tone derisive, 'so how would that benefit me?'

Henry was taken aback. He had been so incensed by Gloria's avariciousness and devious behaviour, he had overlooked that simple fact. In his will he had made ample provision for his daughter, but she would get nothing of the business. And now he had made up his mind that Jimmy would inherit and not Andy.

At his obviously confused silence Ronnie's mouth straightened into a thin line.

'Admit it, Henry,' he said. 'It's more likely that Gloria has designs on *my* money and is scheming to get it. She has duped my mother into helping in her plans,' he said flatly.

Henry realized that sounded very much like Gloria and her scheming ways.

'As you well know,' Ronnie said, 'after my father died on the Somme my grandfather left everything to me.' He looked arrogant again. 'I could buy and sell you twice over, Henry. Gloria knows it, too, and that's why she's anxious for this marriage.'

Henry felt a little foolish now and decided to be pompous to cover it.

'That's all very well, but under the circumstances you and Miriam are no longer welcome in my home,' he said, jutting his chin. 'There'll be no more visits.'

'That's a bit hard on my mother,' Ronnie said shortly. 'She doesn't get out and socialize much.'

'That's hardly my fault,' Henry said shortly.

Miriam Knox was a colourless, rather silly woman. He could well see how easy it would be for Gloria to sway her into any foolishness.

'There'll be no more contact between you and Dorothy,' Henry went on. 'Is that understood?'

Ronnie shrugged nonchalantly. 'Dorothy is a pretty little thing,' he said carelessly, 'but she's of no interest to me.'

Henry nodded. 'Then we do understand each other?'

'Absolutely!'

Henry nodded curtly and went out into the yard. Now that he had got that matter off his chest with Ronnie he was anxious to see Jimmy.

It was the boy's first day. While he had the utmost confidence in Arthur Finch he wanted to be there himself when the lad turned up. It would give Jimmy confidence to see him although he knew he must be careful and not treat him differently from the other lads.

Arthur was standing by the time clock, filling his pipe with tobacco.

'Hasn't Jimmy arrived yet?'

Arthur nodded, puffing at his pipe to get the tobacco burning, and then took it out of his mouth. 'I've sent him into the stores to find a left-handed, triple-edged wrench.'

'Arthur!'

'It's just a bit of fun, Henry,' Arthur said. 'The lad's got a sense of humour. I can tell.'

'I don't want him wasting his time.'

'He's just a young lad. He's got plenty of time.'

Henry sighed, knowing Arthur was a seasoned hand at training apprentices. Perhaps he was fussing too much over his son, but he could not help it. With Andy turning out the way he had, Jimmy was his only hope for the future of the business.

'Let's hope so,' he said.

He looked into his brother-in-law's pleasant face. Arthur had turned out to be his best friend over the years, despite the bitter conflict with Vera over their mother's will. Arthur held no grudges and he could keep a secret. Henry felt grateful for such a friend.

At that moment Jimmy Tomkin's tall figure emerged from the stores.

He grinned widely at Arthur. 'You won't catch me like that again, Mr Finch.'

'Morning, Jimmy,' Henry said eagerly. 'Everything all right?'

'Hello,' Jimmy answered cheerfully. 'I'm fine, Dad.'

Henry gave a loud cough and glanced around to see if anyone else was within earshot.

'I'm Mr Prosser to you when we're at the yard, Jimmy,' he warned in a low voice. 'It'll be easier all round if no one realizes our connection.'

'Sorry, Mr Prosser, I forgot,' Jimmy said. 'It won't happen again.'

'Good man!' Henry said. He looked his boy over and felt proud. 'Mr Finch here will give you a sound training. Pay close attention, son.'

'Yes, Mr Prosser.' Jimmy grinned.

Henry took out his pocket watch. 'Yes, well, I'd better get on with the day's work.' He looked at Arthur. 'There's a building contract on offer at Morriston. I'm going up there today to put in a bid.'

'We don't want to get overstretched, Henry,' Arthur warned.

'We can afford to take on more men if need be,' Henry said confidently. 'What the business can't afford to do is to stand still.'

He patted Jimmy on the back. 'Welcome on board, Jimmy,' he said loudly in case anyone was listening. 'You'll find me a fair employer. Just do your job.'

With that he turned and walked to where his car was parked. Despite problems at home, life wasn't so bad, he thought. He had Jimmy.

Gillian did not know what she was feeling as she rode the tram to work. She could not stifle the little thrill she felt at the prospect of seeing Ronnie Knox, but at the same time she knew her father was right. Ronnie wasn't trustworthy and she thought enough of herself to realize she would not throw her feelings away on someone who was not sincere and honourable.

Her father was still at the yard when she arrived. He had a young man with him whom she had never seen before.

'Still here, Dad?' She glanced up at his companion, hoping for an introduction. 'You're usually off on a job by this time.'

'I've a new apprentice today,' Arthur Finch said. 'I'm showing him the ropes here first. We'll go out on a job later.'

The young man looked interesting and Gillian

decided she would not wait for an introduction.

'I'm Gillian,' she said, smiling up at him. 'Congratulations on your trainer. My father is the best plumber in the town.'

The young man grinned down at her. 'So he keeps telling me,' he said. 'Nice to meet you, Gillian. I'm Jimmy Tomkin.'

'Oh, we've got a Mr Tomkin working here already!' she exclaimed. 'I've seen the name when I help Mr Meeker work on the time sheets on Thursday afternoons.'

'Bert Tomkin is my grandfather,' Jimmy explained.

Gillian liked his cheery grin and his looks in general. He was tall and well built and not bad looking at all. He reminded her strongly of someone but she could not think who it might be.

They stood smiling at each other for a moment.

'Ahem!' Arthur interrupted them. 'We're here to work, remember? You'd better get to your desk, Gill, before Mr Meeker comes looking for you.'

'Oh! Gosh! Yes,' Gillian said. 'See you again, Jimmy.'

'Looking forward to it,' Jimmy said.

Pleased at the look of appreciation she saw in his eyes, Gillian almost skipped off ready to face another day with dour Andy and grumpy Mr Meeker.

Dorothy came down to breakfast reluctantly, waiting until her father had left the house. She felt so miserable she did not want to see anyone.

When she went into the dining room their live-in maid Phoebe was clearing the breakfast debris. The woman's mouth tightened when she saw Dorothy.

'I did breakfast an hour ago,' she said belligerently. 'I've got to get on. I've things to do.'

'It's all right,' Dorothy said dejectedly. 'I'm not hungry. I'll just have a cup of tea, please.'

'Tsk!' Phoebe went out, balancing several dirty plates.

Dorothy sat down and waited, elbows on the table, head in hands. She had had a poor night, going over and over in her mind the things her father had said the day before about Ronnie.

It hurt her that her father was so against him; could not see the wonderful man Ronnie really was. It was the first time in her life that she had felt anything like this, but her father had dismissed her love for Ronnie as though her future happiness was of no importance.

Phoebe came in with the tea and dumped it on the table before her. 'There! I hope that's all because I've got work to do.'

'Thank you, Phoebe.'

Phoebe sniffed. 'Your mother is asking after you,' she said irritably. 'I told her you were in here.' With that the maid marched off.

Not wanting to see anyone, Dorothy stood up, picked up the cup and saucer, deciding to drink the tea quietly in her room. As she was about to leave her mother swept into the room, her hair perfectly styled, her face painted even at this time of the morning.

'Dorothy, you look dreadful,' Gloria said. 'Have you been crying?'

Dorothy bit her lip. She had avoided telling her mother of the previous day's discussion with her father about Ronnie, fearing it would provoke yet another quarrel. Bitter bickering between her parents had become more and more frequent of late and the tension in the home was beginning to set her nerves on edge.

'Well?' Gloria prompted. 'What's the matter?'

Dorothy could not control a little sob. 'Dad has forbidden me to have anything to do with Ronnie.'

'What?' Gloria put her hands on her hips. 'Why on earth not?'

'Dad says Ronnie's reputation with girls is poor. He's untrustworthy. Dad says he'd make a bad husband.'

'Oh! Your father is a fool!'

'Maybe he's right.'

'Your father is never right!' Gloria said angrily. 'Look at the way he disappointed us all in backing out on the purchase of the lovely house in Sketty. I'll never forgive him for that.'

'Was it because of me?'

'Of course not, Dorothy,' Gloria said firmly. 'Your father is determined to upset me, that's all.'

'He has certainly upset me over Ronnie,' Dorothy said tearfully. 'Mother, I'm in love with Ronnie, I really am.'

'Of course you are, dear,' Gloria agreed soothingly, patting Dorothy's arm. 'And Ronnie is in love with you.' She nodded sagely. 'He may not realize it yet, but I can tell by the way he looks at you. A sophisticated woman like me can always read the signs.'

'Do you think so, Mother?' Dorothy asked eagerly. A little bud of hope burst open in her heart. 'Will Ronnie really change when we're married?'

Gloria took the now cold cup of tea from her hand and put it on the chiffonier nearby.

'Now, we've had this discussion before, Dorothy,' she said, her tone confident. 'Of course he'll change. I'm older and wiser than you and I know the way men are and what they want.' Gloria slipped her arm though Dorothy's and led her out through the door towards the drawing room. 'Ronnie only needs a firm hand,' she continued confidently. 'I know what I'm talking about. I'm experienced in these things and you're not. But you'll learn.'

They went into the drawing room and both sat down. Dorothy gazed avidly into her mother's face. 'Will I?'

'Of course,' Gloria said firmly. 'I'll teach you. But you must do what I say and ignore your father. He doesn't understand women.'

'Yes, Mother.'

'I've never told you this before, Dorothy,' Gloria said, her tone confidential, 'but your father had something of a reputation with girls when I met him, but I didn't let that stand in my way.'

Dorothy looked at her mother in astonishment. She could not imagine her father being that sort of man.

Gloria nodded at her surprised expression. 'Oh, yes! He had an eye for the girls, all right. I made that work to my advantage.'

'How?'

Gloria glanced away for a moment as though unable to meet her daughter's innocent gaze. And then Dorothy saw her mother's jaw clench determinedly.

'I worked my womanly wiles on him,' Gloria admitted unashamedly. 'I threw scruples to the wind and gave in to his demands.'

Dorothy stared at her mother for a moment not understanding, but when Gloria glanced down and little pink patches appeared on her cheeks the truth dawned.

'Mother!' Dorothy was more shocked than she had ever been in her life.

'It was the only way to secure him,' Gloria said bitterly. 'You've never been poor, Dorothy. You don't know what it's like to be without and I wanted the good things in life. I deserved them.'

'I can't believe it of you, Mother.'

Gloria was defensive. 'Henry was a good catch with the business doing so well and him in line for management.' She tossed her head. 'I wasn't about to let such an opportunity slip through my fingers just for the sake of a few scruples. Snaring him meant security and a good life.'

'Snaring?'

Gloria shook her head impatiently. 'Call it what you like. The same thing applies to Ronnie. He's everything a woman could wish for and in addition he's very well off. You deserve him, Dorothy. Think of it that way.'

'Mother, what are you suggesting?' Dorothy was scandalized at the idea. 'That I should trick Ronnie into marrying me?'

'I'm suggesting you should be clever,' Gloria said. 'You love him, don't you?'

Dorothy nodded.

'Well, then, go after him with everything you've got,' Gloria said forcefully. 'It's your future you're fighting for. Do whatever you have to. I'll stand by you.'

Dorothy felt breathless. 'But will he change?'

Gloria looked smug. 'I speak from experience, Dorothy. I knew once I told your father I was in the family way he'd do the right thing by me.' She smiled knowingly. 'I trained him well and I can honestly say that since I married him he has never so much as glanced at another woman.'

They met up at half past twelve as arranged and found a table near the window. Bert sipped his tea.

'What do you want to know, Arthur?'

'What really happened to William Prosser?' Arthur asked flatly.

'How would I know?'

'You were working at the yard at the time he disappeared.'

Bert put down his cup. 'All I know is William was there one day and the next he was gone.'

'There must have been talk.'

'Whatever the older men knew they wouldn't let on to us apprentices,' Bert said. Then he hesitated. 'But there was one persistent rumour going around though. It was said that when

98

William left, a large amount of the firm's cash went with him.'

'Embezzlement?' Arthur was uneasy. Vera wouldn't like that if she ever found out.

'No more than idle talk, I reckon,' Bert said. 'Charlie Knox, being the sort of shrewd cuss that he was, wouldn't have let that go. He'd have had the Bobbies in, but he didn't.'

Arthur rubbed his chin. 'But why did William just disappear, Bert? That's the question I'm asking myself ... er ... I mean, Vera is asking herself.'

Bert pursed his lips. 'I reckon it was woman trouble,' he said morosely. 'Women. They can drive a man to drink.'

Andy did not return to his desk after lunch, much to Mr Meeker's obvious annoyance. Ronnie did not make an appearance in the office until well after two o'clock and immediately began conversing with Mr Meeker, not even glancing in Gillian's direction.

She was both relieved and disappointed, but she was very busy with a high pile of invoices and orders in her in-tray and so kept her head down and got on with her work.

She used her key to go to the lavatory. When she came back she was startled and rather embarrassed to see Ronnie perched on the corner of her uncle's desk.

'Oh!' She struggled not to colour up. 'I'm sorry I kept you waiting.'

He smiled that brilliant smile of his that made her want to gasp. 'You're worth waiting for.'

Gillian felt a little quiver of excitement at the compliment but quelled it.

'Excuse me,' she said and tried to step around him to leave the room, but he barred her way.

'Don't rush off,' he said persuasively. 'We hardly ever get to see each other alone.'

Gillian flicked her tongue around her lips nervously. 'Mr Meeker doesn't like me being away from my desk too long,' she said.

'Norman won't know. He's out in the yard dealing with a delivery of materials.' He reached out a hand towards her. 'He'll be a while yet.'

Gillian edged out of reach. 'I'm not one for taking advantage, Mr Knox,' she said.

He lifted an eyebrow in amusement. 'Of course not,' he said, 'but I've been hoping for a little chat with you, Gillian.' He gazed at her, his head on one side. 'You know you're a very pretty girl. I bet you have lots of boyfriends.'

'I'm only seventeen. I'm too young for boy-friends, Mr Knox.'

'Oh, I think seventeen is old enough.' He stepped away from the desk and came closer to her. 'You must call me Ronnie,' he said. 'Mr Knox was my father.'

Gillian shook her head. 'It wouldn't be right to call my employer by his first name.'

'It would if we were good friends.' He smiled at her. 'I tell you what,' he continued. 'Suppose you and I have lunch together tomorrow. I'll take you to the Baltic Lounge.'

Gillian was breathless for a moment and then pulled herself together. 'Is that where you take Dorothy?'

He looked startled. 'Dorothy?'

'My cousin Dorothy. She told me you're practically engaged to be married.'

He recovered quickly and laughed. 'Hardly! I much prefer you, Gillian. You'll like the Baltic Lounge. It's very grand.'

'My father wouldn't like it.'

'I'm not inviting him.'

'Why are you inviting me?'

'You're pretty. A man likes to be seen about with a pretty girl.'

Gillian wetted her lips. 'It's kind of you, but I'm afraid I can't accept your invitation.'

'Why not?'

'My father warned me about you, Mr Knox,' Gillian said in a rush. 'Apparently you're seen about with too many pretty girls.'

He looked taken aback for a moment and then laughed again, but his laugh was strained. Gillian realized he was annoyed and she wondered if she had gone too far.

'Arthur should be careful what he says about his employer,' he said, an edge to his voice. 'He could easily get the sack.'

Gillian looked sceptical. 'I think Uncle Henry would have something to say about that, Mr Knox.' She lifted her chin. 'And besides, Neners have approached Dad with an offer.'

'Neners, the plumbing firm?'

'Yes. They want him to train their apprentices, but Dad turned them down. He's very loyal to Prosser and Knox. After all, he is family.'

'You're missing a good lunch,' he said stiffly. 'And a run in my new motor car.'

101

There was movement in the outer office.

'Excuse me, Mr Knox, but I think Mr Meeker is back. He'll be wondering where I am.'

She moved towards the door and this time he did not stop her. She went straight to her desk and tried not to look flustered under Mr Meeker's eagle eyes.

'I wondered where you were, Gillian,' Mr Meeker said. 'I have to go out for a while. Will you be all right on your own?'

'Yes, Mr Meeker.'

'Well, you have plenty of work to get on with. Answer the telephone and take any messages – carefully, mind.'

'Yes, Mr Meeker.'

'I'll be back well before five.'

'Very well, Mr Meeker.'

He put on his trilby and left. After a while Ronnie Knox came out of the inner office. He strode straight to the door without a word or look. Gillian was relieved to see him go.

After lunch Dorothy stood before the long mirror in her bedroom, looking critically at her reflection. She had on her new floral dress with the dropped waistline and a fine wide-brimmed straw hat.

'You look lovely,' Gloria said. 'Make sure you remain with Miriam until Ronnie comes home.'

'Won't he think it forward of me?'

'Of course not. It's very natural for you to pay a friendly call on Miriam Knox. After all, she's one of our oldest friends.'

'Suppose he's late?' Dorothy asked, worried. 'I

can't hang around without some excuse.'

'If I know Miriam she'll keep you talking as long as she can,' Gloria said. 'She wants this match as much as we do.'

Dorothy sighed heavily. It worried her that she was going against her father's wishes. She had promised him she would be sensible, but in her heart she sought her mother's encouragement. She loved Ronnie and she wanted him for a husband. Was that so wrong?

It was a comparatively short walk to Ronnie's home, a fine detached house surrounded by tall poplars, left to him by his grandfather. It was obviously the house of a well-to-do family.

Gloria made a big thing of Ronnie's wealth, but that wasn't why she loved him, Dorothy told herself and believed it strongly. She loved him for himself alone. She doubted that she'd ever love anyone else. Her father would never be able to accept that.

Miriam Knox was pleased to see her. She was a small woman with fussy, fluttering hands. While Gloria, always fashionable, was only just three years younger, Miriam had a vaguely Edwardian look about her in the clothes she chose and the way her hair was dressed, making her seem much older.

'Oh, how lovely to see you, Dorothy,' Miriam gushed, waving her to a seat. 'And looking so fetching, too. You'll steal my dear boy's heart, I know you will.'

Dorothy smiled faintly and removed her kid gloves. Despite the warm welcome she still felt uneasy at being here at all.

Was it ever right for a girl to chase after a man even if she loved him? Gloria insisted it was the only way to get what one wanted.

Miriam picked up a little brass bell from a side table and rang it. A maid entered almost immediately as though she had been outside the door waiting.

'Some tea, Mabel, please,' Miriam said. 'And some of Cook's famous scones. Our cook's scones are absolutely delicious with cream and jam.'

'Thank you, Mrs Knox.'

Miriam threw up her hands. 'Oh, my dear, you must call me Miriam.' She shook her head playfully. 'After all, we're almost family, aren't we? And a more delightful daughter-in-law I could not wish for.'

Dorothy was bemused and smiled back nervously. 'Has Ronnie said something about me to you, Miriam?'

'Not in so many words, my dear. But mothers always know what their children are thinking,' she said sagely. 'I'm certain Ronnie is planning on settling down. And you are just the sweet, pretty girl for him.'

Mabel brought in the tea and scones. While Miriam fussed with pouring the tea into delicate china cups Dorothy glanced around the drawing room.

While the carpets and drapes were sumptuous, the furniture, although of excellent quality as far as Dorothy could tell, was old-fashioned, like Miriam herself. Dorothy took in everything, knowing her mother would expect a full and detailed account, for much to Gloria's chagrin they had never been invited to Ronnie's home.

Miriam handed Dorothy a cup and saucer. 'Do help yourself to scones, dear.'

'You were speaking of Ronnie marrying,' Dorothy prompted.

Miriam gave her a sweet smile. 'Yes, Ronnie ought to marry soon. My husband George was twenty-one when he married me. Ronnie is now twenty-two and should be starting a family.' She added sadly, 'One never knows what's ahead. My darling George was only twenty-eight when he was killed in France in 1916. I thank the heavens I had his son to love.'

Miriam's eyes were moist, and looking at her Dorothy's heart was touched.

'Is Ronnie like his father?'

Miriam sprang up and rushed to the grand piano at the other end of the room where photographs stood. She brought one back and handed it to Dorothy.

'That's my dearest George,' Miriam said with tenderness in her voice. 'He was tall, handsome, dashing and the most sincere of men.' She shook her head. 'Such a waste.'

Dorothy looked at the photograph. The man in it had a full moustache but otherwise he looked exactly like Ronnie. She understood then how much Miriam had loved her husband.

At that moment the drawing-room door was flung open and Ronnie himself strode in, a scowl darkening his face. 'That bloody girl! Who does she think she is?'

Startled, Dorothy jumped to her feet. Was he angry that she was there?

'You're back early from business today, Ronnie dear,' Miriam said quickly. 'I'm glad because we have a guest.'

Ronnie stared, his face still clouded. 'What?'

'Dorothy has called for afternoon tea, dear. We were just talking about you.'

He walked towards them and Dorothy could see he was struggling to compose his expression. 'Dorothy, how lovely you look.'

She was mollified. 'I hope you don't mind me calling uninvited, Ronnie?'

'Not at all,' he said.

A smile now lifted his expression, but Dorothy felt it was slightly forced and her spirits fell again.

'I'd better go,' she said hesitantly.

'No, don't go,' Ronnie said swiftly. 'It's a delight to see you. Have I said how lovely you look?'

Dorothy felt her cheeks begin to glow.

'Sit down, my dears,' Miriam said. 'I'll tell Mabel to bring more tea.'

She stood up and began to leave the room.

'Aren't you staying, Miriam?' Dorothy asked querulously.

The older woman smiled knowingly. 'I think it best if I leave you two young people alone together. I'm sure you have much to say to each other.'

She left the room, closing the door quietly behind her. Dorothy turned her uncertain gaze at Ronnie, who was smiling.

'You mustn't mind my mother,' he said. 'Her head is full of romantic notions.'

'Oh! I see.' Although she didn't.

Ronnie sat on the sofa and patted the seat beside him. 'Sit down, Dorothy. Mabel will be here with more tea shortly.'

Dorothy sat. She felt her body quiver to be alone with him and so close beside him. Would he kiss her again?

'Funny thing,' Ronnie began. 'I've been thinking a lot about you today.'

'Have you?'

He looked serious. 'You know your father has forbidden me to come to the house again. I can't think what I've done to upset him. Do you know why?'

'No, not really.' She ventured a glance at him. 'But I came today to apologize to your mother – and to you, of course. Dad has a bee in his bonnet. It'll pass.'

'I hope so,' Ronnie said softly.

He reached for her hand and held it in his. Dorothy thought her heart would stop at the thrill of his touch.

'I've been longing to get you alone to talk,' he said. 'I thought we might have lunch one day. What about tomorrow? I'll take you to the Baltic Lounge.'

'Oh!' Dorothy was astonished and overjoyed. 'The Baltic Lounge! I've heard it's very swish and only the best people dine there.'

'Yes, it is rather posh. Just the sort of place a beauty like you should be seen.'

Dorothy could not stop her cheeks flushing at

the compliment. Ronnie would think her very gauche and unsophisticated. She tried to pull herself together and appear at ease.

'That would be perfect,' she said lightly. 'I look forward to it.'

He tenderly stared into her eyes and began to lean towards her. Dorothy closed her eyes and held her breath waiting. And then Mabel suddenly appeared with more tea. She put it on the table in front of them.

'Shall I pour, Mr Knox?'

'No,' he said curtly. 'Leave it.'

Mabel gave a sniff and left.

Without more ado Ronnie poured the tea and offered her a scone. Dorothy was disappointed that the tender moment had passed.

'No, thank you,' she said sombrely.

'You're not worried about your figure, are you?' he said teasingly. 'Because it's perfect as it is.'

'You mustn't tease me,' Dorothy said. She felt shy all of a sudden. 'Because I'm quite a serious girl, you know.'

'You're a beautiful girl, I know that,' he said. 'I was very upset and hurt when your father ordered me to keep away from you. Because I don't know that I can do that, Dorothy, my dear.'

'Oh, Ronnie!'

He reached for her then and held her against him, gently covering her lips with his. Dorothy was ecstatic and leaned into him, ready to give in to any suggestion.

He released her and she felt bereft.

'After lunch tomorrow I'll take you for a long

run down the Gower in my motor car,' he said. 'Would you like that? We'll be all alone.'

'Oh, yes, I'd love to.'

'I'll pick you up about twelve.'

'Come to the house,' Dorothy suggested quickly. 'My father won't be there at that time.'

'I can't wait,' Ronnie said huskily. 'I shan't sleep tonight.'

Dorothy flushed, looking away shyly. 'Neither will I.'

'It's too bad your father has banned me from your home,' Ronnie said. 'But he can't stop you calling here, can he? I mean, you could call to see my mother – often. We could meet here. My mother will see that we have all the time we want to be alone together.'

'Ronnie, that's a wonderful idea.'

'Nothing is going to keep me away from you, Dorothy,' Ronnie said softly. 'You're the girl of my dreams.'

Dorothy felt her heart race with excitement as she looked into his eyes. She would take her mother's advice and not hold back. After all, she and Ronnie wanted the same thing.

Dorothy was glad her mother was still out when she returned home. She felt her moments with Ronnie were too precious to talk about. Gloria would want to analyse every word of conversation that had passed between them; examine every action. That would destroy the dream she walked in.

She stayed in her bedroom, sitting before the dressing-table mirror gazing at her reflection.

Ronnie said she was beautiful. She searched her features, trying to see what he had seen.

She was startled by a gentle tap at her door. She went to open the door and found her aunt Cissie standing outside, her tall gaunt figure dressed in a grey silk suit which had been unfashionable ten years earlier.

'Am I disturbing you, Dorothy?'

Dorothy was fond of her great-aunt. 'No, Aunty Cissie. Come in.'

Dorothy sat at the dressing table again and Cissie sat on the bed, her lined face showing concern. 'Did you see Miriam Knox?'

'Yes,' Dorothy said. 'She was very sweet to me.'

'And Ronnie?'

Dorothy flushed. 'He came home early. He seemed pleased to see me.' Dorothy turned to face her aunt. 'Oh, I do love him, Aunty Cissie. And I think he might love me.'

'Are you sure?'

Dorothy straightened her shoulders. 'You don't approve?'

Cissie leaned her head on one side, smiling. 'It doesn't matter whether I approve or not,' she said. 'I'm thinking of your father and his wishes for your happiness.'

'Ronnie is my happiness,' Dorothy said emphatically. 'I wish Dad could see that as clearly as I do.'

'But perhaps you are blinded by love?'

'I'm eighteen. Grown up. After all, it is *my* life.'

'Yes, you're right. You're old enough to make

your own mistakes,' Cissie agreed. 'I was never given the chance to make mistakes.'

'I'm sorry, Aunty Cissie.'

Cissie shrugged. 'I remember telling my brother William, your grandfather, that I was happy with the life fate had handed to me,' she said. 'And I was at that time. I didn't think it would ever change. I hadn't reckoned on your grandmother, Rose.'

'You never fell in love?'

Cissie smiled sadly. 'My father kept me too busy. My mother died when I was sixteen and I spent my years looking after my father. By the time he died I was too old to look for love.'

'Oh, Aunty Cissie.'

Cissie leaned forward and patted Dorothy's knee. 'Oh, don't be upset, my girl. You're in love yourself, so enjoy it.'

Dorothy squeezed her aunt's hand, feeling glad she had a kindred spirit in her home. She needed that now.

'I think Miriam Knox loved Ronnie's father very much,' Dorothy said. 'It was sad that he died so young.'

'George Knox was one of the nicest, most gentlemanly men I ever knew; so different from his father, Charlie,' Cissie said. 'We were all worried when George enlisted in 1915.' She shook her head. 'There was no need for him to do it. Conscience and a sense of responsibility, I suppose. George was like that.'

'My father didn't enlist,' Dorothy said, wondering.

'Henry and George were partners with Charlie

Knox at that time. Your father had the business to think of. He felt he couldn't leave all the burden of it on Charlie alone,' Cissie said and then stood up.

'Is Ronnie like his father?' Dorothy asked. 'Is he a good man?'

'It's not for me to say,' Cissie said seriously. 'But I'll tell you this. Your father is a good man, Dorothy, like his father William before him. No matter what happens in the future remember that he loves you very much. All he wants is your happiness.'

'All I want is Ronnie.'

Seven

Swansea, April 1891

Cissie opened the front door to them. The April air that buffeted its way inside with their visitors was sharp and crisp. Cissie fancied she could smell snow.

She stood aside to let Charlie and Freda Knox into the large hall. Charlie was carrying his three-year-old son, George, wrapped up like a parcel against the cold air.

'Good morning, Cissie,' Charlie Knox said, smiling. 'Where's the proud couple?'

Tall as she was herself Cissie had to look up at him. She thought, as she always did, that Charlie

Knox was too good-looking for his own good.

'They're both in the drawing room,' she said.

'Rose is up from her confinement bed already?' There was surprise on Freda's pretty features. 'I'd have thought she'd have given herself another week.'

'You know Rose,' Cissie said. 'She won't take telling.'

Charlie chuckled. 'Rose knows her own mind all right.'

'She's too strong-headed by far,' Cissie opined forthrightly. 'She's only nineteen, still a child herself really, but she won't be guided by anyone.'

'A woman after my own heart,' Charlie said.

Cissie glanced down at Freda. Her expression tightened at Charlie's rather insensitive remark and Cissie thought there was sadness in her eyes. She put that down to Charlie's barely concealed philandering and felt sorry for her.

'Let me take your hats and coats,' Cissie suggested.

They shrugged out of their warm outer garments. Freda was small and too thin, Cissie noted. Charlie unwrapped George and then stood holding the child's hand.

George was tall for his three years. Cissie thought he had the face of an angel as he stood looking up at her shyly.

'I think I know where there's a glass of milk and some chocolate biscuits,' she said to him. She looked up at Charlie. 'You go into the drawing room. There's a good fire going. I'll ask Mrs Foster to fetch in the milk and biscuits.'

It took only a few minutes for Cissie to speak to the housekeeper whom William insisted on employing to help ease the burden on her.

Cissie knew she could still take care of this house with one hand tied behind her back, but she let her brother have his way in this, although she suspected, too, that Rose liked the idea of employing their own housekeeper. It was something to boast about and Rose loved to boast. Cissie did not hold it against her sister-in-law. Rose was so young and had never had much to boast about in her life until now.

When Cissie joined the others in the drawing room, William and Charlie were on their feet, shaking hands.

'Congratulations, Will, on your son and heir,' Charlie said enthusiastically.

'Thanks, Charlie,' William said, grinning.

'Aren't you going to congratulate me, too, Charlie?' Rose asked pertly, lifting a hand to push back her dark silky hair from her face. 'I had a hand in it, too, you know.'

She had her legs up on a sofa covered by a rug. Her lovely features were radiant, but there was something in her dark eyes as she gazed up at Charlie Knox that made Cissie uneasy. She might almost suspect that Rose was flirting with him.

'Of course, Rose,' Charlie said smoothly. 'I'm certain a son will mean everything to William. My son George is all in all to me. Every man wants a son to carry on his name.'

Rose grimaced. 'I'd have preferred a daughter,' she said defiantly.

114

'Rose!'

William looked taken aback, but Cissie knew her sister-in-law well enough to realize she was merely being cantankerous in the face of Charlie's chauvinistic remark.

Freda was sitting on the edge of a chair nearby. 'You're tired, Rose,' she said kindly. 'Should you be up yet? It's only three weeks since you gave birth.'

Rose gave her a dismissive glance. 'Five weeks in bed may be necessary for lesser women, but I'm made of sterner stuff.'

Freda lowered her head and Cissie was angry with Rose for that spiteful remark. Freda had had a bad time birthing George and had had to remain bed-fast for five weeks. Even now, three years later, Cissie thought she looked frail still.

'And some women are too full of themselves,' Cissie said pointedly.

'Huh! How would you know, Cissie?' Rose retorted. 'A spinster can have no idea of what it means to give birth.'

There was an awkward silence and then Mrs Foster came in with the milk and biscuits. George sat on an armchair, his little legs dangling. Mrs Foster brought a small table near to him and put his drink on that.

'Thank you, Mrs Foster,' Cissie said.

'Don't leave, Mrs Foster,' Rose said haughtily. 'Please wait by the door. I may need you.'

'Yes, Mrs Prosser.'

Cissie ground her teeth with anger. Rose was showing off before their visitors. She suspected her sister-in-law was trying to impress Charlie.

115

'When are we to see the new baby, then?' Charlie asked. He had stationed himself before the fireplace, his expression whimsical as he looked at Rose.

'I'll go and fetch him from his cot,' Cissie said.

'No!' Rose exclaimed rudely. 'Let Mrs Foster fetch him. That's what she's here for, to run and fetch.' She raised her voice. 'Go and bring my son to me here, Mrs Foster.'

'Yes, Mrs Prosser.'

When the housekeeper had left the room, William spoke. 'Was that necessary, Rose? I think Freda is right. You must be tired.'

'I'm perfectly all right, and if you think you can bury me in that bedroom, you can think again, Will,' Rose said sharply. 'It's time I took charge of this household.'

Mrs Foster returned with the new baby.

'He'll be christened Henry,' Rose announced as she took the baby into her arms. 'That was my grandfather's name.'

'A good, strong name,' Charlie said.

Freda came forward to inspect the baby and to coo over him.

Charlie looked at William. 'Just think of it, Will. Our sons, George and Henry, will be partners in the business after our days. I'm going to make sure that they inherit a thriving business.'

'You've already done that, haven't you, Charlie?' Rose said, looking up at him, her eyes shining, her glance vivacious. 'I think we should congratulate you. In that first year after you were made a partner you brought the business on a treat – and mostly single-handed, too.'

Cissie saw William's colour change. 'Everyone at the yard worked hard, Rose,' he said curtly. 'Charlie couldn't have done so well without the support of all the workforce.'

'Will is right,' Charlie said generously. 'The men were bricks – excuse the unintentional pun. We didn't fall down on one contract. In the last two years Prosser and Knox have built up a good, reliable reputation that will stand us in good stead for the future – a future that belongs to our sons.'

'But it was your leadership that brought it about, Charlie,' Rose said softly. 'You're a go-getter and I admire that immensely in a man.' She glanced at her husband, her look almost disdainful. 'William could learn a lot from you, Charlie, if only he would admit it.'

Cissie saw the expression of humiliation on her brother's face and felt her blood boil. She hoped and prayed that William would never regret the day he married Rose.

Eight

Swansea, 1931

'I can't hang about,' Tom said, shuffling his feet anxiously. 'I've got to get home on time for supper or my mother will play hell.'

Andy, slouching against the wall of Davies the Dairy, kicked at a stone near his shoe. 'You're a proper mammy's boy, you are, Tom,' he said, his lip curling derisively. 'Go on, hurry home and get your nappy changed.'

Tom felt his hackles rise. 'There's no call for that kind of talk,' he said through gritted teeth. 'I respect *my* parents.'

Andy pushed himself away from the wall, his expression vicious. Tom was on guard immediately.

'Don't try it, Andy,' he warned confidently. 'I could beat you to a pulp and you know it.'

Andy leaned back against the wall, a sneer on his thin face.

'Yeah, you're all muscle and no brains,' he said scornfully. He jabbed his finger in his own chest. 'I'm the brains here and don't you forget it.'

Tom felt impatience. His companion was full of smart talk and empty boasts. He wondered briefly why he was pals with Andy Prosser at all. He guessed it was because his mother had forbidden it.

'Well, what is it you want to talk about that's so important?' Tom said.

Andy gave a mocking smile. 'How would you like to get your hands on a couple of hundred pounds?'

'What?'

Andy's smile widened. 'Oh, you're interested now, are you?'

Tom was sceptical. 'What are you talking about? Where would you get money like that?'

'Easy,' Andy said. He stood erect and stepped closer, lowering the tone of his voice. 'It's lying around waiting to be picked up.'

'Eh?'

'From the yard office.'

Tom stared. 'Have you been drinking again?'

Andy tapped his finger against his temple. 'I've worked it all out up here,' he said with confidence. 'It's as easy as taking a lollipop from a baby.'

Tom shook his head. 'You're barmy!' he said. 'I'm going home.'

'Wait!' Andy grabbed at his arm, holding him back. 'Listen, will you? Old Meeker does the men's pay sheets on Thursday mornings and then he goes and gets the money from the bank just before it closes at three o'clock. I've watched and timed him.'

Tom was silent, staring. He could not believe what he was hearing.

'He spends the rest of the day putting up the

pay packets,' Andy continued. 'These are left in the office overnight to pay out to the men on Friday.' He grinned. 'Like I said, just waiting to be picked up.'

'What's that got to do with us?'

'We get into the yard on a Thursday night,' Andy said. 'Take the money at our leisure. No one's the wiser.'

'What? Climb that eight-foot wall? Not likely!'

'I'll take my father's keys,' Andy said. 'We'll walk in.'

'You're bonkers!' Tom said. 'Firstly, I've seen the safe in your father's office. There's no key for that. It's a combination lock.'

'But the money is never put in the safe, that's the beauty of it,' Andy said with a knowing grin. 'Old smart-arse Meeker shoves the pay packets in the top drawer of his desk. He thinks no one has noticed. Ours for the taking, Tom boy!'

'You'd rob your own father?' Tom was aghast.

'He doesn't give a bugger for me,' Andy said bitterly. 'It'll serve him right.' He paused. 'Well, are you in?'

'You're out of your mind, Andy,' Tom said emphatically. 'You won't get away with it. You'll be caught.'

Andy's lip curled with scorn. 'You're a lily-livered coward,' he said with derision. 'For all your muscle you're as weak as water. I'm doing it with or without you.'

'You're crazy, Andy.'

'I'm smart,' Andy said. 'My father thinks he's a big man because he owns the business, but I'll be bigger. I'm not hanging around some stinking builders' office counting paper clips. I'm going to get real money, have everything I want. And I don't care how I do it.'

'Count me out.' Tom was adamant.

Andy looked at him for a moment. 'What about Shirley Thomas from Cromwell Street, who you're crazy about? You want her, don't you?'

Tom was stung by this remark. 'What's Shirley got to do with anything?'

Andy laughed. 'That slut would drop her knickers for you quick enough if you had loads of money to throw at her.'

Tom gave a growl of fury and, hauling back an arm, threw a punch at Andy's smug smile, hitting him squarely in the face. Andy went down like ninepins. He lay on the pavement, his nose bleeding. There was venom in his eyes as he looked up at Tom.

'You'll pay for that, Tom Finch.'

'Oh, aye! And who's going to do it? Not you.'

'I've got brains, I have. I'll fix you good.'

'Huh! The way you're going, you'll fix yourself,' Tom said and turning on his heel strode off. 'You'll end up in clink, you will.'

It was at times like these that she most missed Dorothy's friendship, Gillian reflected as she rode the tram to work. She had no one to talk things over with, especially about boys.

She couldn't seem to get her father's new apprentice out of her head. There was something about Jimmy Tomkin that drew her – and it

121

wasn't just his good looks. She must get to know him better.

She had questioned her father the previous evening. Where did Jimmy live? And did he have a girlfriend? Arthur, usually so talkative about anything connected to his job, had been vague, almost reticent.

'Don't you like Jimmy Tomkin, Dad?' she asked.

'Of course I do,' Arthur said. 'He's a good lad, good worker and he has a sharp mind. He'll get on.'

Since her father had been reluctant to say more, Gillian had given up. Her father liked Jimmy. That was enough. She would get to know him herself.

Since it was his first week Jimmy was still getting his bearings with the job and so he was at the yard with her father most mornings.

They were both there when she arrived at work. She was a little earlier than usual so that she could spend time talking with them before Mr Meeker would expect her at her desk.

'Good morning!' Gillian called gaily and waltzed up to them, feeling trim and neat in her floral dress.

'Good morning, yourself.' Jimmy swung around to face her, his expression smiling and eager. She made a note of that.

Arthur's eyebrows shot up. 'You're early, Gill,' he said. 'Trying to make a good impression on Mr Meeker?'

Gillian could not prevent flushing. 'Something like that.' She looked up at Jimmy. 'Your first week is almost over, Jimmy. How are you getting on? Do you think you'll like being a plumber?'

'Yes, I think so,' Jimmy said, still grinning. 'I've got a good instructor.'

Gillian wetted her lips. 'Dad often asks his apprentices to come to our house for supper, don't you, Dad?'

She was aware that her father was staring at her in astonishment. 'First I've heard of it,' he said.

'He's teasing you, Jimmy,' Gillian said, dismayed that her father had not backed her up. They understood each other so well as a rule. He must realize what she was angling for.

'He does that all the time,' Jimmy said. 'But I've got a few tricks up my sleeve, too.'

'Yes, well, never mind that now,' Arthur said fussily. 'Saturday is half-day, don't forget. We've got a lot of work to get through by one o'clock. We can't stay lolling about here chatting.'

Gillian was disappointed. Her father was being no help at all. She really liked Jimmy. He was the most interesting boy she had met in a long time. None of the other apprentices could hold a candle to him.

Mr Meeker strolled into the yard at that moment. He stopped when he saw Gillian, took out his pocket watch and glanced at it meaningfully.

'I've got to go,' Gillian said with regret.

'Might see you later,' Jimmy said hopefully.

'Get a move on,' said Arthur gruffly.

Gillian stared at him, wondering why he was

being so awkward.

With a smile and a wave to Jimmy she followed Mr Meeker into the office. He had a large pile of invoices ready for her as usual and she set to work obediently.

Around eleven she had just made a pot of tea for their break when Ronnie Knox appeared.

'Is there a cup for me, gorgeous?' He grinned at her impudently. 'And a garibaldi?'

'Yes, Mr Knox,' Gillian said, lowering her gaze from his knowing glance.

She handed him the tea and biscuits. He deliberately grasped her hand tightly as she did so. 'Thank you, beautiful,' he said huskily.

Gillian snatched her hand away quickly. It was strange. Ronnie Knox no longer seemed so handsome and attractive as he had done when she had first seen him. She did not like his pushiness and his arrogant assumption that she was overwhelmed by his charms.

She had been though, her inner voice reminded her. But that was before she had met Jimmy Tomkin.

She compared the two of them in her mind now. They were both tall and good-looking. Ronnie was about five years older. What was most marked was the difference in their attitudes.

She felt that Jimmy would respect her. He met her on her own terms and did not try to bedazzle her with sophistication as Ronnie did. All at once she felt she had learned a valuable lesson in life.

Mr Meeker went into the inner office, obviously to use the lavatory. Ronnie took the opportunity to sit on Gillian's desk and lean close to her.

'That lunch at the Baltic Lounge is still on offer,' he said softly. 'How about joining me later today? I could pick you up at one.'

'No, thank you, Mr Knox.'

He frowned, obviously annoyed. 'Why not?'

She rummaged quickly in her mind to find an excuse. 'I've already made an arrangement for this afternoon.'

'Who with?'

Gillian spoke the name that was uppermost in her mind. 'Jimmy Tomkin.'

'Tomkin?' Ronnie looked astonished. 'That new apprentice?'

'Yes, I've promised to meet him,' Gillian lied. 'I never go back on my word, Mr Knox.'

'Cradle-snatching, are you?'

'He's the same age as me,' she said sharply. 'I don't think it proper for me to go out with older men.'

'Older men?' Ronnie looked taken aback for a moment. 'What do you both plan to do with your afternoon – play hopscotch?'

'Excuse me, Mr Knox,' Gillian said with a toss of her head. 'I have work to do.'

Mr Meeker returned and Ronnie moved swiftly away from her desk to open the drawer of the filing cabinet.

'Want something, Mr Knox?' Mr Meeker enquired helpfully.

'Er, the estimate for the job in York Place,' Ronnie mumbled. 'I think I might have undercosted some materials.'

'Well, it's too late now,' Mr Meeker said. 'Work started at the beginning of the week. The job is practically finished.'

Ronnie's colour changed and for once he looked embarrassed. His glance darted briefly to Gillian.

'Right you are,' he said and strode swiftly out of the office.

While she felt relieved at his going she did feel guilty at lying. Whatever made her say that she was meeting Jimmy? Wishful thinking, she supposed. But Jimmy might have asked her out, given the chance, she told herself.

Later that morning, while Mr Meeker was in the yard, Gillian answered a telephone call for him. She went in search of him and he hurried inside to take the call. Gillian hung back hopefully and, sure enough, within a few minutes Jimmy came out of the stores.

'Hello again,' he said, smiling.

Gillian gathered her courage. 'Hello, Jimmy. I'm glad I've run into you.' She glanced around warily. 'Where's my father?'

'In the stores.'

'Jimmy, could you do me a favour?' Gillian asked in a rush.

'Of course, Gill.' He stepped closer, his expression eager.

'The thing is, Mr Knox asked me out with him this afternoon, but I don't want to go.' She hesitated, swallowing hard. 'I said I was going out with you. I hope you don't mind?'

'Not at all.'

'I was afraid he might say something to you and find out I'd fibbed to him.'

Jimmy shuffled his feet. 'Well, it needn't be a fib, mind,' he said, his cheeks colouring up. 'I mean, we could catch the Mumbles train to Oystermouth this afternoon and stroll on the pier.'

'Oh!' Gillian's heart gave a little jolt. 'That would be lovely. And we could call in Sidoli's for some strawberry ice cream.'

'That sounds grand to me.' Jimmy was smiling from ear to ear. 'Shall I call at your house for you about two o'clock?'

'Er, no,' Gillian said. She did not want anyone at home to know, especially those brothers of hers. 'I'll meet you on the corner of Marlborough Road instead.'

'Right-ho.'

Arthur Finch came out of the stores.

'Not a word,' Gillian whispered. 'Our secret.'

Jimmy winked and, turning on her heel, Gillian went back to the office feeling as though she were walking on air.

They caught the Mumbles train at the Slip and scrambled up to the top deck. She had travelled on the train many times, but today Gillian felt heady with excitement as they rattled along at what seemed like breakneck speed. The rails ran so close to the sea wall in places that one had the impression that the train would topple over into the waves at any moment.

Sitting next to Jimmy she could feel the warmth of his arm against hers and found it very pleasant indeed. There was no awkwardness between them as she had feared. Jimmy had plenty to say and so had she.

They got off the train at the terminus, paid their two pennies entrance fee and then strolled on to the weathered boards of the pier. Gillian always felt nervous when first walking the boards. There were wide gaps between them where one could see the sea swirling angrily around the supports. She could not stop herself imagining what would happen if she fell through, and felt a moment's giddiness.

'Whoa! Steady!' Jimmy said, taking her arm. 'Are you all right?'

'Yes, I'm being silly.'

'Let's stroll down to the lifeboat house,' he suggested. 'I wouldn't mind joining the lifeboat crew myself.'

'The crew are usually village men. I don't think you'd be able to hear the warning siren from Fleet Street,' Gillian joked. 'And I can just imagine my father's face if you suddenly downed tools and ran.'

They laughed together and impulsively Gillian slipped an arm through his. He turned his head to smile at her and the expression in his eyes told her they were in harmony.

When they left the pier they climbed the hill to the coast road and walked down to Oystermouth village. It was quite a long way really, but Gillian enjoyed every step of it.

Calling into Sidoli's Ice Cream Parlour Jimmy bought them both cones filled with delicious strawberry ice cream. They sat on the sea wall opposite to eat them.

'What time is it?' Gillian asked. She did not want the afternoon to end.

Jimmy took out his pocket watch. 'Quarter past five,' he said.

'What?' Gillian leapt off the wall. 'Oh my goodness. I'll be late.'

'Late for what?' Jimmy looked puzzled.

'My mother always serves supper at six. She gets tamping if any one of us is late, including the boarders.' Vera in a temper was not a pretty sight. 'Quick! We must catch that train back.'

Gillian made a dash for the Oystermouth stop and was on pins until the train from the pier terminus swayed into sight along the track.

'You can blame me for being late,' Jimmy said after they had boarded.

Gillian smiled and said nothing. She felt it wouldn't be wise to tell her mother she had been out with a boy and had lost track of time.

'Listen, Gill,' Jimmy said in a rush. 'There's something I want to ask you.' He swallowed hard. 'I like you so much, Gill. Would you consider going out with me again, regular, like?'

'Oh, Jimmy!' Gillian was overwhelmed. 'Yes, I'd love to.'

Jimmy, beaming with delight, put his arm across the back of the seat, resting his hand on her shoulder. 'I'll walk you home,' he suggested.

'To the end of Marlborough Road,' Gillian said.

They left the train and hurried up to Brynmill. On the corner of her street Gillian stopped. 'I'll go on from here, Jimmy. Thank you for a lovely afternoon.' She glanced up at him shyly. 'And thank you for asking me out again.'

He hesitantly tilted his head forward and Gillian responded quickly, accepting his brief but sweet kiss.

'When will we meet again?' he asked breathlessly.

'At the yard on Monday,' Gillian said with a teasing grin. 'If you can dodge my father for a few minutes we can talk and make plans.'

'You'd better be going,' Jimmy said. 'I make the time just on six.'

With a cry of alarm Gillian whirled and raced up the street towards home. She wanted to turn and look back at him, but there wasn't time.

As she ran her heart was filled with joy. Jimmy liked her and wanted to see her again.

'This is a very good sign,' Gloria said, satisfaction clear in her voice. 'When a man asks a girl to Sunday afternoon tea with his mother you can be sure his intentions are serious.'

'I really hope so,' Dorothy said with a sigh.

She had been elated when Ronnie had telephoned the house Saturday afternoon to issue the invitation. She felt now that he was pursuing her instead of the other way around and could therefore keep her pride intact.

Aunt Cissie always declared she despised women who were forever chasing a pair of trousers and Dorothy had to agree. It was degrading.

'Let's see how you look,' Gloria said, standing back a pace or two to view her. 'Beautiful!' She clapped her hands together. 'He won't be able to resist.'

'Resist what?'

'Never mind that for now,' Gloria said, glancing at the clock on the wall. 'It's just gone three but don't hurry. Being fashionably late is always a tease where men are concerned.'

Dorothy smoothed down the skirt of her dress, feeling nervous.

Gloria glanced out of the bedroom window. 'Oh! He's here! He's sitting in that red motor car of his. He's come to pick you up.' She chuckled. 'My word! He is keen.'

Dorothy left the house and walked down the drive to where Ronnie Knox was waiting. He leaned across to open the car door for her and Dorothy slid on to the soft leather seat.

'You look gorgeous,' he said, his glance taking in every detail of what she was wearing. 'In fact, you're a knockout, Dot.'

'Thank you.' Dorothy felt shy and suddenly uncertain. Could she live up to these compliments?

The motor roared into life and they seemed to take off with a skid. Dorothy clung to the edge of her seat with one hand while holding on to her hat with the other as the powerful car charged forward at speed. She was used to her father's careful driving and had never experienced anything like this.

'You're not scared, are you?' Ronnie asked, giving her a sideways glance.

'Of course not,' Dorothy said nervously.

'Well, you don't need to be,' Ronnie said. 'I can handle this bucket with one hand tied behind my back.'

With that his foot pressed down harder on the accelerator. Dorothy's head jerked back and she felt her body being pressed against the back of her seat.

'I'm impressed,' she managed to say. 'But I'd rather you slowed down.'

'All right. Anything to please a lady.'

The car decelerated. It was then that Dorothy noticed they were not travelling towards Miriam's house.

'Where are we going? I thought I was to have tea with you and Miriam?'

He laughed. 'That was for your mother's benefit,' he said. 'We're taking a spin up to Bishopston Common. I know some quiet places to park.'

'But Miriam will be waiting for us.'

'My mother knows nothing about it.'

'It was a trick?'

'Of course it was. We want to be alone, don't we?' Ronnie said. 'Get to know each other better.'

Dorothy wasn't so sure that was what she did want now. Ronnie had deceived her as well as her mother. She was in love with him and if he loved her in return, why would he be so underhanded?

'You're very quiet,' he said after a while.

'I don't like lying to people,' Dorothy said pouting. 'I wasn't brought up like that.'

'It was only a white lie. Harmless.'

The motor sped on and soon they were travelling along narrow roads; to either side of them were the flat open reaches of the common, dotted here and there with isolated cottages.

A few miles further on Ronnie took a side turning that dipped into a small grove of trees and then brought the car to a stop, turning off the engine.

Dorothy looked around her. There was nothing to see but trees, brambles and undergrowth: no sound except birdsong. They were absolutely alone.

'Why are we here, Ronnie?' Dorothy asked. 'I can't walk through the woods in these high-heeled shoes.'

'You don't need to walk. We're staying right here.'

All of a sudden he put his hand on her knee and leaned towards her.

'Ronnie!' Dorothy drew back. 'What are you doing?'

'Oh, come on, Dot,' he said. 'You know perfectly well why I brought you here. We both want the same thing. A little bit of fun.'

'Fun? But I thought...' Dorothy hesitated a moment and then rushed on. 'I thought we were courting.'

'We are, Dot, darling,' Ronnie said easily. 'This is part of courting. There's no harm in a kiss and a cuddle and see what develops.'

A kiss and a cuddle. That was all right, she supposed. Ronnie had kissed her before, but that had happened at her home with people close by.

He sat back in his seat, his hands on the steering wheel. 'Do you want to go back?' he asked coldly. 'Just say the word.'

133

Dorothy thought quickly. Gloria was always urging her to be encouraging with Ronnie. And she wanted him to kiss her.

'No, Ronnie. I do want to be here with you.'

He turned to her immediately with a smile, putting his arm across the back of her seat and drawing her towards him. He lowered his head and kissed her. Dorothy kissed him back, slipping her arm around his neck.

'You're so beautiful, darling, you make my heart race,' he said softly.

Dorothy was ecstatic. It was all going the way she wanted.

'You make my heart race, too, Ronnie, darling. Kiss me again.'

They kissed again. Dorothy felt his hand fumble with the buttons of her dress and the next moment he was fondling her breast, his kiss deepening and his grasp on her tightening.

Alarm bells sounded in her head and suddenly she was frightened. Dorothy struggled to free herself from his embrace and she pushed him away.

'What now?' he asked with some irritation.

'I've changed my mind,' Dorothy said breathlessly, hastily buttoning her dress with trembling fingers. 'I want to go back.'

'It's this place, is it?' Ronnie said. 'You don't like courting outdoors?'

Dorothy drew away from him, pressing herself against the door of the car. 'It's not what I expected, Ronnie.'

'Really? What did you expect?'

'I expect romance, Ronnie, and tenderness.'

He frowned. 'I wasn't rough with you.'

Dorothy swallowed. 'You were taking liberties,' she said. 'I wasn't expecting that.'

'Romance!' He looked at her, his expression set. 'You read too many silly novels, Dot. Real life isn't like that. Men have needs and urges.' He glanced away. 'Anyway, you led me on, you know you did. You're turning into a tease. Men despise teases.'

'I didn't mean to,' Dorothy said meekly. 'I've no experience of these things.'

He turned to her eagerly. 'That's just it. A man doesn't want a wife who won't satisfy him.' He gazed at her lustfully. 'I could teach you so much, Dot. You don't know what you're missing.'

Was that some kind of proposal? Dorothy wondered. Did he really see her as his wife? Maybe she had been hasty in rejecting his advances.

'I want to learn, Ronnie,' she said quietly, her eyes down. 'But not here. This is sordid.'

'All right. I'll let you into a secret. Even though I live at my mother's, I do own a detached house in Treboeth. It's where I'll live when I'm married.'

'Oh!'

'We could go there for an hour or two tomorrow afternoon,' he suggested. 'I'll pick you up about two o'clock. What do you say?'

Dorothy held her breath a moment before answering. She did not want to be a tease. She wanted Ronnie's love and his commitment. Her mother was right. To get those things she must be prepared to put her fear and her scruples aside.

'Yes, Ronnie, I'd love to see your house.'

'Good! That's settled.'

He turned the key to ignite the engine, which roared into life; a shocking sound in the comparative silence.

As they drove back Ronnie had little to say. Glancing sideways at his profile Dorothy sensed his disappointment in her. But she would make it up to him tomorrow, she told herself. She had the rest of the day to gather her courage.

'He mentioned marriage?' Gloria asked excitedly. 'He's definitely interested! Dorothy, my dear, I think we're getting there.' She sounded delighted.

'I was a bit frightened when he touched my breast,' Dorothy admitted.

'That was naughty of him, of course!' her mother said with a chuckle. 'But a girl must expect that kind of thing when she's out with a man.'

'He said I was a tease.'

'Well, prove to him you're not,' Gloria said seriously, taking Dorothy by the shoulders and looking into her face. 'Going to his house tomorrow is a golden opportunity. You must relax, my dear, and not be so prudish. After all, Ronnie Knox is a very good catch.'

Dorothy was still full of doubt. 'Mother, I can't help feeling I'm ... cheapening myself.'

'What nonsense! That sounds like your father talking.' Gloria pulled in her chin. 'Do you want to end up an arid old spinster like your aunt Cissie?'

Dorothy was fond of her aunt and always felt sorry for her. No, she could not go through life without love as Aunt Cissie had done.

'Look, Dorothy, my dear,' Gloria added. 'I'm a woman of the world. I know the way men are. If you want Ronnie then you must go after him and forget your girlish reluctance.'

'I'll do my best, Mother,' Dorothy said meekly.

'That's a good girl,' Gloria said with approval. 'I'm sure he's smitten with you. Become more accommodating, dear, and you'll nab him.'

Nine

'You haven't eaten a thing all day,' Gloria said. 'What's the matter with you?'

'I'm nervous, Mother,' Dorothy said.

Much as she loved Ronnie she was afraid of the unknown and dreaded being alone with him at his house. She was uncertain of what was expected of her; how she should behave, even with her mother's insistence that she be relaxed. If it wasn't for Gloria's insistence she wouldn't go.

'Well, of course you are,' Gloria said. 'But there's always a first time for everything.'

Dorothy wasn't comforted. 'Do I have to

throw myself at him like this?' she asked plaintively. 'He'll think I'm cheap.'

'Nonsense!' Gloria exclaimed impatiently. 'Ronnie Knox is a discerning man of the world – the perfect catch. Every girl is after him. You must show you're more sophisticated and mature than any of them.'

'But I'm not any of those things,' Dorothy said with feeling. 'I just want Ronnie to love me for what I am.'

'Pull your wits about you, Dorothy,' Gloria said sharply. 'To get the man you want you have to trap him. I know what I'm talking about. I had to do that with your father.'

Dorothy turned away, not wanting to hear the story again, but Gloria was unstoppable.

'I was from a poor family,' she said. 'When I first saw Henry Prosser I knew his family had money and I was determined to get him for myself.' Gloria smiled knowingly. 'He was putty in my hands.'

Dorothy said nothing but was thoughtful. For all her mother's scheming were her parents happy together? They were always quarrelling and their arguments grew bitter as the years went by. She did not want to end up like that with Ronnie.

'Don't be namby-pamby, my girl,' Gloria said severely at her daughter's silence. 'You deserve the best, so plan for it.'

'How?'

Gloria gave an impatient snort. 'Use your head, girl! Go with Ronnie to his house. Make the most of your opportunity, like I did.' Gloria glanced out of the bedroom window. 'Here he is now.'

Reluctantly Dorothy went down into the hall, her mother following behind.

'You can tell me everything that happened when you come home. But don't rush away from him.'

Dorothy left the house and walked down the drive on legs that trembled. Ronnie was sitting in the car with the top down. He was so handsome and he was smiling at her in a way that made her heart skip a beat.

'You look like an angel,' he said. 'I'm a lucky man.'

Despite trying to be cool and sophisticated Dorothy could not prevent a blush. 'Thank you, Ronnie.'

She got in and the car surged forward. She was confused when Ronnie took the road that led to the centre of town.

'Aren't we going for a run first?'

'I'm taking you straight to my house in Treboeth,' Ronnie said. 'Don't you remember?'

She said nothing but clutched at her purse. Despite what her mother had said Dorothy still had nagging doubts. It did not seem right that she should have to trick him into marriage. If he loved her, that should be enough for him to propose.

She thought of Gillian Finch. She did miss their friendship. If they hadn't quarrelled she might have talked it over with her friend. Gillian was always a sensible girl.

After twenty minutes they reached Ronnie's

house. Dorothy was impressed. It was a double-fronted, detached stone house with large bay windows on both floors. Lawns stretched front and back, and at the side was a small orchard. Her mother would certainly approve of this.

'Welcome,' Ronnie said when they went inside. 'Would you like a drink?'

Dorothy shook her head. 'I'm still too young to drink,' she said and then wondered if he would find her immature.

'What do you think of my property?'

'It's lovely,' she said, her mouth dry.

'I'll give you the guided tour. Let's look at the bedrooms first.'

'Oh!' She hung back.

'Come on,' he encouraged. He took her arm and led her to the staircase. Ronnie was a gentleman, she told herself. She had nothing to worry about.

They walked into the large front bedroom. 'This is the master bedroom,' he told her.

It was beautifully furnished. Ronnie had wonderful taste.

Dorothy stood by awkwardly, not knowing what to say or do.

Ronnie sat on the bed and patted the counterpane beside him. 'Sit down, Dorothy.'

'Wouldn't we be more comfortable in the drawing room?'

'Come on. I won't bite.'

Gingerly she sat down next to him. 'I can't stay long,' she said nervously.

He took her hand. 'Good gracious! You're trembling.' He smiled. 'You are a darling. So

140

innocent.'

'No, I'm not innocent,' Dorothy blurted out, mindful of her mother's words.

'What?'

She was confused. 'I mean, I'm not as naïve as you might think.'

'I'm glad to hear it.'

She thought he might be laughing at her. 'I'm not a silly girl.'

'I know you're not,' he said softly. 'Otherwise I wouldn't love you so much.'

'Oh! Ronnie.' He loved her. He had said it. Dorothy was overwhelmed with joy.

He put an arm around her waist and drew her closer to him. 'You love me, too, don't you?'

'Yes, yes, I do! I do!'

He gently cupped her face with his free hand and kissed her. Feeling so happy Dorothy responded, putting her arms around his neck.

The kiss deepened and then he gently pressed her down on to the bed. For a moment Dorothy was alarmed and struggled in his embrace.

'What's happening, Ronnie?'

'I want to make love to you so much, Dorothy,' he said huskily. 'We're quite alone here. No one will disturb us or ever know.'

'Ronnie, I'm not sure...'

'But we love each other,' he said persuasively. 'You *do* love me, Dorothy, don't you? You're not just leading me on,' he said, his tone hurt. 'That would be very cruel of you, Dot.'

She remembered he had said he despised girls who teased. She did not want him to despise her. 'No, I'd never tease you, Ronnie. I do love you.'

'Do you trust me?'

Her mother's urgings were ringing in her head. This was the golden opportunity Gloria had been talking about. If she let Ronnie love her then he would be caught. He would have to marry her.

'Yes, I trust you, Ronnie, my dearest,' Dorothy whispered.

'Then, my darling girl, relax. Let me show you what love is all about.'

'Oh! Ronnie!'

Dorothy woke suddenly from deep sleep and, stirring under the bedcovers, opened her eyes to stare in confusion, not knowing where she was for a moment.

And then it all flooded back. Ronnie's love-making had been an awakening, a wonderful experience she would never forget. She thought she understood now what her mother had been trying to tell her.

She reached out a hand to touch him next to her, but found with a stab of disappointment that she was alone in the bed and in the room.

She sat up, confused. 'Ronnie!' she called out. 'Ronnie.'

He walked into the room, fully dressed. 'Get your clothes on, Dorothy,' he said, coolness in his voice. 'It's getting late.'

'What time is it?'

He took out his pocket watch. 'Getting on for six o'clock. I have to meet someone in an hour.'

She reached out both arms to him. 'Ronnie, darling, come here and kiss me.'

'There's no time,' he said brusquely. 'Get

dressed and I'll see you downstairs.'

He turned then and strode from the room. Dorothy stared after him for a moment, frowning. He seemed so distant now. Had she done something wrong? Maybe she was being silly and overly romantic in expecting him to fawn over her. Perhaps sophisticated people did not behave like that.

Dorothy dressed and went downstairs. He was in the drawing room, waiting.

'Ronnie, is everything all right?' she asked uncertainly.

'Of course,' he said. 'I must get you home.'

'Yes, I suppose so,' she said but wished that they could remain and talk over what had happened between them. She wanted to tell him how she felt and know his feelings, too.

He ushered her out of the house without another word and on the drive back his silence continued. She was more uncertain and perplexed. Where did she stand?

'Ronnie?'

'Yes?'

Dorothy bit her lip before speaking. 'Are we engaged now?'

He turned his gaze from the road a moment to stare at her.

'Engaged?' She could not mistake the consternation in his voice and felt keen embarrassment. 'What the devil are you talking about, Dorothy?'

'We made love,' she said simply, trying to steady her voice. 'I thought it meant you wanted to marry me.'

'I never mentioned marriage,' he said defensively, his tone sharp. 'Good God! You *are* naïve!'

'But, Ronnie, you said you loved me.'

'Of course I said it,' he said scathingly. 'Every girl wants to hear that at such times.'

Dorothy drew back against the car door in dismay. 'Didn't you mean it?' She was appalled. 'You mean you lied to me so that I would let you—?'

'Now, don't start throwing a girly fit,' Ronnie snapped. 'You knew what you were doing and you wanted it to happen. I could tell. Don't play so innocent, Dorothy.'

'But my mother said—'

'What the hell has it got to do with your mother?'

In mortified silence Dorothy stared ahead at the road twisting before them, her gloved hand over her mouth. What had she done? What a fool she had been.

She turned towards him. 'But I love you, Ronnie,' she said in a small voice. 'I really do.'

She watched his handsome profile. He was grinding his teeth, obviously in anger, but remained silent. Dorothy wanted to curl up and die.

He stopped the car outside her house. Dorothy made no attempt to get out. He took out his pocket watch again and looked at it.

'I have to be somewhere,' he said dismissively. 'And I'm late already.'

'Ronnie, will I see you again?'

'Yes, of course we can see each other again, Dorothy,' he said frankly. 'As often as you like,

144

but remember I never mentioned marriage.'

Slowly Dorothy opened the car door and got out.

'Goodbye, Ronnie,' she said sadly and walked away.

Gloria was in the hall waiting for her daughter to return.

'Well? What happened?'

Dorothy stared at her mother's expectant expression and burst into tears. She could not help herself. Ronnie had humiliated her. No! She had humiliated herself, Dorothy thought miserably, and now she was so ashamed at what she had done.

'What on earth is the matter?' Gloria was startled.

'What's the matter?' Dorothy wailed, swallowing her tears. 'I'll tell you, Mother. I've been an utter little fool! I let Ronnie take advantage of me.'

'Good.'

'Good!' Dorothy screeched. 'I've made myself cheap. Ronnie has no intention of marrying me, never did. He said so. I'm ruined! Oh, why did I listen to you?'

Dorothy pulled off her gloves and threw them on the hall table together with her hat. She wanted to find a dark hole and hide.

'You didn't mention marriage to him, did you?' Gloria asked, an edge to her voice.

Dorothy sobbed. 'Of course I did once we had...'

Gloria looked dismayed. 'Oh, you stupid girl!'

she said angrily. 'You frightened him off. Have you no sense?'

Dorothy stared at her mother's furious face and felt cold.

'Apparently not,' she said in a low, hopeless voice. 'I let myself be persuaded by you, Mother, didn't I? I went to Ronnie against my better judgement. Now I'm tainted – damaged goods.'

'Rubbish!' Gloria said with an uncaring gesture. 'Ronnie will come around. I know men.'

'Oh, yes, he will.' Dorothy nodded. 'He told me we can be together as often as I like, just so long as I don't expect marriage.' She could not stop a sob erupting. 'He doesn't respect me. I'm easy meat to him now.'

'Ooh!' Gloria's lips tightened. 'Ronnie won't get away with this. I'll speak to your father. Henry will have a word with him. Get him to do the decent thing.'

'Decent thing?' Dorothy blurted out. 'There's no decency in this house.'

'Dorothy! Watch your tongue!'

'You mustn't tell my father what I've done,' Dorothy said frantically. She could not bear it if her father knew how shamefully she had behaved, especially after the promise she had made to him. 'I don't want anyone else to know. Don't you understand how I feel, Mother? I've been used by you as well as Ronnie.'

'Dorothy, what a terrible thing for a girl to say to her mother,' Gloria gasped, scandalized. 'I was thinking only of your future.'

'What future?' Dorothy said tearfully. 'I'm

146

humiliated to the core. I wish I were dead!'

With that Dorothy turned and ran up the stairs, seeking sanctuary in her bedroom. She flung herself on the bed and cried.

She tried not to think of Ronnie, tried not to remember. What had seemed so wonderful an experience just a few hours ago now appeared cheap and sordid to her. She would never get over it.

She did remember painfully the consternation on Ronnie's face when she had mentioned marriage. She believed herself in love with him, now all she felt was deep misery. There was nothing left for her.

Ten

'It'll be all right, Jimmy, I promise you.' Gillian grasped his arm eagerly.

The yard was empty for the moment, her father still in the stores. Gillian was determined to grab a few moments with Jimmy to tell him of her plan before she had to start work.

'Your mother won't like it if I turn up for supper unannounced,' Jimmy said uncertainly. 'I'm not sure how your father will take it either. I'm only his apprentice, remember.'

'And you're *my* ... friend.' She was going to say 'boyfriend' but caught herself in time. Although Jimmy had asked her to go out with him again she did not want to appear too forward.

'Still and all,' Jimmy argued, shaking his head, 'I think you should ask first.'

Gillian pouted. 'Anyone would think you didn't want to meet my family.'

Jimmy laughed. 'I already know half of your family. I see them every day.'

'Well, then!' Gillian said brightly. 'You won't feel out of place with your workmates at the table.' She stepped closer to him, putting her hand on his chest. 'Please say you'll come,' she begged. 'We can go straight from here. I'll wait until you clock off this evening.'

'Well, if you really think it's all right.'

'Of course it is. Look out! Here comes Dad. Not a word, mind.'

Gillian sailed off across the yard towards the office building before her father could speak with her. She was so pleased with her plan she could have hugged herself. Her mother would like Jimmy, she knew she would. It was important to her that all her family liked him.

In the office she was very surprised to see Andy was already at his desk.

'Old Meeker's been looking for you,' he said sourly. 'You should've been at your desk ten minutes ago.'

'You liar!' Gillian burst out. She pointed to the clock on the wall. 'It's only a minute to nine. What are you doing here at this time anyway?' She stuck her tongue out at him. 'Couldn't you sleep?'

'Shut up, you mouthy tart!' Andy barked.

'What did you call me?' Gillian was furious.

'I saw you fawning over that twerp Jimmy Tomkin,' he said. 'Who does he think he is anyway?'

'What do you mean?'

'I heard my father praising him up to the skies the other day,' Andy said. 'He's all too smarmy with my father – and yours, too.' His mouth twisted. 'There's something phoney about him and I'm going to find out what it is.'

'Leave Jimmy alone,' Gillian warned brusquely. 'He's reliable and a good worker, and Uncle Henry appreciates that.' She curled her lip disdainfully. 'He gets precious little work from you.'

'I said shut your mouth or I'll do it for you.'

'Huh!' Gillian swung away, lifting a shoulder in a dismissive gesture. 'You and whose army?'

She wasn't afraid of him, not when she had two hefty brothers to protect her.

Andy's expression was nasty and he started around the desk towards her but drew back when Mr Meeker made an appearance. The older man stared at Andy in shock.

'Miracles do happen, then,' he said sarcastically. His glance turned to Gillian. 'Well, come on, Gillian!' His voice was sharp. 'The cover is still on your typewriter and it's now five past nine.'

'Sorry, Mr Meeker.'

Family members and boarders were all seated at the table when Gillian arrived with Jimmy just after six o'clock,

'Gillian! You're late!' Vera exclaimed loudly.

'I won't have it!'

'Sorry, Mam,' Gillian said meekly, embarrassed in front of Jimmy. 'I had to wait for Jimmy.'

'Who?'

Gillian pulled Jimmy forward and everyone stared.

'I've invited my friend Jimmy Tomkin to supper, Mam,' she said. 'He's Dad's new apprentice.'

Vera looked surprised. 'Oh, is he?'

Gillian carefully avoided looking at her father. 'I thought you wouldn't mind, Mam,' she said hopefully.

Vera looked the newcomer up and down. Gillian knew her mother liked what she saw immediately because the corners of her mouth rose.

'Well, I expect we can find room for him,' Vera said. 'He can sit next to Arthur here.'

Jimmy ducked his head. 'Thank you, Mrs Finch. I hope I'm not a nuisance.'

Vera put a plate of food in front of him. 'Not at all, Jimmy,' she said and sat down. 'You're very welcome.'

Gillian sat next to her mother so that she could look across at Jimmy. He was sitting between her father and her brother Tom – and it was a strange thing, Gillian thought suddenly, how alike Jimmy and Tom were.

'Have we met before, Jimmy?' Vera asked. 'You look familiar. Do I know your mother?'

Arthur Finch cleared his throat noisily. 'Do you follow football, Mr Oglander?' he asked loudly, drowning out Jimmy's reply. 'Sheffield

Wednesday are doing all right in the league. Do you think they stand a chance of getting the cup this year?'

Bemused, Gillian stared at her father. He was not the least interested in football usually. And he had a most strained expression on his face.

'I've no idea, I'm afraid, Mr Finch,' Bill Oglander said pleasantly. 'I'm not a football fan. Cricket is the favourite sport in Australia.'

'Ah! Cricket,' said Mr Gilmore. 'Now that's the sport of princes.'

'You're thinking of horse racing,' said Sam. 'The sport of kings.'

Several animated conversations about various sports broke out around the table then. Gillian looked at her father again. He was eating steadily now, his expression relaxed.

She frowned. Was it her imagination or had he deliberately steered attention away from Vera's questioning of Jimmy? She wondered why.

The meal over, everyone went their separate ways.

'Thank you very much for your hospitality, Mrs Finch,' Jimmy said. 'It was kind of you since I'm a stranger.'

Gillian was pleased to see her mother smile.

'You don't seem like a stranger, Jimmy,' Vera said. 'You must come to supper again.'

'Thank you.' He glanced at Gillian. 'Well, I'd better be going home.'

'I'll walk you to the corner,' Gillian offered.

She enjoyed his company and wished he would stay longer but thought it just as well

151

Jimmy was leaving since her father was hovering in the passage, obviously wanting to speak to her.

When she returned Arthur was sitting on the stairs, smoking his pipe. He got to his feet as she came in through the front door, taking his pipe out of his mouth.

'Gillian, I want a word with you, my girl.'

She stared. 'Have I done something wrong, Dad?'

'That remains to be seen.'

'What?'

He glanced around furtively. 'We need to talk seriously but not here. I don't want Vera to get wind of this.'

He was being very mysterious, Gillian thought. 'Dad, what is it?'

He grabbed for his flat cap off the hallstand. 'Come on. We'll go for a walk.'

'Eh?' Gillian was stumped.

He hustled her out of the front door and started off towards the small park at the end of the street.

'Dad, what's going on? Are you angry because I invited Jimmy to supper without asking permission?'

He glanced over his shoulder. 'Wait until we get to the park,' he said. 'I'll explain.'

The evening air was still warm. Her father led her to a seat and indicated she should sit.

'What is it?' She was getting alarmed now. Had Andy Prosser been telling lies about her and Jimmy?

'This is a very delicate matter,' Arthur said.

'And frankly, embarrassing.'

'Dad, Jimmy and I have done nothing wrong so if someone has been telling you lies—'

'What?' He shook his head. 'No, nothing like that. But it does concern Jimmy Tomkin.'

'What about him?'

Arthur took his pipe out of his pocket, lit it, and sat puffing away for a moment or two in silence. Gillian thought it wise to wait until he was ready to speak.

'Is Jimmy just your friend, or more?' Arthur asked at last. 'Are you becoming fond of him?'

Gillian felt her cheeks flush up. 'Dad! Really! I thought you liked him?'

'I do. Personally, I've got nothing against him,' Arthur said. 'He's a good lad and a credit to his father.

'I didn't know Jimmy's father was still alive.'

'Oh, he's alive all right.'

Arthur puffed heavily on his pipe for a moment more and then, taking it out of his mouth, looked directly at her and she saw how serious his expression was.

'I'm going to tell you something now, Gillian, in utter confidence,' he began sombrely. 'You must never breathe a word of it to anyone, do you understand?'

Gillian nodded in silence.

Her father hesitated a moment and then continued. 'I gave my word not to reveal this to anyone,' he said earnestly. 'But I can see how close you are with Jimmy and you ought to know the truth.'

'What is it, Dad? What's wrong?'

153

'Jimmy is your blood cousin.'

Perplexed, Gillian looked quizzically at her father. 'I don't understand.'

'Jimmy is Uncle Henry's illegitimate son.'

'What?'

'Now, Gill, you've promised to tell no one about this. You must keep your word,' Arthur said urgently. 'Henry confided in me years ago. If your mother ever found out I dread to think what she might do, there being such bad blood between her and Henry over the will.'

'Jimmy is my cousin?' Gillian could not believe it.

'He is also illegitimate.' Arthur shook his head. 'That doesn't lower him in my eyes, but the world has other ideas about illegitimacy. It's a stigma, Gill.'

'Does Jimmy know?'

'Oh, yes.'

Gillian sat back against the seat. Jimmy had known all along that they were cousins and he had not said a word to her. How could he have not told her? He had deliberately deceived her.

Suddenly she understood her puzzlement at the supper table earlier over the likeness between Jimmy and Tom. They could be mistaken for brothers. They were cousins. Vera had sensed something, too.

'Dad, what am I going to do?'

'There's no reason why you shouldn't remain friends with Jimmy,' Arthur said. 'But it would be unwise to get more deeply attached.'

Gillian lifted her chin. 'Cousins have been marrying for centuries.'

It seemed so unfair. She really liked Jimmy, well, more than liked him to be truthful with herself.

'It's not considered wise these days,' Arthur said sternly. 'Besides, you hardly know the boy. Talking of marrying him is absurd.'

'Yes, I know, Dad,' Gillian agreed. 'It's just that it's so disappointing.'

'You mustn't bring him to the house again,' warned Arthur. 'Your mother is far too sharp. If she gets a whiff of this it's all up for Henry.'

'I can hardly believe it.' She felt angry that Jimmy had deliberately left her in the dark about their connection.

'I love your mother dearly,' Arthur said. 'But Vera is in such a state over the will she'll use any weapon against Henry. He doesn't deserve it. But for goodness' sake don't tell your mother I said that.'

Gillian sat with shoulders drooping. She had a great deal to ponder over.

'We'd best be getting back,' Arthur said, standing up. 'The last thing I want is to arouse your mother's curiosity. She won't give me a moment's peace if she thinks I'm keeping secrets.'

Norman Meeker came into the inner office where Henry was making last-minute costing adjustments to some job estimates and put the wages ledger on the desk.

'That's the last of the wages doled out to the men, Mr Prosser,' Norman said and sighed heavily. 'Thank God it's Friday.'

Henry glanced up and smiled. 'You always say

155

that, Norman.'

Norman scratched his head. 'I can never rest easy with all that money about the office on a Thursday night.'

'How long have you worked here now?'

Norman grinned. 'Thirty-six years. I'll never stop worrying now. Old Kitson, my predecessor, was the same. Do you remember him, Mr Prosser? He was yard manager in your father's day.'

Henry frowned. 'No.'

'No, of course not.' Norman nodded. 'You were only a small kid at the time. Old Kitson died a year after your father...' Norman hesitated and glanced away.

'Disappeared?' Henry suggested.

Norman looked embarrassed. 'Sorry, Mr Prosser. I had no right to talk out of turn, bring up bad memories.'

'No, that's all right.' Henry waved a hand. 'I was only seven years old when my father disappeared. I never knew what happened. My mother could never tell me anything. No one seems to know, not even my aunt Cissie.'

Norman looked at his pocket watch. 'I'd better go. If I'm late the wife starts having kittens. I wouldn't put it past her to come here looking for me in case I run off with a belly dancer.'

'What happened, Norman?' Henry looked at him keenly.

'What?'

'What happened to my father? You know something, don't you?'

Norman shook his head. 'It's ancient history,

Mr Prosser. Everyone's long gone; your parents, Charlie Knox. What good would it do to rake up the past?'

Henry rubbed a hand over his face. 'You're right, Norman.' He suddenly felt tired. 'I've got enough on my plate as it is.'

'Goodnight, then.'

After Norman was gone Henry sat with his elbows on the desk. The past didn't matter. The present was all he should be thinking about: Florrie and Jimmy. He sighed heavily. He should be going home, too, but the tension between him and Gloria made him drag his feet. The image of her angry features that morning made his mind up for him. He would not go home. He would spend the night with Florrie again, if she would let him.

He was just clearing the loose papers from his desk when there was a sound in the outer office and the next moment his son Andy was standing in the doorway.

Henry was astonished to see him. 'What the hell are you doing here at this hour?'

'I want some money,' Andy said belligerently. 'Thirty pounds for starters.'

'What?'

'You heard me.'

'Have you been drinking?' Henry was puzzled by the look on his son's face. There was belligerence and triumph, too.

'No, but I will be when I get the money.'

'What the devil are you blathering about?'

Andy swaggered forward, a thin smile on his face.

'I know all about that dirty whore of yours in Fleet Street – and her bastard brat, Jimmy Tomkin,' he said. 'Now, if you don't want Mother to find out I suggest you cough up, and quick.'

Henry's legs felt suddenly weak and he sat down heavily in his chair. 'You're talking drivel,' he managed to say.

'Aw! Come off it, Father,' Andy scoffed. 'I followed you from the yard to Fleet Street. I saw you open the door with your own key. And I saw you pawing her, the ugly slut.'

Henry sprang to his feet. 'Shut your dirty mouth, you snivelling cur,' he bellowed.

'Well, that's a nice way for a father to talk to his legitimate son.'

Henry was speechless for a moment, his mind whirling. Amongst the sudden chaos one thought was uppermost. He must protect Florrie and Jimmy. But paying Andy off was not the answer.

'You won't get a bloody penny out of me,' Henry said in fury. 'So you can forget it, Andy.'

'You'll pay up or else,' Andy said savagely. 'I'll not only tell Mother, I'll tell everyone. That slut and her brat won't be able to hold their heads up. Jimmy will be a laughing stock around the yard.'

Enraged by Andy's words Henry charged around the desk and, lashing out, caught his son across the face with his open hand.

'You good-for-nothing layabout,' he shouted. 'Jimmy is worth twenty of you.'

Andy reeled back, clutching at his reddened cheek. There was hatred in his eyes as he looked at his father.

Henry stepped back from him, startled and appalled at his own violence. That was the first time he had ever laid a hand on any of his children. He silently pledged it would never happen again.

'You'll be sorry you did that,' Andy gasped. 'I'll tell, believe me.'

Henry was at his rope's end. 'Well, go ahead and tell your mother, then,' he yelled. 'Maybe you should. I'm thinking of leaving her anyway.'

'What?'

Henry nodded. 'Are you surprised after what your mother and I have been going through this last year or two? Our marriage is a sham and has been from the start. I'm sick of it!'

'You can't do that,' Andy whined. 'What happens to me if you desert us?'

'Oh, don't worry,' Henry said disdainfully. 'You won't starve. The marriage is over, but you will get money from me and you've still got your job at this office.'

'Bloody pittance!' Andy howled. 'I'm your legitimate son. I deserve much more. You've no right to keep me short of money.'

'Earn it! Everyone has to work for a living,' Henry said. 'Why should you be different? Or maybe your mother has been putting big ideas in your head, eh?'

'You're going to regret this day,' Andy rasped. 'I'm not standing aside for any bastard brat.'

'Get out!' Henry roared. 'Get out of my sight.'

Andy got out and Henry, feeling dizzy with shock, swayed back towards his chair and

159

collapsed into it.

Fate in the shape of his son had made the decision for him. On the edge of his shock was also a sense of relief. He had made the break at last. He and Gloria were finished.

Eleven

William Prosser's house, 1898

William Prosser sat at the big mahogany desk in his oak-panelled study, finishing off some correspondence. Sealing the last envelope, he glanced at the ormolu clock on the mantelpiece. Almost two o'clock. He had promised Henry and Vera that he would take them to Singleton Park to see the monkeys this afternoon. It would be a treat for them on this bright April day.

He stood up as Cissie came into the room.

'William, young Norman Meeker is here,' she said. 'He's asking to speak to you.'

'Norman Meeker?' William frowned in puzzlement. 'What on earth is the boy doing here on his half-day?'

'Will you see him?'

William glanced at the clock again. 'I can give him five minutes, Cissie. Oh, and would you get Henry and Vera into their coats and hats. I'm taking them out.'

Cissie smiled. 'They're already dressed.

They're so excited they were ready half an hour ago.'

'Right.' William chuckled. 'Send Norman in, please. Tell the children I won't keep them waiting much longer.'

William was standing before the fireplace when Norman Meeker came in. The young man, small, rather delicate-looking, stood at the centre of the room, nervously shuffling his feet.

Norman had been employed in the yard office for the past two years, learning the ropes from Mr Kitson, the yard manager, and showed promise. William liked him and knew from Mr Kitson that Norman was intelligent and a hard worker.

'What brings you here on a Saturday afternoon, Norman? Are you in trouble?'

'No, Mr Prosser, sir. Mr Kitson sent me. He'd be obliged if you could come down to the yard right away.'

William was startled. 'There hasn't been a fire at the yard, has there?'

'No, no, nothing like that, sir,' Norman said. 'Mr Kitson needs to see you at the yard.'

William was flummoxed. 'What on earth for?'

'He didn't say, sir, but he did say it was urgent.'

William was in a quandary. 'I'm taking my children out for the afternoon. I don't think I can spare the time to go to the yard today.'

Norman looked agitated. 'Mr Kitson was insistent, sir. I'm not in his confidence of course, Mr Prosser, but I do believe it is a very grave matter.'

161

William frowned, beginning to feel worried. What on earth was Kitson doing at the office on a Saturday afternoon anyway?

'Very well,' William said. 'I'll come. Just let me have a word with my sister.'

In the hall the children were at the bottom of the stairs, jumping about with excitement. Five-year-old Vera skipped up to him.

'Are we going to the park now, Daddy? Are we going?'

'I'm sorry, kids,' William said sadly. 'Daddy has to go out. But I won't be long. We'll go to the park when I come back.'

'But it'll be dark soon,' Henry said, his little face clouding. 'The monkeys will have gone to bed.'

William hated disappointing them. At seven and five, Henry and Vera would take broken promises to heart.

'I'll be as quick as I can.' William turned to his sister. 'Where's Rose? Perhaps she can take them.'

'Rose is visiting at the hospital,' said Cissie.

'Oh, of course,' William said. 'I'd forgotten Freda Knox is in hospital again, poor woman.'

He shrugged into his overcoat. 'I'll be as quick as I can, kids.' He lifted his daughter into his arms. 'Now don't cry, Vera, there's a good girl,' he said gently. 'The monkeys will still be there later.'

William drove down to the yard in a worried frame of mind. Young Norman seated beside him had little to say but William sensed the young man was apprehensive about something, and that worried him even more.

At the office Mr Kitson, the yard manager, was waiting for them. He was a man in his late fifties, tall, stooped with a shock of white hair. His expression was grave when William walked in.

'Ah, Mr Prosser, thank God you're here.'

'What is it, Mr Kitson?'

The older man hesitated for a moment and then glanced at Norman.

'Norman, my boy, I wonder if you'd give us a minute in private.'

'Yes, Mr Kitson,' Norman said and left the office immediately.

'What is it?' William demanded to know, now thoroughly unnerved.

Mr Kitson gave a heavy sigh. 'Embezzlement, Mr Prosser.'

'What?' William was astounded.

Mr Kitson nodded. 'Last week by pure chance I noticed a discrepancy in the accounts.'

'It could be just an error,' William said hopefully.

Mr Kitson shook his head. 'No, Mr Prosser. It's no error. I've been through the books for past years with a fine toothcomb. This afternoon I finally finished.' He looked at William. 'Embezzlement, Mr Prosser; deliberate and consistent. There's no doubt about it.'

'I can't believe it,' William said. 'How much has been taken?'

'By my reckoning it is in the region of ten thousand pounds taken over something like eight years.'

'Good God!' William stared, floored by the revelation. 'But who...?'

'It's not for me to point the finger, Mr Prosser,' Mr Kitson said cautiously. 'But there are only three people who could have done this. Me, you and Mr Knox.'

William felt winded by the shock and sank heavily into a chair.

'I swear to you, Mr Prosser,' Mr Kitson continued fervently. 'I had no hand in it.'

William was silent, staring into space. He could not believe it was true, yet Mr Kitson could hardly have made a mistake about such an important matter. And he believed the man when he vowed he was not to blame. That left only Charlie Knox. And yet that seemed unbelievable. Or was it? He had never really trusted Charlie.

'We must get the auditors in, Mr Prosser,' Mr Kitson said seriously. 'And the police must be informed.'

'No!' William said. 'Not yet. Leave it for the weekend. I'll have a word with Mr Knox. There must be a reasonable explanation for this.'

He hoped this was true for, despite the evidence and his distrust, he was not ready to accuse his partner of such a crime.

'Embezzlement is a deliberate act, Mr Prosser,' Mr Kitson reminded him. 'A serious crime has been committed.'

'We're jumping to conclusions that Mr Knox is involved,' William said hastily. 'I must be sure.'

Mr Kitson's expression tightened. 'Surely you

don't suspect me after I've given you my word that I am innocent?' he asked, a tremor in his voice.

'No, no, Mr Kitson,' William said quickly. 'I don't believe that for one minute.' He hesitated. 'I must talk to Mr Knox. He may be ready to make restitution if he is responsible.'

Mr Kitson nodded. 'As you wish, Mr Prosser.'

'Leave the matter with me,' William said. 'But I ask you not to breathe a word of this to anyone.'

Mr Kitson looked at him, his expression hurt, but he said nothing. He took his coat and hat from the stand nearby.

'I'll see you on Monday, Mr Prosser,' he said solemnly. 'Though I dread to think of what we must now go through in the future.'

The three of them left the yard together, Mr Kitson and Norman finding their own way home.

William knew what he must do. He must confront Charlie Knox immediately, but he felt sickened at the thought of openly accusing his partner of such a crime.

He drove straight away to Charlie's house, a semi-detached villa in well-kept grounds. William rang the bell but there was no answer.

Charlie must be at the hospital, he surmised, and was about to leave when he was aware of the faint sound of music; a gramophone was playing somewhere in the house.

William walked around the pine end of the house to the back and on impulse tried the latch of the back door. To his surprise, it yielded and he walked in. The music was louder now.

He was conscious that he was intruding and was in two minds about what he should do next. He still felt shaken by the shock of Mr Kitson's disturbing discovery. Obviously, Charlie was at home and he must confront him today.

William walked through the kitchen into the hall and stood listening at the foot of the staircase. The music was coming from upstairs and then he heard the murmur of voices.

He was about to shout out, call Charlie by name, when all at once a woman laughed, and the call was stilled in his throat. He stood stock still, the hairs on the back of his neck rising.

That laugh, he knew it so well. That was his wife's laughter. It was unmistakable. But what was Rose doing in Charlie's house?

Slowly, apprehensively William climbed the stairs, pausing on the landing. The music was coming from a bedroom at the front of the house. He walked along the landing towards the door, which was ajar.

Rose gleefully laughed again.

William pushed the door open wider and then stood in the doorway rooted to the spot, staring.

Stark naked, two people stood at the centre of the room clasped tightly in each other's arms, swaying to the rhythm of the music: Rose and Charlie Knox.

William's mouth opened, but he could not speak. He watched in silence as Rose looked up into Charlie's face with an expression of utter delight and abandon; a look that William had never seen on his wife's face before.

He felt a terrible nausea about to overwhelm him and then a great rush of heat to his head, making his vision blur for a moment. He could not bear to see her look at another man that way. As though in a trance, he took a faltering step forward into the room. The entwined couple became aware of him and sprang apart.

'William!' Her face going white, Rose hastily snatched at a wrap nearby, attempting to cover her nakedness, but Charlie just stood where he was, apparently unashamed.

'William, what can I say? You've caught us.'

He did not sound the least contrite. In fact, William thought, there was a degree of amusement in his voice and anger swelled in his breast. The heat seemed to tighten his collar, choking him, and he still struggled to utter a sound.

'William, what are you going to do?' Rose asked, a quiver in her voice. She had slipped into the wrap and now took a step towards him.

'I should kill you both,' William managed to rasp, despite his mouth being so dry. 'You deserve it for such monstrous treachery.'

'Charlie and I love each other,' Rose cried out passionately. 'He's going to leave Freda to be with me.'

'Rose!' Charlie said curtly. 'This isn't the time or place.' He picked up a dressing gown and, putting it on, walked towards William. 'We have to talk, Will,' he said in a placating tone. 'You deserve an explanation.'

Charlie was making light of stealing his wife and William saw red. He heard Rose give a little scream as with a howl he launched himself at

167

Charlie, swinging a punch to the man's face, but Charlie sidestepped and pushed William sideways, sending him sprawling on to the rug.

He was winded. From the floor he gazed up helplessly at the other man. 'You bloody swine,' William grated. 'Not content with stealing from the firm you've taken my wife, too. You filthy scoundrel.'

'What are you talking about?' Charlie stepped back, his expression alert.

William struggled to his feet and faced his opponent.

'You know damned well,' he said bitterly. 'Kitson called me to the office this afternoon. He has uncovered embezzlement on a huge scale. Don't deny it, Charlie.'

'Oh, Charlie!' exclaimed Rose excitedly. 'Did you do it for us?'

'Be quiet, Rose, for pity's sake,' Charlie snapped at her. 'You can't prove it was me,' he said to William, his expression darkening. 'I'll deny everything.'

'Well, you can tell your story to the police,' William said wrathfully. 'I'm calling in the auditors on Monday. Kitson wanted me to inform the police today. Like a fool I told him to wait. I could not believe it of you, Charlie, but now...' William sent a glowering look at Rose. 'Now I know you're capable of anything. You'll go to prison for this.'

'There's no proof that I embezzled a penny,' Charlie asserted strongly. 'I'll deny it and counter-claim that it was either you or Kitson or both. There'll be one hell of a scandal, William. It won't do the firm much good.'

'I'll risk that.'

'Are you ready to risk not only our livelihoods but those of the men who work for us? The business could go under if this comes out. Men could lose their jobs.'

William hesitated at the thought that others would suffer, yet his heart hungered for revenge. Embezzlement had been one thing, bad though that was, but Charlie had gone beyond any degree of decency and loyalty. He had taken William's wife, too.

'You've taken everything from me,' William voiced his thoughts, a catch in his voice. 'Everything.'

'Look, William, we can talk this through,' Charlie said, trying to cajole him. 'We have to save the business from scandal, surely you can see that?'

'We?' William roared. 'Our partnership is over, Charlie. You'll get out. I own sixty per cent of the business. I'll buy you out.'

'I'm not selling, so forget that.' Charlie turned his back for a moment and then swung around again to face William. 'All right!' he snarled. 'Between the three of us here I admit I took the money. I'm worth more than forty per cent. I was the one who kept things going after your father died and I was the one who built up the business to what it is today. I deserved a bigger share so I took it in cash.'

William whirled on Rose. 'You heard him admit it, Rose. You'll bear witness against him.'

'Don't be stupid, William,' Charlie said disdainfully. 'Rose loves me. She'd never do anything to hurt me.'

William stared at Rose but her expression was defiant.

'You're my wife, Rose,' he said. 'It's your duty to stand by me.'

Rose tossed her head. 'It's over between us, William. I'm leaving you. Charlie's right. I love him and I want to be with him.'

'You can't mean it. The children,' William said despairingly. 'What about the children?'

She lifted her chin. 'What about them? I'm entitled to my own life: to happiness. The children have you and your sister, Cissie.'

'This is intolerable,' William said desperately. 'You're destroying us and our lives together.'

'I tell you, it's over and done with,' Rose cried. 'It's me and Charlie from now on. He's leaving Freda for me.'

William flashed a look at Charlie. He could see by the consternation on the other man's face that Rose's assertion annoyed him.

'What about George, Charlie?' William asked. 'Your son is the light of your life, or so you're always telling me. Are you going to leave him, too?'

Charlie's jaw clenched. 'George is the reason why I won't let you kick me out of the business, William,' he said strongly. 'George will inherit my share. It's his birthright. He's the reason why I've worked so hard to build up the business.'

'Is he the reason why you stole from it?' William roared.

'Now look here, William,' Charlie said in a

harsh tone. 'I won't go quietly. I'll accuse you of the embezzlement. There's no proof against me. It's your word against mine.'

'You swine!'

'There's nothing you can do, William,' Charlie said. 'I suggest you forget about the auditors and the police. This is a private matter between you and me. Do you want everyone to know Rose has deceived you with me? You'll be a laughing stock.'

William stared from one to the other. He had never felt more helpless in his life. It was as though everything was collapsing around him. His pride was all he had left.

Without another word William turned on his heel and left them together. He did not know what Rose's immediate plans were and suddenly he did not care. He did not want her to come anywhere near the children.

Outside, he leaned against the closed door, feeling lost and confused. What could he tell the children to explain why their mother was not with them?

There was no one home when he returned, and he was glad of that. He needed time and quiet to think. In the study he sat at his desk, leaned his arms on the top and rested his head on them.

It was as though he was in some kind of nightmare and could not wake up. His whole world had changed: collapsed. He did not know what he ought to do.

Rose would not return home and he did not want her here, not after what he had witnessed.

She would probably stay with Charlie, at least until Freda came out of hospital.

How could he face people? The thought of continuing to work with Charlie made him feel sick to his stomach. The whole truth would come out about Rose's unfaithfulness. Nothing could stop that, but he could not face it. He had to get away, right away. He could not bear to stay here another day.

An hour later he heard voices in the hall and Cissie came into the study with the children. They ran up to him, chattering with excitement.

'We saw the monkeys!'

They ran out into the hall to take off their hats and coats and then dashed along the passage towards the kitchen.

'I want milk and biscuits,' Henry piped up.

'Me, too!' Vera squealed in delight.

'I took them to the park, Will,' Cissie said cheerfully. 'We had a lovely afternoon out.'

'Thanks, Cissie,' William managed to say.

'Is something wrong?'

'No.' He paused, making up his mind not to tell her the truth. 'I have to go away, Cissie, this afternoon.'

'Go away? But why?'

'Business,' he said shortly. 'I'll be away a few days. Will you take care of things here for me and look after the children?'

'Of course, Will,' Cissie said, her tone concerned. 'Will, are you sure there's nothing wrong.'

'I'll go up and pack a few things,' William said, avoiding her anxious gaze.

'What will I tell Rose when she gets home?'

'Rose already knows,' William said shortly. 'And she knows why.'

'This is so strange, Will...'

William took her hand and clasped it tightly. 'Cissie, listen! You're the only one I can rely on. All I ask is that you take care of the house and the children until I return.'

'When will that be?'

'I don't know.'

That was true. All he knew was that he must get away, as far as possible. For the moment he could not envisage returning, not to the wasteland his life had become. Even his deep love for his children could not keep him here to face the humiliation that was bound to fall on him – and them, too.

'I'll write, Cissie. I'll let you know where I am and what's happening.'

Cissie stepped closer to him, her face crumpling with anxiety. 'Will, I'm afraid—'

'You've always been the strong one, Cissie,' William said despairingly. 'You stood up to Father even though he kept you here as his unpaid housekeeper. Be strong again for me. That's all I ask.'

She nodded, and he leaned forward and kissed her on the cheek.

'Thank you,' he said and went upstairs to start packing.

Twelve

Her father and Jimmy Tomkin were just leaving to go out on a job as Gillian reached the yard. Jimmy paused to speak to her. 'Hello, Gill,' he greeted cheerfully. 'I'm glad I caught you. I wanted to say thanks for inviting me to your house for supper yesterday. I really enjoyed myself.'

Gillian stared at him coldly. She could not forgive his deceitfulness. 'I'm surprised you have the nerve to talk to me after what you did.'

'What?' Jimmy looked taken aback.

'I thought we were good friends, Jimmy,' Gillian continued. 'You could have told me the truth.'

Arthur quickened his steps back to where they stood.

'Gill! This is not the time or place for this,' he said hastily in a low voice. 'I asked you to be discreet.'

Gillian threw an irritated glance at her father. 'I've been lied to, deliberately deceived,' she said.

'I've never lied to you,' Jimmy said. 'I don't know what you're talking about.'

174

'Leave it!' Arthur hissed. 'Come on, Jimmy. We have work to do. I'll talk to you later, my girl.'

'So will I, Gill,' Jimmy said forthrightly. 'I want to know what I'm being accused of.'

'As if you don't know,' Gillian said as a parting shot and turned on her heel and marched off.

The clock on the office wall said five o'clock. Andy had slunk out an hour since.

Gillian put the cover on her typewriter. 'Is it all right if I go now, Mr Meeker?' she asked.

'Yes, you get off, Gill,' he said. 'I'll be going home myself in a minute, but I'll be back later. I haven't had a chance to put the wages up this afternoon and have got to go to a funeral tomorrow morning so I'll have to do the pay packets this evening.'

Gillian felt a twinge of guilt. 'Do you want me to come back, too – to help, Mr Meeker?'

He smiled. 'That's good of you, Gill, but I can manage.'

'Goodnight, then.'

'Goodnight, Gill.'

To her consternation Gillian found Jimmy was waiting for her outside the yard gates. She tried to hurry past him, but he caught at her arm, holding her back.

'Wait a minute, Gill,' he said. 'We've got to talk.'

Gillian tossed her head. 'I've got nothing to say to you.'

'Huh! You had plenty to say this morning,' he

175

said sharply. 'And I want to know what you meant by it.'

Gillian looked up into his face and her anger quietened a little. She did like him. That hadn't changed, but she was disappointed in him.

'Why didn't you tell me the truth?' she asked. 'Why didn't you trust me?'

'Trust you with what?'

'Ooh!' Gillian stamped her foot. 'You're still covering up.'

'Gill, you're beginning to annoy me,' Jimmy said brusquely. 'I've no idea what you're talking about.'

Gillian's expression showed her mood. 'Why didn't you tell me that my uncle Henry is your father; that we are blood cousins?'

'Oh!' His face fell. 'That.'

'Did you think I wouldn't find out?' Gillian asked angrily. 'And don't plead ignorance. You *must* have known that my mother is your father's sister.'

'All right!' Jimmy burst out. 'I kept my mouth shut because I don't want to embarrass my father. I love him dearly despite our circumstances. He's very good to my mother and to me. I'll do nothing to hurt him, ever.'

Gillian blinked, flicking back her hair, all of a sudden moved by the emotion in his voice.

'I've no intention of embarrassing Uncle Henry,' she reassured him quietly. 'But I'm family, Jimmy. You should've told me.'

He stared at her stonily. 'Does it make a difference to you that we're cousins? Or maybe it's the fact that I'm illegitimate?' His mouth tightened. 'Perhaps that offends your sensibilities?'

'You know that isn't true,' Gillian said with feeling. 'What angered me was that you deceived me.'

'Can't you understand? It's not my secret to reveal,' Jimmy said. 'Although...' He hesitated. 'I suppose it will come out soon. My father has left his wife. He's now living with Mam and me at Fleet Street.'

'Oh!' Gillian was astonished.

Jimmy sighed deeply. 'I suppose that'll be common knowledge in no time. We'll all have to face the music, even my granddad.'

Gillian did not know what to say. She thought of her mother, wondering what Vera would make of the scandal that was bound to erupt. Vera would go on about it endlessly for weeks.

'I'll stand by you, Jimmy,' Gillian said gently, touching his arm.

'Thanks, Gill. That's good of you. But perhaps your parents won't let you see me any longer. After all, when it's generally known, my illegitimacy will taint everything, family as well as friends.'

'It's so unfair!' Gillian said. 'It's not your fault.'

Jimmy smiled faintly. 'Despite everything I wouldn't change my parents no more than you would change yours,' he said. 'My father and mother love each other very much. I'm lucky.'

Gillian was touched by his devotion to his parents. She could understand that. She felt the same about her own family.

177

'I'm sorry, Jimmy, for being so silly,' Gillian said. 'It's just that I'm so fond of you. I was hurt. I had no right to accuse you. Will you forgive me?'

He took her hand and squeezed it. 'There's nothing to forgive, Gill. You'd better go and catch the tram home. Supper is at six sharp, remember.'

'Oh my goodness!' Gillian exclaimed. 'I'll be late yet again!'

'Off you go,' Jimmy said, more cheerful now. 'I'll see you tomorrow.'

It was just after seven o'clock when Norman Meeker let himself back in through the yard gates and walked across the silent cobbled fore-court. On reaching the door to the office he stopped abruptly, staring in dismay. The door had been forced and was now standing ajar.

Norman hurried inside, fearing the worst. He was astonished to see Andy Prosser at the desk and in his hand was the bank's fawn cloth bag containing the monies for the wages.

'What the hell are you doing with that?'

'Aahh!' Taken by surprise Andy jumped back, dropping the bag on to the desk. 'Meeker!'

'I asked you, what do you think you're doing with that money bag?' Norman demanded. 'You've no right to be here after hours.'

'Shut up, you bloody old goat,' Andy yelled. 'I can do anything I like. My father owns this place.'

'You forced the door.' Norman's eyes narrow-ed. 'You're up to no good.' He jerked his head towards the door. 'You'd better get out now before I call a constable.'

Swiftly, Andy came from behind the desk. 'You're not calling anybody,' he snarled menacingly. 'I'll see to that.'

Norman took a hasty step back. He did not like the look in Andy's eyes.

'I'm going to call your father,' Norman warned him. 'You want your backside kicked hard, you do, you thieving little perisher.'

'You won't tell anybody about this,' Andy said savagely. 'Because I'm going to fix you for good.'

He reached for something lying on the desk and picked it up, brandishing it threateningly. Norman stared apprehensively. It was a hammer and he wondered vaguely what it was doing there.

'What are you going to do?' Norman asked, the hairs on the back of his neck rising in fright.

'Bash your brains in,' Andy threatened nastily. 'You've been asking for this for a long time.'

Andy lunged at him, the hammer raised above his head.

'Stop!' Norman shouted, lifting his arms to protect himself. 'Are you out of your mind?'

His features twisting in hatred, Andy swung the hammer, bringing it down with force. Norman tried to dodge out of the way, but he was not quick enough. He felt a terrible pain on the left side of his head for a brief moment and then he knew no more.

Gloria lay on her back in the double bed, staring

up at the reflections of the street lights from the main road on the ceiling above her. She was sleeping very poorly these days since Henry had stayed away.

He was sulking after their sharp words. He would be back eventually. After all, this was his home. But she wondered where he was staying and with whom. If only he would come home so that they could talk. She could cajole him into a better temper, she told herself confidently.

Even though she was wide awake, the ringing of the front door bell startled her and when she glanced at the clock she noticed it was just after ten thirty. Who could it be at this hour?

She smiled knowingly. That was Henry at last. He must have forgotten his latchkey. She got out of bed and went out on to the landing, looking down into the hall with anticipation. Their live-in maid, Phoebe, wearing a dressing gown, her hair in curling-rags, was just shuffling across the hall below, going to answer the door.

Gloria waited patiently. It would be galling for Henry to be let in at this hour, but it served him right, she thought. His absence from their bed had given her sleepless nights.

The door opened but it was not Henry's voice she heard but that of a stranger.

'Mr Prosser is not here,' Gloria heard Phoebe say. 'Hasn't been home for days. No, I don't know where he is, neither does the missus.'

Gloria was furious at the maid's presumption to speak for her mistress.

'Phoebe!' Gloria screeched over the banister. 'That will be all! I'm coming down. Ask whoever it is to wait.'

'It's the police,' Phoebe called back irreverently. 'Looking for his nibs.'

Gloria dashed back into the bedroom and snatched up a wrap. She hurried downstairs to find a uniformed constable standing in the hall.

She threw back her shoulders and struck an arrogant pose.

'Yes, what is it, my man?'

'I wanted to speak with Mr Prosser, ma'am,' the constable said, removing his helmet.

'What about?'

'Is he here, ma'am?'

Gloria flicked her tongue over her lips. 'No, not at present. Why do you want to see him?'

'Do you know where I can find him, ma'am?'

Gloria drew in her chin. 'Now look here, Constable,' she said arrogantly, 'I'm Mrs Prosser and I demand to know why you want to see my husband.'

'It's an official matter, ma'am. I can't say more until I've spoken to your husband. Do you know his whereabouts?'

Gloria hesitated, reluctant to admit to a stranger that she had no idea where her husband was. 'No,' she said at last. 'He hasn't been home for days.'

The constable frowned. 'Do you mean Mr Prosser is missing?' he asked sharply. 'Have you reported it?'

'Of course not! He's not missing,' Gloria said. 'He's been at his place of business every day. Andy has seen him there.' She lifted her chin haughtily. 'My son Andy has a very important position in my husband's business, you know.'

There was an expression of irritation on the constable's face, which Gloria found very impertinent. She had a good mind to report him to his superiors.

'You'd better speak with his partner, Mr Ronald Knox,' she said stiffly. 'Mr Prosser may be staying with him.'

'He's not with Ronnie.'

Gloria whirled to look at Andy, still dressed, standing nonchalantly on the staircase.

'Andy, go back to bed,' she said firmly. 'Leave this to me.'

Andy ignored her and looked disdainfully at the constable.

'You'll find my father in Fleet Street,' he said. 'At the house he bought for his fancy piece, Florrie Tomkin.'

'Andy!' Gloria was aghast. 'What are you saying? Why are you telling such terrible lies?'

'Mother, you've had your head buried in the sand for years,' Andy said disparagingly. 'You're too busy with your whist drives and coffee mornings to know what Father is doing. Him and that dirty old whore have been at it for years.'

'Andy!' Gloria covered her mouth with her hand, appalled at what he was saying. It could not be true.

'Where in Fleet Street, sir?' the constable asked.

Andy told him the number. 'Why do you want to see him?'

The constable hesitated for a moment before

182

answering.

'There's been a robbery at the builders' yard,' he said at last. 'The manager, Mr Meeker, was savagely attacked. When he did not come home his wife came looking for him.'

'Oh my God!' Gloria said. 'How awful. Who has done this terrible thing?'

'I can tell you who's responsible,' Andy said, swaggering down the rest of the stairs. 'Jimmy Tomkin, Florrie's bastard son. I heard him planning it.' He nodded. 'He's the one that murdered old Meeker.'

The constable regarded him silently for a moment.

'I never said Mr Meeker was dead,' he said, his tone sharp. 'He's very badly hurt and in a coma. There's a fifty-fifty chance he'll recover. If he does, he can tell us who did it to him.' He glanced at them both. 'Well, I must be off. Goodnight.'

In a daze Gloria followed him to the door and closed it after him. She could not believe what was happening and she certainly could not believe the things Andy had said. She turned and stared at him as he stood like a statue in the hall.

'Andy, it can't be true what you told the constable about your father,' she said in a small voice. 'He wouldn't take up with another woman, not while he has me. Why do you tell such awful lies to upset me?'

Andy seemed to shake himself out of a reverie. His face, now very pale, contorted as he looked at her. 'You stupid woman! This is your fault.'

'My fault?' Taken aback Gloria placed her

hand over her heart. 'I don't know what you mean.'

'You turned my father against me with your carping hoity-toity ways,' he bellowed. 'I would not have done it, but you made me, you brainless old cow!'

'Don't you speak to me like that, Andy!' Gloria hooted furiously. 'I'm your mother. Have you no feelings for me?'

His gaze darted around. 'I'll have to get out. I can't stay here now.'

'What?'

'You've driven Father away,' Andy said nastily. 'And now I'm going, too. You've only got yourself to blame.'

'Andy, what are you talking about? Why do you have to leave? I don't understand.'

'The last train to Paddington leaves at about eleven thirty,' he said, as though to himself. 'I can catch that if I hurry.'

He turned and raced back up the stairs.

'Andy!' Gloria screeched after him. 'Andy, what's happening?'

She hurried up the staircase after him. Everything seemed to be falling apart and she had no idea why. Henry's absence from the house had irritated her, but she hadn't been disturbed by it. Now she was frightened. Henry hadn't left her. He wouldn't dare!

She reached Andy's bedroom and went in. He had a small case on the bed and was throwing clothing into it haphazardly.

'What are you doing? This is madness, Andy. Why must you leave home? Anyway, you don't have any money.'

'Huh! I have plenty now,' he said.

He slammed the case shut and, picking it up, pushed his way past her in the doorway.

'Andy, for heaven's sake tell me what's going on,' Gloria cried out as she followed him downstairs. 'I'm your mother. I have a right to know.'

He did not answer but took a raincoat from the hallstand and, draping it over his arm, walked quickly to the front door.

'Andy!'

He turned to look at her. 'I'm going to London, but don't tell them where I am. Say I've gone to Cardiff if they ask.'

'They?'

'Goodbye, Mother.'

Sitting at the breakfast table with the rest of the household, Gillian watched her father keenly across the table. Did he know about Uncle Henry leaving home, she wondered.

'Gillian, start collecting the dirty crockery,' Vera said smartly. 'I don't know why you're dawdling this morning.'

Leaving her seat, Gillian hurried to obey. Sam and her father were already on their feet, but Tom was still seated, wiping his plate around with a piece of bread.

'Leave the pattern on the plate,' she said to him, giving him a playful tap on his head. 'We'll want to use that again.'

'I'll give you a hand, Gill,' offered Mr Oglander. He collected the plates from Mr Gilmore and Miss Philpot and followed her out to the kitchen.

'Is anything wrong, Gill? You look worried.'

Gillian glanced up from stacking the crockery on the table beside the sink. Mr Oglander had a kindly face and she liked him, but the startling news about her uncle Henry was family business and probably a secret as well.

'Everything's fine, Mr Oglander, thank you.'

'If ever you need advice you can always talk to me, you know,' he said.

Gillian smiled. 'Thank you, Mr Oglander. I'll remember that.' She swilled her hands under the tap and then wiped them. 'I must hurry now or I'll be late for the office.'

'Plenty of time yet,' Mr Oglander said. 'It's only quarter past eight.'

Gillian felt her cheeks flush. She wanted to be early to see Jimmy before he went off on a job.

'I like to be early,' she said awkwardly.

Vera came bustling into the kitchen. 'Come along you two, out of my way. That crockery won't wash itself.'

In the drawing room her father was scanning the newspaper, with Sam and Tom looking over his shoulder. They did not seem in a hurry to get to work.

At that moment the front door bell rang.

'I'll get it,' Gillian called out and went to answer the door.

Two men stood outside. The one with the bushy moustache wore a brown three-piece suit and a bowler hat and the other was a uniformed constable.

'Does Thomas Finch live here?' the man in the

186

bowler hat asked in an officious tone.

'Yes,' Gillian nodded, wondering why they were asking for Tom.

'I want to speak with him immediately. My name is Inspector Fenwick and this is Constable Williams. I suggest we come inside, miss.'

Gillian stood back to let them into the hall.

'My brother is in the drawing room,' Gillian said. 'I'll call him out.'

'No need,' Inspector Fenwick said, overbearingly. 'Show us in.'

'But—'

'This is an important police matter, miss,' Inspector Fenwick said, his tone heavy. 'We take obstruction very seriously.'

Gillian pointed to the drawing-room door. 'In there,' she said meekly.

The inspector opened the door and walked in. Gillian turned on her heel and dashed along to the kitchen to fetch her mother.

'Mam!' Gillian cried out in panic. 'Come to the drawing room quickly. The police have called and they want to talk to Tom.'

'The police? Heavens above! What for?' Vera hastily wiped her wet hands.

'I don't know, but they looked awfully grim.'

When she returned to the hall with her mother Gillian was in time to see their three boarders being ushered out of the room by the constable.

Miss Philpot's face was red with anger. 'Well! Really!' she said. 'This country is turning into a police state.'

Vera marched into the sitting room, followed closely by Gillian. She saw her father and

187

brothers were on their feet, their expressions shocked.

'What's going on?' her mother demanded to know loudly. 'What are the police doing in my house?'

'A serious crime has been committed,' Inspector Fenwick said to her. 'We believe Mr Thomas Finch can help us with our inquiries.'

'Crime? What crime?' Vera burst out. 'My son hasn't committed any crime, officer.'

'There was a robbery at the offices of Prosser and Knox last night; a large amount of money was taken. And Mr Meeker, the manager, was attacked with a hammer. He's in hospital in a serious condition.'

'Good God!' Arthur exclaimed. 'But what has this to do with my son?'

'His hammer was used to strike the blows,' Inspector Fenwick replied. 'He has a lot of explaining to do.'

'But, Dad,' Tom said. 'I loaned my hammer to...' He stopped, staring at the police officers. 'I ... er ... I can't remember who I loaned it to.'

'Tom, don't be a fool!' Sam insisted. 'Tell them who had the hammer.'

'I can't remember, I tell you,' Tom said stubbornly, his gaze going to Gillian.

She had the feeling he was trying to tell her something, but she could not think what it might be.

'You'll have to do better than that,' Inspector Fenwick said grimly. 'You're in serious trouble, my lad. You could be sent down for a long time for this.'

'But I didn't do anything!' Tom denied.

'How do you know it was his hammer anyway?' Vera asked belligerently. 'We've only got your word for this.'

'His name has been burned into the handle,' the constable said. 'It's his hammer all right.'

'But you heard what he said,' Vera argued. 'He loaned his hammer to another lad. Talk to him. Leave my son alone.'

'He'll have to come along with us,' Inspector Fenwick said officiously. 'We're taking him in for further questioning.'

'This is outrageous!' Vera flared. 'How dare you accuse my son?'

'Vera, Vera,' Arthur said, going to her and taking hold of her arm. 'Tom had nothing to do with this attack. The truth will come out. We can't obstruct the police. It'll make things worse.'

'Wise words, Mr Finch,' the inspector said. 'If your son is innocent, we'll get to the bottom of it, be assured.'

The constable took Tom by the arm. 'Come along, my lad. Let's not have any trouble.'

Submissively Tom allowed himself to be led to the door.

'I must go with him,' Vera said.

'No,' Arthur said firmly. 'I'll go. You stay here, Vera. I don't want you getting hysterical and landing yourself in trouble.'

'Oh! This is awful,' Vera said tearfully. 'To think we've come to this.'

'Come on, Mam,' Gillian said kindly, taking her arm and helping her into a chair nearby. 'I'll make you a cup of tea.'

She was shocked by what had happened, but she must keep her head, for it looked as though her mother, always dominant as a rule, was going to pieces.

Her father glanced around the door at them from the hall. He had his cap on, ready to leave. 'We won't be long, Vera, love. Don't worry. We'll straighten this out.'

It was mid-afternoon before her father returned. Gillian was relieved to see Tom was with him.

Vera rushed at her son, enveloping him in a hug. 'Oh, my boy! You're back.'

'They've let him go for the moment,' her father said gravely. 'Pending further investigation.'

Vera put her hand to her mouth. 'They can't still think he's guilty,' she said in a quivering voice.

'Mam, I can prove I was nowhere near the yard last evening,' Tom said energetically. 'I was with the boys, watching a game of cricket at St Helens. The boys will vouch for me.'

'If the police believe them,' Arthur said. 'They might think they were all in it together.'

'Oh, Arthur! You must do something!' Vera said plaintively.

Her father sat down heavily into a nearby armchair. Gillian thought he looked completely exhausted.

'The inspector said he would question Tom's pals,' Arthur said. 'We'll have to wait and see.'

Vera also sat down. 'I'll not sleep a wink

tonight,' she said tearfully. Suddenly her eyes flashed. 'I blame Henry for this!'

'Vera! Don't be daft,' Arthur said irritably. 'Your brother is as appalled as we are at what has happened to Mr Meeker and that Tom has been implicated.'

'It's my brother's fault somehow,' Vera mumbled to herself.

'I'll make some tea,' Gillian said and went to the kitchen.

In a moment or two Tom followed her out. He stood by as she put the big iron kettle on the gas ring.

'Gill, listen. I loaned my hammer to Jimmy Tomkin because he'd lost his own and he didn't want to admit to Dad that he'd been careless.'

Gillian swung around to stare at him. 'You're not saying Jimmy had anything to do with this robbery, are you?'

'Of course not,' Tom said, shaking his head. 'But there's something else I haven't told you. I haven't told anyone and perhaps I should've.'

'What is it?'

Tom flicked his tongue over his lips nervously. 'A week or two back Andy Prosser was talking wild about robbing the yard office – taking the wages money.'

'What?'

'He wanted me to help him, but I told him to bugger off. He must have pinched my hammer and planted it to get back at me.'

Gillian bit her lip thoughtfully. 'That doesn't make sense, Tom. The hammer was in Jimmy's tool bag, remember? Andy took it from there.'

'Why implicate Jimmy?' Tom scratched his head. 'I don't get it.'

'I think I do.' Gillian nodded sagely. 'Andy must have found out about Jimmy, and he's done this to spite him and his father.'

'What are you on about?'

Gillian put her hand on her brother's arm. 'Look, Tom, I'm going to break a confidence now so you mustn't tell anyone. Andy could be out for revenge. You see, Jimmy is Uncle Henry's illegitimate son.'

Tom stared at her disbelievingly. 'Don't be daft!'

'It's true. Dad told me, and Jimmy confirmed it,' Gillian said. 'Don't you see? Andy did the robbery, attacked Mr Meeker, and tried to blame it on Jimmy. When he pinched the hammer he didn't notice your name was on it.'

'Good God!' Tom stared at her. 'What are we going to do?'

'You'll have to tell Dad everything; about Jimmy having your hammer and about Andy's plans for the robbery.'

'Gill, are we certain about all this?'

'What other explanation can there be, Tom?'

The kettle was boiling now and she made the tea, arranging some cups on a tray. She started to carry the tray out to the drawing room, but paused.

'Tom, Mam mustn't know anything about Uncle Henry and his relationship to Jimmy. Dad warned me.'

'All right, Gill,' he said. 'I'll get him on his own.' He looked furious for a moment. 'Damn it! I could wring Andy's neck for this.'

'There's been enough violence already,' she said. 'It's Uncle Henry I'm sorry for. If Andy is arrested, the whole thing is bound to come out.'

As she carried the tray into the sitting room Gillian was apprehensive. When the truth did break they would all be touched by the scandal.

Thirteen

As soon as the police indicated later that day that business could resume at the yard Henry was back at his desk. He was still shaken by a constable turning up at Fleet Street so unexpectedly.

The cat was out of the bag. If the police knew his whereabouts then Gloria must know, too. He was not looking forward to the inevitable screaming match with her.

'It's a lot of money to lose,' Ronnie Knox was saying, cutting into his miserable contemplation. 'It'll hit us hard, Henry.' His young partner was lounging on the corner of the desk, dressed to the nines as usual. 'Do you think our insurance will cover it?'

Henry sighed. 'I've no idea, Ronnie,' he said tiredly. 'I'll have to look into it.'

'Who'd have thought young Tom Finch would do a dirty trick like this on us,' Ronnie said bitterly.

'We don't know that he did.'

'The police think so,' Ronnie said. 'I was speaking to Inspector Fenwick earlier on. He reckons they've got him bang to rights.'

At that moment someone tapped on the office door and Arthur Finch came in. 'Can I have a word, Henry?' He glanced at Ronnie. 'In private.'

Ronnie got off the desk. 'Now look, Arthur,' he said curtly. 'I'm sorry for you, but your boy has no one but himself to blame.'

Arthur's face flushed up and he looked furious. 'Tom's innocent, and I can prove it,' he asserted. He glanced at his brother-in-law. 'Henry, we have to talk.'

'Damn it, Arthur!' Ronnie snapped. 'This concerns me as much as Henry. It was my money, too, that Tom stole.'

'Henry, I don't think you'll want Ronnie to hear what I have to say,' Arthur said adamantly. 'It concerns the family only.'

'Leave us, Ronnie, please,' Henry said.

Ronnie uttered an oath but marched out, closing the door behind him.

'Arthur, there's nothing I can do for Tom, you must know that,' Henry said as soon as they were alone. 'It's in the hands of the authorities now.'

'Listen, will you?' Arthur exclaimed loudly. 'Our Tom loaned his hammer to Jimmy because Jimmy had lost his.'

Henry leapt to his feet, looking angry. 'Are you saying that Jimmy—?'

'No,' Arthur interrupted quickly. 'I've now reason to believe it was Andy who did the robbery, attacked Norman Meeker and tried to implicate Jimmy, not Tom.'

'What?' Henry was appalled at the suggestion. 'What gives you the right to accuse *my* son?'

'Sit down,' Arthur said wearily. 'Listen to what I have to tell you.'

Henry sat down heavily and listened as Arthur told him how Andy had tried to persuade Tom to help him rob the office. When Arthur explained about the hammer, Henry knew without doubt that what his brother-in-law said was true. Andy was guilty.

'He found out about me and Florrie,' Henry admitted. 'My own son tried to blackmail me.'

'Henry, you've got to do the decent thing and tell the police what I've just told you,' Arthur said earnestly. 'Tom is innocent.'

Henry was silent. Arthur was right. He must give Andy up to the police. The boy must face up to the consequences. It was serious enough as it stood, but if Norman Meeker did not survive, it would be murder.

Henry felt a chill go through him at the thought. Andy had been a bitter disappointment as a son, so much so that he had largely cut him out of his will. Yet, he was his own flesh and blood. It was a hard and cruel choice that was before him.

'Henry, it's the only thing to do,' Arthur continued in a low voice.

Henry lifted his head. 'Yes, I know,' he said sadly. 'I'll speak to Andy – have it out with him. And then I'll make him give himself up.'

Arthur nodded. 'I'm sorry, Henry,' he said and

left the office.

Henry sat for a few minutes thinking, and then knew that he must go to the house he had once shared with Gloria. He had to face her now – and face Andy, too.

Putting the key in the lock of his previous home Henry felt it was a betrayal of Florrie in some way. He had promised her never to see Gloria again, and he did not want to, but circumstances had changed and he had no choice.

He was nervous as he went into the hall and was startled when Dorothy ran down the staircase.

'Dad! You've come home.' She rushed up to him and threw her arms around his neck. 'Oh, I'm so glad to see you, Dad. I knew Andy was lying all along. You haven't left us.'

Henry embraced his daughter warmly for a moment, feeling guilty. A lump came to his throat. She was the only good thing that had come out of his marriage to Gloria. He was committed to Florrie now, but his heart missed Dorothy sorely.

'Where's Andy?' he asked at last.

'He's not here, Dad. He's—'

'Where's your mother?' Henry interrupted her.

'In the drawing room. She's very upset, of course.'

'I have to talk to her, Dot, privately,' he said, easing her away. 'I'll see you later.'

'But, Dad, there's something I have to tell you.'

'Later, Dot, please.'

He left her in the hall and went into the drawing room. Gloria was sitting on the sofa, her shoulders hunched and a handkerchief to her face. She looked up as he came in and he saw that her face was red and swollen from crying. He was taken aback for a moment to see such obvious emotion. Gloria had always appeared so cold and distant; so totally self-absorbed.

'Henry!' She rose to her feet and stood, trembling visibly.

'I'm sorry you're so upset, Gloria,' he said hesitantly.

He had expected a voluble response to his leaving but not genuine tears.

'Of course I'm upset. My son has left home,' Gloria said, sounding more like her usual self. 'You must go after him, Henry. Otherwise I don't know what will become of him.'

Henry blinked. 'Andy has left home?'

Gloria wiped at her nose. 'Didn't you know?' she said. 'I thought that was why you'd come back.'

'When did he go?'

'Last night, after the police called here.'

Henry's shoulders sagged as the last vestige of hope that he was wrong about Andy shrivelled. His son had bolted. That in itself was evidence of his guilt.

'The young fool!' he said despairingly.

'What attitude is that for a father to take?' Gloria burst out. 'He must be brought back before something happens.'

'Oh, he will be brought back, all right,' Henry said grimly. 'The police will see to it.'

'The police? What are you talking about?'

'Why do you think Andy bolted?' he asked impatiently. 'It was our son who robbed the yard office. He attacked Norman Meeker. He's facing serious charges and that's why he left in such a hurry.'

'I don't believe it!' Gloria straightened up. 'And I can't believe you'd accuse your own son. You're doing this to spite me, Henry.'

'Don't be absurd, woman!' Henry struggled not to lose his temper. 'I came here today to persuade him to give himself up. The police might have gone easier on him. Now he's made things worse.'

'Give himself up! This is outrageous. How could you even think such a thing?'

'Gloria, face up to it,' Henry said. 'Andy is no good.' He felt a stab of grief in his heart to admit it aloud, but it had to be faced. 'He's a thief and he's violent. He attacked a defenceless older man. Norman Meeker is in a coma. They don't know if he'll survive. Andy did that to him.'

'No!'

'It's true. He's a thief and a liar.'

He watched as Gloria's face turned hard and cold.

'Was Andy lying when he told me you'd taken up with a dirty little whore from Fleet Street?' she asked in a stony voice.

He felt shock as though she had struck him in the face.

'If you were a man I'd knock you down for saying that,' he said through gritted teeth. 'I love Florrie and she loves me. She's been faithful to me for years.'

Gloria's mouth dropped open. 'It's been going on for years?' She turned away. 'Oh, the shame of it. Do any of our friends know?'

'Is that all you care about?' Henry asked harshly. 'If it is, you're in for a rough time, Gloria. It's very likely that our son will go to prison for what he's done.'

She turned to face him again, her face stricken. 'No! You must stop that happening, Henry.'

'Where did he go, Gloria?'

She hesitated for a split second before answering. 'Cardiff,' she said.

'Huh! You're lying. I can always tell,' Henry's voice grated. 'You can't shield him any longer.' Henry was silent for a moment. 'I'll have to inform the police straight away,' he said soberly, though he hated the thought of what that would mean to them all.

'How long are you going to stay with this fancy woman of yours?' Gloria asked bitterly. 'Your place is here with your family at such a time.'

'I've left you, Gloria,' Henry said. 'Andy being in trouble makes no difference to that.'

'But you can't leave me alone to face it all.'

'You've got Dorothy.'

'Oh, that silly little fool is useless!'

'What?'

Gloria hesitated, then said, 'I warned her against him, but she wouldn't listen to me. She let that Ronnie Knox take advantage of her in the worst way. He ought to be horsewhipped.'

Henry stared at her, almost speechless with

horror.

'What are you telling me?' he managed to croak at last.

Gloria grimaced. 'I can't put it plainer without being vulgar,' she said. 'But Ronnie tricked her into going to bed with him.'

'Oh my God!' Henry sank down on to the nearest chair.

'Of course, he gave her the cold shoulder afterwards,' Gloria said bitterly. 'He's no gentleman.'

'How can you stand there calmly telling me this about our daughter?' he asked. 'Did you have a hand in it, Gloria?'

'Me?' Defensively she put a hand to her breast. 'It isn't my fault, Henry. The girl has no sense. I can't get it through to her that a woman has to be clever with men.'

'It *is* your doing!' Henry thundered, rising shakily to his feet. 'You and your loose moral values. You've ruined our daughter.'

He raised his fist – the urge to strike her was strong – but lowered it again. Violence achieved nothing and it was against his nature. Gloria was no longer part of his life, but Dorothy was. He would not leave her in this house a minute longer. He must get her away to a safe place.

'That's not fair, Henry,' Gloria said in a grumbling tone. 'Ronnie Knox is well off. He's your partner so I thought he'd be an ideal husband for Dorothy. I was just thinking of her future.'

'You conniving woman!' Henry yelled angrily. 'Even now you don't see the damage you've done.' He stared at her for a moment. 'I'm taking

Dorothy away with me now,' he continued. 'Everything is finished. I'm suing for divorce.'

'No! Henry, you can't! Think of the scandal. I'd never live it down.'

'Then you can divorce me,' he said rashly. 'Either way, I want no more of you, Gloria.'

Gloria started to blubber. Unmoved by it, Henry turned on his heel, strode out into the hall and ran up the staircase.

'Dorothy!' he called loudly. 'Pack a bag. You are leaving this house.'

She came out on to the landing from her bedroom. 'Dad, what's the matter?'

'Your mother has told me about Ronnie Knox.'

'Oh!' Dorothy took a step back, covering her mouth with her hand, staring at him and flushed to the roots of her hair.

'You're not staying here with your mother a minute longer,' Henry said grimly. 'Pack a few things.'

'We can't leave her alone,' Dorothy said hesitantly. 'You do know that Andy has gone away?'

'Your mother and I are finished,' Henry said. 'Andy has buggered up his own life. Now he'll have to face the consequences.'

'What do you mean?'

'Never mind. Get packed. You're coming with me.'

Henry waited impatiently for his daughter in the hall. Gloria did not come out of the drawing room and he was relieved that she was not making a further scene.

Dorothy came down at last, carrying her case.

Henry took it from her hand.

'Come on,' he said. 'Let's go.'

Dorothy held back. 'I have to say goodbye to Mother. I can't just walk out.'

'Then be quick,' he said. 'And don't let her persuade you to stay.'

Henry waited impatiently. Dorothy had been in the drawing room too long, he thought. He went in and called her.

'Dorothy, it's time to go.'

She came towards him, looking distressed. 'Dad, I can't go with you. Mother's so upset. It isn't right to leave her.'

Henry kept his gaze averted from Gloria's face. He knew from experience she was capable of great deceit and was worried that she was working her wiles on her own daughter.

'She'll get over it,' he said curtly. 'You don't know her like I do.'

'Of course I know her!' Dorothy insisted. 'She's my mother!'

'What kind of a mother was she when she persuaded you to fling yourself at Ronnie Knox?'

There was a muffled cry of protest from Gloria, her face buried in a handkerchief. Henry took no notice of her.

Dorothy's face turned pale and she looked at him with a stricken expression. 'Don't! I'm ashamed enough as it is.'

'It's your mother's shame as much as yours, even more so.'

'Perhaps, but are you going to throw it in my face continually, Dad?' she said in a small voice.

He took quick strides to her. 'No, Dot, I won't.

202

But if you stay here, goodness knows what other folly your mother will talk you into.'

'Go with him!' Gloria exclaimed. 'You're as much use to me as a wet blanket anyway. I need Andy.'

'Mother!' Dorothy looked crestfallen.

'Go on, then! I don't need you.' Gloria stood up, looking defiant. 'I don't need any of you. And that goes for your aunt Cissie, too,' she said vehemently. 'You can get that interfering old bag out of my house as soon as you like.'

'This is still my house,' Henry thundered. 'Aunt Cissie stays here until I say otherwise. Is that clear, Gloria?'

She turned her back on them, her shoulders rigid with anger.

'Come on, Dot.' Henry grasped his daughter's arm and led her from the room. 'Let's get out of here.'

Henry's mind was racing as he drove away from the house. It was all very well separating Dorothy from her mother, but where could she go?

He knew Florrie, kind-hearted as she was, would take his daughter in, but it wasn't right. Living over the brush as he was with Florrie it was hardly the right circumstances for a young girl to be in.

He was desperate and there was only one thing he could do. He must ask his sister for help. He had to admit he quailed at facing Vera. They had not spoken together since the reading of their mother's will, and he knew from what Arthur had told him that Vera was incensed to the point of unreason over it.

While he could readily understand Vera's anger at the terms of the will, he did not consider it was his fault that Rose had chosen to ignore her daughter except for a small bequest.

But then, their mother had always been careless of them, even as children, so it had hardly surprised him.

'I'm going to ask your aunt Vera to let you stay with her,' he said. 'She has plenty of room.'

'What?' Dorothy sounded astonished. 'But she hates us.'

'Her quarrel is with me,' Henry said. 'She doesn't hate you. Besides, I'm going to make it worth her while.'

He parked the car in Marlborough Road outside the house that Vera had bought with her small inheritance. It was a tall, double-fronted house on three floors and there was also a basement flat. Henry considered it a very good investment.

With Dorothy at his side Henry knocked at the door. It was opened by his brother-in-law. Arthur Finch's features went through a series of expressions at the sight of him, starting with astonishment through to panic.

'My Gawd, Henry!'

'Can we come in, Arthur?'

Arthur seemed speechless but stood aside for them to enter the hall.

'I want to speak to Vera,' Henry said. 'It's important, Arthur, or I wouldn't be here.'

'It must be,' Arthur said, shaking his head. 'You're taking your life in your hands.'

'Dad, I don't want to stay here,' Dorothy said in a frightened voice.

'Your Uncle Arthur is exaggerating,' Henry said calmly.

'Come into the back room,' Arthur suggested. 'Our boarders are in the drawing room, waiting for supper.'

Arthur showed them into a small room that overlooked the back yard. 'I'll go and break the news to Vera,' he said. 'You'd better sit down.'

It was a while before anyone came near them, but Henry could hear raised voices from the back of the house. Eventually the door opened and Arthur came in with someone following behind him, obviously very reluctantly.

Henry got quickly to his feet as his sister came into the room. Tall and erect, Vera stared at him silently for a moment, pushing back her dark hair in the way he had seen his mother do many times. It struck him with a jolt how like Rose she was in looks.

'What are you doing in my house?' Vera asked him, her voice shaking. 'You have no right to come here under the circumstances.'

Henry wetted his lips nervously. 'I've come to ask a favour, Vera.'

'What?' She looked taken aback. 'What?'

'I want you to take in Dorothy as a boarder,' Henry said quickly. 'I'll pay any rent you want.'

Vera looked startled. 'Your daughter, a boarder here? What on earth for?'

'I've left Gloria,' Henry said. 'Left her for good.'

Vera's mouth dropped open for a moment.

'Well!' she said at last and folded her arms across her chest. 'Well, I must say!' There was a hint of curiosity in her voice.

'Listen, Henry,' Arthur put in. 'What we talked about earlier. Is that why you've left your wife?'

'No,' Henry said. 'I'd moved out of the house days ago. I couldn't stand it another minute—' He stopped himself. 'My reasons don't matter,' he went on.

'Here! Just a minute!' Vera exclaimed. She turned flashing eyes to Arthur. 'What did you talk about earlier with my brother? I have a right to know.'

'Yes, you do,' Henry said. 'The sad truth is, Vera, it was Andy who robbed the office and attacked Norman. He's done a bunk. I haven't told the police yet.'

Vera glared at him, a gleam of triumph in her eyes. 'It's a just punishment on you, Henry, for the shabby way you treated me over Mam's will.'

'Vera!' Arthur sounded appalled. 'For shame! Your own brother.'

'He's no brother of mine. He's proved that.'

Henry looked at her and shook his head. 'You do me an injustice, Vera. And you've never given me a chance to prove you wrong.'

'I'm sorry for your troubles, Henry,' Arthur said quietly.

'What are *you* saying sorry for?' Vera snapped at him. 'It's nothing to do with us. Let him clear up his own mess.'

'Vera, I'm not making excuses for Andy,' Henry said. 'He'll have to pay for what he's

206

done. It's Dorothy I'm concerned about.'

'I don't see the problem,' Vera said sharply. 'You've left Gloria, and by the way I'm not surprised, but why can't Dorothy stay with her mother? It's only natural.'

'Gloria is a bad influence,' Henry rushed to say. 'She's already—'

'Dad!' Dorothy grabbed at his arm. 'Please!'

'I won't have Gloria anywhere near Dorothy,' Henry continued adamantly.

'Oh, you've finally seen her for what she is, then?' Vera said.

'How dare you?' Dorothy showed her anger. 'Who are you to talk about my mother like that?' She turned to her father. 'Come on, Dad. We're not staying here to be insulted by her.'

Vera raised her brows. 'Neither of your children have any manners, I see.'

'Vera, listen,' Henry said pleadingly. 'Dorothy is quite blameless in all this. I'm appealing to you as family to help me.'

'Help you?' Vera snorted. 'You were quick to help yourself when you persuaded Mam to sign her will leaving everything to you. That was a dirty piece of work, I must say!'

'I had nothing to do with it, Vera,' Henry said earnestly. 'I had no idea what she had in mind.'

'Huh! So you say,' Vera sneered.

'You've got a short memory, Vera,' Henry said soberly. 'When did Mam ever take notice of us or put our wishes or needs before her own?'

Vera tilted her head and looked away silently. Henry knew he had struck a chord. Rose had always gone her own way with little thought for

207

her fatherless children.

'God knows what would have happened to us if it hadn't been for Aunt Cissie,' he continued. 'Aunt Cissie was more a mother to us than Rose ever was. I for one will always be grateful to her.'

Vera sniffed but remained silent.

'You know it's true,' Henry said. 'Our mother was a selfish, self-centred woman who did as she pleased.'

'You talk well,' Vera snapped, 'but it's four years since Mam died. You haven't made any effort to put things right between us.'

'Yes, that was wrong of me but I'm ready to make amends now,' Henry said eagerly. 'I've been thinking about it for some time. Look, as soon as Sam finishes his apprenticeship he can come into management. I'll even sign over a small portion of my shares to him. How about that?'

'Henry, that's very generous of you,' Arthur said. He was clearly delighted with the suggestion.

'Not good enough!' Vera snapped. 'My husband's worth to the business should've been recognized years ago. It's Arthur who should go into management.'

'Now look here, Vera,' Arthur said gruffly. 'I go along with most of the things you decide in the home, but I'll thank you not to arrange my working life for me. I'm happy as I am at Prosser and Knox.'

'But you deserve it, Arthur,' Vera said. She sounded a little surprised at his firm tone.

'We'll take Henry's offer for Sam,' Arthur said with finality. 'And another thing. Dorothy is very welcome to lodge with us. Isn't that right, Vera?'

There was a warning note in his voice and Vera, after glancing at her husband sideways, nodded her head.

'We'll find room for Dorothy,' she said. 'But I must ask rent, Henry. I can't afford free board and lodgings.'

Henry felt a wave of relief wash over him. 'I'll meet any terms, Vera, just as long as I know Dorothy is in safe hands.'

Vera sniffed. 'I see she's brought a case. She can share Gillian's room. We can squeeze another single bed in there, I think. You and Arthur can do that now.'

Henry stepped forward, intending to embrace his sister, but she stepped back quickly.

'Don't count your chickens yet, Henry,' Vera said. 'We've a long way to go before I'm satisfied of your sincerity.'

After what seemed a long wait in the back room while the spare bed was manhandled upstairs, Dorothy finally followed Gillian up to the bedroom they were to share.

It was very small, so different from her bedroom at home. Two single beds stood side by side with hardly any room between them to move.

'It'll be a bit of a squeeze, Dot,' Gillian said eagerly. 'But we'll manage. It'll be fun being together again and not having to worry about being found out.'

'It's fine,' Dorothy said apathetically.

While it was such a long time since she had seen her cousin and had missed their friendship, she could take no real pleasure in it at the moment, not with her whole life in turmoil.

Why was she here at all? Why had her father taken the harsh step of splitting up their family? Why must she remain at her aunt's house and be separated from her mother?

She was conscious that Gillian was looking at her with curiosity.

'You must be unhappy, Dot. I'd feel the same if my parents separated.'

'I miss my mother,' she said miserably.

'Of course you do, Dot,' Gillian said. 'But I'm glad you're here.'

Dorothy was annoyed at what she saw as Gillian's insensitivity and selfishness. 'Well, I'm not! I'd prefer to be in my own home with my mother than amongst strangers.'

Gillian looked uncomfortable. 'I didn't mean it like that, Dot. I know it's an upheaval for you and it must be beastly for your parents to be apart, but there's nothing you or I can do about it.'

'I know,' Dorothy agreed sadly and flopped on to the bed which Gillian had indicated was hers.

Gillian sat down beside her. 'It's just that I'm glad we've got a chance to be friends again.'

Dorothy relented. Gillian meant well and it wasn't her fault that things had turned out the way they had.

'Yes, I've missed confiding to you,' she

admitted. 'Why did we ever argue?'

'Wasn't it a silly disagreement over Ronnie Knox?'

At the mention of his name Dorothy felt a wave of nausea and shame engulf her and her fingers automatically clutched at the counterpane. She turned her face away from Gillian's gaze.

'I don't want to talk about Ronnie,' she mumbled.

'You were so keen on him,' Gillian said. 'You thought he was the bee's knees.'

'I hate him now!' Dorothy realized how fierce her tone was. But it was true. She did hate Ronnie for what he had made her do and the constant shame and humiliation that racked her thoughts.

'What?' There was surprise and curiosity in Gillian's voice.

Dorothy jumped up from the bed. 'I've got to unpack,' she said quickly, trying to change the subject.

'I'll help,' Gillian offered. 'There's only room for one wardrobe in here, but we can share it.' She gave a laugh. 'It'll be like having a sister.'

Fourteen

William Prosser's house, Swansea, 1898

'When will I see my mammy, Aunt Cissie?'

Cissie lifted the child up into her arms. 'She'll come home soon, I'm sure,' she said. 'And when she does I'll tell her what a good little girl you've been, Vera, love.'

Vera rubbed her knuckles into her eyes and Cissie knew the child was struggling not to cry. How could Rose stay away from her lovely children for so long? Cissie could not help feeling animosity towards her sister-in-law for her hard-heartedness. Rose was more interested in Charlie Knox than her own family.

She wondered if this was the reason William had gone off so suddenly. She was so worried about him. Two weeks and not a word. If only he would write and explain; set her mind at rest as to his safety.

'Where's my daddy?' Vera asked in a small voice. 'Is he coming home soon, too?'

Cissie bit her lip. It was the question she dreaded for she did not have an answer for it. 'I don't know, Vera, my chick.'

The child let out a sob. 'Henry said Daddy is dead.' Tears began to stream down her little face then. 'Is he dead, Aunt Cissie?'

'No!' Cissie hugged Vera to her fiercely. 'Henry's a naughty boy to tell you that! He'll feel my slipper walloping the seat of his pants.'

Vera laid her silky head on Cissie's shoulder. 'I want my daddy!'

'I know, my lovely.'

Cissie's heart ached for William Prosser as much as his daughter's did.

'Come on, Vera,' Cissie said coaxingly. 'Let's go in the kitchen and find some milk and biscuits, shall we?'

'Yes, Aunt Cissie.'

Cissie was carrying Vera across the hall when the front door opened and Rose Prosser came in.

'Mammy!' Vera struggled in Cissie's arms and she set the child on her feet. Vera immediately rushed at her mother, grasping her around the knees. 'Mammy, where've you been? I've missed you.'

'All right! All right! Let me come in,' Rose said, freeing herself.

'Mammy's back! She's back!' Vera danced a jig around her.

Cissie bent down to talk to the excited child. 'Go and tell Henry your mammy is here,' she suggested and the child ran off giggling and shouting her brother's name.

Cissie gave Rose a penetrating look, wondering how her sister-in-law intended to explain her absence ever since William had left.

'You don't look pleased to see me, Cissie,' Rose said as she took off her hat and coat. There was a sullen air about her.

'It's been two weeks,' Cissie said, trying not to sound accusing. 'The children have been asking for you every day.'

'Huh! I don't doubt you've been molly-coddling them.'

'I'm not their mother,' Cissie said sharply. 'How could you leave them, Rose?'

Rose flicked back her long dark hair indolently. 'Well, I'm back home now, Cissie, so stop carping.'

She turned and walked away towards the drawing room and Cissie followed. She was angered by Rose's brazen attitude. Did her sister-in-law think no one knew she'd been living in Charlie's house these last two weeks? Had she no shame? Everyone knew except Charlie's long-suffering wife.

'Yes, of course, you're back,' Cissie said when they were in the drawing room. 'After all, Freda Knox comes home from hospital today, doesn't she? Charlie wouldn't want her to know you've been taking her place over the past fortnight.'

Rose looked furious. 'You don't know what you're talking about, so mind your own business, Cissie.'

Cissie smiled knowingly. 'Charlie told you to make yourself scarce, didn't he?' She shook her head. 'He'll never leave Freda, not even for you, Rose. She's the mother of his son, and his world revolves around George.'

'Shut up! You dried-up old spinster!'

'Well, at least I'm not bitter,' Cissie said. 'And I wouldn't neglect my children for the sake of a man I can't have.'

214

'You'd better be careful what you say to me, Cissie,' Rose hissed in fury. 'Or I'll have you out of this house, bag and baggage.'

'This is still my brother's house,' Cissie warned. 'Before he went William asked me to take care of everything, including his children. I'm here to stay until my brother tells me different.'

'Well, stay out of my way and keep your nose out of my business!' Rose shouted and stalked from the room.

Rose's threat to evict her was upsetting. Cissie remained where she was, looking around the familiar drawing room. This was the house where she had been born, the only home she had ever known.

William's silence was even more disturbing in the face of that threat. If something did happen to him, Rose would inherit everything. Cissie had no doubt her sister-in-law would oust her as soon as she could. The annuity her father had left her was so small, it would mean cheap lodgings somewhere and she would have to find work. The only thing she knew how to do was keep house. She prayed William would return home soon.

Fifteen

Swansea, 1931

'Now then, Mrs Prosser,' Inspector Fenwick said heavily. 'I understand you were the last person to see Andrew Prosser before he ran off?'

'Andy didn't run off,' Gloria said. She turned an accusing gaze on Henry. 'He's just gone away for a few days, that's all. Is that a crime?'

'You won't do your son or yourself any good by being evasive with the law, Mrs Prosser,' the inspector said sternly. 'I want a full description of what he was wearing when last seen.'

'This is outrageous! You're behaving as though Andy was a criminal.'

'It's no good burying your head in the sand, Gloria,' Henry said wearily. 'He is a criminal after what he's done.'

It had cost him dearly to have to report his own son to the police. He had hardly slept the night before, his mind in turmoil over what he must do. He had talked it over with Florrie that morning and while she had been sympathetic and loving, she could offer him no excuse not to do what he knew was right.

'Norman Meeker is in hospital,' Henry said. 'His condition is still critical. Andy did that and

216

he has to answer for it.'

'How could you?' Gloria wailed. 'How could you give up your own flesh and blood to the police?'

Henry was still hurting and it made him angry. 'If he is my own flesh and blood! I had only your word for that before we married. Anyone could have been his father.'

'Oh!' Gloria turned away, her hands over her face. 'How could you humiliate me – and in front of strangers, too?'

Henry was immediately repentant. Marrying Gloria had cost him a great deal of unhappiness and he blamed her, but perhaps his own youthful immaturity and imprudence had been partly responsible for their disastrous marriage.

'I'm sorry, Gloria, I shouldn't have said that. It was uncalled for.'

She flung him a cutting glance. 'I'll never forgive you, Henry.'

'You must tell the police everything now,' he said. 'Andy must be brought back to face up to the consequences of his actions.'

'He's done nothing wrong!' Gloria cried. 'Nothing at all. You're hounding him and I can't think why.'

Henry's shoulders sagged and he turned to the inspector. 'I can't argue with her any more, Inspector. There's nothing useful I can tell you about my son. I'll leave Mrs Prosser in your hands. Perhaps you can make her see reason.'

'Henry!' Gloria shrieked. 'Don't leave me here alone to face them. Don't go! How could you?'

The pitch of her voice seared his nerves like

217

the squeal of chalk on slate, and he could not move quickly enough to get out of the house and away from her.

He did not have enough heart to return to business. He needed Florrie and her loving kindness to soothe his wretchedness. He had always needed Florrie and always would.

'Gillian, why isn't Dorothy eating her breakfast? Isn't my food good enough for her?'

Startled at the antagonism in her aunt's voice, Dorothy looked up from her plate, and then flushed deeply as each face around the breakfast table was turned to stare at her. She hardly knew her cousins Sam and Tom and her aunt's lodgers were strangers. She felt a complete outsider.

'Mam! It is Dot's first morning,' Gillian spoke up bravely. 'She's not used to a crowd for breakfast.'

'Huh! Well, she'd better get used to it,' Vera said.

Her aunt's sharp tone annoyed Dorothy and gave her a smidgen of courage.

'I'm sitting right here, Aunt Vera,' Dorothy said, lifting her chin. 'Please don't talk over my head. I'm quite capable of answering any questions.'

'Well!' Vera looked taken aback. 'Well!'

'The girl is quite right,' Arthur Finch said emphatically. 'That was rude of you, Vera.'

'Oh!' Vera stared at her husband.

Arthur smiled at Dorothy. 'You're very welcome, Dorothy. We should've introduced everyone before we sat down.'

Dorothy smiled back faintly. 'Thank you, Uncle Arthur.'

Under cover of the tablecloth, Gillian, sitting next to her, squeezed her arm encouragingly. At least she had one ally.

Dorothy prodded the food on her plate – egg, bacon, fried black pudding, mushrooms and fried bread – and knew she would never be able to swallow much of it.

She glanced up again. Everyone else was busy tucking in with gusto, except one of the lodgers: a tall, elderly man at the other end of the table. She had the strangest feeling she had met him before somewhere, but knew she couldn't have. As their eyes met he grinned at her and winked.

Dorothy could not help but grin back in return and soon felt better. With a sigh she tackled the fried egg.

'But what will I do with myself all day while you're at work?' Dorothy asked as Gillian was about to leave for work.

'You could visit some other friends,' Gillian suggested.

Dorothy bit her lip. 'Everyone must know what's happened to my family by now,' she said. 'I'm too ashamed.'

'You could get a job,' Gillian said persuasively. 'It would do you good. I love mine.'

'That's all right for you, Gill,' Dorothy said. 'You've been trained for something. I haven't.'

'Look, I must go or I'll be late,' Gillian said hurriedly. 'We'll talk later before supper. We'll think of something.'

Gillian raced off, leaving Dorothy standing dejectedly in the hall. She had the impulse to skulk back to the bedroom she shared with her cousin but it was so cramped she knew she could not bear that for long.

Taking her courage into her hands, Dorothy went into the drawing room and was relieved to find the room empty. She sat down and took up a discarded newspaper, desperate to find a way to pass the time.

She was startled when someone came into the room. It was the man who had winked at her at breakfast.

'Hello,' he said straight away. 'No one has bothered to introduce us. I'm Mr Oglander and you must be Dorothy.'

'Yes, hello.'

He sat down opposite her. 'I couldn't help overhearing your remarks to Gillian about finding something to do,' he said. 'Might I make a suggestion?'

Dorothy smiled uncertainly, wondering why he was taking the trouble. 'Yes, you may,' she said with curiosity.

He took a pipe and a pouch of tobacco out of his jacket pocket and prepared to light up. 'Vera ... er, I mean Mrs Finch, seems to have a bee in her bonnet about you.'

Dorothy raised her head slightly and tried not to look offended. Was he being nosey?

'It's not idle curiosity on my part,' he said quickly. It was as though he could read her mind. 'Arthur Finch is a great one for conversation. He's told me about the feud between your father,

Henry, and Vera.'

Dorothy blinked at the familiar way he spoke their names. He seemed to be so well informed, she wondered how much he knew about her and decided she must be cautious.

'That's family business,' she said warningly. 'And I've no intention of talking about it to you, Mr Oglander.'

'Quite right, too.' He nodded. 'You're a sensible girl, I can see that.'

Dorothy turned her glance away. If only he knew how foolish she had been and how bitterly she regretted her folly.

He sat forward, elbows on knees. 'It was obvious at breakfast that Vera – Mrs Finch – resents you, but I think I might know how you can get into her good books and solve the problem of how to spend your time.'

Dorothy stared at him. 'How?'

'Offer to make yourself useful.'

'What?'

'There's a great deal of work in a lodging house,' Mr Oglander said sagely. 'It must be hard now Gillian goes out to work. Mrs Finch manages almost single-handedly except for a woman who comes in to do the rough work.' He grinned at her. 'Make yourself indispensable to your aunt, my dear. Take some of the work off her shoulders.'

Dorothy was sceptical. 'She'd never hear of it.'

'Well, you won't know until you try.'

'But I know nothing about such work.'

Mr Oglander raised his eyebrows. 'What do

you need to know about preparing vegetables, making beds and using a sweeping brush? Anyone can do it.'

Dorothy drew in a breath. What would Gloria think if she knew her daughter was reduced to the level of a domestic servant?

'You're not too proud, are you, Dorothy?' Mr Oglander was watching her keenly.

'No, of course not,' Dorothy denied.

She thought for a moment. It would be better than sitting around feeling bored all day, and perhaps Mr Oglander was right. Perhaps her aunt would change her attitude to her if she showed willing.

'I'll think about it, Mr Oglander,' she said cautiously.

'Fair enough!' He stood up. 'Don't think too long.'

Dorothy sat thinking for some time after Mr Oglander left her. His idea was growing in merit in her mind, but was she brave enough to see it through?

Gathering her courage, Dorothy went in search of her aunt. She found her in the kitchen, peeling potatoes. Vera's back looked stiff and forbidding. Now and then she dabbed her forehead with her forearm as though perspiring freely.

Dorothy stood in the doorway for a while, watching and trying to screw up enough nerve to speak out to her aunt.

Vera turned around abruptly and saw her standing there. She frowned at Dorothy and looked annoyed.

'What do you want, my girl?' she asked

quickly, feeling her face go hot. 'But I'm not cut out for it.'

Dorothy and Vera came back with the vegetable dishes and gravy boats.

'You take your seat now, Dorothy,' Vera said quite kindly. 'I'll fetch our plates.'

Dorothy sat down beside Gillian, smiling at her, and Gillian was surprised to see her cousin's earlier worried expression was gone.

'You crafty thing!' Gillian said to her in an undertone. 'What made you do it?'

'We'll talk later,' Dorothy said, amusement in her voice. 'After I've done the washing-up.'

Gillian felt obliged to wipe up in the kitchen after supper and listened as Dorothy explained what had prompted her to offer her services to Vera.

'So, it was Mr Oglander's idea, was it?' Gillian said thoughtfully. 'It's very odd that he's always on hand to give advice, like a guardian angel.'

'I'm very grateful to him,' Dorothy said, drying her hands. 'Shall we go to the drawing room with the others?'

'No,' Gillian said eagerly. 'Come up to our room. I want to tell you something. It's a secret.'

The girls ran upstairs to their shared bedroom. Dorothy sat down on her bed and looked across at her cousin. Gillian's face was glowing and her eyes sparkled. Dorothy was immediately intrigued.

'What is it?' she asked. 'What's your secret?'

'I think I'm in love,' Gillian said breathlessly. 'Really and truly in love.'

irritably.

Dorothy wetted her lips. 'Can I give you a hand with anything, Aunt Vera?'

'Eh?'

'I want to help.'

Vera looked astonished. 'Oh, do you?'

'Yes.' Dorothy came forward and stood beside her aunt at the stone sink. 'It must mean a lot of hard work providing for roomers,' she said cleverly, remembering what Mr Oglander had told her. 'And you seem to be coping all by yourself.'

Vera blinked. 'Well, yes, as a matter of fact I do. There's not much profit in keeping lodgers if you have to pay for domestic help.'

'You wouldn't have to pay me,' Dorothy said quickly. 'I'm family.'

Vera blinked again. 'Family? Yes,' she said as though surprised at the notion. 'Yes, that's right, you are family.'

'I'll have to look for a job, you see, Aunt Vera. I can't hang around doing nothing all day.'

Vera lifted her eyebrows. 'What did you do at home with your mother?'

Dorothy pressed her lips together. 'Not much,' she admitted. 'Mother wouldn't let me do anything around the house.' She looked at her aunt. 'But it was different there. I was at home. Here I'm at a loose end.'

Vera stood back, looking at her for a moment. 'Well, I suppose you could make yourself useful,' she said, pointing at the sink. 'Can you peel potatoes?'

'I'll try.'

'All right then, but don't cut the potatoes down too much or there'll be nothing left to boil.' Vera leaned over the sink. 'Now look. You hold the knife like this and take off a thin slice of peel each time. Have a go.'

Dorothy took the knife and a potato and cut carefully. Her aunt watched her efforts for a while and then sniffed.

'I have to admit it,' Vera said almost affably, 'you're a natural, Dorothy. Our Gillian couldn't do it better.'

'Thank you, Aunt Vera.'

'All right. You finish the potatoes and then I'll find something else for you to turn your hand to.'

Dorothy bent over her task, feeling over the moon with pride. She also felt very grateful to Mr Oglander for his wise advice. She would thank him when she saw him again.

Dorothy smiled to herself. And won't Gillian be surprised when she comes home.

Everyone was taking their seats at the table when Gillian arrived, out of puff through hurrying.

'Just in time!' Vera said meaningfully.

Gillian sat down and noticed the seat beside her was empty. She was feeling guilty. She had promised Dorothy they would talk before their evening meal, but she had stayed too long chatting with Jimmy and hated having to leave him at all; she enjoyed his company so much. Poor Dorothy must be really upset.

'Where's Dorothy, Mam?'

'Still in the kitchen,' Vera said, putting plates of food before Miss Philpot and Mr Gilmore. She sounded a little less harassed than she usually did at mealtimes. 'She's helping me serve the food. Oh, here she is now.'

Gillian stared in astonishment as Dorothy bustled into the room carrying two plates of food, placing one before Gillian's father and the other in front of Mr Oglander and then hurried out again, followed by Vera.

'Bring in the vegetables next, Dorothy,' her mother called out. 'And the gravy boats.'

'What's going on?' Gillian asked, perplexed.

'Dorothy has volunteered her help to Vera,' Arthur said with a wink. 'She's got her head screwed on right, that girl.'

'And Mam is willing?' Gillian asked incredulously.

'Very glad of the offer, it seems.'

'I can hardly believe it.'

'Well, Gillian,' her father said reproachfully, 'you've never been keen to help about the place. Vera works very hard to bring in a few extra shillings.'

'And she keeps the place spotless,' Miss Philpot said approvingly. 'We feel we're very lucky to lodge with Mrs Finch, don't we, Mr Gilmore?'

Mr Gilmore nodded silently, his mouth full.

Gillian was put out at her father's reproach. 'I work hard, too, Dad. I want something better in my life than keeping lodgers.'

Miss Philpot coughed.

'No offence, Miss Philpot,' Gillian said

It was the last thing Dorothy expected to hear. All at once she was alarmed, thinking of Ronnie Knox.

'Who is he?' she asked uneasily.

'His name is Jimmy Tomkin,' Gillian answered. 'He's Dad's apprentice.'

'Oh, I see.' Relieved, Dorothy felt the tension ease in her shoulders.

'Jimmy is really wonderful, Dot,' Gillian said excitedly. 'Everyone likes him; Mam, Dad.'

'You mean they know!'

'He's been here to supper and I could see Mam took a liking to him.' Gillian paused, looking uncertain. 'Dot, you're the first person I've told about how I feel about him,' she said. 'Mam and Dad like him but—'

'But what?'

Gillian paused, her face clouding for a moment before continuing. 'Dot, do you think it's all right for cousins to marry?'

Dorothy was taken aback. 'What a strange question, Gill!'

'That's the problem, you see,' Gillian hurried on. 'Jimmy is my first cousin.'

Dorothy was puzzled. 'But you told me once that your father was an only child,' she said. 'How could he have a nephew?'

Gillian sat back, her eyes widening, obviously startled. She clamped her hand to her mouth and looked alarmed.

'What is it, Gill?'

'Oh, gosh!' Gillian said, sounding flummoxed. 'I shouldn't have said anything. I didn't think...'

She stood up hurriedly, twisting her hands

together nervously. She looked so confused and upset that Dorothy felt a tinge of unease.

'Gill, what's the matter?'

'Forget I said anything, Dot. It doesn't matter.'

'Wait a minute,' Dorothy said, rising to her feet. 'What's going on, Gill? What are you trying to hide?'

Gillian flopped down on the bed again. 'Oh, no! Dad will crown me!' she said. 'What have I done?'

Dorothy stood over her cousin. 'Gillian!' she exclaimed sharply. 'You're beginning to upset me. What secrets are you keeping from me?'

'Jimmy is my cousin,' Gillian said in a small voice. 'But he's on the Prosser side of the family.'

'That doesn't make sense.'

Gillian reached forward and, clasping Dorothy's hand, drew her down to sit beside her. 'Dot, I have something to tell you. It'll be a shock but please don't be upset.'

'I'll be more upset if you don't tell me!' Dorothy said angrily.

Gillian gulped before speaking. 'Jimmy is my cousin, Dot, but he is also your half-brother.'

Dorothy blinked and then shook her head. 'I'm no wiser, Gill,' she said. 'Because you're still not making any sense.'

'Oh, dear. This is awkward.' Gillian looked scared, and Dorothy felt a sense of foreboding. She wasn't sure she wanted to know the truth.

'There's no nice way to tell you the truth, Dot,' Gillian said hurriedly. 'So I'll just come straight out with it. Jimmy is your father's illegitimate son.'

Dorothy could only stare at her. She could not quite take in the meaning of the words. Her father's illegitimate son? It sounded crazy, unbelievable. She jumped to her feet.

'Gillian, I've never heard anything so absurd in my life,' Dorothy said huffily. 'You're making it up.'

'No, I'm not,' Gillian protested. 'Uncle Henry has another family – Jimmy and his mother. They live in Fleet Street. She calls herself Mrs Tomkin, although she's not married.'

Dorothy felt floored. 'How could he? How could he do that to us?' She gave Gillian another flashing glance of anger. 'It's a lie!'

Gillian shook her head sadly. 'Dad told me all about it. Your father confided in him years ago. My dad felt he had to tell me because of Jimmy being my cousin. I think he guessed I'm getting fond of him.'

Dorothy was silent, thinking. She had had no idea of her father's secret life, and she was certain her mother had no inkling either. But now she understood the continual rows between her parents.

All the time, for years, he hadn't really wanted to be with them. Obviously he thought nothing of her as his daughter. After all, he had dumped her on relatives.

She remembered his anger over her foolish behaviour with Ronnie Knox. He had chastised her, making her feel unbearably ashamed yet all the while he had been carrying on with some other woman. She felt crushed by the revelation.

'Are you all right, Dorothy?' Gillian was looking anxiously into her face.

'Of course I'm not!' Dorothy burst out. 'My family has been torn to shreds and now I know why.'

'What are you going to do?'

Dorothy turned her face away. 'I don't want to talk any more, Gill,' she said coldly. 'I'm going to bed now, and I don't want to be disturbed.'

'But it's quite early yet. We could go out for a walk.'

'No. I've a lot to think about,' Dorothy said. 'Company is the last thing I want now. Please close the door on your way out.'

Sixteen

Dorothy was up early to help with the breakfast for the household. She had hardly slept and still felt so miserable at what she had discovered about her father the night before, but the chores Vera gave her took her mind off it for a while.

Gillian had been questioning her ever since they had awakened that morning about what she intended to do. The truth was, she did not know. Yet she felt she must do something, if only to confront her father.

When breakfast was over and she and Vera were clearing away, Dorothy spoke out.

'Aunt Vera, I'd like to go off for a couple of hours this morning. Do you mind?'

Vera sniffed. 'Oh, I see! I thought it wouldn't last long.'

Dorothy shook her head. 'No, I'm not going back on my word. I want to help. In fact, I like the work very much.'

Vera raised her eyebrows. 'Do you?' She sounded surprised. 'Well, I never!'

'There's something I must do; something to do with my family.'

Vera nodded. 'You're going to see your mother, I expect. Well, that's understandable.' She paused. 'I hope you'll be back before one o'clock. I'd like some help at dinner time.'

'I'll be back, I promise,' Dorothy said. What she had to do would not take all that long. 'And this afternoon I'll give the second-floor bedrooms a good clean.'

Vera looked pleased. 'Right you are, then. Off you go. I'll see to the washing-up – just this once.'

Dorothy thought deeply on the long walk to her father's house, having decided she should see her mother first to find out how much she knew about Henry Prosser's secret life.

She did not have a key and so had to ring the bell. She expected Phoebe to answer, but it was her mother who opened the door to her. Gloria was dressed up to the nines and looked astonished to see her daughter.

'I didn't think I'd see you again, Dorothy,' Gloria said.

'Can I come in, Mother?'

231

Gloria stepped aside. Dorothy walked into the hall.

'Is Phoebe out?'

'I've sacked her,' Gloria said shortly. 'I don't need her any longer.'

It was then that Dorothy noticed two suitcases and a portmanteau on the floor at the foot of the stairs.

She whirled to face her mother. 'You're going away, Mother?'

'I will be, quite soon.'

'You'd have gone without a word to me?' Dorothy was upset at the thought.

'I didn't think you were interested. I know your father has poisoned your mind against me.'

'You're my mother. Nothing changes that.'

Gloria looked disgruntled. 'Well, your father has made it impossible for me to stay here. My friends are laughing at me behind my back. I'm so mortified at the shameful thing he's done.'

Dorothy bit her lip. 'You know about the woman he's living with in Fleet Street, then?'

Gloria's features turned stony and her lips tightened.

'I'll thank you not to speak of it,' she said harshly. 'My pain is enough to bear already without my own daughter adding to it.'

'How long have you known?'

'Andy told me the night he left for London. I couldn't believe your father would betray me like that.'

Dorothy was puzzled. 'Why did Andy go to London? I don't understand.'

Gloria's expression became guarded. 'Your

father is telling vile lies about him,' she said. 'Andy is totally innocent.'

'Innocent of what?'

'It's none of your concern, Dorothy,' Gloria said in an offhand tone. 'Now, if you have nothing more to say I must get ready to leave.'

'Why do you all ignore me?' Dorothy burst out angrily. 'I'm the only one who doesn't know what's going on in my own family. Now, Mother, I want to know what trouble Andy is in.'

Gloria's face whitened. 'Your father accused him of robbing the yard office and attacking that old fool, Meeker.'

'What?'

'It's all lies!' Gloria insisted. 'Your father has not only betrayed us all, he hates us as well. A father accusing his son of such a crime – it's scandalous.'

Dorothy leaned a hand against the newel post of the staircase. She felt quite ill. The whole fabric of her life was unravelling before her eyes.

'But why did Andy run away?' she asked weakly. 'Wasn't that foolish?'

'What do you expect him to do?' Gloria flared. 'After such an accusation.'

'But if he's innocent...?'

'It's not your place to ask such questions,' her mother snapped. 'Andy needs me and I'm going to him in London.'

'You're choosing between us?'

Gloria lifted her chin, her expression sour. 'You've done that already, Dorothy, when you meekly left with your father. I didn't hear you

233

stand up for me then.'

'I was angry with you, Mother. If you hadn't encouraged me, I would never have given in to Ronnie Knox. I feel ruined.'

'Oh, that's right! Blame me for your own foolishness. That's just like you.'

She moved towards the staircase and started to climb, then turned to look down on Dorothy standing at the foot of the stairs.

'I wash my hands of you, Dorothy,' she continued coldly. 'You're such a disappointment to me. Any daughter of mine should have more gumption in handling men.'

Gloria continued up the stairs without another word or backward glance. Watching her retreating figure, Dorothy felt dumbfounded and very much alone. This was the last straw and it was all her father's fault.

Turning on her heel she left the house, slamming the door behind her. Both her parents had pushed her aside to pursue their own ends. So be it. From now on she would make her own life, but first she intended to confront her father's mistress and tell her exactly what she thought of her.

Dorothy had prized out of Gillian the number of the house in Fleet Street where her father was now living. She stood on the pavement across from it for a while but did not know what she had expected to see.

The outside looked respectable enough; the lace curtains were clean and the window panes gleamed in the morning sunshine. The front step, too, had been recently scrubbed.

Fleet Street was busy with traffic, but when a lull came Dorothy crossed the road quickly and stood before the freshly painted front door. She drew in a deep breath before reaching for the door knocker and rapping smartly.

In no time it was answered by a woman roughly Gloria's age. She smiled at Dorothy and inclined her head. 'Yes?'

'I'm looking for Henry Prosser,' Dorothy blurted out.

The woman shook her head, still smiling. 'Mr Prosser's not here, dear. You'll find him at the yard.'

Dorothy had guessed that he would be. She wetted her lips and decided to be direct. It was the only way to deal with the embarrassing situation.

'I'm his daughter,' she said bluntly. 'Are you the woman he's living with?'

The woman's smile faltered and she paused a moment before speaking. 'Yes, I'm Florrie Tomkin.'

'Then it's you I've come to see,' Dorothy said sharply.

Florrie Tomkin hesitated for just a moment before she spoke and stood aside. 'You'd better come in.'

Dorothy followed her down the short passage to a back room. The house smelled clean and fresh: the linoleum gleamed and so did highly polished surfaces of furniture.

They stood face to face in the small living room and Dorothy gave the older woman a quick appraisal.

Gloria was always careful to keep her figure fashionably trim, if not thin. Florrie Tomkin was not fat but rounded underneath her flowered wraparound pinafore. She wore no make-up and her hair was loose to her shoulders.

Dorothy studied her features, wondering why her father preferred this rather plain woman to his wife.

'Why did you want to see me?'

Dorothy tossed her head and gave the other woman a challenging look.

'I should think that's obvious,' she said. 'I've come here to tell you exactly what I think of a woman who steals someone else's husband.'

'I see.'

'Well? What have you to say for yourself?'

'Do sit down,' Florrie said calmly. 'It is Dorothy, isn't it? Henry speaks of you often.'

Dorothy tightened her lips, angry that Florrie appeared so composed. 'I will not sit down,' she snapped. 'This isn't a social call.'

'Well, I want to sit,' Florrie said lightly. 'I feel so awkward standing.' She sat down and then indicated a nearby chair. 'Please.'

Momentarily confounded, Dorothy sat. 'Well?'

'I don't know what you want me to say.'

'I want you to assure me that you'll bring this affair with my father to an end.'

Florrie sat back in her chair, her expression thoughtful.

'I've never thought of it as an affair,' she said. There was just a touch of surprise in her voice. 'I couldn't give Henry up after all this time. I

236

feel as though I'm married to him. He bought this house for us. We have a son, you know. Jimmy's a year younger than you.'

'Oh! Have you no shame?'

'Why should Henry and I be ashamed to be in love?' Florrie asked. 'And we do love each other, you know, Dorothy. Very deeply and for a long time.'

'But he's married to my mother.'

Florrie smiled sadly. 'Love is funny like that,' she said. 'It doesn't ask permission to strike.'

'You're making fun of me!'

'No, I'm not,' Florrie said quickly. 'Your father was married three years when I met him and I knew straight away he was unhappy with Gloria.'

'You took advantage!'

'No.' Florrie shook her head emphatically. 'It was a chance meeting in the yard office that brought us together,' she said. 'And without looking for it we both fell for each other and really fell in love for the first time.'

'My father loved my mother.'

Florrie shook her head again and looked down at her hands clasped in her lap.

'I don't want to speak against your mother, Dorothy, and it's not my place to,' she said softly. 'But you should know that Henry married Gloria because she was expecting his child; your brother Andy.' She glanced up and into Dorothy's gaze. 'He did not love her, but he did right by her.'

'I don't believe it!'

'Henry maintains Gloria never loved him

237

either but trapped him because his family had money.'

'How dare you?' Dorothy felt she had to protest out of loyalty to Gloria, but she knew it was true. Hadn't her mother confessed it to her many times?

'I'm sorry, Dorothy,' Florrie said. 'It's your father's place to tell you these truths not mine.' She lifted a hand and waved it around. 'This is Henry's real home. He's always said so. The place where he's loved and cherished for himself; not for who and what he is.'

Despite her own antagonism Dorothy heard the sincerity in Florrie's voice and expression, but she did not want to acknowledge it.

'But you're living in sin!'

'I suppose we are in a way,' Florrie said quietly. 'But can there be sin when there is so much love?'

'You're twisting things to suit yourself,' Dorothy accused her heatedly. 'How can your son hold his head up when he's illegitimate? Have you thought about that?'

Florrie smiled. 'Jimmy isn't ashamed and doesn't blame Henry. He loves his father dearly and doesn't care what others say or think.'

Dorothy was nonplussed. No accusation or argument seemed to touch Florrie's composure.

'Don't you want my father to marry you, then?'

Florrie smiled. 'Of course I'd love to be his legal wife, but I doubt he'll ever divorce your mother. Henry has a strong sense of responsibility. He wouldn't leave her destitute. Your mother's no worse off financially than she was when Henry lived with her.'

'She's alone,' Dorothy said. 'He has deserted her; he's deserted all of us.'

'No, he hasn't,' Florrie said. 'He would've liked for you to live here with us, but he thought it wasn't quite proper.'

'There! You see!' Dorothy exclaimed with energy. 'He knows his behaviour with you is shameful.'

'I feel no shame.' Florrie looked at her kindly. 'I'm sorry you're so upset, Dorothy. Your father will be, too, when he hears that you called.'

'I don't want him to know!'

'Henry and I keep no secrets from each other,' Florrie told her.

Dorothy realized her being there was serving no purpose.

'I'm leaving!' she said. 'I should never have come here.'

'I'm glad you did,' Florrie said. 'You're Henry's child and I'm glad to meet you at last.'

Florrie's affable tone set Dorothy's teeth on edge. Was there no way to shame her?

She started to walk down the passage to the front door when suddenly it opened and her father came in.

He pulled up short and so did Dorothy. She felt embarrassed that he had caught her there, and somehow guilty, too, though she could not think why.

'Dorothy!' His face turned as white as chalk. 'I never thought to find you here.'

'No!' Dorothy shouted. 'You didn't believe I'd

239

find out about your – fancy woman.'

'Don't speak of Florrie in that way!'

Dorothy was disconcerted to see no sign of penitence in his expression or tone of voice.

'It's all right, Henry,' Florrie said in soothing tones. 'It's been a shock for her and she's so young. She doesn't understand.'

'She understands all right and she's not without fault herself.'

'Dad!' Dorothy was appalled at his meaning. How dare he throw her one mistake in her face when he had committed adultery for years? 'How could you bring that up?'

'You can't afford self-righteousness, Dot,' he said. 'You're making judgements about me and Florrie when you know nothing of the situation.'

'I've tried to explain to her,' Florrie said.

Dorothy rounded on her. 'Explain! No explanation can excuse the reprehensible way you live,' she burst out. 'You've both wronged my mother terribly.'

'Don't you mean the way she wronged me when she tricked me into marriage?' Henry asked harshly. 'Or the way she wronged you when she urged you to encourage Ronnie Knox?'

Dorothy stared at her father in dismay. Colour had come back into his face now and he looked angry.

'Dad, how could you?' Dorothy glanced at Florrie. 'I suppose you've told this woman all about it.'

'Henry has never said a word against you, Dorothy,' Florrie said. 'Your father loves you dearly. He's always praising you.'

'Oh, yes. He loves me so much he tore me away from my mother to foist me on relatives,' Dorothy said in a disparaging tone. 'I understand now why he has no time for his real family.'

'I think you'd better go, Dorothy,' Henry said sternly. 'Before you say something I can't forgive. I'll call at your aunt Vera's to talk to you. We need to sort things out.'

'Don't bother!' Dorothy turned on her heel and strode out of the house. 'I don't want to see you ever again, Dad.'

Tears welled as she hurried back to Aunt Vera's and she could not prevent them. She felt betrayed by the one person she should be able to trust implicitly – her own father. He was a hypocrite; preaching to her and living a lie himself.

Her mother had deserted her, her father had deceived her. There was no one, no one at all who she could turn to for comfort and understanding.

It was such a lovely evening. Gillian could not remember when she had been happier. As she and Jimmy strolled along Marlborough Road towards her home she was thrilled when he gently took her hand in his.

Delighted, she glanced up at him as they walked side by side and he was smiling down at her. There was something in his gaze that made her heart flutter.

'Gill, I know you agreed to go out with me again but I want a better understanding between us.' He paused, his colour rising. 'Would you be my steady girl? I mean, I want to court you properly and think about a future together. Will you?'

Gillian stopped. 'Oh, Jimmy! I'd love to be your steady girl.' She had been longing for this. 'I feel the same about you.' She wondered if she might consider herself engaged. 'Perhaps you ought to speak to my dad.'

Jimmy hesitated. 'We'd better not rush things, Gill,' he said cautiously. 'Arthur may kick up a fuss because, well, we're related, aren't we?'

'Jimmy, we can't let being cousins get in our way!' Gillian exclaimed earnestly. 'Besides, that circumstance won't change.'

Jimmy ran his fingers through his hair. 'No, but I thought we could let your family get used to me being around.'

'Jimmy, if we're going to start courting properly then my family should know about it – and yours, too,' Gillian said firmly. 'I don't want to sneak about in secret.' She looked at him pleadingly. 'I'm not very good at keeping secrets.'

'All right,' he said at last. 'I'll speak to Arthur tomorrow. But I know what he's going to say.'

Pleased, Gillian skipped forward, pulling Jimmy along with her. 'Dad might surprise you,' she said. 'He likes you a lot, Jimmy.' She laugh-ed. 'In a way he's your uncle.'

'Gosh!' Jimmy looked somewhat thoughtful. 'I hadn't looked at it that way.'

'Oh, I'm so happy,' Gillian said. 'Wait until I tell Dorothy about this.'

'Perhaps you shouldn't mention it to anyone until I've spoken to your father,' Jimmy said uncertainly.

'Dot's all right,' Gillian said. 'We were friends for years and my mother never found out. I trust her.'

Jimmy smiled. 'Well, you know your cousin best, I suppose.'

Gillian hesitated before speaking. 'You realize she's your half-sister, don't you?'

'I suppose so.' She could tell by his expression that he had not thought of it that way before.

'You should meet her,' Gillian said thoughtfully. 'You should get to know your own sister.'

'Gill, please,' Jimmy said, his voice shaking. 'My father might not like that. I don't want to upset him, or Dorothy either. Let that rest. It's enough that I have to approach Arthur about us.' He paused, his expression sombre. 'Life is getting too complicated.'

'Oh, all right,' Gillian conceded. 'Our future together is all that matters, after all.'

They reached her house and stood outside.

'I'm very fond of you, Jimmy,' Gillian said softly as they stood there hand in hand. 'Very fond.'

'And I'm very fond of you, Gill. In fact...' He hesitated, his face colouring up again. 'In fact, I'm more than fond. I think about you all the time.'

Gillian felt suddenly shy and overwhelmed at his fervent tone. Was he telling her he loved her? She hoped with all her heart that it was true.

In all the weeks they had known each other he had never tried to kiss her properly. She had often wished he would.

'Well, we are courting now, Jimmy. And as far as I'm concerned it's official.' She hesitated, deciding shyness wouldn't do. She must be bold. 'Would you like to kiss me?'

'Oh, Gill!'

She lifted her face to him and their lips met briefly. Too briefly for Gillian.

'Shall we try again?'

Jimmy looked around. 'Not on the street, Gill,' he said. 'What will people think?'

'I suppose you're right.' Gillian sighed in disappointment. She had been dreaming about his kisses. 'I don't want gossip getting back to Mam.'

'We'd better say goodnight,' Jimmy said practically.

Gillian felt bolder. 'Why don't you come inside?'

They could kiss in the hall. No one would see there.

'Best not,' he said with a wide grin and she knew he had read her intention. 'But I'll see you first thing tomorrow at the yard.'

With reluctance Gillian said goodnight, squeezing his hand.

'Do you promise to dream about me?' she whispered.

'I always do, Gill,' he said. 'You're all I dream about.'

She blew him a kiss as she walked to the front door and he was still standing there as she closed it.

Seventeen

Charlie Knox's house, Swansea, 1904

'Freda will be missed at the chapel, Mr Knox. She was so brave in her affliction. I can't tell you how sorry I am for your sad loss.'

Charlie shook the woman's hand and mumbled his thanks, although he had no idea who she was. There had been a large turnout for Freda's funeral. He had been astonished. He had no idea his wife had so many friends and acquaintances.

'Thank you for coming,' he said lamely.

There were more handshakes and mumbled thanks before the final mourner left. Charlie stood in the hall for a moment, feeling suddenly overcome. Freda was gone. It was only just beginning to sink in. There were just him and George left now, and the boy was taking his mother's death so badly.

He felt at a loss, not knowing what he should do next. He should find George. The boy needed him now more than ever. And his son meant the world to him. Everything he had ever done was for him.

Charlie walked slowly into the drawing room but pulled up short when he saw Rose Prosser standing near the fireplace, slender in her black silk, full-skirted mourning dress.

'I thought you'd left with the others,' he said sharply.

Rose stepped towards him, the silken hem of her dress rustling as she moved. 'We have things to talk about, Charlie.'

There was a determined edge to her voice, which irritated him. Even on the day of Freda's funeral Rose had to push herself forward.

'Where's George?' he asked.

'Gone to his room to sulk, I suppose.'

'Sulk!' Charlie was angry. 'The boy has just lost his mother, for God's sake. He's devastated.'

Rose turned her head, sulking herself.

'I think you'd better go, Rose. We can talk some other time.'

'No!' Rose's eyes flashed in anger as she turned her head to glare at him. 'We must talk now. I've waited, Charlie, waited so long. Now you're free to marry me. We must start planning.'

He stared at her in dismay. 'How insensitive can someone be?' he exclaimed. 'I've just buried my wife today. Have you no decency, Rose?'

Her lips twisted. 'I gave up decency when I first jumped into bed with you,' she flared. 'And you're being a hypocrite, Charlie. You didn't love Freda so don't pretend now that you did.' Her look was challenging. 'You love me.'

Charlie shook his head in disbelief. 'This is low even for you, Rose,' he said quietly. 'Today of all days. I always knew you were self-absorbed, but what you're doing now disgusts me.'

'Don't speak to me like that, Charlie.'

'What do you expect? I've lost my wife. I did

love her once and I always respected her.' He paused, feeling suddenly guilty. 'Even when I was deceiving her with you.'

'How touching!' Rose sneered. 'I'd kill you if you ever deceived me like that.'

Charlie looked at the passion in her dark eyes and knew she meant it. It was this passion which had first drawn him to her and had captured him. She was like a drug to him, one from which he could never be free. His mood softened, remembering the years they had been lovers.

'I know it,' he said gently. 'I do love you, Rose, but this is neither the time nor the place to talk about our relationship.' He went to her and put his arms around her. 'We're still together. We're fine as we are for the time being.'

'I want marriage,' Rose said firmly, looking up at him challengingly. 'I should have married you instead of William.'

'And that's another point,' Charlie said reasonably. 'You're still married to William.'

'He's dead!' Rose said irritably. 'It's been over five years since he disappeared and not one word or sign that he's still alive.'

'There's no proof that he's dead.'

'He must be!' Rose insisted petulantly. 'Not even Cissie has heard a word from him. If he was still alive he would've been in touch with her.'

'Nevertheless,' Charlie said. 'Legally, you're still married to him.' He shook his head. 'We can't think of marrying until William is officially declared dead, Rose and that's going to take time – years.'

He was counting on that. He could not live without her, yet he was not at all sure he wanted to marry her, not after all this time. Their relationship suited him as it was.

She pulled away from him. 'I'll see my lawyer tomorrow,' she said. 'Something must be done.'

Charlie shook his head. 'Seven years is the legal period of waiting before a person can be declared officially dead.'

'You mean we have to wait nearly two years?' Rose looked stunned. 'It's not fair that I should have to wait so long to be your wife.'

'That's the law, Rose.'

She was silent.

'You'd better go,' he said. 'I have to be with George now. He needs me.'

'Oh, for heaven's sake,' Rose said irritably. 'He's fifteen. You're treating him like a baby. What about me? I need you, too.'

'Please, Rose.'

With a sullen glance and a lift of her shoulder Rose went into the hall. Charlie got her coat and helped her into it. She leaned into him as he did so.

'When will I see you, Charlie?' she asked huskily.

'I'll come around to the house,' he said.

'Make it soon.'

He kissed her as she stood at the open doorway and then she was gone. Charlie turned back into the hall and then started guiltily to see his son standing on the staircase. George had been watching them together.

'I thought she'd never go, Dad,' George said.

'Why did she stay so long?'

'She was your mother's best friend,' Charlie said lamely.

He was disconcerted to see an expression of derision cross his son's usually pleasant face as he came down the rest of the stairs and stood at the foot.

'I'm not a child, Dad. I know what's been going on.'

'George!' Charlie was dismayed. 'I don't know what it is you believe you know, but you're mistaken.'

'I'm not a fool either, Dad,' George said. 'Rose Prosser was no friend of Mam's. I don't like her. I never did. Must you have anything more to do with her?'

'You don't understand, George,' Charlie said. 'You will when you're older.'

The open scorn on his son's face hurt him. 'We've just buried my mother, your wife, Dad,' George said solemnly. 'At the moment I don't want to understand anything but that.'

George turned on his heel and ran up the stairs two at a time.

Charlie could only stand at the bottom staring up the staircase after him. He felt chastened by his son's words.

When he and Rose were together she fired up his blood as no other woman had ever been able to do before and he could not imagine living without that passion now.

But much as he wanted Rose he knew he loved and needed George even more. His only son was the world to him and his happiness and future were all that mattered.

If he could avoid marriage to Rose, he would – for George's sake.

Eighteen

Swansea, 1931

'Jimmy! Don't stand there staring into space, lad,' Arthur said impatiently. 'You should've finished wiping that joint by now.'

'Sorry, Arthur. I was thinking.'

'Well, don't think on the job unless it's about plumbing,' Arthur said. 'The client isn't paying us to think. She wants us out of the house as quick as you like.'

'Sorry, Arthur.'

Arthur grunted, wiping his hands on a rag. He couldn't make out what was amiss with the boy today. Usually Jimmy was as keen as mustard.

'What's wrong?'

Jimmy opened his mouth to reply, but at that moment the house owner came into the bathroom where they were working, carrying a tray.

'Here's a cup of tea each,' she said, 'and a few Welsh cakes.'

'That's very good of you, Mrs Morgan,' Arthur said pleasantly. 'We'll just take five minutes off, no more.'

Jimmy spoke his thanks, too, and took the tray

from her to balance it on the wash-hand basin as she left. He squatted on the floor to drink his tea while Arthur sat precariously on the edge of the bath.

'Well, what's the matter?' Arthur said, taking a sip. His curiosity was piqued when Jimmy coloured deeply and looked embarrassed. 'Spit it out.'

'It's about Gill,' Jimmy said cautiously.

'What about her?' Arthur was suddenly alert.

'Well, you know Gill and me are friends,' Jimmy said hurriedly. 'I'm very fond of her, Arthur, very fond, and I'd like your permission to court her, serious like.'

'What!' Arthur jerked to his feet, spilling the tea on the linoleum. 'What?'

Jimmy scrambled to his feet, too. 'Gill and I have talked it over seriously. It's something we both want, Arthur.'

'Gill is only seventeen,' Arthur said. 'She's too young to know her own mind.'

'But my intentions are honest, Arthur, and it would be years and years before—'

'It's out of the question,' Arthur spluttered.

'Why?'

Flummoxed, Arthur looked up at his young apprentice. 'Because...' He paused, confused at his own thoughts. 'Because you're a blood relation of Gill's,' he said. 'It just won't do, Jimmy. You must see that.'

'People marry their cousins all the time,' Jimmy protested.

Arthur realized the boy was only repeating what Gillian had said.

251

'Not in my family they don't!' Arthur was adamant.

'The gentry do.'

'Yes, well, there's a reason for them to do it,' Arthur said, exasperated. 'It's to keep the wealth in the family, but we're not gentry.'

'It's not illegal, Arthur.' Jimmy shook his head. 'I asked our insurance man, Mr Parsons. He knows a lot about the law, does Mr Parsons.'

'Blast and damn it, Jimmy!' Arthur exploded. 'Have you been discussing family business with every Tom, Dick and Harry?'

'No, Arthur,' Jimmy said quickly. 'It was hypothetical, I told him.'

Arthur was sceptical and let his expression show it.

'I never mentioned Gill's name, Arthur,' Jimmy said fervently. 'I promise you.'

To gain time to think Arthur bent down to wipe up the spilled tea with the rag. He liked the lad well enough. Jimmy was a good worker and honest as the day was long, but his family history was such a mess. If Vera ever found out...

He straightened up and looked into Jimmy's eager eyes.

'I'm sorry, lad,' he said kindly. 'But I can't give my permission. Think what it would mean. My wife would have to know the truth about you.'

'So that's it!' Jimmy said angrily. 'I might've guessed. It's because I'm illegitimate, isn't it? You and your family would be ashamed. Well, Gill isn't ashamed of me.'

'I don't care two hoots about your parentage,

Jimmy,' Arthur assured him, and it was true. 'But others feel different. You know it is a stigma to the world.' Arthur was trying to sound reasonable. 'Gill's a romantic young girl who doesn't understand what that could mean.'

Arthur saw the lad was injured by his remarks, and he must wound him further. He was very sorry about that but there was no help for it.

'Jimmy, you mustn't see Gill any more.'

'Well, that'll be difficult. We work at the same yard.'

'You know what I mean,' Arthur said sharply. 'You're not to see my daughter socially from now on. It can't come to anything and I've told you why.'

Jimmy stared at him for a moment without speaking, but his expression showed his utter devastation at Arthur's edict.

'I mean it, Jimmy.'

Jimmy swallowed heavily. 'Is that your last word, Arthur?'

'Yes, lad, it is.' Arthur put his cup on the tray and gave Jimmy a meaningful look. 'We're being paid to do a job, Jimmy,' he said. 'Let's get on with it.'

Gillian hung around the office last thing, waiting for Jimmy and her father to return from a job. She watched them come into the yard from the office window and knew immediately that something was amiss between them. Alarmed, she ran out to the yard.

'Jimmy?'

Jimmy started towards her, but halted as

Arthur said something to him and then just stood there.

Ignoring her father, Gill ran to Jimmy. 'What's the matter, Jimmy?'

Arthur came forward hurriedly to her. 'Gill, why are you still here? You should've gone home half an hour ago.'

'I'm waiting for Jimmy,' she replied. 'To make arrangements to go for a walk on the prom later.'

Her father ran his tongue over his lips nervously. 'No, Gill,' he said firmly. 'I've told Jimmy here that you can't be friends any more.'

'What?' Gillian was appalled at his words. 'But why?' She stared at Jimmy. His face was as white as a sheet and he looked back at her helplessly. 'Dad, what's happened?'

'We'll talk at home,' he said. 'Now go back in the office and wait for me. We'll go home together.'

'But, Dad—!'

'Gillian!' Arthur burst out. 'Do as you're told!'

'Jimmy?' She looked at him appealingly.

Jimmy shook his head. 'It's no good, Gill,' he said sadly. 'Your father has forbidden me to see you again.'

'I'm sure he didn't mean it.' She could not believe it of her father.

'I do mean it and I have my reasons, as you well know, Jimmy,' Arthur snapped.

Gillian was taken aback at his sharp tone and she noticed, too, that he looked worried. Despite her anxiety she realized it was not the right time to challenge him.

'Fair enough, Dad,' she said obediently. 'We'll

straighten this out at home.' She glanced at Jimmy and tried to smile reassuringly. 'Good-night, Jimmy. Don't worry. Everything will be all right. I promise you.'

'We'll walk home, Gill,' her father said when he eventually clocked off work. 'Then we can talk.'

'But we won't get home before six o'clock,' Gillian said. 'Mam will have a fit with both of us being late.'

'It can't be helped,' Arthur said. 'Our talk can't wait. And besides, there's not a lot of privacy at home, now is there?'

Gillian fell into step beside him. It was the first time she had ever tried to oppose her father's wishes and she knew she had a fight on her hands. But she wanted to be with Jimmy and she was willing to do battle with anyone.

'What's this about me not seeing Jimmy again, Dad?' she asked pertly. She glanced sideways at him and saw his lips tighten.

'He asked if he could court you,' Arthur said flatly. 'I told him it's out of the question.'

'But why?'

'Use your head, Gill. Have a bit of gumption,' Arthur said with impatience. 'In the first place Jimmy is your blood cousin and secondly, he's illegitimate.'

'I don't care a fig about that!'

'No, *you* might not, but others will turn away. I don't want my daughter pilloried because she married illegitimacy.'

'Married?' Gillian gave a short laugh. 'Jimmy and I couldn't marry for years. We'd have to save up first and Jimmy would have to finish his apprenticeship before he could take on such responsibility.'

Her father glanced at her. 'You've worked this out.'

'Yes,' Gillian said. 'I'm not a child, Dad.'

'You are in my eyes and your mother's, too,' Arthur said firmly. 'And that's another thing. Can you imagine what would happen if Vera found out that Henry has an illegitimate son?'

'Why should she care about that?'

'Huh! Don't you know anything about your mother?' asked Arthur, frustrated. 'She's still proud of the Prosser name. Henry has besmirched it. There'd be hell to pay, especially on top of her feud with him over the will.'

Gillian felt angered. 'Why should Jimmy and I suffer because of Mam's pride?' she exclaimed. 'It's my future happiness that's at stake here.'

'Gill, you're young yet,' said Arthur. 'There are plenty of young men who'd be far more suitable. I suggest you wait. Don't rush into anything. Make no promises.'

Gillian stopped in her tracks and stared at her father. 'But I'm in love with Jimmy.'

She was not ashamed to put a name to her feelings for Jimmy. He was in her thoughts constantly. She could not bear the notion that they did not have a future together, and all because of prejudice.

'Nonsense!' Arthur said loudly. 'You don't know what love is.'

'How dare you belittle my feelings, Dad!' Gillian burst out heatedly. She stared at him accusingly and then saw his face soften a little.

'I don't mean to do that, Gill, love,' he said patiently. 'But I'm your father and it's up to me to protect you.'

Gillian frowned and shook her head. 'Against what?'

'Against your own foolishness amongst other things,' Arthur said heatedly. 'You don't know what you're letting yourself in for.'

'Jimmy doesn't get any prejudice at work.'

'That's because the other men don't know he's Henry's illegitimate son,' Arthur said. 'His grandfather, Bert, told everyone that Jimmy's father is dead.' Arthur paused and looked at her beseechingly. 'How long do you think it will take them to find out the truth? The men will turn their backs on him and on anyone associated with him, like family.'

Gillian's lips twisted. 'You're thinking of yourself,' she accused. 'Afraid you'll lose the respect the men have for you if Jimmy and I start courting. Your pride will be dented.'

'That's not true, Gillian,' Arthur said. 'I'm concerned for you and for your mother. She'd have to be told about Henry, and God help us all then.'

'You're exaggerating,' Gillian said. 'Anyone would think you're afraid of Mam.'

Arthur was silent and walked on. Gillian ran to catch up with him.

'You can't stop me from seeing Jimmy,' she said defiantly.

'Yes, I can. I'm your father.'

Gillian was silent for a few minutes as they

continued to walk.

'Mam likes Jimmy,' she said. 'I know she does. I'm going to tell her that you've forbidden me to see him again. She'll be on my side.'

Arthur stopped dead in his tracks, his expression dismayed.

'Gillian, you can't mention it to her,' he said anxiously. 'You'll cause serious trouble between me and your mother, and not only that, it'll widen the rift between her and Henry.'

'I don't intend to tell her the truth about Jimmy,' Gillian said. 'I'll tell her only as much as she needs to know.'

Arthur ground his teeth. 'Gillian, you're walking on dangerous ground. You don't realize the bitterness you'll create.'

Gillian tossed her head stubbornly. 'I'm fighting for my right to love whom I choose,' she said loftily. 'I'm not giving Jimmy up; not now, not ever.'

Vera was already in bed and sitting up when Arthur pulled back the covers to get into bed himself.

'Don't put out the lamp yet, Arthur,' Vera said. 'I want to talk to you about Gill.'

Arthur's heart sank, but he tried not to show he was disturbed. 'What about her?'

'She tells me you've stopped her from seeing that nice boy, Jimmy Tomkin,' Vera said. 'It's not like you, Arthur, to be so heavy-handed. What's the reason?'

Arthur felt like a rat caught in a trap as he put his head on the pillow and pulled the covers up around his ears.

'Not now, Vera, love,' he mumbled. 'I'm too tired to talk.'

'Gill is very upset,' Vera continued. 'I think she fancies she's in love with him.' She gave a laugh. 'It's nonsense, of course, but you can't tell a young girl that. She has her dreams.'

'Go to sleep, Vera, love.' He reached out a hand and put out the lamp, leaving the room in darkness.

'You've done the wrong thing in forbidding their friendship, Arthur,' Vera said. 'If you'd left them to it I'd give it a month. By that time Gill's fancy would have turned elsewhere.'

Arthur was silent, pretending to be asleep. Although he knew he wouldn't get much sleep tonight. Knowing Vera as he did she wouldn't let the matter rest. What the heck was he to say to her in the morning?

Gillian, the little minx! he thought. She was growing more like her mother every day.

Vera's features froze when she answered the door the following morning to find Henry standing on the step.

'What do you want?' she asked abrasively.

'I thought we had a truce, Vera.'

'Think again. Now why are you here?'

'I've come to see Dorothy,' Henry said. There was a tremor in his voice and Vera wondered at it. 'How long must I stand here on the doorstep?'

Vera grudgingly moved aside and Henry came into the hall.

'It's not very convenient at the moment,' she

259

said stiffly.

Henry frowned. 'I hardly think I need an appointment to see my own daughter.'

Vera sniffed. Although her relationship with Dorothy had changed she still felt animosity towards her brother. She wasn't convinced he could be trusted.

'She's upstairs, cleaning the bedrooms,' she told him.

Henry raised his eyebrows. 'You talk as though she's a domestic servant. I'm paying her way, Vera, remember.'

'It's her idea to do housework,' she said defensively. 'And she's very good at it – very thorough.'

Henry looked surprised. 'Well, can I see her, please?'

'Go into the back room,' Vera said. 'I'll tell her you're here.'

Henry went down the passage while Vera climbed the stairs to find Dorothy. She found her in the second-floor bedroom at the back. Dorothy was on her hands and knees, applying lavender polish to the linoleum.

Vera permitted herself a secret smile. She had to admit that she could never see Gillian getting down to work like that. Dorothy had a lot of Prosser in her.

'Your father's here to see you,' Vera announced.

Dorothy straightened up but remained on her knees, her head bowed. 'I don't want to see him,' she said quietly.

'What?'

'I mean it, Aunt Vera,' Dorothy insisted. 'Tell him to go away. I've nothing to say to him.'

'Well!'

Dorothy bent forward again and began to polish vigorously, even angrily, Vera thought with curiosity.

'Tell him he can forget me as he's forgotten the rest of my family.'

'Dorothy, are you sure you know what—'

'I'm finished with him!'

Vera left the girl where she was and went downstairs. She was pensive as she made her way to the back room, wondering how Henry would take the news that his daughter had washed her hands of him. But why? That's what Vera wanted to know.

'She doesn't want to see you,' Vera said, watching his face carefully. She saw pain cross his face.

'She must see me,' he said. 'I have to talk to her to explain.'

'I don't think she's interested, Henry,' Vera said. 'In fact, she told me to say she's finished with you.'

He put his hand to his forehead and bowed his head. 'I wouldn't have had this happen for the world,' he said miserably. 'I have to make her understand.'

'Understand what?' asked Vera. 'Is it because you've left Gloria?'

Henry looked up at her, his glance wary. Vera's curiosity was stirred further.

'I'll just go upstairs and see her,' he said, walking towards the door.

261

Vera moved quickly to intercept him. 'No, Henry,' she said brusquely. 'Dorothy's made up her mind.'

'But she's my daughter!'

'And this is *my* house, remember,' said Vera firmly. 'You'd better leave.'

His shoulders sagged and he walked dejectedly into the passage. Vera followed him to the front door. There was something going on here between her brother and her niece that she did not understand.

She had no secrets herself and always spoke her mind without fear or favour. The thought that she was being kept in ignorance of family matters riled her. She would get to the bottom of this.

Henry paused on the doorstep. 'I'll call tomorrow round about the same time,' he said. 'Perhaps she'll see me after sleeping on it.'

Vera lifted her chin. 'I wouldn't count on it, Henry. To me she seems a very determined young woman who knows her own mind.'

He opened his mouth to reply and then seemed to think better of it. He nodded to her and strode away down the street towards his car.

Vera stood on the step, watching him until he drove away, and then she turned and marched swiftly up the stairs. Dorothy had finished the linoleum and was now giving the wardrobe a good going-over.

'Put down that duster, Dorothy,' Vera commanded. 'I want to talk to you properly.'

Dorothy kept her back turned. 'I've nothing to say.'

'Oh, I think you have, my girl. And you owe me an explanation.'

Reluctantly Dorothy turned around and Vera saw with surprise that her eyes were red with crying.

'What on earth is the matter?'

'I can't talk about it. I'm too ashamed.'

Vera jerked back in horror. 'Good heavens, Dorothy! You're not in any trouble, are you? You know what I mean.'

'No!' Her denial came with flushed cheeks and an averted gaze that Vera noted.

'Then what's all this fuss with your father?'

'He's betrayed us all!' Dorothy blurted out. She rushed to the bed and flopped on to it, wiping away tears.

'Well, I've discovered he's shifty and conniving to my cost,' she said. 'But how has he betrayed you?'

Dorothy swallowed her sobs with obvious difficulty. She looked up, giving Vera an accusing glance.

'Oh, you *must* know,' she said, her tone sarcastic. 'You're his sister, after all. Uncle Arthur knows and so does Gill. She's the one who told me.'

Vera pursed her lips and sat on the bed, trying to keep control of her growing anger.

'Told you what, my girl?'

Dorothy stared at her with surprise in her eyes.

'Don't you know that he's been keeping a fancy woman on the side for years and years?' She paused as a great sob escaped her. Her eyes were filled with tears and she continued. 'Don't

263

you know about his illegitimate son?'

Vera bounced off the bed. 'What?'

Dorothy rose, too, dabbing at her wet eyes with a handkerchief.

'His fancy woman lives in Fleet Street.' She gulped. 'I've been there. I've seen her. She's as plain as mutton. Not a bit fashionable like my mother.'

Vera could hardly believe her ears. She had known ever since their mother's will had been read that her brother was underhanded and devious, but now it appeared he had sunk to further depths of depravity. Had she ever really known him?

'What's the name of this flibbertigibbet who's got her claws into him?'

'Florrie Tomkin,' Dorothy told her.

Vera paused, puzzled. 'Tomkin? Where have I heard that name before?'

'Jimmy Tomkin,' Dorothy volunteered. 'He's Uncle Arthur's apprentice.'

Vera's mouth dropped open and she was speechless for a moment.

'Oh my God!' she said at last. 'He's been here under my roof.' She sat down on the bed again. 'Now I begin to understand what Arthur is up to.'

She had puzzled over Arthur's uncharacteristic behaviour in banning Gillian's friend, Jimmy. Now everything was clear. Her husband must have known who this young lad was all along. And he had kept it from her. Infuriated, Vera ground her teeth.

'I can't forgive my father,' Dorothy said with

another sob. 'I don't think I ever will.'

'I know exactly how you feel,' Vera said ominously. 'Arthur has a lot of explaining to do.' She glanced at the sobbing girl. 'Go and make yourself a cup of tea and I'll have one, too. You can finish off the bedrooms later.'

Gillian came home from work first, but Vera said nothing to her about what she had discovered. She was saving her ire for Arthur. She was beside herself with rage to think that after all the years they had been married he had kept quiet about such an important family matter.

He came into the kitchen, still in his overalls as usual, and dumped his tin lunch box on the table.

'I'll have some pickled onions with my corned beef sandwiches tomorrow, love,' he said cheerfully.

His happy and contented expression was too much for her.

The rolling pin was still on the table. Vera picked it up and then brought it down on the tabletop with a tremendous crash.

'Whaaat!'

She felt some satisfaction when Arthur nearly jumped six feet into the air. His eyes were bulging as he stared at her.

'Vera! What the hell—?'

'How dare you?' she asked pithily. 'How dare you keep me in the dark about what's happening in my own family?'

Arthur blinked. 'Keeping you in the dark? I don't know what you mean, Vera, love.'

'Don't come the old soldier with me, Arthur

Finch!' Vera howled. 'How long have you known about Henry's fancy piece?'

Arthur's face turned white and then red. His lips moved but no words came out.

'Well?' Vera glared at him, waiting.

He made a pacifying motion with his hands. 'Vera, love, let's quieten down, shall we?' he said breathlessly. 'I don't understand.'

'Liar!' Vera shrieked. 'You've been keeping secrets from me; things about my own family that I should know. How could you, Arthur?'

He pulled out a chair from under the table and sat. 'Now don't get all up in the air, Vera, love. You're making something out of nothing.'

'Nothing?' Vera screwed her lips in fury. 'I find out that my brother has been keeping another woman for years and has an illegitimate son by her and all you can say is it's nothing.'

Arthur ran his tongue over his lips nervously. 'Henry made me promise.'

'I'm your wife!' Vera shouted. 'You and I don't have secrets.' She stared accusingly at him. 'At least I thought we didn't. I'm beginning to wonder what kind of a treacherous monster I married.'

Arthur jumped to his feet. 'Now steady on, Vera,' he said, his tone grumpy. 'That's a bit strong. Henry told me in confidence about his relationship with Florrie Tomkin, and he is my boss, don't forget.'

'He's also my brother and your brother-in-law,' Vera said. 'I had a right to know.'

'Oh, and what would you have done about it if I had told you?'

Vera flicked her tongue over her lips, bewildered for a moment. 'I'd have faced him about it,' she said at last.

'Yes, making trouble, when it's none of your business,' Arthur rejoined quickly.

'It is my business,' Vera said. Indignant, she stretched her neck. 'Henry has besmirched my family name with his sinful behaviour.'

'Huh!' Arthur looked impatient. 'Piffle! I might have done the same if I'd been married to Gloria.'

'I tell you Prossers have always been looked up to around here,' Vera insisted angrily.

'Oh, really! Well, what about your father, William?' Arthur asked sharply. 'Him disappearing and, from what I've heard, a lot of money disappeared at the same time.'

'What?' Vera was incensed. 'That's not true. You've just made that up to spite me, Arthur.'

'I'm sorry, Vera, love. You're right and I shouldn't have said it.' Arthur took a step towards her. 'Don't let's quarrel over this, love. It's Henry's business. Nothing to do with us.'

'What I can't forgive, Arthur, is that you deceived me by keeping quiet,' Vera said. 'I have a right to know.' She took in a deep breath. 'You saw fit to enlighten our daughter, I see. Gillian blabbed to Dorothy about it and now Dorothy won't have anything to do with her father.'

Arthur put his hand to his face and rubbed his jaw. 'I had to tell Gill,' he said reasonably. 'She was getting too fond of that lad Jimmy. I had to warn her he was her blood cousin.'

Vera had to concede that made sense, but it still

rankled. 'You could've told me, too.'

'I thought what you didn't know wouldn't hurt you,' Arthur said. 'I was in a bind, Vera, love. Henry made me promise.' He smiled at her tentatively. 'And you know I'm a man who always keeps his promises.'

Vera lifted her chin. 'It's no good, Arthur,' she said stiffly. 'I'm in no mood to forgive you.'

Arthur took another step towards her but hesitated when Gillian came running into the kitchen.

'What's happening, Mam? Has there been an accident or something?' Gillian asked looking anxiously from one to the other. 'It's ten past six! Everybody's waiting to eat. I've never known you be late with a meal before.'

Vera shook herself together with difficulty.

'Where's Dorothy?' she asked sharply. 'Ask her to give me a hand serving the plates. And you can help, too, miss!' Vera went on. 'After we've eaten I've a bone to pick with you, too.'

After another puzzled look at both of them, Gillian went out.

Uncharacteristically, Vera felt she wanted to cry but struggled with it.

'Vera, love?' Arthur's voice was soft, coaxing.

She turned her back on him. 'I don't think I'll get over this, Arthur,' she said through quivering lips. 'I feel let down by my family. I trusted you. You're my husband.'

'I'm sorry.'

Vera sniffed back the tears and then swung around to face him.

'And so you should be!' she exclaimed loudly,

her spirit returning. 'You can sleep in the boys' room tonight.'

'What?'

'You heard me.' Vera marched to the stove, where pots and pans were simmering. 'Now, get out of the kitchen, please. I have a meal to serve.'

Nineteen

The following morning Gillian came into the inner office, her eyes as round as saucers.

'Uncle Henry, there's a policeman outside. He wants to talk to you.'

Henry rose to his feet, feeling a tremor of alarm. His thoughts went immediately to Norman Meeker. He had forgotten to ring the hospital this morning. If the man died Andy would be facing a manslaughter charge, if not murder.

'Send him in, Gill.'

The uniformed man strode in and Henry recognized him as Constable Williams.

'Morning, sir.' The constable took off his helmet.

'Has something happened, officer?' Henry felt his mouth go dry with fear.

'Yes, sir,' the constable said. 'Mr Meeker has recovered consciousness.'

Henry put his hand to his forehead and sat

down heavily. 'Thank God!'

'He has named his attacker,' the constable continued in an official tone. 'Andrew Prosser is now wanted for robbery with violence; a very serious charge, sir.'

Resigned, Henry nodded. 'I realize that, officer,' he said.

It was no more than he had expected, but at the same time it was a blow that it was now official.

'Do you know where your son is at the moment, sir?'

'No, I'm not sure, Constable,' Henry hedged.

'Well, we know where he is, sir,' Constable Williams said smugly. 'He's been under observation for some time. Two officers went up the Smoke earlier today to fetch him back.' He paused, giving Henry a keen look. 'Him and his mother.'

'What do you want with my wife?'

'I have to advise you that Mrs Prosser is also likely to be put on a charge.'

Henry wetted his lips nervously. Even though he could never live with her again – disliked her, even – he did not want her to go through that disgrace.

'But she was only doing what any mother would do,' he said reasonably. 'Looking after her son.'

'The law sees it different.' Williams shrugged. 'Anyway, my superiors are looking into that.'

'I see.'

'Andrew Prosser will be taken into custody,' Williams said. 'Mrs Prosser will be allowed to return home – for the moment.'

Henry nodded. He did not know what to say or think.

Constable Williams put on his helmet and adjusted the strap under his chin.

'Well, that's all for now, sir,' he said in a more cheerful tone. 'We'll inform you when your son is officially charged. You may want to be present.'

'Yes, thank you,' Henry said vaguely, his mind in a whirl.

When the police officer had gone Henry went into the outer office. He had not had the heart to get a replacement for Norman Meeker, but Gillian was coping remarkably well under the circumstances and he was glad he had taken her on.

'Gill, I've got to go out,' he said distractedly. 'Keep everything ticking over, will you? I'll be back as soon as I can.'

'Yes, Uncle Henry.'

He was just about to go through the door when he remembered to ask. 'By the way, how is Dorothy?'

Gillian's gaze shifted away from his. 'She's all right,' she answered with reticence.

Henry gave a heavy sigh. 'I understand, Gill. I was just asking.'

He went immediately to his former home. His aunt Cissie was in the kitchen, making a pot of tea.

'I wondered when you would remember I live here and am still alive,' she said to him. There was just a touch of reproach in her tone.

'I'm sorry, Aunt Cissie. There's so much going on.'

She sat down and poured him a cup of tea also.

'Andy has been arrested,' he said gloomily as he took a seat at the table, drawing the cup and saucer towards him. 'The police are bringing him and Gloria back to Swansea today.'

He knew it was inevitable and was only what the lad deserved, but it was hard to accept.

'Gloria must be furious.'

'She may be charged, too.'

Cissie's eyebrows shot up. 'Oh, dear!'

'They'll probably arrive in Swansea late this evening. Gloria will be coming home. I thought I'd warn you.'

Cissie looked thoughtful. 'She'll never let me stay here now. She won't rest until I'm out.'

'I won't have it!' Henry exclaimed heatedly.

'It's best I go, Henry. I don't want to make more trouble between you,' she said. 'You've got enough on your plate, as it is.'

'Where will you go?'

'I'll find lodgings,' she said. 'I had to do it before when your mother sold my old home from under me when she married Charlie Knox.' She gave a wan smile. 'I'll survive. I always do.'

Henry reached across the table and took her wrinkled hand in his.

'I hate this happening to you, Aunt Cissie,' he said sincerely. 'You've been more a mother to me and Vera than Rose ever was. All she cared about was Charlie.'

'Yes, well, I love you both like you were my own.' She paused. 'I go over and visit Vera often for a cup of tea, you know. We're still close in spite of her quarrel with you.'

Henry put his hand to his chin pondering. 'Vera might have room for you,' he said. 'I'll ask her.'

'I don't want charity,' Cissie said quickly. 'I can pay my way.'

'You won't pay for anything, Aunt Cissie,' Henry said firmly. 'Not while I'm alive and kicking.'

Cissie smiled at him. 'You were always a generous lad, Henry.' She winked at him. 'Generous with your love, too, I hear.'

Embarrassed to hear such words from his aunt, Henry felt hot blood flood his face. 'How long have you known?'

She chuckled. 'Almost from the start. I know Florrie Tomkin slightly. Always liked her. She has a fine son, too.'

Henry lifted his chin. 'Yes, I'm proud of Jimmy,' he said. 'And I'm just as ashamed of Andy.'

'Now, Henry, don't be too hard on Andy. He is your flesh and blood, too. And, if you don't mind me saying so, he's had a handicap in the shape of his mother.'

With a deep sigh Henry nodded. 'You're right, Aunt Cissie. And now Andy's about to pay for her stupidity.'

He thought of Dorothy. Gloria's lack of moral understanding had caused problems for their daughter, too.

'I do miss Dorothy,' Cissie said, and Henry thought she must have read his thoughts. 'How is she, Henry?'

'Very angry with me over Florrie and Jimmy,' Henry said sadly. 'She refuses to see me.'

'If Vera agrees to take me as a boarder, I'll talk Dorothy around,' Cissie said. 'Leave her to me.'

Henry stood up, leaned across and kissed his aunt's cheek.

'You're a wonder, Aunt Cissie,' he said, feeling the fondness for her in his heart grow even stronger. She was the only real mother he had ever known.

'Oh, go on with you, you soppy thing!' she said, smiling. 'Run along. You've got a business to see to.'

Later that day Henry followed Arthur through the front door and into the hall in Marlborough Road.

'I'm not sure this is a good idea, after all, Henry,' Arthur said. He sounded apprehensive and Henry had a similar feeling. 'Vera's still upset with me and she's not pleased with you at all.'

'I don't doubt it,' Henry said. 'But I know she'd shut the door in my face if I called in the normal way.'

Arthur turned to look at him anxiously. 'You'd better go in the back room. More private there. I'll tell Vera you're here.' He glanced at his pocket watch. 'But it's nearly six. Supper waits for no man in this house.'

Arthur went and Henry walked into the room and waited. He was too het up to sit and went over and over in his mind what he would say to his sister.

He waited for some considerable time. Finally the door opened and Vera walked in, shoulders back, chin high. Her eyes flashed sparks at him.

'How dare you set foot in my respectable home, you depraved womaniser!'

'Vera, please!'

'Don't you "Vera, please" me!' she snapped. 'I'm ashamed of your behaviour. My own brother, living over the brush with a wanton woman no better than she should be.'

Henry's anger flared. He did not care what was said about him, but he would not have Florrie's name sullied.

'Florrie is none of those things, Vera,' he burst out hotly. 'She's a loving wife and a good mother.'

'She's not your wife, though, is she?'

'As good as,' Henry declared. 'And she would have been if I'd met her first, before Gloria got her claws into me.'

'She's a scarlet woman!'

'I won't have you insult her,' Henry said strongly. 'I love Florrie dearly. As far as I'm concerned she is my wife.'

Vera's nostrils flared. 'You can't play fast and loose with morals and get away with it. You've disgraced the Prosser name.'

'To hell with the Prosser name!' Henry bellowed. 'What have the Prossers got to be proud of? A runaway father who didn't give a damn about his children.' Henry swallowed hard. 'He was probably an embezzler, too.'

'Ooh!' Vera took a step back, her hands to her

face. 'That is a vicious lie! How could you, Henry? Our own father.'

'Because it's true, Vera,' Henry said. 'Yes, I've come to that conclusion.'

'Dorothy is humiliated, too,' Vera said defensively.

Henry did not need to be reminded. 'She doesn't understand,' he said. 'My life with Gloria was miserable from the beginning. Meeting Florrie opened my eyes to what love really is.'

Vera clapped both hands over her ears. 'I don't want to hear such disgraceful talk,' she said hurriedly. 'I do want you to leave my house this minute.'

'You don't know what I've come for yet.'

'I don't want to know.'

'It's about Aunt Cissie,' Henry persisted, ignoring her denial. 'Gloria is about to evict her. She has nowhere to go. I was hoping you'd take her as a boarder. I'll pay any costs.'

'No!'

Henry looked at her aghast. 'What?' He frowned. 'You refuse to help your aunt, your own flesh and blood, and a Prosser to boot.' Vera sniffed, looked obstinate but remained silent. 'Aren't you forgetting what Aunt Cissie did for us?' he added. 'She brought us up after Dad left. God knows what would've happened to us if it hadn't been for her.' He stared at her closed expression for a moment. 'Now she's old and vulnerable and you turn your back on her. You're the one that should be ashamed, Vera.'

'How dare you?'

'You're angry with me, Vera, but why take it out on Aunt Cissie? She's the least culpable member of our family.'

Vera sat down heavily in the nearest chair. 'I do care about her,' she insisted. 'I'm very fond of Aunt Cissie. She often comes for a chat and a cup of tea. I enjoy her visits.'

'Well, then?'

Vera looked up at him, her lips thin. 'I might be able to make room. I'm willing to take in Aunt Cissie purely for her sake,' she said. 'But you're not welcome here, Henry. I want nothing more to do with you. You're a disgrace!'

Henry was relieved that she had agreed to take Cissie. It was a load lifted from his shoulders.

'There is something else I should tell you,' Henry said. 'The Prosser name will have mud slung at it again. The police have Andy in custody for the robbery at the yard and for the attack on Norman Meeker. It'll be all over the *Cambrian Leader* in a day or two, I expect.' He paused. 'Gloria might also be charged with something.'

Vera looked crestfallen. 'I won't be able to hold my head up at the Co-op. Everyone will be whispering behind my back.'

'You'll survive,' Henry said dryly. 'You're the sort that always does.'

She flashed him a look of anger. He knew it was no good asking after Dorothy and it would only stir things up more if he insisted. He put on his trilby.

'I'll go now, Vera,' he said. 'Florrie will be wondering where I am.'

277

Vera gave a disparaging sniff but remained silent.

'I'll tell Aunt Cissie she can move in any time she likes, right?'

She nodded, her glance averted.

'Well, goodbye, Vera, and thank you.' He strode towards the door. 'I'll see myself out.'

Henry decided he must be at the house when Gloria returned. He stationed himself at the front drawing-room window and waited. He'd heard it would be today. It was quite late when a police car dropped her outside the entrance. She walked slowly down the drive, shoulders hunched and head bowed. Henry was struck by the fact that she looked older.

He met her in the hall. Her expression froze when she saw him. 'What are *you* doing here?'

'I want to know what's happening to Andy,' he said. 'How bad is it?'

She stared at him silently, seething in rage. She pulled off her kid gloves and then turned her back to take off her hat and coat.

'Well?'

She rounded on him, eyes flashing. 'Don't pretend you care, Henry. Get back to that slut you're living with and leave us alone.'

Henry held his temper with difficulty. 'Andy will need a lawyer,' he said through gritted teeth. 'Who do you think is going to pay for that?'

'So you should!' she exclaimed. 'Are you complaining?'

Before he could answer she walked swiftly into the drawing room. Henry quickly followed.

Another row was looming, but he was beyond caring.

'As a matter of fact, yes,' he barked. 'I blame you, Gloria, for the way Andy has turned out.' She spun around, her expression furious. 'Oh! That's rich!' she retorted. 'When did you ever give time to Andy? You were too busy with your other family; pampering your bastard son.'

He wanted to strike her but resisted with difficulty. He would not sink to those depths.

'I wouldn't be here now if I wasn't concerned for Andy,' Henry said. 'He's turned bad, but he's still my son.'

Gloria did not answer. She sat down on the sofa, opened her handbag, and took out a packet of cigarettes. 'Give me a light,' she muttered morosely.

Henry took his lighter out of his pocket and lit her cigarette. He had always hated to see her smoking, but Gloria thought herself a very modern woman.

'Andy's in the cells at the police station in Alexandra Road. I was there when he was charged.' She glanced up at Henry. 'He's very frightened, Henry, and so am I. What will become of him?'

'He'll have to pay, Gloria. He almost killed Norman Meeker – and for what?'

'It wasn't his fault!' Gloria whimpered. 'He was led astray. He told me.'

'By whom?'

'Tom Finch and that Tomkin boy; your illegitimate son.' She glowered. 'They planned it. They were in it together, but Andy got caught.'

Henry shook his head. 'He's lying, Gloria,' he said harshly. 'Norman Meeker came out of his coma in the early hours this morning. He named Andy as the only attacker.'

'Meeker's covering up for the others,' Gloria whimpered.

'Don't be a bloody fool, Gloria!' Henry exclaimed impatiently. 'Why would he do that?' He was silent for a moment and when he spoke his tone was gentler. 'Face facts, Gloria. Andy's no good.'

It hurt him to admit it.

She leapt to her feet. 'Get out!' she screamed at him. 'And take your bloody aunt with you!'

'Aunt Cissie is coming with me, don't you worry,' Henry said angrily. 'I knew you'd take your spite out on her. I've already made arrangements for her to lodge with my sister.'

'For God's sake take her and go! Go! The pair of you.'

Too livid to speak another word to her, Henry went out into the hall and ran up the stairs two at a time. He hurried along the passage to his aunt's room and knocked. He went in when she called out.

She was sitting on the bed, dressed to go out, two small suitcases at her feet.

'I'm ready, Henry,' she said calmly.

He indicated the suitcases. 'Is this all you're taking?'

She gave him a wan smile. 'I've never owned much in my life. Just a few bits of clothes.' She pressed her lips together. 'Not much to show for myself after all these years.'

'Possessions don't mean a thing,' Henry said bitterly. 'Look at Gloria for example. You are loved, Aunt Cissie. Believe me, that's all that counts.'

Cissie stood up. 'We'd better go.'

'Yes,' Henry said, picking up the cases. 'Let's get the hell out of this house for good.'

Twenty

Charlie Knox's house, 1906

Charlie felt a little disconcerted to find Rose standing on the doorstep of his home at midday on the last day of November. There was an expression of elation on her face.

'I wasn't expecting you, Rose,' he said shortly as she pushed past him and walked confidently into the drawing room. 'George and I are just about to sit down to eat. Then we both have to get back to the yard.'

He followed her into the sitting room.

'You may not want to go back to work once you've heard my news,' she said, and he could see she was overexcited.

She stood in the middle of the room, waving some documents at him. 'It's official, Charlie. William is declared dead! I'm a widow at last!'

He stared at her in consternation. She flicked her dark hair back over her shoulder in an impatient gesture.

'Well? Don't just stand there. Say something, Charlie!' she exclaimed. 'This is what we've both been waiting for. Now we can get married as soon as we like.'

'When did the papers arrive?' He wanted to play for time. He had banked on the whole process taking longer. Rose had made the application only a few months ago. He wasn't sure he was prepared for that last step after all this time.

'This morning's post,' she answered.

She slipped her coat off her shoulders, threw it on the nearest chair and then whirled around, looking about her at the room.

'First thing I'll do is redecorate, starting with this room.' There was a disdainful smile on her face. 'Freda never had much sense of style, did she? But then she was rather unremarkable herself,' she said airily. 'I don't know why you married her.'

'Redecorate? What are you talking about?'

'Well, after we're married I'll be moving in here with you, of course.'

'I see.'

'I'm selling William's house.' She laughed delightedly. 'Well, it's my house now. I'm putting it on the market this afternoon.'

Charlie ran his tongue over his lips. 'Don't you think you're rushing things?'

She stared at him. 'Rushing things? I've been waiting seven years to marry you, Charlie. That's a long time for a woman to wait.'

He arched his eyebrows. 'Yes, and we were all in all to each other all those years, too, as though we *were* married,' he reminded her. 'What's the rush to change things now?'

She stood stock still, her nostrils flaring. 'What's happening, Charlie? Are you telling me you don't want to marry me?'

'Of course I'm not saying that,' Charlie answered quickly.

He wondered for a moment whether he really meant it. The arrangement they had suited him fine. Marriage might change what they had.

She lifted her chin challengingly. 'Then get a special licence tomorrow,' she said. Her dark gaze pierced his. 'Have you another woman on the string, Charlie? Is that it?'

'No!'

'Then why hesitate?' She stared at him. 'What's changed between us?'

He shook his head. 'Nothing's changed.'

He did not know what he was feeling. He needed her, could not live without her, but something bothered him.

She came towards him and put her hand on his chest, looking up into his face with that certain smile that never failed to send his heart racing like a locomotive.

'Is it George?' she asked softly. 'You can tell him I've no intention of taking Freda's place in his life.' She laughed. 'He's too old for a mamma anyway.'

She had hit a nerve and Charlie pushed her away, suddenly angered. 'George's opinion is important in any decision I make.'

George had made his dislike of Rose very plain over the years. At eighteen his son was a man now and his opinion counted. Maybe marriage with Rose was not such a good idea if it alienated his only son.

'You're putting George first, before me!' Her face twisted in fury. 'You swine! You've been leading me on all these years.'

'No!'

He was worried all at once. He wanted their arrangement to remain as it was, but he could not lose her either. He must be clever.

'I do want to marry you,' he evaded. 'In fact, I want to make life as easy as possible for you, Rose. When we marry you can make over all your share of the business to me.'

He knew her well enough to guess how she would react to that. But even if he was wrong, gaining complete control of the business might make the marriage worthwhile.

She stepped away and looked at him, her face expressionless now. 'Is that a condition, Charlie?' she asked, her tone cold.

In silence he swung away and walked to the fireplace to lean an elbow on it and then turned his head to look at her.

'I wouldn't put it quite like that,' he said carefully. 'I think I should get something out of the marriage, too.'

'You get me, what more could you want?' she asked acidly.

'Rose, be reasonable,' he said. 'It makes sense that when you're my wife I have complete control of the business now that William is declared dead.'

Her lips twisted into a smirk. 'You must think

I'm as big a fool as Freda was,' she said. 'I know what you're after. If anything happened to you, George would inherit everything and Henry would get nothing from the business his father built up.'

Stung and further angered, Charlie stepped away from the fireplace.

'I built up the business, Rose. Me!' He walked quickly towards her. 'After old Samuel died I kept that place going single-handed. William was still apprenticing.' He ground his teeth in anger. 'Your husband never had a clue about business.' He poked at his chest with his forefinger. 'It was *me*. I made it a success. And I continued to do that after William buggered off.'

'We both know why he did that.'

'Oh, come on, Rose, don't pretend his going bothered you one bit.'

She gave him a haughty look. 'Frankly, I was glad to see the back of him.'

'Well, then,' Charlie said. 'You admit I have an exclusive right to the business.'

'No!' She looked stubborn. 'I won't sign my share over to you. That goes to Henry when I'm gone.'

'Then there's no point in my marrying you, Rose, is there?' he said in an offhand way.

'Oh, you'll marry me, Charlie,' she said triumphantly. 'You're forgetting about the money.'

'What money?'

'The money you embezzled.' She smiled. 'You let William take the blame for that. It was so convenient for you that he pushed off as soon as the money was discovered missing.'

'William took it.'

'No, he didn't, Charlie.' She shook her head. 'I was there in your bedroom when you confessed to him, remember? Besides, I can prove it.'

He stared at her. 'How? William is gone, so is old Kitson. They were the only ones who knew the truth.'

She gave him a knowing look. 'Wrong! Norman Meeker knew, too. He told me about it the day after William disappeared. He's known it was you all along.'

'What are you going to do?'

'Nothing, Charlie. I'll soon be your ever-loving wife.'

Charlie sat pondering in the drawing room after Rose left. He had underestimated her and she now believed she had the upper hand.

He was so deep in thought he did not hear that someone had come into the room until he spoke.

'She's got you exactly where she wants you, hasn't she, Dad?'

Charlie lifted his head to gaze up at his son. George was tall and broad-shouldered, even brawny, but he had the gentle eyes of his mother, Freda.

'You seem to make a habit of eavesdropping,' Charlie answered sourly.

'I'd have to be stone deaf not to hear what was said between you,' George said. 'Is it true, Dad? Did you take that money?'

Charlie rose to his feet. 'It's none of your business, George.'

'You never give a straight answer to anything,

do you, Dad?' George said heatedly. 'You could tie poor Mam up in knots with your evasiveness, but not me.'

'All right!' Charlie burst out. 'I took it. William was useless, while I was breaking my back making something of that business. I earned that money.'

'It was theft.'

'It's ancient history.'

'Rose doesn't think so,' George said quickly. He hesitated before saying, 'You know how much I despise her, Dad. I can't forgive her for the way she hurt Mam. The both of you broke Mam's heart.'

'No,' Charlie denied emphatically. 'Your mother never knew. I was careful.'

'Huh!' George scoffed with disdain. 'You deceive yourself as much as you deceive others, Dad. But you'd better think again about marrying Rose Prosser because you'll regret it.'

'I'll do what I must!'

George's expression was despairing. 'Mam was gentle, loving and loyal, while Rose is as cold as snow in winter,' he said quietly.

'You're too young to understand, George.'

'Well, young as I am, I understand this. Rose Prosser is no good and the day she comes into this house as your wife is the day I move out to lodgings, Dad.' He shook his head. 'I mean it. I won't live under the same roof as that woman.'

George turned on his heel and strode from the room.

'George! Wait!'

But his son had gone and Charlie heard the

front door slam shut. Slowly he sat down again.

George was angry. He didn't mean it about leaving home, Charlie thought. Anyway, he would have to marry Rose now; he had no choice. Eventually he would persuade her to hand over her share of the yard, he was certain. He had always planned that George would get everything in the end. And so he would.

'Henry! Take your finger out of that mixing bowl!'

Henry jerked his hand away from the bowl on the kitchen table and then licked his finger, grinning.

'Tastes nice,' he said. 'What are you making, Aunt Cissie?'

'Welsh cakes for tea,' she said, grinning back.

'Can we have fairy cakes as well?' Vera asked.

'I'll see,' Cissie said. She smiled fondly at her niece. 'It's about time you started learning to cook yourself, Vera. After all, you are thirteen now; nearly a woman.'

'I'm taking cooking classes in school,' Vera said proudly.

'Huh!' Cissie grunted. 'I can teach you all you need to know right here.'

'Where's Mam?' Henry asked. 'She had a letter this morning and seemed excited about it. Who was it from, Aunt Cissie?'

'Your mother doesn't take me into her confidence,' Cissie said dryly.

It was more than secretiveness on Rose's part. Cissie knew her sister-in-law looked upon her as more of an unpaid servant than a relative and did not consider her opinion of family matters as important.

'If it's about the business I think she ought to tell *me*,' Henry said peevishly. 'I'll be sixteen next year. I'll be starting my apprenticeship a year after that. I'm entitled to know.'

'Your mother will do exactly as she pleases, as usual,' Cissie said.

She thought about her brother William then, as she often did. It was more than seven years since he had left – disappeared under a cloud, many people thought – but she would never believe the rumours that he had embezzled money from the business. It just was not in his nature.

If only he had made his reasons for leaving clear at the start, but there had never been one word from him or a sign that he was still alive in all that time. It was as though he was dead. She had finished grieving a long time ago.

'I think she's gone over to Uncle Charlie's,' Vera opined, pushing her long, dark hair behind one ear as she studied Cissie's cookery book. 'I saw her putting rouge on.'

Cissie exchanged a glance with Henry, who looked away quickly, obviously embarrassed.

'The letter must be about business, then,' Cissie said matter-of-factly. 'She's gone to talk to him about it.' She bustled over to the sink. 'Come on, you two. Help me with the washing-up.'

They had just finished when Rose walked into the kitchen. Her face was flushed, Cissie noticed, and her glance sparked. Immediately

Cissie knew something unpleasant was about to happen.

'Cissie, I want to talk to you in private in the drawing room,' Rose said without preamble.

'I'm just doing a bit of cooking,' Cissie said. 'Can't it wait?'

'No, it can't!' Rose said forcefully.

'What was in that letter, Mam?' Henry asked. 'I've as much right to know about the business as Uncle Charlie.'

Rose's lips stretched into a thin line. 'You'll be told when I'm ready to tell you, so be quiet,' she said. 'Cissie! Now!'

Cissie wiped her hands on a cloth before complying. Looking at Rose's hard face she was filled with foreboding. Whatever Rose wanted to say to her, it was a serious matter.

Suddenly she wondered if there had been news of William.

'Is it about my brother?' she asked apprehensively. 'Have you heard anything about his whereabouts?'

'No,' Rose said.

Cissie followed her into the drawing room, the children on her heels.

'You two are not wanted in here,' Rose said to them. 'Go back to the kitchen until I call you.'

'But, Mam, I think—' Henry started, but Rose cut him short.

'Do as you're told for once!' she exclaimed loudly. 'And stay out of mischief.'

After one look of hopeless appeal to his aunt, Henry went out, taking Vera along with him.

'You're wrong to treat Henry like a child,'

Cissie said, feeling sorry for the boy. 'He understands more than you give him credit for.'

'How I treat my children is none of your concern,' Rose snapped.

'In my opinion—' Cissie began, but Rose talked her down.

'I'm not interested in *your* opinion, Cissie, or in you for that matter,' Rose said. 'You're always interfering between me and the children.' She looked triumphant. 'Well, that will stop now because I'm selling this house. You'll have to go elsewhere.'

Cissie was taken aback. 'What?'

'You might as well know,' Rose continued. 'I'll be marrying Charlie Knox quite soon. The children and I will be moving into his house. There will be no room for you.'

'Selling William's house?' Cissie was aghast. 'You can't do that. It's not yours to sell.'

Rose took an envelope out of her pocket and withdrew a legal-looking document.

'The house and everything else is mine,' she stated, giving Cissie a challenging look. 'I have had William declared officially dead. I am his sole beneficiary.' She thrust the document towards Cissie. 'Go on. Read it for yourself.'

Cissie took the document with shaking fingers, read the contents and then looked up at Rose in a daze.

'But this house is the Prosser family home,' she said shakily. 'My father built it. I was born here. I've never lived anywhere else.'

Rose sniffed disdainfully. 'Well, here's a chance for you to make a new start somewhere else.'

'Somewhere else?' Cissie knew a growing sense of panic. 'But where? I've nowhere else to go.'

'Yes, well that's been half the trouble, hasn't it?' Rose said spitefully. 'You've had it pretty easy all these years, cosseted first by your father and then William. It's about time you learned what it's like in the real world.'

'Easy!' Cissie felt her self-control snap. 'Easy! I've worked my fingers to the bone all my life!' she burst out heatedly. 'And you were quick to make a skivvy out of me, too.'

'What?' Rose's eyes sparked again.

'I've cooked, I've cleaned,' Cissie continued. 'And I've brought up your children while you were busy entertaining yourself with Charlie Knox.'

Rose gave a loud gasp of disbelief.

'Oh! Don't deny it, Rose!' Cissie shouted. 'You've made use of me as an unpaid servant from the day you married William.'

'How dare you?'

'All my life I've had to watch my P's and Q's, being dependent on others,' Cissie flared wrathfully. 'Well now, since you're chucking me out, out of the only home I have ever known, I can say what I think at last.'

'Why, you dried up old hag,' Rose screeched. 'Don't you speak to me like that. Who do you think you are?'

'I'll tell you who I am,' Cissie yelled. 'I'm the one who kept your home together when you couldn't be bothered, and this is all the thanks I

292

get. Evicted for my trouble.'

Rose's face was stony cold. 'I was prepared to give you a month's notice for you to find suitable lodgings,' she said harshly. 'But after this performance you can get out as soon as you like.'

'That suits me!' Cissie stormed as Henry and Vera came dashing into the room.

'What's happening, Aunt Cissie?' Henry cried out. 'Why are you both quarrelling?'

'Your mother is evicting me, that's what,' Cissie said angrily. 'She's selling this house from under us.'

'Mam? What's Aunt Cissie talking about? You can't sell Dad's house.' Henry hesitated, his face whitening. 'He might come back.'

'Your father is dead!' Rose exclaimed callously.

'My dad's not dead!' Vera sobbed. 'No, he's not!' She burst into tears and ran to Cissie.

Cissie quickly put her arms around the weeping girl.

'There, there, my lovely,' she said, trying to quell her own anger and sound soothing. 'Don't cry.'

Cissie was suddenly apprehensive for her. Vera was a sensitive girl and took things to heart so easily. Rose was careless of her daughter's feelings and lacked understanding.

'Stop that snivelling, Vera!' Rose ordered curtly. 'My God! Anyone would think you were three not thirteen.'

'Dad's not dead,' Vera wailed. 'I hate you for saying he is!'

'How would you like a slap, Vera?' Rose asked. 'You should be ashamed, talking to your mother like that. I wouldn't dare do that to my mother.'

Cissie noticed Henry's silence. He was just standing there, staring at his mother. He looked so much like his father at that moment that Cissie's heart received a jolt of pain.

'Henry, are you all right, love?' Cissie asked.

'If you're selling Dad's house,' Henry said to his mother, 'where will we live?'

Rose hesitated, pushing back her hair over one shoulder.

'I'll be marrying Uncle Charlie very soon,' she said carefully. 'We'll be living at his house.' She paused. 'Cissie is going into lodgings. There's no room for her at Uncle Charlie's.'

'I'm going with Aunt Cissie,' Vera declared. She had stopped crying now and there was a hint of stubbornness in her tone which reminded Cissie of Rose.

'You'll do as you're told, my girl!' Rose shouted. 'I won't put up with any nonsense from either of you, understand?'

'You can't marry Charlie,' Henry said flatly. 'You're still married to Dad.'

'Your father has been declared dead,' Rose said brusquely, and Cissie thought how insensitive she was with her children's feelings. 'It's all legal and here's the document to prove it. I'm free to marry again and I intend to marry Charlie.'

Henry looked appealingly at Cissie, but she shook her head helplessly.

'There's nothing I can do, Henry, love. Your mother has the law on her side.'

'I'm glad you finally understand that, Cissie,' Rose said exultantly. 'Now I don't want to be unfair. I'll give you a week to find another place. There are always plenty of rooms to let along the main road. I suggest you start looking tomorrow early.'

Rose turned to leave the room, ushering the protesting children out before her. Cissie flopped on to the nearest chair, her legs feeling weak all at once.

She permitted herself a sad smile as she considered her future. At least she wasn't destitute. It was a good thing that she had been careful with the small annuity her father had left her, but her savings would not last for ever either.

She would have to find a job. She was no stranger to hard work and there wasn't much she could not turn her hand to after keeping house first for her father and then her brother.

What hurt most about her new situation was the thought of leaving her old home. She would miss it so much. She doubted she would ever be happy again.

Cissie was in her room much later, packing her few belongings into two carpet bags. She would not cry, she told herself; at forty-seven she was far too old for that weakness.

She was just closing the bags and making them secure when she looked up and found Henry standing in the bedroom doorway. His young face was white and drawn. He was obviously unhappy, and she felt so sorry for him.

'I hate it that this is happening to you, Aunt Cissie,' he said with a catch in his voice. 'It's not fair. Vera's in her room, crying her eyes out over it.'

Cissie smiled at him. 'Life is rarely fair, Henry, love.'

'Vera and I will miss you, Aunt Cissie.' His voice faltered. 'There'll be no one to love us.'

'Oh, Henry, love!' Cissie went to him and put her arm around his shoulders. At fifteen he was almost as tall as she was. 'Your Mam loves you, deep down.'

'Huh! She never shows it.' He was struggling to hold back tears. 'All she cares about is Uncle Charlie.'

Cissie squeezed his shoulder. 'I'm not going to the ends of the earth, Henry, love,' she said, trying to sound light-hearted. 'I happen to know of a room I can rent in Ysgol Street. You and Vera can visit me as often as you like.'

'I wish we could come and live with you, Aunt Cissie,' he said. 'But I promise you faithfully that as soon as I have a home of my own you'll come and live with me.'

Cissie hugged him warmly. 'Henry, you're a sweet-natured boy. And I believe you will look after me in my old age.'

Henry left his aunt to the rest of her packing and went in search of his mother. At the risk of making her angry he was determined to speak his mind.

He found her in the sitting room, smoking a

cigarette at the end of a long holder and winced at the sight. He came and stood in front of her, planting his feet firmly on the hearth rug.

'I think the way you're treating Aunt Cissie is beastly!' he blurted out.

'You're just a child,' Rose said dismissively. 'You don't understand.'

'I understand that Vera and I will suffer from Aunt Cissie's leaving,' he said bitterly. 'At least she cares what happens to us. You don't care, Mam. You've neglected us all our lives. Aunt Cissie is more a mother than you'll ever be.'

Rose sprang to her feet, her expression furious. 'Why, you ungrateful little tyke!'

'Why should me and Vera be grateful to you?' Henry flared. 'We always come second to Charlie Knox.'

Without warning Rose stepped forward and struck him hard across his face with the flat of her hand. Henry recoiled, more shocked by her unexpected attack than by the pain in his cheek.

'You're as sanctimonious as your father was,' she grated.

'At least my father was honest,' Henry gasped, his hand still pressed against his stinging cheek.

'What is that supposed to mean?'

Henry could not answer. He had spoken out of instinct, and his instinct warned him that there was more to Charlie Knox than met the eye.

Rose stared at him for a moment, her expression cold.

'I'll tell you why you should be grateful to me,' she said in a hard voice. 'Charlie wanted my share of the business on our marriage. I refused because I want you to inherit and not George.' She glared at him. 'But after this outburst I may have to think again, Henry.'

Henry curled his lip. 'Do as you like, Mam,' he said, still holding his smacked cheek. 'You always do anyway.'

Twenty-One

Swansea, 1931

'Vera, you know I have no quarrel with your aunt coming to lodge here,' Arthur said reasonably as he buttoned up the coat of his flannelette pyjamas, 'but our Gill can't sleep on the settee in the drawing room for ever.'

'It's only for tonight,' Vera said.

'But where will we put Cissie? All the bedrooms are taken. We can't ask Miss Philpot to share.'

'Of course not,' Vera said, gathering her long hair into a hair net. 'Tomorrow we'll turn the back room into a bedroom. Gillian and Dorothy can share that. Aunt Cissie can have their room. It's really too small for two single beds anyway.'

Arthur climbed into bed. 'Well, as always, you have everything worked out, love.'

'Oh, yes,' Vera said with satisfaction. 'And Henry's under obligation to me. I'll teach him to cheat me!'

Arthur gave a heavy sigh. 'Can't we have done with that, Vera?' he said wearily. 'Henry's got a lot on his plate. Andy comes before the magistrates next week. It looks bad. There's bound to be a court case. I can't see him avoiding a jail sentence.'

'Huh! It's no surprise to me the way that boy has turned out,' Vera said disparagingly. 'Not with a father who swindles his own sister and brazenly lives over the brush with a loose woman. If my father were alive he'd die of shame.'

Arthur turned over in bed. 'Goodnight, love,' he said resignedly.

'I feel I'm causing a lot of trouble,' Cissie said as she watched Tom, Sam and Arthur lug furniture up and down the staircase after supper the following evening.

'It's no trouble at all,' Vera assured her. 'It was lucky Mrs Cornelius next door had a single bed to sell. Her daughter got married last week.'

'You're very good to me, Vera.'

Vera turned to look at her, a smile curving her lips. 'I remember how you looked after me when I was young, Aunt Cissie,' she said. 'Now it's my turn to look after you.'

Cissie felt a lump in her throat. Over the years she had been passed around the family like an unwanted piece of furniture. The only home she had ever loved was the house where she was born, but today, for the first time in a long while, she felt comfortable.

'I want to help all I can about the place,' Cissie

said eagerly. 'I'm not one to sit around idly.'

'Good gracious, Aunt Cissie! You're seventy-two now! You've earned a rest.' Vera patted her arm. 'You've done your share of work over the years,' she continued. 'I have good help in Dorothy. She's a wonder, that girl.' Vera sniffed. 'I can hardly believe she's Henry's child.'

'Don't be hard on him, Vera,' Cissie chided. 'He's a good man.'

'Oh, is he?' Vera turned flashing eyes on her and Cissie was instantly reminded of Rose. 'Henry did me out of a lot of money, Aunt Cissie,' she said loudly. 'I'm surprised you're standing up for him.'

'He's got no one else to do that,' Cissie said quickly. 'I speak as I find, and not only that, I love him like the son I never had.' Cissie touched Vera's hand. 'And I love you like a daughter.'

Vera's expression softened. 'Let's get you settled into your room, shall we?'

A week had passed since she moved into Vera's house, and Cissie could not remember when she had been more comfortable and, indeed, content. The family, including the youngsters, were friendly and respectful. She got on well with the other boarders, especially Miss Philpot, with whom she had much in common even though the woman was considerably younger.

Yes, everyone was courteous and friendly. Except that foreigner from Australia. She had not met him face to face yet. He seemed to be deliberately avoiding her and Cissie found him deeply disturbing.

300

On Sunday Cissie insisted on helping Vera with the washing-up after supper as Dorothy and Gillian had gone out together for the evening. She could not help sharing her doubts.

'That man from the Colonies is a mystery,' Cissie began as she wiped the plates. 'He's very outlandish from the fleeting glimpses I've had of him. I'm not sure he's trustworthy. You can never tell with foreigners.'

'What? Mr Oglander?' Vera turned her head to give her a surprised look. 'Our Gillian thinks the sun shines out of his eyes.'

Cissie blinked in surprise. 'But you have to admit, Vera, there's something odd about him,' she persisted. 'He misses meals. He makes a point of dodging me. I can't imagine why.'

Vera shrugged, her hands in the washing-up water. 'He gets on well with everyone, especially my Arthur.'

'On the odd occasion that he comes to dinner, when we sit down to eat he always finds a place at the far end of the table and then rushes off before the meal is finished.' Cissie nodded sagely. 'He's afraid to show his face like a wanted criminal.'

'It's your imagination, Aunt Cissie.'

Cissie shook her head. 'No, Vera, it isn't.'

The man seemed to go out of his way to distance himself and Cissie found that disconcerting.

'This morning, as I passed him on the top landing, I wished him "Good morning". He hurried past without a word, his head down.' Cissie shook her head. 'I think he's very ... peculiar.'

She had thought to describe him as sinister, but decided against it. She did not want to frighten her niece.

Vera paused in washing up to stare at her. 'Aunt Cissie, you haven't said something to upset him, have you?'

'Certainly not!' Cissie exclaimed, slightly miffed at the question. 'I have not spoken one word to the man since I've been here.'

'But you must have. I introduced you to everyone around the table that first evening you had supper with us.'

'Mr Oglander wasn't at supper that evening,' Cissie said triumphantly. 'I remember Gill took a tray up to him because he wasn't feeling well.'

'Aunt Cissie, what are you trying to say?'

'I don't know, Vera, my dear,' Cissie said uncertainly. 'But there's something about Mr Oglander that makes me feel ... anxious.'

'The bathroom is free,' Gillian said cheerfully to Dorothy as she returned to the bedroom they shared, rubbing her wet hair with a towel. 'You'd better be quick before somebody else grabs it.'

Dorothy did not answer and Gillian glanced at her. Her cousin was sitting on her bed, her head down.

'Breakfast will be in three-quarters of an hour,' Gillian reminded her. 'Mam will be wondering where you are.' Gillian gave a giggle. 'She reckons she can't do without your help these days.'

Silently, Dorothy stood up and picked up her

toiletry bag but still didn't make a move to the door.

'Listen, Dot,' Gillian went on, 'I'm meeting Jimmy again this evening. Can you pretend that we're going out together as usual?'

Dorothy kept her back turned and mumbled something Gillian did not hear properly, but it sounded like a refusal.

'Please, Dot,' Gillian pleaded. 'It's not fair that Jimmy and I are kept apart. We love each other and you promised you'd help me.'

Dorothy sat down on the bed again and put both hands to cover her face.

'Dot! What is it?'

Dorothy lifted her head and Gillian saw she had been crying. Alarmed, she sat down beside her.

'Tell me what the matter is, Dot.'

Dorothy's lips were trembling. 'Gill, I think I'm in trouble.'

'Trouble? What on earth do you mean?'

Dorothy's head sank and she hunched her shoulders. 'I think I'm in the family way.'

'What?' Gillian was flabbergasted.

'I've missed, you know, the curse.'

'But that happens, Dot,' Gillian said. 'Perhaps you're a bit run-down. And besides, how can you be in the family way?'

'Oh, Gill, I've been so stupid,' Dorothy said miserably. 'My mother said I had to be ... agreeable ... to catch a husband with money. You know how keen I was on Ronnie Knox...'

'Yes, we had that silly quarrel over him.'

Dorothy dipped her head again. 'My mother

303

said he was a very good catch and if I played my cards right I could get him to marry me.' Dorothy peered at her in misery. 'I took her advice.'

Gillian stared at her in growing dismay. 'Oh, Dorothy, you didn't?'

Dorothy nodded. 'He took me to his new house. I was confused. I thought I was in love with him and that he was in love with me. I thought it would mean we were engaged. But afterwards he laughed at me. Oh, I'm so ashamed!'

Gillian did not know what she should say or do for a moment. Finally she said, 'But you're not certain about being...' She could not bring herself to say the word.

'Pregnant?' Dorothy said it for her. 'Something's not right, Gill. My body feels ... different somehow.'

'Oh, Dot!' Gillian put her hand to cover her mouth. 'What are you going to do?'

'I don't know.'

'You must tell someone.'

'No!' Dorothy cried out. 'It's too humiliating. People will think I'm loose.'

'But you must tell someone before your condition becomes obvious,' Gillian insisted. She put a comforting arm around Dorothy's shoulders. 'Tell your father. He'll know what to do.'

'No, not him!' Dorothy shrugged Gillian's arm away. 'I want nothing more to do with my father. He has betrayed me, all of us.'

'But Uncle Henry can make Ronnie do the right thing by you,' Gillian said. 'He must marry you now.'

Dorothy gave a bitter laugh and stood up quickly. 'Ronnie Knox is the last man I'd marry. I hate him!'

Gillian stood up, too. She felt appalled at what had happened to her cousin, but knew they could not face this calamity alone.

'Dot, I'm going to tell my mother,' she said firmly. 'You're upset now and can't think straight, but I believe I know what's best.'

Dorothy looked up, fright in her eyes. 'Aunt Vera will throw me out!'

Gillian bit her lip. Knowing her mother's almost puritanical views she thought it likely, but would not say so to her cousin. However, she could see no other alternative.

Dorothy squared her shoulders. 'I'll go and see my own mother,' she said resolutely. 'I took her advice so it's partly her fault, after all. Now she must help me.'

'Shall I come with you, Dot?'

Dorothy shook her head. 'No, but thank you, Gill,' she said sadly. 'My mother will go off the deep end if she thinks I've told someone else.'

Her Aunt Vera was quite amenable when Dorothy told her she needed to go and see her mother that morning and could not help with the housework.

'You don't have to ask me,' Aunt Vera said. 'You can come and go as you like, Dorothy, my dear. You're not a servant.'

Dorothy felt a jab of shame, feeling she was being deceitful in the face of her aunt's kindness.

She set out on foot to the house her parents had once shared. As she approached and walked down the drive she was filled with trepidation. Surely her mother would not blame her for what had happened. Gloria should take some of the responsibility for her ill advice. Suddenly Dorothy was uncertain that she was doing the right thing in revealing her predicament to her mother.

Gloria opened the door and looked very surprised to see her.

'What's brought you here again?' she asked belligerently. 'I thought your father had forbidden you to see me.'

'I have to talk to you, Mother.'

Gloria sighed heavily but stood aside for her to enter.

The luggage that Gloria had brought back from London was still in the hall, still unpacked, and had been added to. It looked as though her mother intended to leave again and was taking with her everything she could carry.

Gloria noticed Dorothy's glance at the piled baggage.

'You're lucky to have caught me,' she said huffily.

'Where are you going?' Dorothy asked. 'You're not leaving before we know what's to happen to Andy?'

'No, but soon.'

They went into the drawing room. Gloria stood before the fireplace, her hands clasped before her. She did not ask Dorothy to sit, and the girl felt like a mere visitor in her former home.

'You'd better sit down, Mother,' Dorothy said. 'I've got some news.'

'Did your father send you?' Gloria asked waspishly, making no move to take a seat.

'No,' Dorothy said, sitting down herself.

Now she was on the point of revealing the awful truth, her legs felt weak as she wondered how her mother would take it.

'Well, what is it, then?'

'Mother, I think I'm in the family way.'

Gloria stared at her in stony silence.

'Did you hear what I said, Mother?' Dorothy said nervously. 'I'm sure I'm pregnant.'

Gloria jutted out her chin. 'What are you telling me for?' she asked icily.

'You're my mother!' Dorothy said in dismay. 'And besides, you encouraged me to ... to give in to Ronnie Knox. I didn't really want to.'

She wasn't sure that was completely true. She had thought herself in love with him. Even so, she felt she would have been more cautious if Gloria had not insisted she be 'clever'.

'I'm not responsible for your stupid mistakes,' Gloria exclaimed. 'You've made your bed. You lie on it.'

'Mother!' Dorothy was devastated at her words.

Gloria began to walk quickly about the room. 'I've got my own problems,' she said harshly. 'Andy came before the magistrate yesterday. He has to appear in court again next Wednesday.' She swung around and glared at Dorothy. 'The poor boy is facing a jail sentence. I blame your father!'

'What about me?' Dorothy said, jumping to her feet. 'Andy committed a crime, so he has to pay. I've done nothing wrong except listen to your stupid advice, Mother.'

'That's enough!' Gloria stared at her, her mouth hard. 'I can't help you, Dorothy. I've got my hands full. I've seen a solicitor. I'm divorcing your father.'

'Divorce!' Dorothy was shocked. 'But it'll be in all the papers. Think of the scandal.'

'Huh! It'll be your father's scandal – him and that floozy he lives with. I'm citing her as co-respondent.'

'Mother, are you sure...?'

'I'm leaving Swansea straight after Andy's case is settled,' Gloria said flatly. 'He'll probably go to prison, but I can't help that and I can't help you either.' She sniffed. 'I wash my hands of both of you.'

'Mother, for heaven's sake...!'

'My husband, my children – you have all been a great disappointment to me.' Gloria lifted her chin. 'I'm young enough to start over, and I intend to.'

'How could you be so cold and unfeeling?' Dorothy said. 'You're my mother!'

'What about *my* feelings?' Gloria snapped. 'I tried to advise you the best way to make a clever marriage, but you're so dense, Dorothy. There's nothing more I can do.' She began to walk towards the hall. 'You'd better leave now,' she said distantly. 'I have arrangements to make and a lot more packing to do.'

Dorothy stood where she was, staring at her

mother, hardly able to believe she really meant it.

Gloria paused at the doorway. She glanced back at Dorothy, her nostrils flaring.

'I hope you're not going to be difficult, Dorothy,' she said archly. 'Whether you like it or not, this is the parting of the ways.'

Without another word or a glance at her mother, Dorothy hurried out. When the front door slammed behind her, the sound was like a shaft through her heart. She was alone now. She no longer had a family.

Twenty-Two

'Mam, can I talk to you a minute?'

Vera turned from washing up to look at her daughter. 'I thought you and Dorothy were going out for a stroll this evening,' she said.

Gill ran her tongue over her lips. 'Dot isn't feeling very well.'

'I thought she looked peaky at supper,' Aunt Cissie commented as she wiped a plate and put it on a shelf of the Welsh dresser. 'Perhaps she needs a tonic.'

'Mam, can I have a word with you?' Gillian asked again, her tone agitated. 'In private.'

Vera wiped her wet hands on a towel. 'Private?' she repeated somewhat puzzled. She saw her daughter's glance slide warily towards

Aunt Cissie.

'There are no secrets in this house, Gillian,' she said promptly. 'There's nothing that Aunty Cissie can't hear.'

Gillian bit her lip and was silent, looking very uncertain.

'Well, good gracious!' Vera exclaimed, beginning to feel uneasy. 'What on earth is the matter?'

'It's poor Dot,' Gillian began in a rush of words. 'Mam! She's in awful trouble.'

'Trouble?' Vera stared at her daughter, wondering at the paleness of her face. 'What are you talking about?'

Gillian wrung her hands. 'Dot's in the family way, Mam. And she's desperate with worry.'

'What?'

Vera and Aunt Cissie looked at each other in dismay. 'It can't be true.'

'It is, Mam,' Gillian insisted. 'Dot told her mother this morning and Aunty Gloria pushed her off. Dot's so upset, she's crying all the time. Please help her, Mam. It's not her fault.'

Vera felt stunned. How could it possibly be true? She looked at Aunt Cissie again to see deep concern on the older woman's face.

'But how could this have happened?' she asked of no one in particular.

'Can you come along to our bedroom, Mam?' Gillian pleaded. 'Dot can explain.'

They followed Gillian along the passage to the room that used to be the back room, where the girls now slept. Dorothy was lying face down on her bed, sobbing, her shoulders shaking.

Immediately Aunt Cissie went to her, gathered her into a sitting position and put an arm around her heaving shoulders.

'There! There! My poor girl,' Aunt Cissie said gently. 'Stop crying now. You're amongst your family. You can tell us anything. We'll understand.'

'Will we?' Vera exclaimed sharply. She wasn't so sure. 'Gillian, you'd better leave the room.'

'Mam! Don't be daft, will you?' Gillian said hotly. 'I'm not a child.'

'Well, Gill, go and make Dorothy a strong cup of tea,' Aunt Cissie suggested. 'She needs something.'

Gill hesitated a moment before leaving the room. 'It's all Aunt Gloria's fault anyway!' she said loudly and left.

'All right, Dorothy, my dear,' Aunt Cissie said soothingly. 'Tell your Aunt Vera and me what has happened to you.'

Dorothy lifted her face to look at them for the first time. Vera was concerned to see how wretched her young face was.

'I've been so foolish, Aunt Vera,' she said through trembling lips. 'I believed Mother when she drummed it into me that it was the only way to get a wealthy husband.'

'Heavens above!' Vera was appalled as the meaning of the girl's words dawned on her. 'Your own mother condoned this behaviour?'

Vera pursed her lips in anger. She had always considered Henry's wife to be witless and shallow, but to encourage her own daughter to loose behaviour was criminal.

'But what made you believe her, Dorothy? Surely you knew it was wrong?'

Dorothy turned her miserable gaze at Aunt Cissie. 'Mam insisted it was the way she managed to catch Dad and make him marry her.' Tears glistened in her eyes. 'Mother said I was useless when I told her I'd rather not.'

'Oh my God!' Vera said and sat down heavily on the nearest chair. 'This is the worst thing I've ever heard. Your mother needs to be horse-whipped.'

'Mother was so keen for me to marry Ronnie Knox because he's well off and owns part of Dad's business,' Dorothy said, twisting a damp handkerchief between her fingers. 'I thought I loved him and he loved me. But he laughed at me after...' With a whimper she turned her face into Aunt Cissie's thin shoulder. 'Oh, I'm ruined. My life is finished.'

'There! There! We mustn't despair.' Aunt Cissie held her in comforting arms. 'Now think, Dorothy, dear, when did this happen?'

Dorothy brushed a strand of hair away from her eyes with trembling fingers. 'I'll never forget. It was the first week of June.'

Vera and Cissie glanced at each other. 'When was your last period?' Vera asked.

'Just before,' Dorothy answered. 'It should have come on at the beginning of this month, July, but it didn't happen.' She burst into tears again.

At that moment Gillian returned with a tray of tea for everyone. She poured out the brew, strong and fragrant. Dorothy took her cup and saucer with shaking hands.

'I'll have to leave Swansea,' she said, her lips trembling. 'I can never face anyone ever again.'

Feeling calmer now, Vera was silent as she sipped her tea, but her mind was still in a whirl. First Henry had acted scandalously in leaving his wife and living with another woman, and now Dorothy was following in his footsteps.

'Vera, Dorothy is not to blame here,' Aunt Cissie said quickly as though reading her mind. 'She's a young innocent girl who has been led astray by an imprudent and avaricious mother.'

Vera nodded. 'I agree. I'm just wondering what we can do to keep it quiet.'

'The truth is bound to come out!' Dorothy wailed.

Vera sniffed. 'I think we should wait and see. After all, it's just over a month. We can't be certain yet that you've ... caught. Periods can be interrupted by all kinds of things.'

'Yes,' Cissie said. 'You've been working hard.'

Miffed, Vera stared at Cissie. 'I don't force her to work about the place, you know,' she said quickly. 'It's Dorothy's choice.'

'And I love it, Aunt Vera,' Dorothy said. 'I want to learn all I can about keeping a boarding house.' She looked down at her lap. 'After all, no man will want to marry me with an illegitimate child in tow. I'll have to fend for myself somehow.'

'Nonsense!' Cissie said. 'Your family will stand by you.' She looked meaningfully at Vera. 'I agree we should keep quiet about this for the moment, but Henry must be told.'

'No!' Dorothy exclaimed loudly. 'I don't want to see my father's face, let alone talk to him.' She shook her head emphatically. 'I can't forgive him for what he's done.'

'Dorothy, have some sympathy for him,' Cissie said gently. 'You can blame your mother for the predicament you may be in. Think what your father has been through with Gloria all these years.'

Dorothy reflected. 'They quarrelled all the time.'

'Your father is human,' Cissie said. 'Gloria isn't capable of giving love and affection, as I think you'll agree. Henry found someone who is. Can we blame him?'

'I suppose not,' Dorothy murmured reluctantly. 'But it's so sordid.'

'It's no more sordid than Gloria tricking your father into marriage,' Cissie remarked. 'Or encouraging you to folly.'

There was a pause when no one spoke.

'Right, it's settled,' Vera said brightly at last. 'Arthur will ask your father to call around tomorrow. Now don't worry, Dorothy,' she added. 'Everything is going to be all right.'

Dorothy looked at her with misery still in her eyes.

'There's something I haven't told you,' she said in a small voice. 'When I saw my mother this morning she told me she is suing my father for divorce and citing *that* woman.'

Vera threw up her hands in despair. Would the scandals never end?

* * *

314

Vera let her brother into the hall early the following morning. She guessed he must have hurried around as soon as Arthur had given him her message.

Henry smiled and his gaze was eager as he came in. 'Good morning, Vera,' he said. 'It's good of you to let me call. Is Dorothy about?'

Vera gave a murmured reply. She wondered how happy he would be when he learned why she had sent for him.

'Go into the drawing room, please, Henry,' she said. 'I'll just tell Aunt Cissie you've arrived.'

He looked puzzled. 'Aunt Cissie? What has she to do with anything?'

'Just wait, Henry.'

Vera pushed open the door of the drawing room and glanced in. She was disconcerted to see Mr Oglander was still there sitting reading a newspaper.

That was awkward. She hoped he would have the good manners to leave when she and Aunt Cissie came in.

Henry strolled in obligingly and nodded to Mr Oglander. 'Good morning, sir.'

Mr Oglander rose to his feet. 'Good morning, Mr Prosser.'

As she closed the door behind her she could hear the two men start a conversation. Vera went back to the kitchen where her aunt was finishing off washing the breakfast crockery.

'Henry's here,' Vera announced. 'Come on, Aunt Cissie. We'd better talk to him; get it over and done with.'

They went to the drawing room, Cissie leading

315

the way. She opened the door, strode in without preamble and then stopped dead in her tracks, making a strange choking sound.

Taken by surprise, Vera bumped into her. 'Aunt Cissie! What's the matter?'

Henry and Mr Oglander were standing shoulder to shoulder before the fireplace while Cissie stared at them transfixed. Vera took her arm and looked into her aunt's face. She had gone as white as a sheet and was trembling violently.

'Oh my God!' Cissie said in a strangled voice. 'It is him.'

Whereupon, her knees buckled and her mouth went slack. She would have fallen to the floor had not Henry dashed forward and caught her thin frame in his arms.

'What's the matter with her?' Vera cried out, thoroughly alarmed. 'Oh, Henry, has she had a stroke?'

'I don't know.' Henry carried his aunt to a sofa and laid her gently on it. 'Better get the smelling salts, Vera,' he said. He sounded very worried.

As Vera turned around to fetch the salts she saw Mr Oglander sidling furtively towards the door. There was fright in his eyes and his skin looked pasty under his weathered complexion.

'I'll get out of your way,' he said in a reedy voice which wasn't like his usual strong tones. 'This is a family matter.'

Vera was immediately curious about his distracted demeanour, but had no time to wonder at it, not with her aunt lying unconscious on the sofa, so she hurried on past him to fetch the bottle of smelling salts she always kept in the drawer in the kitchen.

When she returned Vera held the bottle under her aunt's nose. Cissie stirred and then pushed the bottle away from her nose with a grunt.

'Aunt Cissie, what happened?' Henry exclaimed, his voice shaky with concern. 'Are you ill?'

Cissie looked up at them, a strange light in her eyes. 'Where is he?'

'Who?'

'She means Mr Oglander,' Vera told him quietly. 'I know she's taken a strong dislike to the man for some reason, but this is beyond anything.'

'It's not like Aunt Cissie to take against someone,' Henry said. 'He must have upset her in some way.'

Cissie struggled up into a sitting position. 'Has he gone?' she asked.

'Yes, he has gone,' Henry assured her. 'He won't hurt you.'

'Huh! A bit late for that,' his aunt said in a startling, strong voice. She flapped her hands at them. 'Don't fuss, the pair of you! I'm all right. It was a shock, that's all.'

Vera frowned, perplexed. 'What was a shock? I don't understand, Aunt Cissie.'

Cissie's expression was cautious. 'An old woman's fancy,' she said. 'Take no notice of me.' She pulled herself together. 'Have you told Henry why he's here?'

Annoyed, Vera pursed her lips. She had had such a fright, her aunt collapsing like that.

'I haven't had a chance with you fainting all over the place,' she said caustically.

'Sit down, Henry,' Cissie said. She patted the seat beside her on the sofa. 'It's about Dorothy.'

Henry sat. 'What is it?'

'There's a possibility Dorothy may be – well, in the family way, Henry,' Cissie said calmly. 'Now, don't get het up! It isn't confirmed yet.'

'My God! That swine, Ronnie Knox!'

'You knew about him and Dorothy, then?' Vera asked, staring at him in astonishment. 'Why in heaven's name didn't you put a stop to it before it was too late?'

'I warned Gloria not to encourage the association,' Henry said defensively. 'And Dorothy promised me she'd have nothing more to do with him, but I hadn't considered Gloria's greed and lack of moral fibre.'

'Worthless woman!' Vera hissed.

Henry looked crestfallen. 'I was beside myself when Dorothy told me Ronnie had taken advantage of her.' He glanced at them appealingly. 'You mustn't condemn her. She was too much under Gloria's influence to know better, and I was blind not to see it sooner.'

'Yes, well!' Vera said with a disdainful sniff. 'You were too busy with your fancy woman, I've no doubt.'

'Vera! You're not helping with that attitude,' Cissie said sharply. 'What's done is done. Now we have to deal with the situation.'

'He'll have to marry her,' Henry said firmly. 'He got her into this mess.'

'I don't think that's the solution,' Cissie said.

'Well, anything else is unthinkable,' Henry said, getting to his feet. 'Knox had better be ready to marry her or I'll give him the beating of his life.'

'Oh, talk sense,' Vera said irritably. 'Threats of violence are no good. He's years younger than you, Henry. You'll make a complete fool of yourself and humiliate Dorothy as well.'

'I think you should talk to your daughter,' Cissie said. 'After all, it's her future we're discussing.'

'I'll go and fetch her,' Vera offered and left the room to go to the girls' bedroom next door. She knocked and went in.

'Your father is here, Dorothy,' Vera told her.

'I won't see him!'

'Now, look here, my girl!' Vera said heatedly. 'You've already agreed to face him. There'll be no more of this childish shilly-shallying. You're in a mess and your father wants to help.'

Dorothy's face took on a stubborn expression.

'Now, don't play me up!' Vera exclaimed loudly. 'I'm worried to death about Aunt Cissie. She just fainted away a moment ago.'

'What?' Dorothy jumped to her feet, looking alarmed now. 'Is she ill?' Her face crumpled as though she were about to burst into tears again. 'Has it anything to do with the mess I'm in?'

'No, it's not you,' Vera assured her hastily. She wondered then what on earth could have upset her aunt so much. Cissie Prosser was such a strong, well-balanced woman. 'It's her age, I think. I must get the doctor to see her,' Vera continued. 'Come along, your father is waiting.'

Dorothy still hung back.

Vera's voice softened. 'He's not angry with

you, Dorothy, and doesn't blame you. Be brave and face him.'

Vera put an arm around the girl's shoulders. She could sense how reluctant she was as she led her to the drawing room. Cissie was chiding Henry as they went in.

'Henry, go easy on young Dorothy,' Vera heard Cissie say. 'She's frightened and very ashamed.'

'I don't blame her,' Henry replied. 'If anyone's to blame it's me. I should've protected my daughter against Gloria's low moral outlook.'

Dorothy flinched when she came face to face with her father, her expression closing up again, and she turned away from him.

Henry stepped forward. 'Dorothy, my dearest girl, don't turn from me. You're breaking my heart.'

She looked directly at him then. 'You turned away from your legitimate family,' she accused him with deep reproach in her voice. 'What can you expect from me?'

He nodded. 'I know I deserve that. But I want to help you now.'

'No one can help me,' Dorothy said miserably. 'I'm ruined.'

'Not if I have anything to do with it,' Henry said strongly. 'I'll make that swine Ronnie Knox marry you. That way you can keep your reputation.'

Dorothy shook her head vehemently. 'I won't marry Ronnie!' she cried out passionately. 'I despise him. He's the last man I'd marry. I'd rather be dead!'

'Dorothy, be reasonable,' Henry said. 'Life

will be intolerable for you as an unwed mother. You'll never be able to hold your head up again. People will point and whisper as you walk down the street.'

'I tell you I'd rather be dead than be Ronnie's wife,' Dorothy cried out. 'I'll go away where no one knows me.' She gave her father a disdainful stare. 'Don't worry. I won't be a burden on you. I'll make my own way.'

'You can't remain unmarried,' Henry said. 'Marriage to Ronnie is better than nothing.'

'Is it, Henry?' Cissie cut in loudly. 'Was your marriage to Gloria better than nothing?'

Henry whirled around and stared at his aunt. 'That was different.'

'No, it wasn't.' Cissie gave him a hard stare. 'You married Gloria because she was in the family way and you've had a hell of a life with her ever since.'

Henry sat down heavily on the nearest chair and was silent.

'Anyway,' Vera interposed, 'we're not absolutely certain Dorothy is ... well, ruined,' she said. 'We must wait and see. But whatever the outcome, we'll all stand by her.'

'Of course we will,' Cissie agreed strongly.

Vera put an arm around her niece's shoulders. 'Dorothy will have a home with me and Arthur for as long as she wants.'

'Thank you, Aunt Vera,' Dorothy said, and kissed Vera on the cheek. She went to Cissie, sitting on the sofa, and kissed her, too. 'Thank you both for standing by me.'

'You are welcome, my dear girl,' Cissie said.

Henry stood up. 'That's very good of you, Vera. How can I ever thank you?'

Vera pursed her lips. 'I still have my doubts about you, Henry,' she said pithily. 'So don't get the wrong idea.'

He moved towards Dorothy as though he would embrace her, but she turned away. 'I'll go back to my room for the time being, Aunt Vera,' she said without looking at her father. 'But I'll be ready to help with dinner.'

Dorothy turned then and left the room.

Cissie struggled up from the sofa. 'I'll go after her,' she said. 'She's still very upset. She needs someone with her.'

Henry looked helpless as his aunt followed his daughter. He gave Vera a wry smile.

'Will Dorothy ever trust me again?'

Vera inclined her head. 'I don't know,' she said. She felt like reminding him that he only had himself to blame. 'I know I don't.'

'Vera, you must believe me. I was not responsible for the terms of Mam's will.'

Vera sniffed disparagingly. How could she ever believe him?

He looked at her with a resigned expression on his face. 'My offer still stands for Sam,' he said. 'I won't go back on my word if that's what you're thinking.'

She remembered Dorothy's other news. 'There's one more thing you should know, Henry. Gloria intends to divorce you. She told Dorothy she'll cite Florrie Tomkin as co-respondent.'

'What?' His face turned white with consternation. 'She can't do that!'

She sniffed again. 'More scandal for this family to bear.'

Henry let himself into the house and stood in the hall, shouting her name. He was consumed with fury but steeled himself not to lose control.

'Gloria! Where the hell are you, you bitch?'

She appeared at the drawing-room door immediately, her cheeks pink with anger.

'How dare you barge your way into this house?' she cried out. 'Get out!'

'This is still my house,' he reminded her wrathfully.

'And you can keep it,' she rasped. 'But I'll demand a substantial settlement when we're divorced.'

He looked at her coiffured hair and carefully painted face and felt nothing but deep dislike verging on hatred. He immediately felt ashamed.

'You're deluding yourself, Gloria,' he said. 'Divorce is difficult to come by, even for a man.'

'I'm determined to try,' Gloria said resolutely. 'I deserve a new beginning.'

'Getting the courts to grant a divorce to a woman is well-nigh impossible,' Henry said bluntly.

'It has been done.'

Henry shook his head, provoked even further by her stubbornness.

'The courts are rigorous about the grounds on which a wife can sue her husband,' he persisted. 'Besides which, Gloria, it's an extremely costly business and you don't have the money.'

'You have money, Henry,' she said. 'You'll pay all costs and provide the grounds I need as well.'

'You're out of your mind,' he scoffed.

'Perhaps you don't want to marry this fancy woman of yours, then?' she asked. 'Make an honest woman of her.' She laughed bitterly. 'Well, in name anyway.'

Henry paused. Marry Florrie? His heart had longed for that for many years.

'You'll keep Florrie's name out of it.'

'Oh, no!' Gloria said nastily. 'I'm going to show her up for what she is. A dirty little slut!'

'You malicious bitch!'

Gloria's lips twisted in derision. 'Call me what you like,' she said. 'But I'll get what's owed to me, Henry. I'm the wronged wife, remember? By the time I've finished dragging you and your whore through the courts she'll wish she was dead.'

Henry controlled himself with difficulty. In all the years of provocation he had never raised a hand to her and he would not start now, even though she deserved it.

'This really is the last time we'll speak together, Gloria,' Henry said heavily. 'I never want to look at your spiteful and avaricious face ever again.'

'Well, that suits me!' She sounded triumphant.

He swung away to leave and then looked back at her.

'You'll never be happy anywhere, Gloria,' he said disparagingly. 'Because you're incapable of loving anyone but yourself.'

'Get out, you philandering swine!'

Twenty-Three

Cissie had been sitting, waiting, at the bottom of the stairs to the top landing for some time and now her old bones were beginning to ache, but she was determined to stick it out. He would not elude her this time.

She had seen him go out earlier and knew he would be back soon. He was never late for supper.

Her fingers trembled a little at the thought of the coming confrontation. Would she know what to say to him? Was she mistaken?

An image came into her mind again of the two men standing shoulder to shoulder before the fireplace earlier in the day and the tremendous shock she had received when she thought her heart would stop. She wasn't mistaken.

A sound alerted her. Someone was climbing the stairs. Cissie struggled up from the stair and looked over the banister.

It was him. For a few minutes she watched his tall, lanky frame climb slowly and then she hurried as fast as her old legs would carry her to the door of the bathroom opposite his room and positioned herself just inside.

Holding the door slightly ajar Cissie peered through the narrow opening as Mr Oglander reached his room. He opened the door and stepped inside. As quickly as she could Cissie came out of hiding and reached forward, putting her hand against the door to prevent him closing it.

He was startled to see her appear so suddenly and she saw panic in his eyes. 'Miss Prosser!' he exclaimed breathily. 'Good gracious! You took me by surprise.'

'Don't you Miss Prosser me, you – you sly deceiver!' Cissie said strongly.

'What?'

Cissie set her jaw and glared at him. 'Do you think I'm too old or too stupid not to know who you really are?'

'Miss Prosser, are you sure you're well?' he said nervously. 'You did faint earlier, and I was worried.'

'Oh, you were worried, were you?' Cissie said sharply. 'Worried that you'd been found out.'

'Really, Miss Prosser! I don't understand—'

'Stop it! Stop pretending!' Cissie cried out wrathfully. 'I'm old but I'm of sound mind. Do you think I wouldn't know my own brother when he stood right before my eyes, even though he supposedly died thirty-odd years ago?'

He put his thumb and forefinger to his mouth and pinched his lower lip. 'Ah!'

'What happened, William?' Cissie asked, a catch in her voice. 'Why did you desert your dear children and desert me, too?'

William Prosser swallowed heavily, his face now pale. He stepped back. 'Cissie, come in and shut the door,' he said quietly.

Cissie shut the door and then turned to him.

'You left us to our fates,' she accused him heatedly. 'How could you do that to us – the ones who loved you?'

She looked up into his face. Despite ageing and the ravages of the hot Australian sun his features were as she remembered them and she was filled with conflicting emotions: anger at his thoughtless desertion of his family and at the same time relief that he was alive and well. It was like a miracle, yet she was still hurting.

'What in God's name happened, Will?'

It was unforgivable that he had gone off, leaving his children, Henry and Vera, to the far from tender mercies of Rose. And he had left his sister, too, to struggle on as best she might. Hadn't he given them one thought over the years? It appeared not.

'The children and I thought you were dead and gone,' she said in a strangled voice. 'And we grieved for you.'

'I'm sorry, Cissie.'

'Sorry?' Cissie snapped at him. 'Is that all you have to say for yourself? I deserve an explanation, Will.'

His face was pale. 'God knows I've regretted it, Cissie, for many, many years.'

'That's not an explanation, Will,' Cissie said harshly. 'Not one word, not one sign that you were alive. Did you think so little of us?'

All at once overwhelmed by her emotions she sat down on the bed, her shaking legs unable to support her frame.

'That was just it,' William said solemnly. 'I couldn't think clearly, not after witnessing the truth about Rose and Charlie Knox.'

He sat on the bed next to her, his head hanging forward.

'I caught them, Cissie,' he murmured. 'Charlie and Rose; caught them together in his bedroom...'

He put his hand up to rub his face as though to rub away the memory.

'Oh! Will!' Cissie was dismayed.

'I was stunned.' He shook his head. 'Devastated.' He looked up at her, misery in his eyes. 'We argued violently, Charlie and me, right there with Rose looking on,' he said in a low tone. 'He humiliated me in front of her.'

'Rose wasn't worth it.'

'She was to me, Cissie,' William insisted. 'I loved her.'

Cissie shook her head sadly. 'I'm so sorry, Will.'

'Before the beating he gave me I'd challenged Charlie about the money he had embezzled. He admitted it to me brazenly! But he knew I wouldn't want a scandal and Rose said she was leaving me anyway.'

'But why run away?'

'Don't you understand, Cissie?' William exclaimed, looking at her pleadingly. 'I was desperate, distraught; out of my mind with the humiliation. I couldn't face going on working with Charlie, and losing Rose to him was the last straw. The pair of them would have destroyed me completely. I had to get away. I didn't mean for it to be for ever.'

'Thirty-odd years seems like for ever,' Cissie said pithily.

'I'm sorry,' William said.

He reached forward and tried to take her hand but Cissie snatched it away. She realized he had suffered, but so had she and the children. There was no forgiveness for him in her heart just yet.

'But not a word,' Cissie repeated aggrieved. 'Didn't you give one thought to the children?'

'Of course I did!' William said with energy. 'I wanted them with me – and you, too, Cissie. I knew I'd have to start again somewhere far away from Rose and Charlie.'

'You could have taken me and the children with you,' Cissie said reproachfully.

'I wanted to,' William said. 'But I didn't have enough money to support us all. I heard about cheap one-way fares to Australia for tradesmen and that's when I decided to emigrate.'

'To the ends of the earth!'

'I lived from hand to mouth for quite a while,' William said. 'Then I found work on a sheep farm. Within five years I had a small spread of my own, but it was a hard life.'

'Did you think of us back home?' Cissie asked plaintively.

Not one day had gone by when she had not thought of her brother and what had become of him.

'The children and you were always in my thoughts, Cissie,' he said. 'Every year I'd think about sending for all of you. Ten years passed before the sheep farm started to pay, but I knew by then that I'd left it too late.'

'Rose had you declared dead after seven years,' Cissie told him. 'She couldn't wait to marry Charlie the same year.'

'Yes, I know.'

She looked into his face. She could not hide her feelings any longer. He was her brother and she was prepared to forgive him. She patted his hand.

'I'm so thankful you are alive, Will, despite everything that's happened.'

William rose to his feet, pulling her up with him, and embraced her warmly. 'Forgive me, Cissie, for leaving you all alone to cope. I'm going to make it up to you, I promise.'

Cissie clung to her brother for a moment more. She knew he was sorry, but it was too late. There was no way he could make up for the years of loneliness she had endured.

At that moment the supper gong sounded. Both of them jumped at the sound.

'We must go down,' Cissie said with a wry smile. 'Your daughter will go off the deep end if we're late for our meal.'

William grinned. 'My little Vera! Isn't she wonderful?'

'Oh my God!' Cissie felt her features stiffen with sudden fright and she put up both her hands to cover her face. 'What will Vera say when she learns that her father has returned from the dead?'

William looked alarmed, too, and held up a warning hand.

'Please, Cissie, we must say nothing for the

330

moment,' he warned urgently. 'I'm in the middle of some important negotiations. I don't want my true identity known yet.'

'But, Will—'

'Mr Oglander to you!' William said with a smile. 'I'll explain about my plans after supper. Try to sneak up to my room then.'

Cissie did not know whether she could contain herself in front of their family. It was dawning on her that with William's return everything would change.

He took her arm gently. 'Come on, old girl,' he said. 'We mustn't keep Vera waiting.'

As it turned out it was Tom who was late for supper and he got it in the neck good and proper from Vera.

'I work my fingers to the bone to keep this house going!' she railed. 'Is it too much to expect that my family keep to the rules?'

'You do a splendid job, Mrs Finch,' said Mr Gilmore heartily. 'Splendid!'

'Hear, hear!' said Mr Oglander from the far end of the table, and Cissie tried to hide a smile with her napkin.

Their praise did not seem to mollify their landlady.

'I cook, I clean, I provide,' Vera lamented plaintively. 'And then my ungrateful son strolls in any time he likes. It's too much for any hard-working mother to bear.'

'I've said I'm sorry, Mam,' Tom muttered. 'Shall I wear sackcloth and ashes?'

'Ooh!'

'Now, that's enough from you, Tom,' Arthur

said sternly. 'Get about eating the food your mother has provided.'

'I think Tom should be made to do the dishes,' Gillian opined with a sniff. 'As a just punishment for upsetting Mam.'

'You little toady!' Tom exploded. 'I do the dishes while you scuttle off to meet Jimmy Tomkin. You think nobody knows.'

'What?' Vera looked from one twin to the other, her lips set in a hard line. 'Gillian? Have you been seeing that Tomkin boy behind our backs?'

'I ... I...' She rounded on her brother. 'Oh, you beast, Tom!' She jumped up from the table. 'You horrid beast!'

'Sit down, my girl!' thundered Vera. 'Your father and I will have a word with you later. Meanwhile no one leaves this table until the meal is finished.'

Gillian resumed her seat, but Cissie saw she hardly touched her food. The girl was foolish to disobey her parents yet Cissie felt sorry for her.

Personally, she liked Jimmy Tomkin. The boy had a lot of his father in him, and to Cissie that counted for quality. What harm was there in letting the youngsters be friends?

'I'll lend a hand with the dishes,' Cissie offered later when they were clearing away.

'No!' Vera said firmly. 'Our Gill will do that before Arthur and I have a talk with her. I can't believe she disobeyed us.'

'Surely there's no harm in letting them be friends,' Cissie ventured cautiously. 'The both of them are as innocent as new lambs.'

332

'You don't have any daughters to worry about, Aunt Cissie,' Vera snapped. 'Look at the trouble Dorothy is in.' She sniffed. 'Besides, he's kin.'

Cissie had no option but to leave it at that and as soon as the coast was clear made her way to William's room.

'Did anyone see you come up?' he asked in a conspiratorial voice.

'No. Don't worry.' Cissie was amused at his caution.

She sat on the bed and her brother sat next to her. His face showed a very sad expression.

'What is it, Will?'

'There's so much I regret,' he said. 'Particularly missing watching my children grow up. Vera is a fine woman, but it pains me that I had no hand in her upbringing. Perhaps Rose was a better mother than I imagined.'

'Huh!' Cissie grunted. 'Rose was a selfish, self-centred woman, and she never changed,' she said. 'She evicted me from our father's house, sold it and then moved in with Charlie Knox.'

'That wasn't fair on the children,' William said.

'They hated it,' Cissie confirmed. 'They spent more time with me at my lodgings than at home. They told me everything that was going on and there were plenty of rows and ructions, according to them.'

'Are you saying Rose and Charlie weren't happy together?'

'Rose soon discovered that his son George was the only person Charlie truly loved,' Cissie said. 'I don't doubt the real reason he married her was to get control of the business. Henry told me that Charlie frequently badgered Rose to sign everything over to him, but she wouldn't.'

'Poor Rose!'

'Huh!' Cissie was impatient. 'She got what she deserved – and remember, she treated you like dirt, Will.'

'I wanted nothing more than to make her happy,' William said sadly. 'I'm sorry she didn't find what she yearned for with Charlie.'

'Rose made her bed, Will, so she had to lie on it,' Cissie said flatly, feeling no sympathy for her sister-in-law. 'They'd been married ten years when George Knox was killed on the Somme in 1916,' she said. 'It finished Charlie completely. He never recovered from that blow and died five years later of a broken heart. He was a beaten man.'

William put his hand on her shoulder and smiled into her eyes. 'Then I have you to thank, Cissie, for my children's good upbringing,' he said.

'I love them like my own. That's why I worry so much about Henry,' Cissie said. 'He made a disastrous marriage. His son is facing prison and Dorothy is in...'

Cissie paused, remembering the girl's plight was to be kept secret.

'What about Dorothy?' William looked concerned.

'I've spoken out of turn,' Cissie said hastily. 'Please don't press me for an answer, Will.'

'Cissie, I have a right to know. I'm her grandfather,' William said strongly. 'Now tell me.'

Cissie felt Dorothy's shame as her own as she related what had happened to the girl.

'She isn't to blame, Will,' she said quickly.

'I'm not blaming her,' William said. 'Ronnie Knox is as rotten as his grandfather,' he said bitterly. 'It puts Henry in a nasty spot, though.' He paused, his expression thoughtful. 'How can he go on working with that swine Ronnie? I know the hell he's going through, believe me. I couldn't face it myself.'

William fell into silence, obviously deeply absorbed.

Cissie watched him for a moment, remembering the days when they were young and living in the old family home. She yearned for those days.

'You mentioned plans, Will,' she prompted him.

He glanced at her, his face brightening. 'Cissie, old girl, I've got some news. I had to wait until completion.'

'What is it?'

'I've bought back the old house,' he said. 'It's in Prosser hands again. Back where it belongs.'

'Oh, Will!' She stared at him in disbelief. 'But how?'

'How could I afford it?' He grinned. 'I made a fortune with sheep farming,' he said cheerfully. 'I mean a real fortune. I'm very wealthy, Cissie, and I intend to make up for everything I threw away all those years ago.'

'I can't believe it.' Cissie felt overwhelmed.

'I'm going to live there again and I want you with me,' he said. 'We're going home, Cissie.'

'Oh, Will!' Cissie suddenly had a lump in her throat and was lost for more words. She felt as though she were in a dream.

'But I don't want it known yet,' William cautioned. 'There are so many things I have to put right first.'

'You can't stay in hiding for ever, Will,' Cissie said. 'You have to face your family.'

'I know,' he said.

There was anxiety in his tone and Cissie understood why. How would Henry and Vera take their father's return from the grave? She felt her heart sink with dread. There were bound to be recriminations and bitterness; more family upheaval, as if there wasn't enough already.

Seething with anger, Gillian sat on her bed, her arms folded tightly across her chest like a shield. Her cousin Dorothy sat opposite her.

'How could Tom betray me like that? My own brother!' she said bitterly. 'Oh! I could kill him, I really could!'

'I don't think he meant to,' Dorothy said. 'He was cross because your mother was getting at him.'

Gillian could not be mollified. 'It was spite, sheer spite!'

'Tom isn't like that,' Dorothy said soothingly. 'If it was Andy now, that would be different. He enjoys making trouble.'

Gillian set her chin stubbornly. 'I will not give up Jimmy,' she said strongly. 'My parents can do as they please; throw me out if they like.'

Dorothy smiled. 'I can't see Aunt Vera doing

336

that, or your father letting her either.'

Gillian relaxed her arms from the defensive attitude she had adopted. Her parents were taking their time in coming to confront her. It was a war of nerves, she decided. Well, she would not be intimidated.

'I don't care what they say, I shall go on seeing Jimmy as often as I like,' she said defiantly and then gave her cousin a cautious glance. 'I just can't be parted from him, Dot. I'm in love with him.'

Dorothy gave a faint smile. 'It must be nice to be in love,' she said wistfully. 'And not have disgrace hanging over your head like a dark cloud.'

Gillian was immediately contrite. 'Dot, I'm sorry. I'm prattling on about my woes. It's nothing compared to the trouble you're in.'

Dorothy hung her head. 'I thought I was in love, too,' she said. 'I was wrong about that.' She looked up. 'I think Aunt Vera is afraid the same thing will happen to you.'

'Jimmy is nothing like that weasel, Ronnie Knox,' she burst out. 'Jimmy is honourable. He'd do nothing to harm me.' Gillian tossed her head. 'And besides, I wouldn't be so daft as to get myself up the spout.'

'Gillian!' Dorothy's mouth dropped open, and she stared in consternation, her colour draining. 'How could you be so crude and insensitive?'

'I'm sorry,' Gillian said. 'But our circumstances are quite different. Jimmy has never said or done anything out of place. He respects me and I love him for it.'

337

Dorothy stood up. 'I'd better go before your parents come in,' she said stiffly.

'No, Dot. Wait!' Gillian pleaded. 'Stay and help me face them.'

Dorothy sat down again reluctantly, and Gillian chided herself for being so unfeeling with her cousin. Dorothy was the only true friend she had apart from Jimmy.

At that moment the bedroom door opened and Vera came in with Arthur right behind her. Gillian saw her mother's face was tight with suppressed anger and knew there was going to be an almighty row. She rose quickly to face them.

Vera's glance swept over Dorothy. 'You'll excuse us, please, Dorothy,' she said stiffly.

Dorothy jumped up with alacrity. Gillian saw she was eager to leave, and she felt abandoned by her.

'I want Dorothy to stay,' she said quickly.

Dorothy looked apologetic. 'I'd better go, Gill,' she said. 'After all, it's nothing to do with me.'

Dorothy hurried out and Gillian faced her parents, glancing from one to the other. There was a mixture of anger and disappointment on her mother's face and all at once she felt apprehensive.

'It's not fair, Mam,' Gillian said defensively. 'Why can't Jimmy and me be friends? What's so terrible about it?'

'It's not terrible,' Arthur said, sadness in his eyes. 'It's just not suitable, Gill. You must see that.'

'No! I don't see!'

'The boy is your cousin,' Vera said severely. 'And apart from that, he's illegitimate. It's a stigma, Gillian. And that kind of social stain rubs off.'

'I've never heard anything so stupid in my life!' Gillian burst out. 'This is the twentieth century for heaven's sake. I can be friends with whoever I like.'

'Don't try to be clever with me,' Vera flared. 'You're not too old for a slap, my girl.'

'You're treating me like a child!'

'You're only seventeen so you still are a child according to law,' Vera said. 'When you're twenty-one you can do as you like.'

'Four years!' Gillian howled. 'I have to wait four years? Well, I can't wait,' she said stubbornly. 'I won't let you keep me and Jimmy apart. I won't!'

'You'll do as you're told,' Vera said. 'Otherwise you'll stop working at the yard. I will not have you disobey me.'

Gillian was horrified. 'You can't do that!' She glanced appealingly at her father. 'Dad, you know I love my job. I'm keeping Mr Meeker's position open for him and Uncle Henry says I'm doing a really good job of it, too.'

'I'm with your mother in this,' Arthur said flatly. 'Either you stop seeing Jimmy on the sly or you give the job up. It's up to you, Gill.'

Gillian stood still, staring from one to the other and feeling helpless. She could not understand their point of view.

'You both act as though you think Jimmy and

I are irresponsible, not to mention stupid,' she said tightly. 'He may be illegitimate,' she continued, 'but that doesn't make him bad. He would no more get me into trouble than he would jump in the River Tawe.'

'Gill, you are too young to understand ... men,' Arthur said awkwardly. 'Feelings are sometimes too powerful to resist.'

'Men?' Gillian said scornfully. 'Jimmy is the same age as me, so he's still a child, according to you.'

'Don't you try to be clever with us, my girl,' Vera exploded. 'You'll do as you're told and we'll hear no more about it.'

'I will not!' Gillian shouted. 'Even if you make me leave my job, I'll still see Jimmy. You can't keep us apart!'

'What's all the shouting? You can be heard on the top landing.'

They all turned to see Cissie standing in the doorway.

'It's private, Aunt Cissie,' Vera said quickly. 'Nothing for you to worry about. Close the door on your way out, please.'

'No, stay!' Gillian exclaimed loudly, sensing an ally. 'We'll see what Aunt Cissie thinks of it all.'

'Gillian!' Vera said, obviously riled by her daughter. 'You stubborn, wilful girl!'

Gillian moved quickly to her great-aunt and, taking her arm, drew her further into the room.

'Mam and Dad want me to stop being friends with Jimmy Tomkin, Aunt Cissie,' Gillian said. 'And I think it's so unfair. They're misjudging

340

him just because he's illegitimate.'

Gillian looked at her great-aunt hopefully. She had always thought of her as a level-headed, unprejudiced woman. She would see the unfairness of it all.

Cissie gave a long sigh. 'I do think you're going about this the wrong way, Vera,' she said. 'I see no harm in Gillian and Jimmy being friends.'

Vera sniffed disdainfully. 'Aunt Cissie, being unmarried yourself you know nothing of life and the ways of men,' she said severely. 'I'm trying to protect my daughter from harm.'

'Is it just Jimmy she must avoid?' Cissie asked sharply. 'Or all young men?'

'What?'

'Well, it seems to me,' Cissie said matter-of-factly, 'you don't trust Gill's judgement or sense of morality. If that's the case, she can never be friends with any young man for fear of being harmed.'

'That's absurd!'

'Oh, so you think Jimmy's a bad lot, then?' Cissie asked quickly. 'Your own brother's son.'

'Illegitimate son!' Vera said with emphasis. 'I don't want her ending up like poor Dorothy.'

'You don't give me much credit!' Gillian said. 'I'm sorry for Dorothy, but she did allow Ronnie Knox to make a fool of her. I'm not so silly.'

'Yes, well, Gloria helped there,' Cissie said with irony. She glanced at Arthur. 'You're not saying much, Arthur. What's your opinion of Jimmy?'

He looked very uncomfortable to be put on the

341

spot, especially in front of Vera.

'I've nothing against the boy,' he said defensively. 'He's a good worker and he's respectful to his elders.'

'Yes, he's just a boy,' Cissie pointed out. 'They're both no more than children. By forcing them apart you bring them closer together, don't you see?'

'Aunt Cissie, I'll be glad if you'll mind your own business,' Vera said in a lively tone.

'There's no harm in their friendship,' Cissie persisted in her opinion. 'They're so young yet. They will grow out of it; meet other people, make new friendships. The whole thing will fizzle out eventually if only you'll stop opposing it.'

Gillian studied her great-aunt's expression. She really seemed to believe what she was saying, but Gillian knew better. Her feelings for Jimmy were stronger than that, but she kept silent. Aunt Cissie was doing just fine.

'Aunt Cissie, you can't possibly know a mother's anxiety for her daughter's welfare,' Vera said condescendingly. 'You talk so lightly on the matter.'

'Mr Oglander thinks as I do,' Cissie said emphatically. 'He said himself that the youngsters should be allowed to find their own way.'

'Mr Oglander?' Vera stared. 'My lodger has an opinion on a personal family issue?' She looked outraged. 'Aunt Cissie, have you been discussing family matters with a relative stranger?'

Cissie looked confused for a moment and then an expression of caution stole over her face.

Gillian wondered at it. If she didn't know better she might have thought her great-aunt was feeling guilty about something.

'I don't gossip with strangers,' Cissie said. 'Mr Oglander said it in passing as we were chatting earlier.'

Vera raised her brows. 'Chatting? My word, you've changed your tune, Aunt Cissie,' she said sarcastically. 'Yesterday Mr Oglander was the devil's own kin, according to you.'

Cissie blinked and her cheeks turned pink. She glanced at Gillian.

'I'm sorry to say it, Gill, but your mother is as opinionated and pig-headed as your grandmother Rose was. Rose never learned from her mistakes. I'd always hoped Vera was different.' She gave her niece a straight look. 'I see I was wrong.'

'Well, really, Aunt Cissie,' Vera said.

'You think carefully about Gillian's best interests,' Cissie insisted. 'Gloria interfered, thinking she knew better, and it all went wrong.'

'Don't you lump me with her!'

'Well, use a bit of common sense, then!' Cissie said as a parting shot and stalked out of the room.

There was silence for a moment. Gillian watched her parents carefully. There was a look of doubt on her father's face, which filled her with new hope.

'Vera, love, perhaps Cissie is right,' he said warily, looking apprehensively at his wife. 'It boils down to this. Do we trust our daughter to act properly in her friendship with any boy?'

Gillian held her breath as she saw her mother hesitate before answering.

'It isn't that I don't trust you, Gillian,' Vera said at last, and Gillian heard an element of doubt in her tone. 'Of course I do. You've been brought up right.' She shook her head. 'It's just that I worry. You're young and inexperienced.'

'I thought you liked Jimmy, Mam,' Gillian said.

Vera sniffed. 'I did, until I knew who he was.'

'Mam, that doesn't make sense.'

Vera inclined her head and looked uneasy. 'What do you and Jimmy get up to when you go out together?'

'We stroll on the prom, go the pictures or play tennis with friends,' Gillian said eagerly. 'Other times we listen to the brass bands in Singleton Park.' Gillian took a step towards her mother. 'You must admit, Mam, I'm never out late. Jimmy insists I get home by half past nine. He's a decent boy, Mam.'

'Vera?' Arthur put his hand gently on his wife's arm. 'Are we exaggerating the situation? I wouldn't like to think we're being prejudiced against the boy.'

Vera put her hand to her face. 'I don't know, I'm sure!'

'Bring Jimmy round to supper tomorrow,' Arthur suggested. 'It's time I had another word with the boy. I've been a bit harsh, I think, on reflection.'

'Oh, Dad! Thank you!' Gillian flung her arms around her father's neck. 'Thank you. You won't regret it, I promise.'

344

'Arthur! I hope you know what you're doing,' Vera said worriedly.

'I'm trusting my only daughter,' Arthur said. He gave Gillian a hug before continuing. 'And not before time, too, eh, Gill?'

'Oh, Dad, you're the best father ever.'

'Flattery will get you nowhere, my girl,' he said with a grin. 'Now go and make a pot of tea for me and your mother before we die of thirst.'

Twenty-Four

The courtroom was crowded. Henry was not surprised. The story was front-page news in the *Cambrian Leader*.

Gloria, attending court each day up until Andy's conviction, was now absent on the day of judgement. Henry knew she was furious that Andy's lawyer Mr Burden-Rees had persuaded him to plead guilty. All that was left was for the judge Mr Justice Routledge to pass sentence.

From the public seats Henry watched his son with an aching heart. Seated next to his lawyer Andy looked small and insignificant today, with drooping shoulders and lowered head.

Henry longed to go to him, clasp him in his arms and tell him everything was going to be all right. But he knew it would not be so. Andy was convicted of a callous criminal act and must pay.

All those present stood as the judge entered the

court and took his seat. When everyone else sat down again, Andy and his lawyer remained standing.

A cold shiver ran through Henry when the judge determined that Andy must serve five years' imprisonment for his crime of robbery with violence.

When the proceedings were all over Henry remained sitting where he was while the other spectators trooped out. With tears in his eyes he watched as Andy was led away by officers of the court. His son did not glance up but allowed himself to be taken without a murmur.

He would stand by his son, Henry pledged to himself; make sure the boy knew he was not deserted completely. Gloria may have turned her back on him, but Andy was still his son.

Overwhelmed with sadness Henry left the courtroom and was in time to see Mr Burden-Rees about to depart. He caught up with him, anxious for a word.

'Mr Burden-Rees! You remember me. I'm Andy's father.'

The man stopped immediately. 'Yes, of course, Mr Prosser.'

Henry swallowed convulsively. 'Five years,' he said with a catch in his voice. 'That's such a long time to serve in prison.' He wondered how Andy would ever bear it.

'It could've been worse,' the lawyer said matter-of-factly. 'He might have been facing a charge of murder had his victim died.'

'I'm well aware of that,' Henry said stiffly. 'But five years? He has never been in trouble before. He's a boy.'

'He's twenty years old, Mr Prosser, and therefore responsible for his actions,' Mr Burden-Rees said and then frowned. 'I gave him sound advice if you're implying anything different,' he said curtly. 'If he had pleaded not guilty as his mother wanted, with all the evidence the prosecution had, he'd have got much longer.'

'Yes, thank you,' Henry said, resigned. 'I'm not blaming you.' He hesitated. 'What are the chances of a successful appeal?'

Mr Burden-Rees shook his head, his expression grim. 'Save your money, Mr Prosser. I see no grounds for an appeal.'

It had been a vague hope in Henry's heart, but now he must put it aside. 'I was wondering,' he continued hesitantly, 'if you'd heard from my wife recently.'

'Yes, I have,' the lawyer said. 'Mrs Prosser has washed her hands of the whole thing, so she informs me, and has left Swansea for good.' The lawyer's disapproval was obvious. 'I'm surprised you didn't know.'

Henry averted his gaze from the other man's eyes and felt ashamed for Gloria.

'Thank you, Mr Burden-Rees, for all that you've done,' Henry said with finality. 'I, of course, will settle all fees.'

The man nodded and left him standing there.

Henry felt miserable. He wanted to see Andy but knew he must wait. He went to his car but going back to the yard today, facing Ronnie Knox and trying to act normal, was unthinkable in his wretched state so he drove home to Fleet

Street, longing for the comforting embrace of Florrie.

She did not fail him. Sitting on the sofa, he broke down and cried as he told her of Andy's sentence. Her warm soothing arms were a salve to his pain as they sat together for a long while.

He was tempted to tell her about his anxiety for Dorothy but hesitated. It wasn't his secret to reveal.

'We must plan for the future,' Florrie said at last. 'Time will pass and when Andy comes out he's welcome to make his home with us if he wishes. He's your son, Henry, and I know you love him no matter what has happened.'

Henry felt a stab of guilt. 'There's something I haven't told you,' he said. 'Gloria is suing me for divorce.' He looked at her lovingly. 'Florrie, love, I'm afraid she intends to cite you as co-respondent.'

'I see.' Florrie's expression was impassive and for once he could not guess what she was feeling or thinking.

'It's just spite on her part,' he continued quickly. 'I don't know if she'll succeed in getting a divorce, but there will be a mighty scandal in the process.'

Florrie touched his face and smiled and Henry's heart lifted. 'Henry, love, I've lived with scandal for the past seventeen years,' she said gently. 'People have gossiped about me since we met.'

Life must have been hard for her, but she had never rebuked him.

'Florrie, love, I'm so sorry.'

She shook her head. 'There's nothing for you to be sorry about,' she said. 'I found the only man for me was you. I love you and nothing can touch me so long as you still love me, Henry.'

Henry kissed her lovingly. Florrie was everything a wife should be, and he loved her more than his own life.

'I'm going to make damned sure Gloria gets her divorce,' Henry said emphatically as he held her close to him. 'Florrie, love, I'll be free to marry.'

She gave a little gasp.

He took her face in his hands and looked into her eyes. 'Will you marry me, Florrie?'

'Yes, Henry, I'd love to marry you.'

Holding her, Henry felt healed by her love. Things had gone badly wrong with Andy and Dorothy, but now he felt a new strength surge through him.

The thought of having to work and associate with Ronnie Knox, the man who had ruined his daughter, had made him feel physically sick over the last few days, but now he felt up to the task of dealing with him. Florrie's love made him strong and whole.

Henry was at the yard early next morning, ready to deal with Ronnie. He knew every man there must be talking about his son's disgrace, perhaps blaming him, but he squared his shoulders to face it.

Arthur Finch came into the office first thing and he welcomed his brother-in-law's easy attitude as they discussed the various jobs that were on hand that day. He knew in Arthur he had a friend he could trust and depend on.

When Ronnie arrived at the office later that morning Henry asked Gillian to leave them alone for a while. The girl's eyes were round as she studied them both for a moment, and then she scuttled off.

'You've been avoiding me, Ronnie,' Henry began without preamble. 'Bloody guilty conscience.'

Ronnie picked up some invoices and pretended to scrutinize them. 'I don't know what you're talking about.'

'Dorothy may be pregnant,' Henry said, pointblank. 'You're responsible.'

Ronnie threw down the papers he was holding.

'Don't take me for a bloody fool, Henry,' he bellowed, his expression sneering. 'I'm not carrying the can. The father could be anyone.'

With a roar Henry lunged at him, catching the younger man full on the mouth with his balled fist. Ronnie fell sprawling backwards over a desk, his lip split and bleeding, his eyes wide with astonishment.

'You foul-mouthed scoundrel,' Henry shouted at him as he lay there. 'You're as corrupt as your grandfather was. I know because I had no choice but to live under the same roof as him.'

Ronnie struggled to his feet, his fingers gingerly examining his swelling lip.

'You're a lunatic!' he said painfully. 'Look what you've done!'

'I'd like to beat you over the head with a brick,' Henry raged. He was astonished at his

350

own violence. 'You deserve it for taking advantage of my innocent daughter.'

He saw derision in Ronnie's eyes and took a threatening step towards him.

'Don't say it, Ronnie,' Henry warned with a snarl. 'Or I'll not be responsible for my actions.'

Ronnie moved so that there was distance between them.

'I won't take responsibility for the mess Dorothy has got herself into,' he said morosely. 'Why should I?'

Henry's lip curled with derision. 'You're a rotter and no mistake,' he said gutturally, feeling deep aversion to the man standing before him. 'I don't want you in this business any longer. I'll buy you out.'

Ronnie dabbed at his bleeding lip with his handkerchief.

'You're too late,' he said, triumph in his eyes. 'I've already sold my share and for a good price, too.'

'What?' Henry was dumbfounded.

Ronnie smirked and then winced, touching his mouth gingerly.

'You've got a new partner, Henry,' he said with difficulty. 'I wonder how you'll like working with a stranger.'

'Who is this new partner?' He wondered if Ronnie was lying to get himself out of a tight spot.

'I don't know,' Ronnie said. 'The deal was done through lawyers, but it's obviously someone with plenty of money. They gave me a damn good price.'

'You swine! You went behind my back,' Henry hooted with anger. 'I should've been consulted.'

'You've held me back for years with your small-minded ways, Henry,' Ronnie said belligerently. 'I'm glad to get out of our partnership. I intend to start up on my own. I have the capital now, thanks to your new partner.'

'The business was good enough for your grandfather,' Henry countered. 'He was always scheming to take control of it.'

'If he had he'd have made something of it,' Ronnie said thickly. 'This place is going nowhere, but perhaps your new partner will turn it upside down.'

'Get out!'

'I'll go when I'm good and ready,' Ronnie said.

'Clear off!' Henry shouted, raising his fist. 'Or I'll beat you to a pulp!'

With an oath, Ronnie walked out.

Henry sat down behind his desk, shaking. Violence was not in his nature normally, but Ronnie Knox had tried him more than even a saint could bear.

Very worried, he sat for a long while thinking about his new situation. He had thought things could not get worse. Well, now they had. This new partner, whoever he was, might have ideas of edging him out of the business altogether. He did not like not knowing whom he was up against.

Gillian could not wait to get home to tell Dorothy about what had happened at the yard. She even cut short her chat with Jimmy before leaving. 'See you later, Jimmy,' she called out as she went.

She got home at half past five and, as usual, Dorothy was in the kitchen helping prepare supper.

Gillian did not even bother to take off her hat and coat in the hall before barging in.

'Dot! Dot!'

Her cousin was washing cabbage leaves in a colander at the sink. Gillian was relieved to find her alone for the moment.

Dorothy looked up, surprised at her sudden appearance.

'What's the rush, Gill? What are you looking so excited about?'

'I've got news!' Gillian said breathlessly. 'Look! Leave the cabbage for the minute. Come into the bedroom. It's important.'

'I can't. Aunt Vera wants—'

'Never mind about Mam!' Gillian exclaimed. She looked over her shoulder at the door, worried at being overheard. 'I've got news about that weasel, Ronnie Knox.'

Dorothy looked startled.

'Come on!' Gillian urged. 'Before Mam comes in.'

She had no doubt Vera would get to know about the fracas at the yard quickly enough when her father came home, but she wanted to be the one to tell Dorothy.

'I don't want to hear anything about Ronnie,' Dorothy said stiffly, holding back. 'As far as I'm concerned, he doesn't exist.'

'Listen, will you?' Gillian said quickly. 'There has been a fight at the yard over you.'

'What?' Dorothy was taken aback. 'What on earth—?'

'We can't talk here,' Gillian said urgently. 'Come on, do!'

Gillian drew her cousin hurriedly into their bedroom and, sitting on one of the beds, pulled her down beside her.

'Gillian, what's going on?'

'Uncle Henry and Ronnie came to blows this morning over you and blood was spilled,' Gillian said cheerfully.

Looking dismayed, Dorothy put her hand to her mouth. 'Oh, no! Oh my goodness!' She gulped. 'Did you see it?'

Gillian nodded. 'Through the crack in the open door,' she said. 'Uncle Henry sent me out of the office as soon as Ronnie arrived, but I didn't go far. I knew something was going to happen.'

'Is my father hurt? What did that beast Ronnie do to him?'

Dorothy looked so worried Gillian thought she might burst into tears. For all her protestations of despising her father, Gillian could see that was far from the truth.

'Uncle Henry didn't get a scratch,' Gillian reassured her. 'But Ronnie got a split lip and a bruised ego.' She laughed. 'Uncle Henry was magnificent,' she said gleefully. 'He said he'd beat Ronnie to a pulp, and I believed him. So did Ronnie, I think, because he pushed off as quick as you like.'

Dorothy covered her face with both hands and

hung her head.

'Oh, Gill, I feel so stupid,' she said in a small voice.

'Stupid?' Gillian frowned. 'What do you mean?'

Dorothy bit her lip before answering.

'I've got some news, too.' She looked at Gillian, tears in her eyes. 'I'm not in the family way, after all, Gill,' she said shakily. 'My period started earlier today.'

Overjoyed, Gillian leapt to her feet. 'Oh, Dorothy! That's wonderful. I'm so glad for you. But why are you crying?'

'I've caused terrible trouble,' she sobbed. 'Dad has attacked Ronnie for nothing. He'll be arrested. It's all my fault.'

'Nonsense!' Gillian said emphatically. 'Ronnie got everything he deserved, the scoundrel!'

'But Dad will get into trouble over it,' Dorothy said tearfully. 'My brother being in prison is bad enough. I don't want that to happen to my father, too.'

Gillian put an arm around her cousin's shoulders. 'Ronnie won't make trouble,' she said soothingly. 'He'd have to admit in court that he took advantage of you. He thinks too much of himself for that.'

'Oh, Gill.' Tears ran down Dorothy's face. 'My family is torn apart. I feel so alone. Andy and my mother are gone from me. All I have left is my father, but he only wants his other family.'

'Now, that's not true, Dorothy,' Gillian said firmly. 'Uncle Henry thinks the world of you. Good heavens! He's proved that today.'

Dorothy looked unconvinced.

'You've been pushing him away, Dot,' Gillian said severely. 'And that's so unfair of you. Now is your chance to reconcile with him. He'll be overjoyed to know you're not in the pudding club!'

'Gillian!' Dorothy looked shocked at the expression. 'What a thing to say.' But she smiled through her tears. 'You are awful!'

'Have you told anyone yet?'

'No.' Dorothy shook her head. 'I'm too embarrassed.'

'Come on,' Gillian urged. 'We must tell my mother straight away. I know she'll be so relieved.'

'I hope she won't blame me for causing such a fuss,' Dorothy said. 'I made a complete fool of myself over Ronnie.'

Gillian was reminded of her other piece of news.

'I've something else to tell you, Dot,' she said. 'I overheard Ronnie tell your father that he has sold his share of the business to a complete stranger.'

'Oh, no!' Dorothy turned an apprehensive glance on Gillian. 'What does that mean? Will everyone lose their jobs?'

'I don't know,' Gillian said glumly. 'But Uncle Henry looked very worried for the rest of the day.'

On that uncertain note they went in search of Vera and found her in the kitchen, deep in conversation with Arthur.

Gillian could tell by the startled expression on

her mother's face that she had been told about the change of part ownership of the yard.

'But who is this new partner?' Vera asked with energy.

'No one knows,' Arthur said. 'We'll have to wait and see. I only hope it's not some big concern planning to take us over. That would be serious. Jobs could be lost.'

'Huh!' Vera exclaimed bitterly. 'So much for my brother's empty promise to bring Sam into management. I bet he's known about this all along. It's another trick to do me down!'

'Whisht, woman!' Arthur said with unaccustomed sternness. 'It's not Henry's fault. It's that blackguard, Ronnie Knox. I'd like to split his other lip for him!'

'Oh, it makes my blood boil,' Vera said heatedly. 'The Knoxes have always run rings around the Prossers.'

'Henry must come around here to supper tomorrow,' Arthur said firmly. 'We should discuss this as a family.'

Vera's lips tightened and Gillian thought it was a good moment to put in her piece of news.

'Dad's right, Mam,' she said. 'Besides, we've something to celebrate. Dorothy isn't in trouble, after all.' She nodded at the unasked question which sprang into her mother's eyes. 'Yes, Mam, you-know-what has settled the matter.'

'Oh, Dorothy, my dear girl!' Vera said, coming forward to embrace her niece. 'I'm so glad. You deserve a second chance.'

Arthur looked uncomfortable but patted Dorothy's shoulder.

'Hear! Hear!' he said awkwardly and Gillian realized with amusement he was completely out of his depth.

'I'll invite Henry first thing tomorrow,' Arthur continued. He looked at Gillian. 'It might be a good time to have Jimmy around to supper, too, father and son together.'

'My goodness!' Vera exclaimed caustically. 'You'll be inviting Henry's fancy woman next!'

Arthur frowned. 'That was uncalled for, Vera,' he said.

Vera sniffed. 'I've a right to say what I like in my own house.'

'Well, when Henry and Jimmy are here tomorrow,' Arthur said severely, 'let's try to keep things amicable. After all, we're facing a family crisis. It could be the end of Prosser and Knox for good.'

When Gillian came into the office the following morning she found her uncle Henry sitting at Mr Meeker's desk.

'Morning, Uncle Henry!' she said. She was bubbling to tell him the good news about Dorothy, but refrained. It was her cousin's place to do that.

'Morning, Gill,' he said. 'You'll be glad to know Mr Meeker will be back with us next week. Of course, he'll have to take things much slower than before, so he'll need all your help, Gill.'

'Yes, Uncle Henry.'

'Good girl! I know I can rely on you.'

She was glad Mr Meeker had recovered sufficiently to return to his position, but at the same time felt disappointed. She had run the office very efficiently in his absence and would miss that responsibility.

'How is Dorothy?' Henry asked anxiously. 'I worry about her continually. God knows what the future holds for her.'

'She's fine,' Gillian said eagerly. 'As a matter of fact—'

Before she could finish, her father came into the office and straight away issued his invitation to supper that evening. Henry looked quite astonished at first and then appeared delighted.

'Thanks, Arthur,' he said with feeling. 'But is it all right with Vera?'

Arthur assured him that the invitation was with Vera's approval.

'We eat at six on the dot, mind,' he reminded his brother-in-law. 'Vera will eventually forgive most things but not being late for a meal. Anyway, come early. We need to talk.'

It was mid-morning when someone knocked on the office door and waited before coming in. Curious, Gillian went to see who it was and was surprised to find her mother's newest lodger, Mr Oglander, standing there.

'Hello, Gillian, my dear,' he said, taking off his wide-brimmed hat and holding it against his chest. 'Is Mr Prosser in? Could I have a word with him?'

'He is in,' Gillian said cautiously. 'But he's a bit busy, I'm afraid.'

She liked Mr Oglander a lot, finding him a very interesting man to talk with, but she was sure under the circumstances that Uncle Henry would be in no mood for idle chit-chat.

'I won't keep him a minute,' Mr Oglander assured her. 'It is rather important that I see him, though.'

'Mr Oglander!' Henry looked perplexed as Gillian showed in his visitor. If he was annoyed at the interruption he did not show it. He rose and came around from the desk, his hand outstretched. 'Nice to see you again, sir.'

'I thought I should come to see you, Mr Prosser,' Mr Oglander said. 'I realized it wasn't fair keeping you in the dark any longer.'

Henry looked even more flummoxed. 'I don't understand.'

Without being asked, Mr Oglander sat down. 'It's a matter of business.'

Gillian turned to leave the room, but Mr Oglander held up a hand.

'Please stay, Gillian. This concerns you, too, since you're employed here.'

Gillian was immediately filled with curiosity and moved closer while Henry resumed his seat behind his desk.

'You'd better explain, Mr Oglander,' he said, curiosity in his voice.

Mr Oglander sighed deeply. 'To put it in a nutshell, my boy,' he said, 'I'm your new partner.'

'What?'

'I'm not without means, in fact, I'm rather well off,' the older man said without any side. 'I've been looking for an investment locally for some weeks. It came to my attention that Mr Knox

360

was interested in selling his share. I pride myself that I know a good thing when I see it and so I bought him out.'

Henry looked flabbergasted while Gillian was delighted at the news. Her father's fears of some kind of takeover were unfounded.

'I've taken the wind out of your sails, Mr Prosser,' Mr Oglander remarked. There was a hint of amusement in his voice. 'Perhaps you're disappointed?'

'No, not at all,' Henry said, but Gillian could see he was totally at a loss. 'It's just that I expected something quite different.'

'I'm a silent partner only,' Mr Oglander said. 'The business remains entirely in your hands. But you can rely on me to provide any extra finance you may need – for expansion, for example.'

Henry was silent for a moment, but Gillian could tell by his expression that his mind was working at full speed.

'This seems too good to be true, Mr Oglander,' he said cautiously at last. 'What's the catch?'

'There isn't one, I assure you,' the older man said sincerely. 'This business is a sound investment, especially under your management. You have my utmost confidence, Mr Prosser.'

'Thank you,' Henry said. He still looked floored. 'At least now I know where I stand.'

With a nod Mr Oglander rose to his feet. 'I'll leave you now to get on with business as usual,' he said. 'Feel free to call on me at any time. Good morning to you both.'

He put on his hat and, with a little bow in

361

Gillian's direction, left the office.

Gillian turned to her uncle, who continued to sit.

'What a surprise, Uncle Henry,' she said. 'It is good news, isn't it?'

Henry glanced up at her. 'I don't know, Gill,' he said dubiously. 'I've a feeling there's more to Mr Oglander than meets the eye. Aunt Cissie has a great aversion to him and she's rarely wrong about people.'

'Oh, no, Uncle Henry,' Gillian assured him quickly. 'She's changed her mind about him. Mr Oglander and Aunt Cissie are now as thick as thieves.'

Twenty-Five

'You didn't say anything to him, did you?' Dorothy asked Gillian. 'I want to be the one to tell him.'

'I never said a word to Uncle Henry,' Gillian assured her cousin. 'I wouldn't steal your thunder, Dot.'

She had not said a word to anyone about what had transpired at the office earlier either. She felt somehow that it was stupendous news but it was Uncle Henry's place to tell the family about Mr Oglander.

They were in the kitchen. Every time the front

362

door opened Dorothy dashed into the hall, obviously expecting to see her father at any moment.

'He's late,' she said in a worried tone. 'Or perhaps he's changed his mind. Maybe he can't face Aunt Vera.'

'Oh, he'll be here all right,' Gillian told her with confidence. 'Don't you worry about that!'

At last Uncle Henry arrived. Dorothy ran out to meet him in the hall while Gillian trailed behind. Uncle Henry looked somewhat bewildered at the unexpected warmth of his daughter's greeting, after she had treated him with disdain these last weeks. He looked perplexed as Dorothy grasped his arm.

'Are you all right, Dad?' she asked him worriedly. 'I heard there was trouble with Ronnie.'

Uncle Henry looked at the back of his right hand and Gillian could see the skin on his knuckles was raw. 'Right as rain now, Dot, love,' he said.

'Thank goodness!' Dorothy paused, still clinging to his arm. 'Dad, I've something important to tell you.'

'Take him into our bedroom,' Gillian suggested to her cousin. 'You won't get any privacy in the sitting room.'

Gillian watched as father and daughter went inside the bedroom and then she went back to the kitchen.

'Where's Dorothy?' Vera asked as she came bustling in straight after.

'Giving Uncle Henry the glad tidings,' Gillian said. She felt smug in knowing something her

363

mother didn't. 'This is going to be a supper time to remember.'

'What on earth do you mean, Gill?'

'Wait and see!'

'Tsk!' Vera looked impatient. 'Your brain is filled with nonsense, my girl,' she said sharply. 'You want to pull your socks up. Dorothy can jump over your head when it comes to common sense.'

Just before six o'clock everyone trooped into the dining room, family, boarders and guests mingling. Gillian made sure Jimmy sat next to her and felt excited at his presence, intending to hold his hand under cover of the tablecloth. She felt certain he would win her parents over after tonight.

Uncle Henry sat opposite with Dorothy next to him. Her uncle looked happier than she had seen him in a long time. Gillian felt glad. She liked her uncle Henry a lot.

She glanced around at the assembled faces, feeling smug again at her knowledge. Everyone was going to get a big surprise.

At the far end of the long table sat Mr Oglander in deep but hushed conversation with Aunt Cissie, who was sitting next to him.

Gillian was intrigued. What could this elderly pair have to say to each other that was so intense?

Vera presided over the assembly as usual.

'Dorothy, fetch the vegetable tureens, please,' she ordered. 'And you, too, Gillian. Bring the gravy boats. It's time you did your share.'

Finally everyone was served and tucking into

the food, while pockets of conversation broke out the length and breadth of the table.

'Mrs Finch!' Mr Oglander said loudly above the din. 'I have some bottles of wine here for the adults. Later I want to raise a toast.'

'Wine!' Vera lifted her chin and her eyes widened. 'Wine?' She looked at him aghast. 'I've never heard anything so outlandish! You're not in the colonies now, Mr Oglander. This is a teetotal house.'

Mr Oglander's lips twitched. 'Of course, Mrs Finch,' he said mildly. 'But I thought on *this* occasion you might make an exception.'

Vera frowned. 'And what occasion is that, may I ask?' she asked tartly.

Mr Oglander rose to his feet. 'I'm sure Mr Prosser won't mind if I make the announcement.'

He glanced enquiringly at Henry, who waved a hand nonchalantly. 'You go right ahead, Mr Oglander.'

Mr Oglander nodded his thanks. Remaining on his feet, he struck a pose, putting his thumbs in the top pockets of his waistcoat.

Gillian's heart sank. It looked like this was to be a long-winded speech when all she wanted was to get the meal over and spend the rest of the evening alone with Jimmy.

'As you are all aware, I'm sure,' Mr Oglander began, looking around the faces turned to him, 'Mr Knox has left the business.'

'And good riddance!' Tom piped up with a snort of disdain. 'Him and his flashy car.'

'Quite so!' said Mr Oglander. 'I hope you will

all be pleased to learn that it was I who bought him out. I am Mr Prosser's new partner.'

There was an astonished silence for a moment and then everyone began to talk at once.

'Well! I'll go to the foot of our stairs!' Arthur said, clearly flabbergasted. He got to his feet, too. 'My goodness! This is good news. Not knowing was very worrying.'

'No cause for worry,' Mr Oglander said reassuringly. 'The business will continue as before and, indeed, expand and prosper with Mr Prosser in full charge.'

'Yes, that is good news,' Vera said stiffly. 'Now, please sit down – and you, too, Arthur. I'll not have a mealtime disrupted.'

Mr Oglander sat down obediently but Arthur continued to stand.

'Vera, this is important,' he said, plainly exasperated. 'It means jobs are safe. You of all people should know how worried I've been; not only for myself but for the boys as well. Mr Oglander has saved the day.'

Vera's expression was stubborn. 'We're grateful, I'm sure,' she said pertly. 'Now please, everyone, finish your food. I'm about to serve afters.'

Arthur sat down, shaking his head at her obstinacy. Knives and forks began to clatter on crockery again. Gillian was relieved that the speech had been cut short.

'Hurry and finish your pudding,' she whispered to Jimmy. 'Then we can go and sit on the stairs together and cuddle.'

'I don't think your father would like that,'

Jimmy murmured uncertainly.

'He's not invited,' Gillian said with a giggle.

'We shouldn't be rash, Gill,' Jimmy said cautiously. 'I'm here in your home on sufferance, remember.'

The pudding was served and everyone was halfway through when to Gillian's annoyance Aunt Cissie got to her feet.

'Please listen, everyone,' Cissie began loudly. 'Mr Oglander has something further to tell you.'

'Oh, no!' Gill muttered to Jimmy. 'What now?'

'Cissie, please!' Mr Oglander exclaimed. His face had turned quite pale. 'This is not the time or the place.'

'It's exactly the time and place,' Cissie insisted. 'You must tell them now.'

'Aunt Cissie,' Vera said angrily, 'I'm willing to put up with a lot, but this really is the last straw. Has everyone gone mad?'

Cissie ignored her outburst but put her hand on Mr Oglander's shoulder beside her.

'Face up to it!' she urged him.

Mr Oglander rose to his feet, obviously reluctantly, and looked around at the faces surrounding him. Gillian expected him to strike a pose again, but instead he looked anxious, almost fearful and suddenly older. Everyone waited for him to speak.

He began in a trembling tone. 'Thirty-odd years ago—'

'This is absurd!' Vera burst out an interruption. 'I've never known such behaviour at a mealtime. Really! I must protest—'

'Be quiet, Vera, for once,' Cissie told her. 'You might learn something.'

'Well! Really!' Vera looked flabbergasted.

Delighted at her mother's consternation, Gillian could hardly stifle a giggle, which drew a warning glance from her father.

'Go on!' Cissie urged Mr Oglander.

He started again, his voice still trembling. 'Thirty-odd years ago I lived around these parts. I had a wife, children and a thriving business.'

There was a loud sigh of irritation from Vera. Gillian could see her mother was keeping silent with some difficulty.

'Then one morning,' Mr Oglander continued, 'I woke to find that my business partner had stolen a large sum of money from the business. But worse still, he had stolen my wife also.'

There was complete silence around the table. Mr Oglander had their full attention now.

He swallowed hard, his eyes cast down, and his shoulders seemed to slump. 'I'm ashamed to say that I did a very cowardly thing,' he said. 'I ran away.'

'Why are you telling us this?' Vera asked sharply, obviously unable to contain herself another minute. 'None of us are remotely interested in your private life.'

Mr Oglander looked at her helplessly without speaking and would have sat down, but then Henry spoke up.

'That's not true, Vera,' he said loudly. 'Go on, Mr Oglander. I'm interested.'

Mr Oglander nodded at Henry in appreciation. 'Thank you, my boy.'

There was a grunt of exasperation from Vera.

'Coward that I was,' Mr Oglander continued, 'I could not bear the prospect of continuing to work alongside the man who had betrayed me, particularly as my wife had abandoned my bed for his.'

Mr Oglander seemed overcome at the memory and reached for a glass of water from the table. His hand shook so much the water spilled and Gillian felt very sorry for him.

'Are you all right, Mr Oglander?' she asked, concerned, getting to her feet.

Mr Oglander gave her a weak smile. 'You're a good girl, Gillian,' he said softly. 'A credit to your parents.'

'Don't stop now,' Cissie insisted as Gillian sat down again.

Mr Oglander pulled himself together. 'When I left I expected to be away for just a few days to think things out.' He paused, a spasm of pain crossing his features. 'But I could not find the courage to return.'

'What did you do?' asked Arthur, his gaze intent on the older man's face.

'To my great dishonour I deserted my son and daughter, and the rest of my family, Mr Finch,' Mr Oglander said in a broken voice. 'I put my own pain and humiliation before them and I've bitterly regretted it ever since.'

Arthur got to his feet, his expression solemn. 'Oglander isn't your real name, is it?'

The older man waited before answering. 'No,' he said. 'My name is Prosser, William Prosser.' He glanced at Henry and then at Vera. 'Henry,

Vera, I am your father. I've come home to my family.'

The revelation was not what Gillian had been expecting and she was stunned.

'I will not listen to this nonsense a moment longer,' Vera said. She rose to her feet, throwing down her table napkin. 'I don't believe a word of it!'

'I'm looking for forgiveness from my children, Vera,' William Prosser said with deep emotion. 'I need your forgiveness, and Henry's, too, before I end my days.'

'Forgiveness!' Red patches appeared on Vera's cheeks and she looked furious. 'This is some monstrous trick. You're a fraud. My father is dead!'

'Vera, my dearest girl, my only daughter—' William began.

'How dare you be so familiar with me?' Vera stormed an interruption. 'I'm not your daughter. I'm no more to you than your landlady.' She stepped away from the table. 'And as from this moment I'm not even that.'

'Vera, love!' Arthur cried out, but she ignored him.

She was trembling visibly as she glared at the man who claimed to be her father.

'You'll vacate your room by midday tomorrow, Mr Oglander. You are no longer welcome in this house.'

Cissie looked furious. 'How dare you speak to your father like that?' she said. 'Apologize at once!'

With an expression of defiance on her face,

Vera marched from the room.

'What have I done?' William mumbled and sank on to his chair again. Gillian thought he had shrunk into himself.

'Vera gets more like Rose every day,' Cissie grumbled bitterly. 'Selfish, wilful and opinionated.'

Henry stood up. 'My father! I can hardly believe it.' He shook his head wonderingly. 'Yet I've been drawn to you since the day we met.'

William looked up eagerly. Gillian saw there were tears in his eyes and her heart went out to him. He was her grandfather.

'Henry, my son,' he said in broken tones. 'Can you ever forgive me for my shameful desertion of you?' He got shakily to his feet. 'But after what I did I've no right to ask your forgiveness, Henry,' he continued sombrely. 'I understand if you hate me for it.'

'Father.' Henry stepped towards him and put his arm around the older man's shoulders. 'You are my father,' he said, his voice thick with feeling. 'I feel no resentment towards you. I thank God you've returned to us.'

'Henry,' Arthur said quickly, 'take your father into the drawing room where you can have some privacy.'

Henry nodded his thanks and then escorted William from the room, followed by Cissie.

Arthur glanced at those left around the table. 'Everyone stay and finish your meal,' he said.

'Wait a minute, Dad!' Gillian exclaimed. She glanced across at her cousin Dorothy and her brothers, who were looking as astounded as she was feeling. 'Me and the boys, and Dot and Jimmy, too, should be allowed to hear what's going on.'

'This is a grown-up matter and doesn't concern you,' Arthur said in an offhand manner.

'We're not children, Dad,' Sam said strongly. He got to his feet and Gillian could see he was deeply offended. 'This man is the grandfather we never knew we had. We've a right to know the whole truth.'

'Yes, we have!' Gillian said in support.

Arthur looked uncertain for a moment. 'Oh, very well,' he conceded at last. 'But you're all to sit and keep your mouths shut, do you understand?'

Gillian grasped Jimmy's hand tightly as they all trooped out.

'Please excuse us,' Arthur said to their two silent boarders, who were still sitting. 'This is a private family matter.'

When they entered the sitting room Arthur waved them to the far end of the room, giving them a stern warning glance. Grasping Jimmy's hand Gillian sat, pulling him down next to her.

Her newly discovered grandfather was seated in an armchair near the fireplace, Cissie and Henry at his side. William looked pale and drawn, so unlike the exuberant Mr Oglander she had known.

Arthur went across to him. 'I'm sorry, Mr Prosser, for Vera's behaviour. She's shocked and upset,' he said hesitantly. 'Of course you're welcome in this house.'

'I should hope so!' Cissie exclaimed fervently.

'Disgraceful behaviour. Vera must apologize.'

'Call me William, Arthur,' the older man said wearily. 'After all, I am your father-in-law.'

'Vera didn't know what she was saying,' Arthur continued. 'It's not like her at all.'

Cissie gave an indignant tut-tut. The excuse was too much for Gillian, too.

'Dad, it's exactly like her!' she said. 'Don't make excuses.'

'Do be quiet, Gillian,' Arthur said angrily.

'I could do with a stiff drink,' William said rather weakly. 'Open one of those bottles of wine, Henry, will you?'

'Hold on. I've something better,' Arthur said.

He took a small key out of the pocket of his waistcoat and opened one door of the sideboard, taking out a bottle of whisky.

'For emergencies,' he explained to the surprised onlookers. 'What Vera doesn't know won't harm her. Tom, go and get a tumbler for your grandfather.'

Tom hurried about his errand and Gillian took time to study William Prosser. He sat with his head resting against the back of his chair. Like her uncle Henry, she had been drawn to the man from the start. Maybe she had secretly, in the back of her mind, wished that he were her grandfather. It was as though her unacknowledged wish had come true.

Tom came back with the tumbler and after pouring out a stiff shot Arthur handed the glass to William. He took it eagerly and downed half of it.

'That's better,' he said, and indeed he sounded

stronger. He beamed up at Henry, still standing at his side.

'Why did you come back?' Tom burst out.

'Tom!' Arthur exclaimed, furious.

William waved a hand. 'It's all right, Arthur. The boy has a right to the truth like the rest of my family.'

'What have you been doing all these years?' Sam asked. 'How did you live?'

William smiled wryly. 'Sheep,' he said. 'I've made a fortune sheep farming. More money than I know what to do with. I wanted to see my family again and share the wealth I have.'

'Is that why you bought out Ronnie Knox?' Sam asked.

'Partly,' William said. 'Charlie Knox ruined my life. Ronnie appeared to be like his grandfather so I was determined to get the Knoxes out of the business once and for all.'

'What plans do you have now, Grandfather?' Gillian ventured shyly.

'I'm getting old,' he said. 'But I have a yen to live in my old home again, where the Prossers have lived for decades. So, I've bought our old home in Aberdyberthy Street.'

'What?' Henry looked astonished. 'It's an old mausoleum of a place,' he said. 'And dreadfully run-down now.'

'Rose always called it a mausoleum,' William reminisced. 'She never appreciated the place as I did.'

'Rose never appreciated anything, especially not her family,' Cissie said bitterly. Her face brightened. 'William promises we'll live there again, he and I.'

'Surely not, Father,' Henry said, uncertainty in his voice.

'I'll renovate it,' William assured him. 'And then Cissie and I will spend the rest of our lives there.'

'It's like a dream come true, Will,' Cissie said softly.

He reached towards her as she stood next to his chair and grasped her careworn hand.

'When all else failed me, Cissie was always there.'

At that moment the drawing-room door was thrown open and Vera marched in. Her eyes were puffy and reddened and clearly she had been crying. But the light in her gaze told Gillian that the fireworks were not extinguished.

Arthur moved towards her quickly, concern on his pleasant features. 'Vera, love. Are you all right?'

He tried to put his arm around her but to his obvious consternation she pushed him away. Instead she stalked across to stand in front of William, who struggled to his feet.

'Vera...'

Vera's expression was stony. 'How dare you turn my life upside down like this?' she blurted. 'Why couldn't you stay dead?'

There was a chorus of gasps and protests.

'Vera!' Arthur sounded shocked to the core.

Fury was etched on Cissie's face. 'What a terrible thing to say to your own father,' she cried out. 'You should be ashamed, Vera.'

William's expression was one of patience and

compassion.

'Vera, you look so like your mother,' he said. 'Especially when you're angry.'

'I'm *not* like her!' Vera stated and then gave a sob, holding a damp handkerchief to her nose. 'All my life I've striven not to be like her,' she continued. 'I care for my family. I work my hands to the bone for them. I don't neglect them as she neglected her children.'

Arthur went to her and gently led her to a chair.

'There, there, love,' he said tenderly. 'William isn't criticizing you. Give him a chance. This reunion is painful for him, too.'

Vera regained control and challenged her father with her stare.

'Mother neglected us, but you deserted us, which was worse,' she accused. 'You didn't care. You had no feelings for Henry and me.' She gave a deep sob. 'We were too young to be left like that.' She buried her face in her hands.

William came forward, his hands outstretched to her.

'I can't tell you how much remorse I feel for that, Vera,' he said sincerely, his voice trembling. 'There are no excuses for me, only that I was nearly out of my mind at the time and didn't know what I was about.'

Vera lifted a tear-stained face to him. 'But no word came, nothing,' she said. She shook her head. 'I loved you so, Father. One day you were there and the next you were gone. I felt so alone, so unloved.'

'Oh, my dearest daughter!' William drew her to her feet and held her. 'I loved you, Vera, you and Henry, and I never stopped in all these years.'

'Father.' Henry came forward quickly and William, still with his arm around Vera, put his hand on his son's shoulder.

'I have so much to make up for,' he said, his voice still quivering with emotion. 'To both of you.'

Vera released herself from her father's embrace and looked up at him challengingly.

'Can you put right the wrong that Henry has done me?' she asked him belligerently. 'He and my mother conspired to do me out of my rightful inheritance – a share in the business.'

'Vera, please!' Henry said with obvious annoyance. 'I did not conspire against you. I had no hand in our mother's will.'

'I believe you, Henry,' William said. 'Vera, you must put this bitterness against your brother out of your head for your own good, otherwise it will become a canker in your soul.'

Vera's expression remained defiant. 'That's all very well, Father,' she said stiffly. 'But the fact remains that I *was* cheated and it isn't right!'

'Sit down, both of you,' William instructed. 'I've studied Rose's will, and I believe I understand why she did what she did.'

'I might have known you'd be on Henry's side!' Vera said. 'You probably always loved him more than me.'

'Now that is not true, Vera,' William said emphatically. 'And you know it, my girl!'

'I was left with just five hundred pounds,' Vera complained bitterly. 'When I'm sure the business is worth twenty times that, if not more.'

'Five hundred pounds is quite a handsome sum,' William pointed out. 'It was more than enough for you to buy this house and the free-hold; a good investment.'

'Well, yes.' Vera seemed reluctant to agree.

'You've made the most of it, too,' he continued. 'I judge your boarders bring in a tidy second income.' He smiled at her. 'You're a Prosser through and through, Vera.'

Gillian could see her mother was a little mollified by this compliment.

'I still think Mother's will was unfair,' Vera persisted. 'Why only Henry?'

'I've told you over and over again, Vera. I'm more than content as I am,' Arthur protested.

'There speaks a happy man,' William said, and Gillian thought she detected a hint of envy in her grandfather's voice.

'I have all I want,' Arthur agreed.

William turned his gaze back to Vera.

'Rose, give her her due, did her best to protect and preserve the business for her son,' he said. 'Charlie Knox schemed to get it all, right from the beginning, when my father willed him a share.' He nodded. 'Rose knew if Charlie got his way he'd leave everything to his son George, and the Prossers would be edged out.'

Vera would not give in, it seemed. 'But what about me? I—'

William lifted his hand to interrupt.

'Rose knew better than to split her share of the business between you and Henry,' he explained patiently. 'That would have weakened

378

the Prosser holdings and if Charlie had outlived her she knew he'd find a way of gaining control. Rose may not have been a good mother, but she was no fool in business.'

'I've always thought that was the reason,' Henry said. 'I'm sorry Vera could not see the truth also.'

'Well, that's all behind us,' William said. 'I have another fortune to leave and I'll distribute it fairly between both when my days are over.'

'Oh, William,' Cissie said. 'Don't talk of such things. You'll break my heart.'

'I've tried to make amends, too,' Henry said. 'Sam will be coming into the management side when he's finished his apprenticeship in two years' time.' He gave his father a grateful glance. 'And with your help, Father, I'll expand. There will be room on the management side for Jimmy and Tom, too, if he wants it.'

'You see, Vera,' Arthur said cheerfully. 'William and Henry between them have set things right. Surely you're satisfied now?'

Gillian could see her mother was struggling with her pride. Vera had kept alive this feud with Henry for so long she was reluctant to let it go.

'Vera!' There was a cautionary tone in Arthur's voice. 'Don't be stubborn, like your mother.'

'Arthur! How could you?'

Gillian held her breath for a moment, expecting a further outburst. She was relieved to see her mother's lips twitch, which then expanded into a rueful smile.

'Why don't you offer my father some of that whisky you keep in the sideboard for emergencies?' she asked pertly of her husband. 'I think Henry could do with some, too.'

Arthur gaped. 'Vera,' he said with astonishment, 'you never cease to flummox me.'

Gillian snuggled her cheek close to Jimmy's as they sat in the semi-darkness of the staircase. Everyone else, family and boarders, was in the drawing room. She could hear laughter and lively chatter. But she did not want to be part of that. She just wanted to be alone with Jimmy.

'Isn't life wonderful?' she murmured.

'Extraordinary,' Jimmy said, wonder in his voice. 'All my life it has just been Grandpa Bert, Mam and Dad, and now I have so many relatives my head is spinning.'

'I knew they'd love you as much as I do,' Gillian said softly.

Jimmy was silent.

Gillian lifted her head away to look at him. The light was too dim to see his expression clearly.

'What's the matter, Jimmy?'

'Tonight the truth came home to me, Gill,' he said seriously. 'We have the same grandfather.'

'Yes, of course.'

'I hadn't really thought about our blood relationship properly until tonight.' He sounded disturbed. 'Suddenly my family circle is tightening around me. It makes me wonder, Gill – about us.'

'There's nothing wrong in cousins loving each other, Jimmy, and marrying, too,' Gillian said quickly.

Jimmy laughed. 'We're a bit young to be talking of marriage,' he said. 'I've only just begun my apprenticeship. It'll be years before I earn a decent wage. I wouldn't want to hold you to any promises, Gill. There's a whole world we haven't seen yet.'

'We'll see it together,' Gillian said with confidence.

'Well, maybe we will. Who knows?'

'I love you, Jimmy,' Gillian murmured. 'Do you love me?'

Jimmy chuckled. 'I'm thinking I'd better or else!'

Gillian snuggled close to him again.

'They believe we'll grow out of each other,' she said. 'To them we're just children still.' Gillian sighed. 'I'm sorry for them. They're too old to understand love.'

ABERDEEN
CITY
LIBRARIES